BEC MCMASTER

HEXBOUND

THE DARK ARTS SERIES

Hexbound: A Dark Arts Novel
Copyright (c) Bec McMaster

Edited by: Hot Tree Editing
Print formatting by: Cover Me Darling and Athena Interior Book Design
Cover Art (c) Damonza.com

ALSO AVAILABLE BY BEC MCMASTER

LONDON STEAMPUNK SERIES
Kiss Of Steel
Heart Of Iron
My Lady Quicksilver
Forged By Desire
Of Silk And Steam
Novellas in same series:
Tarnished Knight
The Curious Case Of The Clockwork Menace

LONDON STEAMPUNK: THE BLUE BLOOD CONSPIRACY
Mission: Improper

DARK ARTS SERIES
Shadowbound
Hexbound

BURNED LANDS SERIES
Nobody's Hero
The Last True Hero

OTHER
The Many Lives Of Hadley Monroe

PROLOGUE

London, 1894

ADRIAN BISHOP WOKE quietly, his eyelids fluttering open and his skin tingling as if every sense was suddenly on fire. He held his breath, listening intently to the cold, dark silence of his house. Nothing moved. Not a whisper, not a creak, not even a mouse.

Except....

Someone stepped through one of the invisible wards he'd set throughout the mansion. It clung like spider silk to their body, giving him an instant beacon of awareness: the intruder was in the second guest bedroom with the revolving fireplace that hid a secret room. Whoever it was, they moved with deliberate purpose, as if they knew exactly where they were going and most likely what they were looking for.

Sicarii, then? Like himself?

Highly trained, the Sicarii were the lethal edge of the sorcerous Order of the Dawn Star, and only the ruling Prime knew all of their identities. Their purpose was absolute; protect the Order, serve the Prime, remove all threats. It was lonely, bloody work, but he'd known nothing else all of his life.

Bishop eased back the covers, slipping naked from his bed. He dragged on a pair of the loose black trousers he wore for training purposes, and opened himself up to his sorcery. Energy slipped and slid into his skin, the temperature of the room plunging abruptly to freezing as he prepared himself, drawing power from the world around him. Heated breath spilled in a fine mist around his mouth as he glided silently past the windows.

Another ward tripped just as the downstairs clock began to chime midnight. *BONG. BONG. BONG.* There. He closed his eyes, head tilting upwards as the clock droned on. His thief had found the fireplace, which meant he had no time to spare. Forging a knife of raw matter, he cut his hand and pressed his bloody palm against the walls of the house.

"Hecarah as di mentos," he whispered, breathing a spill of Power into the words. The words meant nothing; ritual was the key in training his mind to accept simple codes, and he had chosen his words wisely so many years ago.

Nothing happened but he could sense the house coming alive, awakening to his touch and anticipating his commands. It, too, held its breath.

Above him the thief paused, just for a second.

And that was when he realized that he was facing a master adversary. The house wards were inverted. Nobody should have felt it waking, but from the sudden fierce patter of footsteps the thief had given up all pretense of stealth and was opting for speed.

Done then. Bishop moved like a wraith. The tracking ward jerked forward, almost as if it were leaping from place to place, but he was swiftly gaining as he thundered up the staircase. The thief might be heading directly toward the object of their desire, but they were moving in a straight line and certain obstacles, walls for example, kept interfering.

His blood was up, the fierce hunting edge keening through him. Death rode him hard, hungering for a taste of blood, and Bishop forced it back upon its leash. Some sorcerers found increased energy through blood or sex, but only a kill gave him that edge, that sweet ride of power, like an aurora awakening in his veins. He could tear London apart with but a thought following the hot gush of blood, but such power came with a weakness: the hunger for the kill grew every time he took a life. One day he would be a dangerous force to be reckoned with, the sweet addiction stronger than his will, and then another of the Sicarii would be sent to remove him.

But he was not there yet.

Racing silently up the hidden staircase behind the fireplace, Bishop saw the faint bobbing glow of a mage sphere through the partly opened panel that led to his secret room. A single creak betrayed him.

Bishop threw himself into the room in a roll, beneath a hastily flung wave of force that would have smashed him back through at least three walls, and came to his feet just in time to face a masked adversary.

No time to think. The rosy mage globe the thief wielded for light spun into twelve that circled their head, and began to spin faster and faster. One shot directly toward him and he flung both arms up, crossing them at the wrists as a single protective ward formed around him. The globe the thief had flung burst into heated, liquid light that bathed the thin, shimmering ward then dripped to the floor. Molten sparks burned straight through the floorboards.

"Well," said the thief, in a faintly amused, very feminine voice, "I see the rumors of your skills were not exaggerated."

His first shock of the evening—the Chalice that he'd sworn to protect with his life was already hanging from her belt. It gleamed silvery against her all-black men's attire, along with a dozen small devices of unknown origin.

It should have taken her nearly ten minutes to crack through the safeguards on his safe. A safe that hung open on the wall, its heavy steel-lined door hanging limply from its grooves.

"I don't believe we've had the pleasure," Bishop replied, straightening and letting the silvery gleam of the ward disintegrate with a static crackle. It would take only a thought to re-form it.

A faint smile curled over the woman's lips. Her chin and mouth were all that he could see, apart from the gleam of pale eyes behind her black lace mask. The battle globes spun lazily around her head, warming her creamy skin as she slowly circled him. Though she wore a black shirt, it had been cinched in with some sort of outer corset that thrust her breasts high. The entire effect was... provocative.

"And here I thought you a stranger to pleasure?" she purred. "Or so they all say."

Bishop didn't move. The only way out was through the doorway directly behind him. His smile was cold. "I'd be careful about listening to rumors. Sometimes I start them myself."

"Oh, I know," she whispered as she sauntered slowly around the room, crossing one foot over another. "Let's just say I've spent the last month learning everything there is to know about you. I've watched you paint these walls with your blood and your wards, trying to protect against thieves. And I've watched you move quietly through the house each night, restless, unable to sleep. All alone at night in this dark house. Why do you send your servants away? Do you not want them seeing the mess of your body that you hide beneath your clothes? Or perhaps you're afraid they'll hear your nightmares? It's the one mystery I haven't been able to crack yet."

Bishop's gaze flattened.

"Didn't you notice me?" Her smile was positively wicked. "And here I thought you had eyes in the back of your head."

Every muscle in his gut tightened and he took the time to reexamine her. He was very, very good at what he did. The fact that he hadn't noticed the surveillance made him wonder if she was better.

They faced each other on light feet, their bodies tense with implied movement. Those slim hips were encased in a pair of trousers that were positively indecent, but she looked lean and strong, and she moved with a kind of supple grace he'd rarely seen before.

"Who are you?"

"Madame Noir."

"Should that mean something to me?" he replied, and from the flattening of her eyes, it should have. Or she'd have liked it to.

"I call myself a reclamation agent," she said, circling the desk that stood between them, keeping pace with him.

"A thief, then."

"One does what one must," she replied, casting a gaze across the room, then sneering. "We aren't all born with a silver spoon in our mouths. Some of us have to get our blunt elsewhere."

9

If she only knew....

He'd earned this house through his service in the East Indies, and then taken the bounties that passed down from the Prime. Silent assassinations to keep him in pocket. Blood money. Execution warrants when sorcerers went rogue. Sometimes he sold some of the magical trinkets he created when he couldn't sleep, but he was a far cry away from having deep pockets.

"How did you hear about the Chalice?" he asked.

Another intriguing smile. "I have friends in low places, you could say."

Its whereabouts shouldn't be common knowledge. He'd only received it a month ago, when its previous owner had been forced to give it to him to protect it. Morgana Devereaux, the Prime's ex-wife, had been collecting the three Relics Infernal; the only things that could control a demon. She'd blackmailed her way to possession of the Blade, and the Wand had gone missing sometime earlier, suspected to be in her hands, which left only the Chalice. Without it, she was powerless. With it, she'd own a demon, the only thing potentially capable of matching the Prime's power.

Morgana was also the only person who might have any idea of who had the Chalice.

Which made the thief's appearance doubly suspicious.

"Are you working for Morgana?" he demanded bluntly, and this time his voice held the edge of a threat to it. Morgana wanted to destroy the Prime—his father. Bishop would do anything to get his hands on her first.

"Who?" she arched a brow in disdain. "My employer is none of your business."

So she *was* working for someone else. "I think you're wrong about that. I'm very interested in learning who you're working for."

Bishop launched himself forward to grab her, and—

The sound of a distant thunderclap echoed right near his ear. His arms clapped shut around nothing but air.

She'd vanished.

A creak alerted him. Bishop swung around and there was his thief, leaning against the doorframe, examining her nails. "Well, it's been lovely making your acquaintance," she said, giving him a mocking finger wave. The handle of the Chalice swirled negligently around one finger. "But I really must be going. People to see. Relics to sell. Toodle-oo."

And then she was gone.

She'd... teleported. That was a rare talent, and he couldn't remember ever meeting anyone who'd owned that ability.

But the Chalice. Hell. This was a disaster. Bishop scrambled after the thief as she hurtled down the staircase. She was fast, streaking ahead every three or four steps, every time he got close enough to almost reach out and touch her.

Either she was taunting him, or she was limited in how far she could teleport.

They hit the main staircase and his thief launched a hip onto the bannister and rode it to the ground. Bishop thundered after her, his heart hammering.

"Stop!" Bishop threw himself forward as he hit the ground floor, his body slamming into hers hard. They both went down, a mess of arms and legs, and Bishop took a knee to his thigh that almost—almost—unmanned him. No time to think of it though. He grunted and flipped her over the top of him, sending her sprawling onto the hall runner, taking most of it in a slide across the black marble.

Then he was up. And so was she.

Both of them were breathing hard.

Bishop held his fists up in a pugilist's stance, but a wash of green light ran over the back of his knuckles and down his arms. One punch would be backed by pure force.

And then he paused, because that was how he would treat a dangerous adversary, and the thief was a woman. He wasn't quite certain how to deal with her. Nonlethally, if he had a preference.

"You're fast," she breathed.

"You're faster. How did you learn to do that?"

"Do what?" She teleported to his left and smashed her fist into his ribs. Then she was gone again, coming up in front of him as he tried to get his bearings.

A hard jab to the solar plexus. Then a right hook that almost slammed his chin up through his skull. He blocked the next one. And the next. His hands moved like a blur, but so did hers, and he was reluctant to unleash his deadlier talents, at least until he knew who she worked for.

Slamming a flat hand into her chest, he sent her staggering into the door to his parlor. Her weight flung it open, smashing it into the wall, and his thief tumbled to the floor, rolling back over her shoulder onto her hands and feet.

The light caught her eyes as he strode forward, and he realized that they were green. Green and utterly devilish. Much like her. Her pretty mouth curled up in a smile.

"You can only teleport short range," he told her, fists curled up in front of him defensively. "Five feet or so, at the maximum."

His thief tipped her chin up. "Is that so, Lord Death?"

Lord Death. His nostrils flared, but the only other sign of discomfort he showed was a faint narrowing of the eyes. "It seems a night for hidden talents," he remarked. "Want me to show you some of mine?"

"I bet you say that to all the girls."

Bishop smiled a not-nice smile and triggered one of the spells built into his rings. The room vanished, plunged into an inky black. There was a faint detonating *boom* to his right and another sound, almost a silent crackle to his left an instant after it, as she teleported.

There.

He could feel the tingle of his spiderweb ward, still clinging to her. The same place as that faint, crackling sound had come from.

"It seems to me, Lord Death, that this spell inconveniences you just as much as it does me." He was correct. She was standing exactly where he'd predicted her.

"Does it?" he murmured.

Boom. Crack. A whisper of noise close to the armchair he sometimes sat in. Bishop moved silently, feinting to the right as if drawn in. "I suppose we shall see."

He leapt back the other way, just as she teleported again... straight into his arms.

A gasp.

Bishop caught her wrists and slammed her back against the nearest wall. Every inch of her struggled, but he was far larger than she, and stronger. The sharp edge of the Chalice ground into his hip as he used his body to press her against the wall. Leaning closer, he whispered in her ear, "The interesting thing is... you thought the darkness was my talent."

"My first mistake." She didn't sound remotely cowed.

"Darkness is but a home to me."

"Home to thieves, assassins, and whores." She turned her face, her breath warm against his cheek. Bishop tensed, but she merely laughed, a husky sound that vibrated through his chest. "Now the interesting question remains: what are you going to do with me?"

And he hesitated.

She felt it. The tension in the room ratcheted higher, both of their bodies steel. "Well, now," she almost purred. "That *is* interesting. You don't know. I didn't think you'd hesitate to take a life."

I don't kill women or children. Not after that one time, that one mistake. His heart wrenched in his chest, but he forced the thought aside. Not now. Not when one sign of weakness could cost him everything. "I want answers first."

"Perhaps I can be accommodating."

Testing the grip he had on her wrists, she let all her weight hang there and lifted those legs, wrapping them around his hips.

His cock hardened. He sucked in a sharp breath. *Jesus,* she was brazen. "That's not going to get you anywhere."

"Maybe I'm right where I want to be?" That whisper did damage to his willpower as she reached forward and brushed her mouth along his jaw.

Bishop trembled. Her lips were like silk, and he could feel the crush of her breasts against his chest. The inky black cloud was starting to dissipate as his attention slipped, and he caught a glimpse of her pale face, his hands tightening on her wrists.

"Where did you get your scars from?" she whispered, licking the one that ran along his jawline.

That congealed his sagging willpower like nothing else. It felt amazing; wet velvet over raw silk, but with it came the damning memories.

"That's none of your business," he growled, and wrestled her toward the desk.

"You shouldn't be so serious all of the time."

"I'm not your friend."

"Pity."

Somehow she turned the tables on him. He almost had her pinned to the desk, prying her legs from around his waist and disentangling her arms, when she hammered a blow into his jaw. His foot slipped on the rug beneath him, and he fell to the floor.

He cracked his head on the marble and the spell dissipated completely. Light sprang back into being just as a whirlwind of action accumulated in the doorway.

His thief smiled as Bishop lay sprawled on his back.

"Such a shame. Just when we were getting to know each other." Her gaze slid down over the hard, naked planes of his chest, almost regretfully. "Just as an aside, I *can* teleport further than five feet, but a part of me wanted to get to know you a little better." His thief blew him a kiss. "Sometimes the thrill is in the chase."

Boom. Crackle.

She was gone. And so was his tracking ward.

"No!" Bishop darted for the window and slammed his hands on the ledge, but the gardens outside were silent and empty.

Nothing moved.

His heart hammered in his chest. Guilt and failure formed a bitter stew in his gut. He'd never been so distracted that he'd lost his mark before.

Damn it. He had to get the Chalice back before someone dangerous got their hands on it.

And now it was personal.

CHAPTER ONE

Three days later...

SOMETIMES IT PAID not to reveal the full extent of your talents.

Verity staggered along the street, one hand clapped against her ribs and the bloodied gash there, and the other trailing along brick walls she could barely see. *Bloody bastards. Bloody swiving rotters!* The world swam and suddenly she found herself up against an iron-railing fence with little idea of how she'd gotten there.

"She's been this way!" someone shouted behind her. "I've got her trail again!"

Her blood. They were tracking her blood. Verity swayed. Pain had left her lightheaded, and now only determination fueled her. Mother of night, where was the house? Bishop couldn't be far away. She'd spent weeks tracking this house, watching it, watching him....

Only place those behind her wouldn't dare follow.

If Mercy were here, she'd be the first to tell Verity what a bleeding stupid idea this was. *But, ah, Mercy-love, not a lot of choices. We're down to our last hand here, and it's not a great one. Sometimes you've just got to play it.*

"There she is!"

Verity's heart hammered behind her ribs. She curled her power up tight and small inside her, and then released it like a punch. She was weightless, senseless, a mere flicker... and then the world kicked in around her, slamming her back into tired, leaden bones as she found herself in a garden.

Roses. She staggered to her knees, feeling the weight of her pain riding her down into the ground. A door formed in her vision, almost taunting her. A black lacquered door, stark in the imposing white walls. How many weeks had she stared at that door, wondering about the silent man who lived inside and moved through a ghost world?

Nearly there....

Footsteps swarmed over the gravel behind her and she sucked in the last shred of her strength, unleashing it in a whirlwind of power around her. Instantly she lurched through time and space, using the door as her focus. Then she was there, and she couldn't remember coming back. The twitching of Bishop's wards settled over her skin like an invisible net that itched, just faintly. Relief swept through her. He'd kept them up then. Now he'd at least know that someone was there.

If he was home, that was.

Bishop rarely leaves the house. Why would he be out now?

Searching for you, said her far-too-nimble mind.

"Help." A little stronger this time. "Help!"

Reaching out, Verity hammered her fist on the door, leaving a bloodied smear against the lacquer. *Hurry, damn you.* A brief glance behind showed it was too late. The men chasing her stepped out of the shadows, wearing faceless masks beneath their top hats. Even behind the mask, she could sense one of them grinning.

There was no way in hell she was going to die like this. Grabbing the doorknob, Verity dragged herself upright. "Come on then, you rotters! Come on!"

One of them took a step toward her—

And then the door opened abruptly, and she fell inside.

The last person Bishop had ever expected to answer his door to fell heavily against his chest.

"What in the bloody hell—?"

"Shut the d-door," the young woman breathed, glancing back over her shoulder.

There was nothing out there but fog, but he could tell from the little pinpricks against his skin as his wards trembled that there had been. Five of them, to be exact. Swirls of fog proclaimed where they'd been standing, and the faint sound of running feet against cobbles echoed like dull hammer blows in the still night.

And then the world sprang into sharp realization. He could smell something rich and coppery. Blood.

"Thank goodness," the woman said. It was *his thief's* voice and *her* magic that trembled against his wards. He just hadn't expected that pert, upturned face with the faint cleft in her chin, and her full, slightly trembling mouth. A tumble of dark brown hair was knotted in a loose chignon that had seen better days, and she had the biggest, greenest eyes he'd ever seen.

She was also far younger than he'd expected.

"What the hell are you doing here?" He'd spent three sleepless days and nights hunting for her, and suddenly she was in his arms.

"Thought I'd p-pop in and see if you were any friendlier on reacquaintance."

She was bleeding quite badly. Bishop pressed a hand against her side where the worst of the blood seeped through her linen shirt.

"You *are* aware that you stole a very precious item from me but three days ago?" He eased her onto her back on the floor. "What makes you think for one second that I would help you?"

"Because," she panted, "I can get it back for you. I'm the only one w-who... can find it." She glanced down at her side, her face going white. "Oh, God." Then her eyes rolled back in her head and her weight slumped heavily into his arms.

Bishop froze, cradling her gently. "Bloody hell," he cursed under his breath, then dragged her into his arms and strode toward the stairs. Her head slumped back and a tangle of dark brown hair tumbled over his arm. He was hardly a Healer—his skills ran in another direction entirely—but when one knew how to stop a heart in a man's chest with a thought, or tear holes in the walls of an artery, then you also knew the basics in doing the opposite.

"—says she can get it back?" The voice was near, a low, firm tone that brooked no nonsense.

"So she claims. I'm inclined to believe her. She made a mockery of me but four nights ago. Moved through this bloody place like the Chalice was a magnet."

Verity stirred. She knew that voice. Had spent hours listening to it during her surveillance.

Adrian Bishop. He had a beautiful voice, low and smooth like gravel and honey. His face matched the voice; all sharp edges, strong jawline, and typically masculine features, matched by the prettiest eyes she'd ever seen on a man. They were so dark they looked almost bottomless. Cold eyes, she'd thought the first time she saw him, but they hadn't been cold the other night when he pinned her against the wall.

A little shiver ran through her, which was rather surprising. The victory of her theft had had her blood up the other night, and she was always riding the edge of her nerves in those moments, but she hadn't realized the attraction to him remained.

Maybe it was his sheer height? Or the memories of the lean, sculpted planes of his body, gilded by moonlight?

Maybe it was simply the fact that when he moved he looked like a predator, fast and strong and utterly in control of himself. A man who knew how to use his body.

Verity blushed. She was no innocent. No girl from Seven Dials ever could be, but sex had been somewhat lacking in her experience. Sweaty, thrusting intervals that earned her little enjoyment.

Bishop did not look like the fumbling sort at all. Sex with him would be dangerously intense, she just knew it.

"Hell and ashes," the other man snarled, and shadows danced between her eyelashes as she turned her head toward the pair of them, catching a glimpse of the stranger leaning heavily on his cane.

Instant trepidation crept through her veins, but she stayed very still. Spending most of her adolescence on the streets, Verity knew danger when she saw it. The older man might wear a crisp suit and waistcoat, and he was still handsome with streaks of silver at his temples, but there was something about the way he held himself, even his manner, that made her think that this man feared no one, and had good reason not to.

"Why would someone want the Chalice?" the older man demanded. "It's useless now, without the other two relics."

"That doesn't make me any less uneasy," Bishop demurred. "Combined, the Relics Infernal could control a greater demon. By themselves, their powers are still dangerous and unpredictable. The Blade might have been destroyed last month but what can the Chalice and the Wand do together? From what I remember, by itself the Chalice improves the potency of spells, but who practices alchemy anymore?"

The powerful man paused before the fireplace, his hands resting on his cane as he stared into the flickering flames. Verity finally got a good look at one of the rings on his hand, and her blood ran cold at the sight of the chips of diamond within the thin gold triangle symbol that represented the Order of the Dawn Star. Catching herself before she blurted out her surprise, she tried to ease her breathing. This wasn't simply another sorcerer, but the Prime himself, the man who ruled the Order!

Enemy to all Hex mages like herself, who had either been cast out of the Order or who slipped through its grasp. The Order represented laws and rules that defined what a practitioner was allowed to do with their magic, and punished those who refused to submit. They served the crown and therefore had the backing of the might of the British Empire behind them, whereas she was an unregistered mage whose very presence was a crime.

"The Chalice can do more than simply improve spell potency. It is a vessel that can create an elixir that can bring the very dead to life. It's still dangerous. We need it back." The Prime considered something. "There's not a single sorcerer I'd trust with it."

"You gave it to *me*," Bishop replied.

"You're my son. You're an exception to the rule."

"I'm your bastard, and you have another," Bishop countered, and there was heat in his voice. "Do you trust him too?"

Verity sucked in a sharp breath. Adrian Bishop was the *Prime's* son? Of all the revelations.... This information was worth its weight in gold!

"Lucien has made his peace with me," the Prime said, finally.

"And the other?" Bishop hesitated. "No sign of his body yet?"

The Prime shook his head, a swift dismissal that made her curious. "The excavations of the house continue. If he's... buried beneath that rubble, then we will find him."

"Perhaps it was for the best," Bishop murmured. "His power was immense, and dangerously unpredictable."

"That's enough," the Prime snapped. "Losing one of your sons is never *'for the best.'* Besides—" His mercurial gaze turned to the bed, spearing hers through the gauzy curtains. "Your charge is awake. I believe you're going to have to add eavesdropping to her list of sins."

Bishop strode toward her. As he snatched at the bed drapery and flung it open, she scrambled back, drawing her knees up to her chest and trying to take stock. One nightgown, a bandage still wrapped around her middle, and a pair of strange beaten bracelets around her wrists.

Not a single weapon, except perhaps the ability to escape.

Those dark, emotionless brown eyes turned molten as he examined her.

"Well, hello again," she said, using bravado to mask that brief hot clench of uncertainty that speared through her.

"You're awake."

Not quite the friendly greeting she'd hoped for.

"What's your name, girl?" The Prime moved into view, pouring himself a goblet of wine.

"What would you like it to be?" Verity murmured, glancing up at the Prime from beneath her lashes. Names were dangerous. And whilst she'd had little choice but to return to the scene of her crime, now she needed to keep her wits. She'd known when Murphy accepted this commission on her behalf that she was playing dangerous games, but the price had been too tempting to turn down and there was no refusing Murphy. He owned her, body and soul.

"The truth," Bishop replied, easing onto the bed and turning a hooded gaze her way.

Why that look left her feeling faintly breathless, she didn't know. Or perhaps she did. It was a cheap thrill, a dangerous undercurrent between them. Her fingers twitched, tempted to reach out and stroke the soft velvet of his coat, or perhaps tuck the long strands of his dark hair behind his ear. It was unfashionably long, and as he cocked his head she wondered if he kept it that way to try and hide the scarring on the left side of his face.

Control yourself.

"Tell me what your name is," he demanded, and something clamped down hard within her. The bracelet around her wrist locked tight, a lash of pure electric sensation short-circuiting her brain.

"Verity Hawkins," she said promptly, then her eyes widened. What on earth...? Clapping a hand over her mouth, she stared at him in shock. The last time she'd told anybody her true name she'd been eight and staring up at the grim master of the workhouse. That was also the last time she'd ever trusted another man.

"Thank you, Miss Hawkins."

"You bastard," she spat, levering to her knees. Lace dripped down her sleeves, getting in her way, but the shackle around her wrist abruptly loosened. Giving it a wiggle, she inspected the thin manacle of pure gold closely. The other one remained dormant. Perhaps it had another use? "What did you do to me? What is this?" Her fingers tore at the manacle, but it was smooth, without a single latch. "Get it off! Get it off me!"

"It's an Occam's Shackle. It means that you are entirely dependent upon my goodwill for the moment." He was enjoying this far too much, though only someone who'd studied the hard planes of his face for hours would notice the faint softening of his firm mouth, and the sparkle in his dark eyes. Chips of obsidian, they were, but now they burned like dark fire. "Did you truly think that I'd trust you?"

It took a second longer to regain her temper. Her nostrils flared, and she smiled, a dangerous thing indeed. "Fair enough." Turning around, she eyed the Prime. "Thought mind-magic was against the law."

"It is." He glanced at Bishop.

Bishop shook his head. "The Sicarii *can* act outside the law in extreme circumstances. Appeal denied. She stole a dangerous relic. I consider the circumstances extreme enough."

Sicarii. That explained a great deal. A shiver of cold worked through her. The Sicarii were the Order's death dealers—shadows in the dark who hunted those who defied the Order, or those who had committed crimes against its laws. You never saw them coming, rumor whispered.

The Prime frowned, as if the argument didn't quite sway him, which interested her. A moral man, perhaps? "Why did you steal the Chalice?"

"Thought it would look pretty on my mantelpiece," she replied. A warming tingle lit through her veins. Say too much, and she would bear the consequences. Murphy had seen to that.

"Verity," Bishop warned. Pressure increased through the manacle at her wrist, a whip of pure lightning streaking through her nerves.

The words burned inside her, her gut clenching and her throat spasming as magic bit deep within her. She shook her head as the burning tingle within her met the lash of power that Bishop wielded. The two opposing forces collided and her body became the battlefield.

It hurt.

Verity screamed as she fought her way through it. Then she was on her back on the bed, panting as the heat left her bones, a concerned face peering down at her. The Prime's hand clasped her forehead and a cool tingle of sorcery worked its way through her, dispelling the heat of the opposing forces.

"It's a compulsion," the Prime said, for Bishop's benefit, she thought. He looked troubled, then turned and stepped away. "She's been blocked from answering certain questions. Something else is there too... a memory block perhaps. Take the manacle off her."

Bishop's gaze cut to the Prime's. "My lord—"

"That wasn't a question." The Prime's voice was pure steel. "I will not see her will compromised. Not even in events such as these."

"This is a mistake," Bishop murmured as he took a menacing step toward her. "She's a criminal."

"We shall see," the Prime replied, watching her carefully.

Verity held up her wrist with a smug smile.

"Not that one," Bishop replied.

"What *can* you tell us?" the Prime asked as Bishop unlatched the shackle from her wrist with those cool, graceful hands. "The names of the men who hired you to steal the Chalice?"

"Nothing," she replied, trying to play his good nature. "It will only hurt me."

"The only one who can remove that compulsion is the one who gave it," the Prime muttered thoughtfully. "Though Lady Eberhardt might know some way around it."

"You want me to talk to Agatha?" Bishop tucked the horrid shackle in his pocket.

"Could be worth a visit," the Prime replied, as if she weren't in the room.

"I'm not talking to anybody!" Verity told them. She slid to the edge of the bed and hopped out of it. "I'm done with this. The only reason I came here is because the drop-off point was nearby, and I was wounded and needed to get them as were on my heels, off it. Now, kind gentlemen, I thank you for your efforts in healing me"—she genuinely meant it too, as she locked eyes with Bishop—"but getting caught up in all of this nonsense is a death sentence, by the sound of it."

Time to get out of here, nightgown and all. She blew Bishop one last kiss, gathered her power, and...

...slammed into the door as she re-formed. Tumbling backwards, she landed flat on her backside with an *oof.*

Bishop held up his wrist, with a matching manacle attached to it. "You can't leave the room, despite your skills."

"You cock-broking bawd-monger! Get it off me. Now!"

Eyebrows rose throughout the room. Verity had her hands up in front of her, somewhat defensively. She lowered them, though she still felt somewhat backed into a corner, like a wild animal. She hadn't wanted this; any of it. Murphy had pushed her into the theft and there'd been little choice but to go along with it. Now that it had blown up in their faces, she wanted out.

"No," Bishop replied, crossing his arms over his broad chest. He didn't smile, but looked faintly pleased with himself.

"I'm sorry," she blurted. "I didn't want anything to do with this. I... I work on commission." Better than mentioning Murphy or the One-Eyed Crows. "This wasn't my choice."

"Choice or not, Miss Hawkins, your actions have caused a considerable amount of danger to the Order, and to the rest of London. Do you understand what this means?" the Prime asked gently. "You stole a dangerous relic that could set entire graveyards walking among the streets should a necromancer with the right skillset get his hands upon it. And that's the least of my concerns with what it might be used for. I would be within my rights to demand your head for this, and the Queen herself would see you hang."

"What's stopping you?" For something was, she realized. "That's what the Order does, doesn't it? Crush the weak? Execute those who don't fit their fancy mold? Not everyone wants to be on a leash and chain, *my lord*. Just because I have occult ability and don't ascribe to your practices doesn't mean you can grind me beneath your heel."

The Prime considered her. "You have a very curious idea of what it means to belong to the Order. No," the Prime mused. "No. I have a better idea. I need to know who commissioned the theft, and I need to get the Chalice back." His silver gaze pierced her right through. "You tracked the item with your powers—and don't try and pretend otherwise—and you're the only one who knows who you gave that relic to. Earn your reprieve, Miss Hawkins, and I will protect you. From the rest of the Order, from whatever you're scared of, from the men who wanted you dead."

"You want me to fetch the Chalice back?" Disbelief strained her voice. Despite the fuzziness in her head whenever she thought of the man who'd commissioned this theft—and her anger that he'd tampered with her memories in the first place—she still couldn't escape that eerie sense of danger whenever she thought of him.

It was a sensation that had stopped her from making deadly mistakes in the past. Sometimes she even wondered if it was a hint of precognition that she'd never learned to train. "Are you barmy?" Verity breathed out a humorless laugh. "I can point you in the right direction, but if this"— she gestured to her bandages—"is any indication of their intentions toward me, then thank you, but no."

The Prime crossed his arms over his chest in a gesture somewhat reminiscent of his son. "They know where you are, Miss Hawkins, and they know who you came to. What are your alternatives? Escape? To where? They obviously know who you are and what you do—that's how they came to you in the first place. Do you truly believe that they cannot find you again? Do you not have family that might be at home, who these people might go after?"

The words crawled inside her stomach. Murphy's face flashed to mind, pleasantly cheerful as he cuffed the back of her head and leaned close. *"Someone wants to meet you, pet, and I wants you to be nice to them. They've got a little job to do, and they're offering enough blunt to help you keep young Mercy with a roof over her head, eh?"*

The threat to Mercy had forced her to meet with them.

She'd been thinking about this all wrongly.

If she didn't sort this out, Mercy might be in danger. Heat drained out of her face. Who knew what these people would do to her friends? If they couldn't find her, then maybe they'd go after the One-Eyed Crows to get their hands on her?

"Adrian will protect you," the Prime continued, though Bishop looked about as pleased with this suggestion as she felt. "And if you help get the Chalice back then I shall acquit you of all charges against the Order. Think wisely about your decision, Miss Hawkins, as the Order could be the best ally you have right now, and the only ones who might be able to stop these people before they do worse. We both have similar aims."

She knew he was manipulating her, but it all made too much sense, damn him.

Murphy would have her head if she agreed to this, but what choice did she have? Murphy might protect Mercy, but were the Crows strong enough to deal with these people? She might not be able to remember who'd commissioned the theft, but she remembered everything afterwards, including the fact that the men who'd jumped her were dangerous, and powerful sorcerers.

Verity met the Prime's eye grimly. "I'm not agreeing to anything else until we have a deal signed in blood."

"Signed in blood?" The Prime arched a brow.

He might as well have said, "how primitive." But that was how Verity had grown up, cutting deals in Seven Dials among curse workers and exiled sorcerers. Some sorcerers there could do blood magic, so an oath signed in blood was bindingly legal unless one wanted to experience the worst kind of backlash a broken oath could cause.

She tipped her chin up. "I'll work for you to find this Chalice, but in return, you clear all charges and protect me from the people who stole it."

The Prime considered her then held out his hand to Bishop for a knife. "We have a deal, Miss Hawkins."

The second the Prime had gone, Bishop turned to her. "Let's make one thing entirely clear. I don't trust you. But I will protect you, if you do your part of this deal. However, if you think for one second that I will let you hurt him in some way, then you and I will be enemies." He brushed past her, heading for the door. "Trust me, Miss Hawkins. You don't want to be my enemy."

She was used to dangerous men and threats. Her entire life seemed to be filled with them. And Adrian Bishop, for all his smoldering stares, owned some sense of morality. Not like Murphy, or Daniel Guthrie. She could use that. She just needed to get under his skin a little, and judging from their encounter the night of the theft, it wouldn't be difficult.

Bishop lived like a monk; that didn't mean that he had the same appetites as one.

"You care for your father." It surprised her a little.

Bishop paused in the doorway. "Of course I do. And you would be wise to keep that little tidbit to yourself."

"Not common knowledge?" She arched a brow. "Is he ashamed of you?"

Those sensual lips thinned. "Drake is ashamed of nothing. It was my idea to keep the connection between us quiet, so that nobody would suspect he has a Sicarii assassin on hand."

What would that feel like, to deny your own heritage? She nibbled on her lip. "That sounds entirely practical, and quite horrible. I'd give anything to know who my father was."

His expression actually softened. "You don't know him?"

Verity shrugged. "He walked out on us when I was two. Had another mistress."

"Ah. I see."

Not quite. She smiled bitterly. "He liked gin too much. A common occurrence in my neck of the woods."

Silence settled between them. She could see that he didn't like thinking of her as a person with her own losses to deal with.

"Well," Verity said, arching a brow and offering a faint shrug, just enough to draw his attention to the thin cotton night rail she wore. "Where to first?"

"First we get you some clothes," he muttered. "Then, you tell me."

CHAPTER TWO

"THIS DOESN'T LOOK like Seven Dials."

Bishop ignored Miss Hawkins, alighting from the hack and passing a pair of shillings up to the driver. Tucking his collar up against the late morning drizzle, he turned his gaze toward the house.

Forbidding black iron fences guarded the perimeter, along with overgrown hedges that seemed as though anything could lurk within. Small watchful chitters sounded and the leaves rustled. Miss Hawkins looked around sharply, pressing closer to his side as he gestured her through the gate. Bishop had found her a black gown—an old one belonging to the Prime's ex-ward, Ianthe, who'd left it behind at his house once—but it fit poorly, and clung in some areas whilst gaping in others. She'd dressed her hair in a simple chignon, and the effect was... troubling.

The little thief should not look like an innocent country lass with her cheeks all rosy and her skin dewy. Especially not when she was just as likely to slit your purse, steal your entire life savings, and sell your soul to the devil, all the while blinking up at you with those innocent eyes. She could make a fortune at the card tables.

Christ. How old was she? She couldn't have more than two decades on her, which made him uncomfortable. She certainly didn't act like it, though he suspected growing up without a father might have been difficult, especially if she'd lived in Seven Dials as she claimed. Maybe she'd been forced to grow up early?

And he was *not* going to start feeling sorry for her.

"Bishop," Miss Hawkins warned. "I thought you wanted me to take you to the Dials. I need to see... my friend... and ask if he knows about any of this. Those people had the token he was meant to give them if they paid the right amount."

"I lied. We have a stop to make first. I don't like going into a situation blind, and you could be planning anything."

That drew her sharp green gaze. "I'm not leading you into a trap."

"We shall see," he replied as he strode up the front path then around to the side of the gloomy manor. "Come. And keep your tongue polite. Our host shall not be pleased to meet you to begin with."

"Our host? Where are we?" Miss Hawkins looked up at the house, her gaze sliding over the iron fence and the lush sprawl of gardens barely tamed. Some trick of the weather saw that the windows appeared made of gray glass—completely opaque. From the rooftop a raven watched with a beady eye, ruffling under its wing with its beak.

"We're here to see Lady Eberhardt," he told her, strolling through the door to the servants' quarters as if he belonged here.

Which, in a way, he did. Lady Eberhardt had been his second master during his sorcery apprenticeship, and

33

though the old harridan breathed fire on her better days, for some strange reason she'd taken him under her wing as if he were her own. Scarred by his mother's death—both physically and mentally—and haunted by the events surrounding the transfer of his apprentice bond from his previous master to Lady Eberhardt, young Adrian Bishop had been looking for a home.

And with Lady Eberhardt, who had never borne children of her own, he'd found it. Or the closest thing to a home that he could imagine since his mother's passing.

"The Prime said something about her—and the compulsion laid upon me." For the first time, Miss Hawkins looked nervous as she stepped over the lintel, gasping as Lady Eberhardt's wards touched her and clung like spidersilk. "Do you think she can remove the compulsion?"

"Perhaps. If she decides she likes you." Agatha was notoriously testy. This was going to be interesting.

Miss Hawkins's pretty green eyes narrowed. "Who could not like me?"

"Oh, I've a person or two in mind."

The sudden smile she graced him with made him uncomfortable. "That's because you've barely had a chance to get to know me. I'll grow on you, Bishop."

"Like ivy, no doubt."

"Well," she murmured under her breath as she pressed close to his side. "I didn't realize that you wanted me to get so close to you. Perhaps if you smiled a little more, I might consider wrapping myself *all* over you. Like ivy, as you say. You do have pretty eyes, after all."

Someone could have knocked him over with a feather. Bishop stared down at her, at that pretty heart-shaped face and those teasing eyes, and realized that he'd stopped in his tracks. She was an outrageous flirt and he... he had little defense against such notions.

It wasn't the first time a woman had propositioned him. It was the first time, however, when he'd felt any sort of answering stir below the belt. As if aware of every thought that was currently occupying his head—if he could be said to be thinking at all in this moment—she reached out, fiddling with the edges of his coat. Glorious mischief filled those almond-shaped eyes, one shoulder lifting coyly.

"Look at that," Miss Hawkins whispered. "Cat got your tongue, Mr. Bishop? Or are you struck dumb just imagining all of the things that I could do to you?"

"You're incorrigible." Somehow he forced himself to catch hold of her wrists, just in case she decided to explore further. He wasn't certain he'd have the willpower to protest.

"Be honest with me," she whispered, taking a step forward. Somehow his back met the wall, but there was no escape, for she was right in front of him, skirts brushing against his trousers, the faint perfume of her soap—his soap—warming the air around her. "That night when you were chasing me... did you ever think about what you'd do with me, if you caught me?"

Every. Damn. Night. Bishop stared down at her, swallowing hard.

Sound intruded: the door swinging open. Bishop pushed away as the butler clattered into the kitchen. Maxwell let out a sigh of relief when he realized who was standing there. "Master Bishop. You could use the front door, you know?"

"I know." As he reached the door, Miss Hawkins gasped, and he looked around to find her staggering after him, drawn by the shackle around her wrist.

"I thought this kept me in the same room as you?" Miss Hawkins threw all of her body weight against it and he had the bizarre thought that if he took off his own shackle, she'd fall straight onto that delectable little backside.

"It's not the room. With this on, I'm the Anchor. Step lively."

The look she shot him wasn't nice. "I've never heard of such a thing."

"That's because I created it." Something to do in the dark hours of the night, when he couldn't sleep. Although his sorcerous talents ran toward destruction and death, he'd always been driven by the urge to create. It helped to assuage the dark hunger that gnawed at him as the call grew worse. It was something every practitioner of the Grave Arts had to watch for, and so far, creating devices in the depths of his laboratory was the only thing that took his mind off that dark hunger, even if it was only for a few hours. Offering his arm, Bishop quirked a brow. "Would you care to follow me?"

"*Care?*" Miss Hawkins growled under her breath, pointedly ignoring his arm. "It's not as though I have a choice, is it? Besides, I should hardly wish to be dragged and bumped up the stairs like some carpet bag."

Bishop leaned closer to her, his gaze drifting to the soft curve of that dangerous mouth. "The second I can trust you is the second I release you."

"And when will that be?"

"Most likely never." Holding open the door, he gestured her through it. "Fool me once, shame on you; fool me twice, however...."

"That sounds like a challenge," Miss Hawkins murmured, and this time her gaze slid down his coat, locking on the powerful planes of his chest. She looked up swiftly, catching his flustered gaze. Those gloved fingertips brushed against his shirt, directly over his heart. "I like playing games, sir. And I like stealing more than just pretty baubles and strange relics."

"I don't have a heart."

The smile grew. Turned dangerous. Bishop's breath caught and those fingers marched down his chest, turning into a slow glide before he caught her wrist just above the glint of his belt buckle.

Shit. Every thought rushed out of his head as his blood ran south.

"I've often found the way to a man's wits lies in other areas of his body, my lord." Verity glanced up from beneath thick, dark lashes. "Who said I was talking about your heart?"

Bloody hell. "I'm not interested," he lied.

"Mmm." That purr was dangerously smug. "We'll see."

Pushing away from him, she reached up to unclip her jaunty black hat as she swept through the doors.

Not much to do but follow her, and Bishop cursed as he realized just how neatly she'd turned the tables on him. Bloody, rotting hell. He'd never been much adept at polite conversation or flirtation, but the feeling of being distinctly out of his depth left him unsettled.

And aroused.

"Upstairs?" Miss Hawkins asked, waiting for him at the bottom of the staircase.

"Follow me," he growled, and her laugh floated up the stairs behind him.

The scent of patchouli and the soft murmur of voices lured him toward the private sitting room that Agatha often preferred.

Inside, he found a pair of older ladies near the window. Agatha's head twisted sharply toward him, relaxing when she realized who it was. She was leaning over Marie's shoulder, pointing out some discrepancy in what her secretary had been writing. From their muttered tones, it was clear they'd been disagreeing over something.

"Good morning, Marie," he called.

Marie looked up and smiled. Thin, steel-rimmed spectacles obscured the secretary's gray eyes, and her graying hair was bound into a tight chignon. She wore a waistcoat over a loose shirt rolled up at her elbows, and a pair of breeches, though only here in the privacy of the house. "Good morning, Adrian. What a pleasant surprise."

And she meant it.

"Surprise?" Lady Eberhardt harrumphed. "Perhaps. Pleasant is yet to be seen." With a faint groan, she reached out for the cane she sometimes used. The inclement weather would be plaguing her joints.

"It's always enjoyable to have Adrian visit us," Marie protested.

"Always is a strong word. As to the Ascension protocol, do as you will then, dearest." Lady Eberhardt kissed Marie on the cheek while Bishop respectfully averted his gaze. He was the only one who ever bore witness to these endearments, a sign of trust. If someone else realized the precise relationship between the women, then they would be lucky to escape an asylum for their "indecent" behavior. As far as he knew, even Lady Eberhardt's previous husband had been entirely oblivious to what was going on between his wife and her secretary.

The door pushed open, revealing Miss Hawkins. Like a summer sky swiftly clouding over, Agatha's gruff smile faded and she eyed Miss Hawkins like a bug pinned to a lepidopterist's board. "Adrian. You should have warned me that you had company."

He crossed to her side, reaching down to buss his lips against her cheeks. "Sorry. I didn't realize you weren't alone."

Agatha's hand cupped his face and she looked up into his eyes, reading almost everything within him, he was certain. The bond between master and apprentice remained, a sentiment from other times that neither of them was quite ready to dispense with.

"You're troubled," Agatha said telepathically. *"Is it the girl?"*

"She's the thief I've been searching for."

"The Chalice?"

"Already passed hands, unfortunately. She turned up at my doorstep bleeding. Whoever she gave it to tried to kill her."

A light touch stroked within his mind, chasing scattered sensations. *"That's part of it, but not all. What has she done to unnerve you so?"*

Bishop kissed her palm then stepped away from her, discreetly shutting the mental door between them. "Lady Eberhardt, may I introduce Miss Verity Hawkins, thief extraordinaire and reluctant accomplice in the quest to get the Chalice back. Verity, this is Agatha, Lady Eberhardt, and her secretary, Marie Adams." He looked to Agatha. "Verity's under a compulsion denying her the means to give me information about those who commissioned the theft."

"I see." No sign of what she thought of the young woman. "You want me to take a look?"

"If you would." Bishop collapsed into one of her sleek chairs, noticing a platter of lemon tarts on the table in front of him. He reached for one. "Drake seems to think there's a memory block too."

Agatha prowled toward Verity in a swish of skirts. "If you get this boy hurt, I *will* find you. Then I will skin you alive, do you understand me?"

"Agatha!" he protested, spraying tart crumbs as Marie echoed him.

"It's all right," Verity replied, crossing her arms over her chest and returning Agatha's gimlet stare with a slightly challenging one of her own. "She'd have to catch me first, which as you've learned, Bishop, is no easy task."

"You don't know who you're dealing with," he told her. "I have only half of Agatha's skills."

Verity gave him a very steady look, then straightened as HMS Eberhardt sailed into her orbit. Very few people could meet Agatha's stare when it held those icy tones, but Verity was giving it her best shot.

Dusting crumbs from his fingers, he considered that. Grudging admiration bloomed within his chest. "Careful. She teleports."

"Is that how she escaped you?" Agatha asked, then flexed her left hand with a disgruntled expression on her face.

"Yes. Are you all right?"

Her inner shields engaged, locking him brutally out of her mind. Bishop felt as though she'd slapped him but she merely scowled and flexed her arm. "A slight pain, which comes and goes. Nothing much to worry about."

He exchanged a glance with Marie, who shrugged. Agatha didn't know the meaning of the word vulnerable, so it was sometimes difficult to ascertain whether a "slight pain" meant just that, or whether she was in agony and hiding it.

"*I'll watch her,*" Marie mouthed over Agatha's shoulder, to which he nodded and looked away.

Catching them in a conspiracy against her would only arouse her ire.

Agatha caught Miss Hawkins's chin, turning it this way and that. "Hmm," she said, reaching for the girl's left glove and tugging it off. There was a tattoo on the back of her hand, though he couldn't see what it was. "I wouldn't have to chase you, girl. All I'd have to do is go straight to Seven Dials, wouldn't I? Perhaps I'd catch you in a house with a black door?"

Miss Hawkins gasped, drawing her hand against her chest. "How did you—"

"Mr. Murphy is someone I keep my eye upon," Agatha said, prowling around her. She poked Miss Hawkins in the ribs. "He's obviously not feeding his little crows enough, is he? Help yourself to the lemon tarts before Adrian demolishes them." With that, Agatha strode to the tea service and began pouring.

Miss Hawkins gaped after her. As if noticing his interest in this, she shut her mouth and then crept closer. "How did you know about... Murphy?"

Agatha sat and stirred her tea. "Murphy? Or the Hex?"

Hex? Bishop sat up straighter. "You're part of the *Hex* Society?"

"Witches, mischief-makers, and dabblers," Agatha pronounced, sipping her tea. "If you want to find something of a magical nature that's gone missing in the East End, then you hie straight for the Burrow before it can be sold. Mr. Murphy runs a fine trade in fleeced goods and he wields an entire household of little crows who scurry about and do his work for him. He prefers not to dip his fingers in the Order's pools, however, which makes it interesting to consider that he might have had something to do with the Chalice's theft. He's not usually so stupid. Or bold."

"You're not supposed to know about us," Miss Hawkins blurted, sitting hesitantly on the sofa beside him. "If you know about us.... The Order frequently puts Hex witches to death when they can find them—"

41

"And boils their babies alive," Agatha added with a faintly raised brow. "Don't forget we like to burn their houses and salt the ground."

A mulish expression crossed Miss Hawkins's face. "I've *seen* sorcerers burn a Hex house to the ground and salt the earth."

"But did you ever wonder what they were doing inside that house, hmm?" Agatha leaned closer. "Did you ever wonder whether the ground *needed* to be salted?"

"Salt purifies," Bishop murmured when he saw her perplexed expression. "If there was something bad raised inside...."

"Precisely." Agatha sniffed, and sipped her tea. "We don't want that sort of rot popping out of the Shadow Dimensions willy-nilly."

"Demons and hell spawn," he added, as Miss Hawkins might know nothing of the Shadow Dimensions. "Imps, sometimes. Depends on how strong the sorcerer was that raised them, or whether they sacrificed something."

He'd never seen Miss Hawkins so disconcerted. "This is not right," she finally said, eyeing the platter of lemon tarts. "We're supposed to be a secret."

Marie, ever the nurturer, poured Miss Hawkins a cup of tea and patted her gently on the shoulder in sympathy as she handed it over. Agatha might be the blunt cosh a thief used, but Marie was the velvet glove. Verity couldn't take her eyes off the tarts now, and Marie noticed, handing her a small plate.

"There's very little that I'm unaware of when it comes to occult forces, though I'll concede that few within the Order have the extent of my knowledge, or Adrian's. Perhaps only a half dozen people," Agatha admitted, tipping her head toward him. "The Hex, however, are constantly monitored. If they play within the lines then we pretend we haven't noticed them. Sometimes a young misguided sorcerer needs a place to go when he's cast out of the Order, and they're considerably good at picking up minor Talent off the streets and keeping it from burning half of London to the ground. They know our rules and so they teach their members to control themselves, at least minimally, and keep their heads down. Nobody wants some young fool ripping the roof off a house because he can't control his temper. It's in all of our best interests to keep magic and sorcery out of the papers, and away from those who would use word of it to further their cause in parliament. The Order is busy. We don't have time to police the entirety of London, so we allow them to continue unmolested."

"I just... I cannot believe, all this time...." Verity sprayed crumbs as she shoveled lemon tart in her mouth.

When was the last time she'd eaten? Bishop frowned.

"Shocking, isn't it?" Agatha's smile looked predatory. "Now drink your tea up so that I can read your future in the tea leaves. There's more than one way to slip a compulsion, and I'm very interested in discovering who's been skirting around certain laws."

CHAPTER THREE

"THAT WOMAN IS terrifying," Verity grumbled as Bishop helped her down from the carriage. She could still see those dark eyes glaring right through to her soul, the claws of Lady Eberhardt's magic trying to pierce her compulsion... and failing. All it had left Verity with was a slightly throbbing headache, and the impression from Lady Eberhardt's murmured, "Hmm," that she was going to be hounded until this mystery could be solved.

If only you knew who'd placed the compulsion upon you and ordered this theft. Life would be so much easier, wouldn't it?

For she could be leading them into a trap, right now. Bishop wanted to retrace her steps on the day she'd been given the commission. It would be easier if she remembered what those steps were. Verity had argued against it, determined to see if Mercy and the rest of the Crows were all right.

"I actually think she liked you," Bishop told her, scanning the area. One would have to get up early in the morning to get a jump on the shadowy assassin.

"What gave you that impression?"

"The fact that she offered you her lemon tarts. Trust me," Bishop threw over his shoulder as he stepped out of the gutter onto the footpath. "Agatha's very fond of lemon tarts, and she doesn't just share them with anyone. Besides, she wouldn't have called you 'girl.' It would have been something far more disparaging, believe me."

"She threatened to skin me alive," Verity muttered, snagging a handful of skirts and following him.

"That's only because she likes me, and you stole my Chalice."

The broad planes of his back met her gaze. *Or, because she's worried I'm going to get my "hooks" into you.* Which was precisely what the old witch had muttered as she'd snagged Verity's arm whilst Bishop exited the room first.

The sundial that portrayed the heart of Seven Dials loomed in the gloomy afternoon sunshine. The rain had stopped, though heavy clouds threatened another shower sometime in the near future. Seven roads scythed out from the sundial, leading to a variety of paths—and fortunes. There was a pub on each corner of the roads, and outside each sat a man or woman on a stool. Some were reading the paper and surreptitiously watching the streets. Some leaned against the walls, picking their nails or fiddling with a straight razor, as if to proclaim an aura of danger. One stared at her directly, his fingers twitching as if to reach for the weapon tucked in his belt, no doubt a hex-thrower. Every single one of the them wore only one glove, and there was a tattoo on the back of each of their ungloved left hands proclaiming their allegiance to their gang: a scorpion, a black cat, a one-eyed crow, a white rabbit's foot, a clock face, a bat, and a four-leaf clover.

"This way," Verity said, leading Bishop down the only road that was safe for her. The Hex had distinct rules that they referred to as the Code. Step outside the rules and you were considered easy prey, with no consequences from the Hex Society leaders.

Bishop looked around with interest at the distilleries and gin sellers along the street. No sewers or dustbins here. The Seven Dials rookery of St. Giles was a sprawl of filth, and the pair of them stood out like sore thumbs. It had been cleaned up somewhat when the Hex took over the Dials, but signs of gang warfare revealed itself in sooty scorch marks against brick walls, and a shop window had been smashed out and hastily boarded over. On the boards a pentagram within a circle had been painted.

"You grew up here?" he finally asked.

"I wasn't born here," she admitted, stepping lively and looking as if she knew exactly where she was going. "My mother died when I was seven, and I ended up in the workhouse. Colin Murphy offered me a position in the One-Eyed Crows when I was twelve."

A vastly abbreviated version of her history, one that sounded almost sanitary. How could a man like Bishop even begin to understand what life had been like for a young girl of twelve who knew what the alternatives were if she didn't accept Murphy's offer? Twelve was a dangerous age, after all, for a girl.

Verity's gaze slid over a pair of whores prowling their particular corners. A very dangerous age.

"You don't sound anything at all like I'd expect for these parts," he replied. "Unless you're cursing at me."

Heat found her cheeks. "My mother was a serving maid, once upon a time. When Murphy took me in, my dialect was good enough, but he insisted upon me learning how to pass in the West End."

"Why?"

"Why do you think?" she retorted. "I'm the decoy when he's got a bit of breaking and entering on the mind, or a better-racket planned. I spent hours on Bond and Oxford Streets, mimicking my *betters* and dipping pockets. It's strange, but a rum cove will let any girl get close enough to pluck the very eyes from his sockets if he can see halfway down her dress and she sounds all polite and fancy-like." Verity rolled her eyes. "If I knew my numbers and letters and how to speak, then it meant I didn't have to lift skirt. Gives a girl a little incentive to learn."

The look he gave her made her anger fire.

"Why?" she demanded, feeling the urge to prick at him. "Not quite like the silk sheets you were born on, my lord?"

"Silk sheets?" he replied in an unimpressed tone. "I thought you said you'd studied me?" He hesitated. "And I wasn't sneering at you. It sounds horrible. I can't... blame you for doing what was necessary to escape these circumstances."

"Including your Chalice?"

He shot her a look that melted her all the way through. "I wouldn't go that far."

"Yes, well." She stared straight along the streets. "What do you mean you weren't born on silk sheets?"

All of the easiness fled from his expression. "Just that. I'm illegitimate, Miss Hawkins."

With that, he strode ahead of her, one hand sliding to his belt as a pair of youths took a step in their direction then thought better of it.

He handled threats well. Confidence was its own armor here and Bishop somehow made it seem like he was the predator, not the prey. The fact that he towered over most of the street lads, and looked big enough to fight "Diamond" Jim Purcell in fisticuffs also gave them all pause.

You've fallen in with a dangerous man, Verity Anne.

One who didn't quite fit the mold that she'd expected of him. "If not silk sheets, then where?" she muttered to herself as she followed him.

Bishop paused in the next intersection.

"What's going on?" Verity stood on her tiptoes, but the street was clearly blocked. Men were arguing up ahead and some sighed under their breath, as if this had been going on for some time. There were children about, hands held palm up, which she always hated to see. And her without a single coin on her.

Verity caught a glimpse of the obstruction; a dray carrying coal was wedged sideways in the street, blocking traffic. Someone had obviously tried to turn it around, and now the horses were stuck in their traces and clearly weary of it.

"This way," Bishop said, gesturing her down an alley.

"If we go down there, we enter neutral territory," she protested, then added to clarify, "It means we're going to have to be careful of other gangs."

A small, dangerous smile played over his mouth. "I should like to see them try to assault me. But we'll skirt back around into Crows' territory the second we get a chance."

His confidence was infectious, even though she knew better. "As *soon* as we get the chance," she repeated, then hesitated once again.

Bishop, however, had made up his mind. Verity scurried after him, using her hat to shield her face as she entered the gloom of the alley. It opened up into the next street over, which could have been identical to the one they'd been on if only all of the hairs along her arms hadn't risen.

"Seven gangs," Bishop murmured, offering his arm to her. "How did the Hex form? I don't know a lot about it."

She accepted his arm, pasting her body close to his side. All the better to hide her face. "The founding members of the Hex got together in 1789, barely a decade after the Order of the Dawn Star formed. Some of them were outcasts from the Order; some couldn't conform to the rigid ways the Order expected them to use their power; and some were simply hedge witches and occult tinkerers. Forming the Hex Society protected them as individuals and they took over the Seven Dials, either by forcing other gangs out or assimilating them."

"Hence the use of superstitious symbols as gang flags," he murmured. "One-Eyed Crows, what does that mean?"

"That we see all." A group of children rollicked past them. "The original founder of the Crows was Norse."

The scrimmage of street children ended as one tore loose from the others; casting a nasty hex under his arm as he grabbed the puppy they'd all been chasing. A young lad, barely ten or eleven, whistled under his breath, winking into the shadows of an alleyway.

Verity watched him, suspicion dawning.

"Oh, hells," she blurted, slamming to a halt as a trio of young men slipped out of the alley directly in front of them. They'd been made.

Another slunk off a barrel, cupping his hands around a thin cheroot that he lit with the flame flaring off his finger. There was a splash of black ink tattooed on the back of his hand, and Verity didn't need to look closer to know which gang he ran with.

"Friends of yours?" Bishop asked.

"No," she said emphatically. "They're members of the Black Cats. The Black Cats are curse throwers, con artists, and grave robbers."

"Trouble?"

"Could be. But we're not in their streets," Verity replied, checking to make sure that, yes, they were still on Monmouth and hadn't yet crossed into Clare Avenue. "So they won't start a fight unless they're interested in a turf war, but I'm not sure what they want." At his confusion, she added. "Monmouth Street splits territories in the Dials. This is neutral ground. Nobody wants the Hex to go to war with each other. It's bad for... business." Not to mention hell on walls and buildings, and pretty much anything softer. Like flesh.

"Madame Noir," called the man with the cheroot, tipping his cap back as if to get a better look at her. "Fancy seeing you here, sweet pickles."

"Zachariah." Verity smiled flirtatiously, adding a little swing to her step to hide her nervousness.

"Who's the bit of bread and butter?" Zachariah asked, strolling around Bishop as if sizing him up. Zachariah Morrissey was the main enforcer for Harry "Hex" Perkins, who ran the Black Cats. He liked flashy tweed waistcoats, strangler hexes, and the butcher knife that was no doubt hidden somewhere on his person. He could spit a curse at twenty paces and have it stick like glue, which was his main source of amusement.

"A friend."

"Smells like burnt cinnamon to me," Zachariah said, taking a puff of the cheroot and blowing the smoke in Bishop's face.

Oh, shit. Verity stiffened, but—

"Burnt cinnamon?" Bishop muttered under his breath.

"Sorcery," she whispered. "Zachariah's a Sniffer. Can spot Talent a mile away."

"A new lad, eh?" Zachariah's grin split his face in half. "You want me to introduce him to the rules 'round here?"

"I don't think you want to do that, Zach," she warned, her hands held up to placate him. *Come on, stand down, you cocky little shit.* Energy swelled within her as she drew in whispers of power. If he pointed a single finger in her direction then she was legging it out of there. Zach's curses tended to be cruel, with an edge of humor—as long as you weren't the intended recipient.

"Hex Perkins and Murphy got an alliance, pretty. That don't mean no stranger on our turf can walk 'round like he owns this here joint. There's a peckin' order here, boss. And you're on the lower rungs of it." Zachariah stopped an inch away from Bishop's face, even if he had to lift onto his toes to meet the sorcerer's eyes.

Please don't, she tried to tell Bishop as those dark eyes glanced her way, then back to Zachariah.

Bishop merely stared the enforcer down. Then brushed at his coat as though some riffraff off Zach's person had landed on him.

Oh, hell.

"If you're hoping to provoke a scuttle," she said, stepping forward hurriedly as Zach's eyes began to narrow, "you're looking in the wrong place. Mr. Bishop is...."— searching, searching for the right way to introduce one of the Sicarii—"He's a client."

"Aye, lads. Listen to the little dollymop," Zachariah said flatly. "Usin' all them big words, like she's tryin' to prove that she got an ed-u-cay-tion and don't work flat on her back for a bit of spit-and-polish, eh, boys?"

"He's not my lover," she shot back.

"And you'd do well to treat the lady with some respect," Bishop announced, which sent the four of them into gales of laughter.

Verity turned long enough to raise her eyebrows at him—*you're not helping*—then stepped between him and Zach. "Murphy's got me on a side job, you understand? Mess with us, and you'll bring Murphy's wrath down upon your head. Hex Perkins won't want that."

Zach pushed her in the chest, forcing her to stagger back a step. "Aye, now there's a problem with that little story, there is. Ain't you heard?"

"Heard what?"

He grinned at his boys. "Murphy ain't gonna do nothin' if we have us a little fun with his leashed bitch."

Verity went cold. What the hell was he talking about? She'd only been gone for a day and a night. What had happened?

"That's enough of that," Bishop muttered.

Zach's grin was nasty and he shot his finger under one arm as he dove for cover, shouting, "*Crie vexus!*"

Curse! Verity punched into nothingness and reappeared five feet away, kicking Zach in the chin as he landed on his belly behind a set of crates. Hearing footsteps behind her, she spun, lashing out with her magic. The world drew close and tight and then power exploded out around her, taking her with it. Two feet to the right. The second she re-formed, she drove the flat chop of her hand into Zach's fat thug friend's throat, and he went down with a groan.

"Step back," she warned the other gang members.

Where the bloody hell was Bishop? She'd been anticipating blood and ooze leaking out of ears, but they were all still standing. A quick glance showed the sorcerer on his knees, breathing hard as he pressed his knuckles to the cobbles.

Realization dawned. She'd been standing in front of him when Zach flung that curse. Which meant that when she'd translocated, he'd taken the full force of the blow. "Bishop, are you all right?"

He grunted.

And Zach laughed, which was when Verity saw red.

A second later she re-formed, shoving a knee into Zach's back to keep him down.

"What did you hit him with?" she snarled, yanking Zach's head back by a fistful of hair and pressing her knife to his throat.

Everybody froze. The Black Cats turned into statues, watching the knife in her hand. She couldn't use it. Not without breaking the Code, but the threat of it made everyone realize just how serious she was.

"Verity?" Bishop said, a strangled sound coming from his throat, as he slowly stood, moving carefully. Sweat broke out on his forehead and he half took a step toward her before forcing himself back into stillness and clenching his eyes shut.

"He'll be... fine." Zach gasped. "Stiff as a corpse for a few hours, but—"

"*What* was it?"

"A little Lover Boy," Zach bleated, "though it was meant for you."

Lover Boy... or Ladies Luck, as they called it in the vernacular. Because it would be amusing to see the unattainable Madame Noir lift her skirts and try to ride Bishop like a pony in the middle of the alley, overcome by lust. Verity's hands quivered with rage and she punched him in the face. All of the Dials came out in her, cutting through her clean Verity Hawkins persona. "You son of a bitch! What's the counter-curse?"

Zach flinched, shielding his face. She punched him again, keeping an eye on Bishop just in case he lost control of the curse. "Counter-curse him, you little prick, or I'll cut yours off!"

"Can't!" he gasped.

"What do you mean, 'can't'?"

"I don't have a counter-curse," he gasped. "Not for Lover Boy."

God damn it. Verity withheld her fist, trying to mull her way through this.

"It'll wear off in an hour or two." Zach rolled into a ball, using the chance to move away from her knife. He found his hands and feet, resting on his fingertips as he met her gaze. They both knew he couldn't escape her. "Meant nothin' by it, Madame. Just a friendly little hex."

"'Friendly' my Aunt Nelly," she snapped, but he'd played within the rules of the Code and there was not much she could do about it. If it had hit her, then she'd have borne the consequences. The seven gang leaders who ruled the Hex might have considered the matter in Hex Gathering, but whilst they might have insisted Zach pay a tithe to her, secretly they'd have been stroking their moustaches to hide small smiles. The curse wasn't fatal. Zach would have won considerable esteem without causing any major damage, and that would have earned him man-about-town status whilst she was the one laughed about.

Bishop stared at her, his nostrils flaring and his hands clenched, with a very prominent erection.

"Cor," whispered someone behind her, "he's actually holding against it...."

"That's bullshit," someone else muttered. "Can't nobody stand against Lover Boy."

"Are you certain you're all right?" she asked. She'd seen grown men wade into whorehouses, forgetting about their wives and children, while under the influence of Lover Boy. A proud widow protesting the gin houses in St. Giles had taken four men in a back alley before it wore off.

Black eyes shot open. The way he looked at her.... "Fine," he pronounced, very slowly and very clearly. "But I need to get out of here, right now. Before I turn a certain someone into a greasy smear on the cobbles."

Before he lost control.

Taking a few careful steps back toward him, she kept the knife in her hand. "Zachariah?"

"Yes?" he asked warily.

"I would have preferred to keep this business to myself, but you've just made it impossible." Verity let a nasty smile show. "You just cursed an Order sorcerer of the Grave Arts. This isn't over. We have business to conclude, which means we can't take the time to teach you a lesson, but if I were you, I would sleep with one eye open."

Zachariah turned pale.

"If I were you," Bishop growled, straining with sweat, "then I wouldn't sleep at all. Ever."

Then he turned and strode toward the mouth of the alley, forcing her to follow.

"I am so, so sorry," Verity said, hurrying after him and reaching for his arm.

"*Don't touch me*," Bishop snarled, then froze as the curse crashed over him with intensity, sensing her proximity and trying to drown him in her nearness.

The scent of her, all hot, wet woman.... He was almost overwhelmed by the sudden urge to press her against the wall, drag up her skirts, and fuck his way into her. The memory of that night she'd stolen the Chalice blinded him. He could almost feel her smooth skin under his touch.

Verity froze like a rabbit in the hunter's sights. "You could... take care of that," she whispered. "I have rooms at the Crows, but there's another place I have when I want some privacy. If you wanted to... you know...."

Bishop swallowed. Hard. *Jesus bloody Christ.* Was she suggesting what he thought she was?

"It's not going to go away," Verity explained, clearing her throat as though she felt some sort of guilt for the matter.

"Does this happen regularly?" Somehow the words formed.

"Everyone's got their own little curse. Zach's just tend to be nastier than others."

Curses and hexes. He couldn't imagine sorcerers scrubbing around in the dirt like this and using their talents for two-bit entertainment. There was no training here, no rituals, no control. Just bottom-feeders like Zachariah, and from the way he'd treated Verity, this wasn't the first time he'd made a nuisance of himself. Anger swelled. "Has he ever hit you with this?"

Verity's eyes went round. "No. But I've seen what it does."

"This... is not right."

"I know," she whispered. "I'm so sorry. I didn't think. I didn't factor in the fact that you were standing directly behind me."

He was going to kill someone. Or four someones. All it would take would be to reach out with one hand and squeeze his fist, and they'd all four drop dead in the middle of the street, their hearts crushed with a thought....

Do it, whispered the craving, the rushing temptation of the call of the Grave. All of that sweet, sweet power... his for the taking as he rode their death throes, drained them of every last....

Bishop's eyes shot wide and he grabbed Verity by the shoulders. "Kiss me!"

"What—?"

"I'm going to kill them if you don't—"

Verity grabbed his collar and hauled his body against hers. Bishop staggered, catching her by the upper arms and feeling all of that soft flesh pressed against his. She was so small, her cheeks revealing the fact that she didn't eat well, or often, but all he could think about right now was shoving a hand under her skirts and stroking the sleek skin there. Her mouth met his, and he lost his mind.

Sweet. Soft. Tasting faintly of lemon tarts. It wasn't a gentle kiss, but she seemed to know what she was doing, and so he followed her actions, darting his tongue against hers and earning a soft gasp.

Somehow her back hit the wall, and then he was sliding his mouth down her throat, his hands catching her up beneath the thighs as he shoved his hips into the vee of her legs. Good God. It felt amazing. He thrust against her, feeling the curse overwhelm him.

"Bishop!" She dragged his face up with a fistful of hair.

He caught a glimpse of green eyes, then his mouth was on hers again. He just wanted to kiss her. Forever. All over. To taste every inch of her skin.

"Bishop," she gasped again, and this time he heard the protest.

No. She was saying no. And if he were in his right mind, he'd be saying it too.

It took everything he had in him to let go of her wrists. He couldn't even remember grabbing them. His cock ached, and somehow he let her slide down between his body and the building.

He shoved away from her, breathing furiously. The curse had counteracted the crushing weight of his killing addiction, but he wasn't certain that was any better, for now he had the raging desire to slam her up against the wall and have his way with her. He could barely think of anything else.

"Private rooms. Now," he growled. "Then fetch me some bloody ice, or cold water, or something."

Before he lost his virginity in a back alley in the slums.

An hour later, Bishop still soaked in the small copper bath in Verity's spare set of rooms, gritting his teeth against the chill of the ice she kept dumping into the water. He didn't know where she was getting it from, but as she reappeared in the room again and again, he realized that not much could stop a sorcerer who didn't consider walls to be much of a hindrance.

As the curse wore off, he finally began to realize something.

He was naked.

Oh, he'd been aware of that in a peripheral way—*get her in the bath, against his wet, naked flesh, kiss her, drive her beneath him*—but until now, he hadn't had the ability to consider the implications of that.

She hadn't said a thing about the burn scars.

Or the fact that his cock was trying to resemble the mainmast of a ship, despite his best attempts not to. Bishop pressed his hand to his temple. He still wanted to kill

Zachariah. He also wanted to sink under the water and pretend she wasn't there to see this humiliation.

"I'm sorry," Verity said, sitting on the edge of the bath and biting her lip. "I–I'm not used to working with another person, and I think I assumed you'd deflect the curse.... It all happened so quickly."

Bishop dragged his knees up, trying to shield his nakedness. Heat flushed through his cheeks. What the hell kind of woman just sat there, as if they were talking about the weather over tea and scones, whilst he was naught but skin?

"It's fine. I'm not used to people being able to teleport. You were between us, so it didn't occur to me that I'd be the one hit by the curse." No, he'd been about to fling a ward in front of her, trying to angle it correctly, to deflect the bloody curse.

Unfortunately for him, Verity hadn't needed protection.

"I just didn't want you to think that I tried to save my own skin at the expense of yours," she replied, and trailed her fingertips through the water, brushing them against a half-melted chunk of ice. Green eyes locked on his. "I'm not that kind of girl."

And what kind of girl was she? Nostrils flaring, he leaned his head back against the bath. That way lay trouble. A muscle in his jaw throbbed. He was attracted to her. He couldn't deny that. But he had to keep his mind focused. The Order depended upon him. Drake depended on him.

And with his father half-lost to the grief of losing a son last month, Bishop couldn't afford to think of his own needs. One more blow might shatter the man, though this morning had been the first time he'd seen his father halfway back to normal.

"You wield an impressive weapon, Mr. Bishop."

Good God, was she referring to— She was. He swallowed. "Miss Hawkins—"

"Verity," she reminded him, looking all lazy and relaxed, like a cat. As though she weren't trailing her fingertips through the water of his bath.

One last burst of the curse sank its hooks within him. He blinked and realized that he was holding on to her wrist, and couldn't remember when he'd moved. Their stares met. Verity seemed to be considering something, biting that lip again. That bloody lip. His vision glazed as it filled his vision until it was all he could see.

"Please," he begged. "Please leave me alone, at least until this wears off."

"I'm not going to take advantage of you," she said.

"That's not what I'm afraid of." It was difficult to admit. And shameful.

Verity's gaze softened as she searched his. "Most men I know wouldn't bother to try."

"I'm not most men."

"I know." Verity looked away. "I also wanted you to know that you didn't force that kiss in the alley. I wanted it."

His breath exploded out of him. He'd needed that, he realized.

She seemed to understand, as she stood and fetched him a towel. "Well, now. I'd say we've got at least an hour of this left in us, and then we might be able to go see Murphy. Something about what Zach said makes me uneasy. I'll go see what they're saying on the streets. Give you some privacy." She shot a glance over her shoulder as she turned to go, taking in every inch of him with an unabashed interest. "Just in case you *do* want to take care of that."

Bishop smashed the water with his fist in frustration, sending a surge of it in her direction. Verity vanished with a squeal and a laugh, leaving him alone in a bath of ice water.

Where, after some careful consideration, he did take care of "that."

CHAPTER FOUR

"FOLLOW MY LEAD, keep your mouth shut, and for God's sake, don't reveal your sorcery," Verity warned, dragging a fistful of her black crepe skirts up the rickety staircase at the back of the Grey Goose Inn. "Let me do the talking. Colin Murphy isn't a man who cares for sorcerers or their ilk, and he particularly dislikes challenges to his authority. You're on his turf now, so don't forget it."

"As you wish," Bishop murmured.

At the top of the stairs, Verity turned to see if he was mocking her. Those warm brown eyes met hers and Bishop graced her with a faint smile. It transformed his face from not quite handsome to extraordinary.

And it quite stole her breath.

"Your move," he reminded her, with a twitch of his dark brows. "You're in charge."

Turning around, Verity knocked sharply on the door to Murphy's private rooms and then stepped inside as if she belonged. Which she did.

Only... Verity's head lifted, taking in the removal of Murphy's landscapes that he'd painted himself, and the lack of furniture. His books were all gone too and the room reeked of... some kind of smoky scent, rather than the Irish whisky that Murphy liked to drink. Only a desk remained, and a handful of people were gathered around it. Nobody in the streets had been willing to admit they knew anything, which made her nervous, and now this.

"Verity!" Mercy's voice was shocked as she saw them.

"Merce," she said, noticing the signs of damage to the walls and the smear of black that had scorched the curling wallpaper. "What happened here?" That was when the crowd stepped back from the desk and she realized who was sitting behind it. "Guthrie, what are you doing? Where's Murphy?"

Daniel Guthrie pushed his chair back, dark eyes flickering to Bishop at her side. "Thought you was dead."

"Almost," she admitted warily, for she and Daniel shared a turbulent history. And nobody should be sitting in Murphy's chair like that. The old man would have a fit. But... there was no sign of him. Only Conrad's looming dark hulk, Betsy Gibbons in her array of bright red ruffles and painted lips, and whip-thin Nigel Cremorne, who you never dared take your eyes off. All three of them Murphy's inner circle, but splayed around Guthrie as if....

As if leadership had changed.

"Murphy's dead, Verity," Mercy said, stepping away from Guthrie for the first time, her long lanky legs swathed in their usual trousers. "The attack happened the night you vanished, right here in this room."

The same day those... men... had tried to kill her. Mercy knew where she'd been and what she'd been up to, but Verity nodded vaguely, still reeling from the news. This was what Zach had meant. Murphy wasn't here to protect her anymore and Daniel... Daniel had his own grudges against her.

"Do we know who?" She didn't like the way Daniel was examining her, as if Verity were some bizarre object that he didn't recognize. "The Clover Lads? The Black Cats? They accosted me in an alley earlier. I thought they were bolder than usual."

Conrad and Nigel exchanged glances at that.

"What's going on?" she demanded.

"Perhaps you can explain?" Daniel rasped in his hoarse voice. Someone had tried to hang him once and failed. There was a cheroot sitting in the ashtray by his fingers, but he didn't move. Only watched her. "Heard you and Murph were workin' on some kind of job. Heard you bailed."

Mercy tried to shoot her a warning look from beneath the brown bowler's hat that covered her mousy hair. A smear of black kohl razored across her face, making her green eyes stand out in the shadows, but Verity rather thought she'd been crying recently, and that made her feel protective. At sixteen, the girl was several years younger than her, but they'd grown up together in the workhouse and when Murphy offered her the gig, she'd insisted upon Mercy coming too.

Madame Noir, and Murphy's Wraith. Thief and assassin. And allies.

"I didn't bail!" Verity spat. "They tried to break the terms of the deal. As soon as I delivered the goods, one of them stabbed me."

"Who?" Guthrie's fingers twitched.

And Verity froze. "I-I don't know. Someone put some kind of memory hex on me."

"A compulsion," Bishop added, and all of a sudden every eye in the room was upon him.

"This is Mr. Bishop," she said, mentally cursing him. "We're working together to discover who betrayed us."

"And who the fuck are you?" Guthrie's gaze locked on Bishop.

"A friend of Verity's," Bishop replied calmly, as if the tension in the room hadn't just ratcheted up ten degrees.

"Seems awful convenient, Verity." Guthrie focused those shark's eyes on her. "Murphy cuts you in on a deal that he doesn't mention to any of us, then you go missing and he winds up dead, and all of a sudden you can't remember anything."

"Convenient or not, that's what happened."

"Show us the wound."

She paused. "I can't. Mr. Bishop healed it."

Guthrie sank back in his chair as if her words proved her guilt.

"Merce," she said, drawing her friend's attention. "We need to know what happened to Murphy. Were they men wearing blank masks?"

"Mercy belongs to me now, Ver." Guthrie's hand closed over her friend's fist, and Mercy looked away.

Verity's eyes narrowed, her mind chasing down all of the potential meanings to that and coming across one that chilled her. "What do you mean? I paid her debt. That's what this entire job was about! She's free to come and go as she pleases."

Guthrie arched a brow. "Seems there's been some kind of mistake. I've been through Murphy's ledgers. There's no payment, Verity. Mercy owes a hundred pounds to the Crows."

No! Verity's hands crashed on the desk, and she leaned over it. "That's bullshite and you know it. The debt stood at eighty-eight pounds three weeks ago, and if I did this little job for Murphy then the debt was clear—"

"Interest," Guthrie spat. "Debt's a hundred quid. And it's your word against ours. If Murphy made such a promise, then why is it that none of the others have heard about it? Murphy told Betsy and Conrad everything. He wouldn't keep this a secret."

A secret.... The words shifted a memory in her head, of Murphy settling those smoke-stained hands over a letter and toying with the edges of it. *"Can't nobody know, Verity-lass. This one's top dollar, and dangerous. You're the best and they've asked for the best...."*

Verity blinked. That conversation had happened right here in this room, the night before she set out to observe Bishop's house.

She looked around. "He mustn't have written it down in his ledger. Said it was a secret. Top-dollar gig."

Guthrie simply smiled and she wanted to punch him in his smug face. This was wrong. Mercy wouldn't look at her, as if ashamed.

I bloody well told you to stop gaming!

"I've never lied in my life, not to the Crows," she told them all. "All I ever wanted... all *we* ever wanted was to...." *To be free.* "To pay our debts." She looked desperately at Mercy, knowing that their dream was crashing into dust, right here in this room. Every time they came closer to earning their way free of the Crows, someone hammered another nail into the coffin. There was always something: food, board, a roof over their heads, weapons training.... As if they hadn't been the best things that Colin Murphy had hauled out of that workhouse. "I can pay her debt. Just... I need time." Time to think. Why did Murphy not write it down? He wrote everything down!

"Tick tock," Guthrie said. "Every day earns extra interest."

How the hell was she going to get the money?

"Or..." Guthrie drew the word out. "You could come back and work for me. Do some high-risk jobs, fetch in some coin. Maybe we could offer special terms of interest to see the debt cleared quicker. And yours too, I might add." Guthrie flipped open a ledger. "I believe you're almost within fifty quid of being free."

"You son of a bitch," she whispered, seeing the noose all of a sudden. This was what he wanted. Because Verity's debt was so close to being cleared, so close she could almost smell it, and Guthrie had always wanted to own her. He'd never let her see that debt paid. Not now when he was trying to consolidate his hold over the Crows. "How do we know that you didn't kill Murphy, just so you could fill his shoes? Just so you could trap me like this?"

Guthrie's eyes narrowed.

"Because the air smells like brimstone," Bishop murmured, pressing his fingertips to the ashy smear on the wall and then rubbing the residue between his gloved fingers. "A demon was here, not too long ago."

Everybody looked at him, as if remembering he was in the room.

"What?" Guthrie demanded.

Demons? A little chill down Verity's spine, however, remembered that smell, as if her inner self was trying to warn her about something.

Conrad's dark-skinned fist curled over the axe at his side. "The Crows don't hold no truck with the Shadow Dimensions."

"Don't they?" Bishop looked supremely disinterested in that statement. "What was the state of the room when Mr. Murphy's body was found, and what did the body look like? I presume it *was* found?"

Silence. Deafening, thundering silence.

Then Mercy spoke. "The smear marks on the walls are from Murphy's curses. He's a hex witch of formidable power and could strip a man's skin from his bones with one flick of his wrist. But... something deflected the curses. The chair where Murphy had been sitting was burned to its seat, and the body was slumped over the desk. It looked almost normal until one lifted his head off the desk." Mercy paled, which was a damned unusual sight indeed. "It looked as though something had eaten his face."

Bishop arched a brow at Guthrie. "And you think Verity did this?"

"What are we supposed to think? He wasn't scheduled for a meeting and the entire house was guarded. Conrad himself was sitting at the door when it all happened, and he didn't see or hear anything unusual. Not a sound, not even the smell of burning. No signs of break-in, and the windows were barred from the inside." Guthrie shot her a glare. "The only person who could have possibly entered unseen was our Verity."

"While I agree that Miss Hawkins has unusual talents, she's not the only person who could get into a locked and guarded room."

"Oh?" Guthrie challenged.

"I myself could do it, as well as at least four others whom I know."

"And who, precisely, are you?" Guthrie demanded, sinking back into his chair, his hands curling over the armrests. "Some kind of theft specialist?"

In answer, Bishop slowly stripped his leather glove off his left hand, revealing the four rings that circled his fingers, their glittering obsidian stones winking in the candlelight.

Nigel almost leapt out of his skin. "G-grave Arts!" he stammered, scrambling back against the wall. "He's a sorcerer!"

That catapulted them all into action. Verity caught Mercy's arm as the girl reach for her blades, and shook her head sharply. Their eyes met and Mercy's hand slowly relaxed on the blade, but her green eyes were wary when they returned to Bishop.

Guthrie's nostrils flared. "Order?"

"Of course." Bishop nonchalantly slipped his glove back on, as if this sort of thing happened on a daily basis. "I'm an adept of the seventh level."

Conrad's fingers clenched around his axe. "What I want to know," Conrad said, shooting her a look, "is how, precisely, you come to know 'im. You been conspiring to get out, Ver?"

"No. God." She waved a hand. "Bishop was the target. Murphy made me steal a relic from him. When the commission tried to kill me, he was the one who saved me. We've cut a deal. The Order won't crucify me if I help him get the relic back."

"We could stop them from touching you," Guthrie said, like a rat seeing a way in.

"No, you couldn't. And I'm fairly certain none of you could stop him from walking out of here, just in case you're planning on burying the evidence." She rolled her eyes.

"That depends." Guthrie stood, aiming a faint smirk at Bishop. Cockiness was his stock in trade, but she knew him well enough to see that he was sweating. "There's five of us and only one of him."

"The only person here who could cause me any consternation is the girl." Bishop tipped his head toward Mercy, who watched him with glittering eyes. "But she's untrained, isn't she?"

Verity, despite her alliance with him, took a half step closer to Mercy. For if trouble erupted, Bishop was the sort to take down his most dangerous enemies first. And how the hell had he known about Mercy's talents? Mercy could kill with but a clench of her fist.

It's what he does, said a whisper in her head. *Like recognizing like.*

"I'm not going to hurt her, Verity," he said. "I have no intentions of hurting anyone." *Unless provoked*, seemed to hover in the air.

"So we're at an impasse," Guthrie said. "We don't know who killed Murphy, and there ain't no sign of Murphy clearing this theft, except for Verity's word on it, as it ain't in his ledger. Now you come nosing—"

"Wait!" Verity hovered in the middle of the office. *Ledgers!* What if Murphy had kept a secret one? It went against the Crow code, but if Murphy were skimming, and he didn't want anyone to see.... "One second." Verity slipped around the desk and dragged a chair out of the corner. She withdrew her knife from her sleeve and used it to pry up one of the floorboards. "I always wondered why there were scratches on the floor here, and I once caught Murphy trying to pretend he hadn't been hiding something in this corner."

The floorboard came loose and Verity caught her breath, dragging out three old, heavy-set books. Not as thick or well-used as Murphy's ledgers, but... secret ledgers. Full of dates, jobs, figures....

"He did write the job down!" she said, rifling through it and finding the last entry. Then she realized that there was no mention of Mercy, or how much the commission would have given Verity. Damn it!

"Let me see that," Guthrie snapped and there was a brief tussle over the ledger, which Verity won.

She needed to know who Murphy—and she—had been meeting with the night of the commission.

A closer look at the name listed in the register stole her breath. "Noah Guthrie," she whispered, meeting Daniel Guthrie's eyes.

He snatched the register out of her hand. "Noah was here?"

"Noah was involved," she said, suddenly certain. "He was the one who met with Murphy to commission the theft." And swirling behind her eyes was the memory of Noah's face, smiling at her across a table she didn't recognize, as though the words had unlocked some key in her mind.

Verity blinked. Her head began to throb. The memory vanished. Noah might be Daniel's younger brother, but he'd always been kind to her. She couldn't equate the image of his sneering smile with the Noah that she'd known.

But she had other problems. "Date, time of meeting, and record of it." Verity forced her voice to harden. "Clearly I wasn't lying."

"Only says Noah was 'ere and wanted the job. But Noah ain't no master of memory hexes," Guthrie pointed out.

"Who knows what Noah is master of?" As much as she missed him, Noah had been a troubled soul, drawn to drinking and finally to the opium dens that ruled the East End. Murphy had been forced to throw him out of the Crows, and Noah had simply vanished one foggy morning. "It's been years since he graced the Dials. We all knew he ran with a bad crowd. Perhaps they taught him more of his magic?"

"Noah didn't have the capacity for it," Betsy said. "His mind was rotted from the opium. Even if he had the strength to perform such hex work, he wouldn't have had the will. Noah ain't your culprit."

"And ain't no sign of what Murphy were paying." Guthrie snapped the book shut. "Which means you still owe fifty quid."

Verity's fingernails bit into her palms, but she knew the way the game was played. "You'll have your fifty quid. As soon as I can get a chance to work it off, but until then I need to focus on Murphy's murderer. I want a stall on the interest."

"Denied." Guthrie looked smug.

"Denied," Conrad echoed, and then Betsy and Nigel. The three of them hovered around the desk, making it clear whose lead they followed.

Damn them. Verity glared back. If it weren't for her, Conrad wouldn't still have both hands, and Nigel owed her for that little job she'd kept quiet about five years ago.

A couple of twenty-pound notes landed on the desk. Bishop plucked several more from his pocketbook, then counted them out. "One hundred pounds, which is all I'm carrying at the moment. That's more than enough to pay out Verity's debt to the Crows, and to make a good start on the other young lady's debt. Yes?"

"What?" Verity's jaw dropped open. "You don't have to give them money!"

"Yes." Bishop gave her that look, the one that said she might as well save her breath. "I do."

"So I can be beholden to you instead?"

A shocked look met her words, then he turned toward the Crows.

"The debt is paid," Bishop said, and taking her arm, he linked it through his. "Verity is free and I'm of a mind to see you write it down in your precious little ledger."

Guthrie stared at the money. "And if I refuse?"

He suddenly gasped, staggering against the desk. Betsy whipped around, knife in hand again, but Bishop merely clenched his fist and she went to her knees too, clutching at her chest.

"I have kept my tongue throughout this entire proceeding," Bishop said, and turned those flat eyes on Conrad when the big man took a step toward him, as if in warning. "I have watched you try to force this young woman into a corner, treating her like a criminal, and I have not yet taken umbrage. Because she asked me not to."

Guthrie choked on nothing, his eyeballs flaring in fear and his hands scrabbling at the papers on the desk.

"I have paid you the money that she owes." Bishop stepped forward and even Nigel scrambled out of his way as he placed his gloved hands on the desk and leaned over it to stare into Guthrie's face. "If you refuse to take it and clear her debt, then I shall treat you as the miserable pox you are, and wipe you from the face of this earth. It's as easy to me as simply... seizing the breath in your lungs."

Guthrie's face turned a particular shade of red.

"In fact," Bishop warned, his voice lowering, becoming almost hypnotic, as if he hungered for it. "The thought of your death pleases me... very much."

Something was wrong.

"I would like to kill you," Bishop crooned. "I can feel the blood rushing through your veins, right now. I can hear your heart racing." He closed his eyes, like a man listening to a symphony composed by the masters. "That little shudder as it pulses for oxygen...."

"Bishop," Verity whispered, catching his sleeve.

His head swiveled toward her and she forced herself to hold firm in the face of that stark expression. This was not the man she knew. Then he blinked, as if realizing who stood in front of him and dared to touch him.

"Please, stop," she whispered.

Dark lashes fluttered over his eyes. "Because you asked," he murmured, and his fingers flung wide, releasing whatever kind of hold he had on the pair of them.

Guthrie sucked in a huge breath, staggering back into his chair and collapsing. Betsy managed to push herself up onto her hands and knees, her back heaving as she sucked in mouthfuls of precious air. Her thin arms were shaking.

Mercy watched on with an almost anticipatory air to her expression.

"Heed this warning," Bishop suggested, once again slipping Verity's hand into the crook of his elbow. "The only reason you're still alive is by her good graces and sense of sentimentality. If it were up to me... well." His thin smile said it all, really, as he turned toward the door.

Verity met Guthrie's furious eyes, and saw there her future. *Oh, sweet Jesus.* He'd ruined everything.

CHAPTER FIVE

VERITY GASPED FAINTLY as they exited the building. "You j-just.... Do you have any idea what you've just done to me?"

"Rescued you from this filth," Bishop replied with a faint snarl. His temples were throbbing and he desperately, madly wanted to kill something. What a vile cesspool of people. This place ought to be burned to the ground. No wonder the Order despised the Hex Society.

"*Rescued* me?" Verity darted in front of him, stabbing a finger into his chest. "I sold my soul to the One-Eyed Crows when I was twelve and it wasn't because I had some hankering to join a curse-workers gang! It was because it was the *only* option for a girl like me in these streets. Without the Crows I'm nothing but prey, and there are people here who would enjoy repaying certain debts, thanks to the Crows!" She looked as though she'd just realized something. "You just signed my death warrant. I can't come back here. I'll have to... flee the country."

Bishop's temper flared. "You weren't coming back here in the first place."

"And who made that decision?" The finger stabbed him in the middle of the chest again. "You? Let me guess, you have a little side offer you're willing to offer me... as long as I *entertain* you. A little way to help pay off the debt I now owe *you*."

He was growing quite tired of that finger. It kept jabbing into the one spot. Grabbing her wrist, Adrian glared at her. "If you're referring to what I think you're referring, then you're quite wrong—"

"Oh? So you don't want to get me flat on my back?"

"No—"

"Because you certainly don't look at me as though you're devouring me with your eyes," she scoffed. "And you've taken me under your wing out of the sheer goodness of your heart. Why, one would think that you give these things freely, wouldn't they? If one was a blind, naïve little waif without a thought in one's head—"

"Are you quite done?"

Verity's lips thinned and she regarded him with suspicious green eyes. "Tell me that you haven't thought about it."

He'd thought about it. There was something about her that drove him crazy, something that reminded him of the way he'd felt about Mya. *And you know how well that worked out.* "I am not the type of man who preys on young women. Whilst we might have started out on the wrong foot, let me assure you that you owe me no debt for the nights you spend under my roof, or even the money that I just paid to the Crows. Work it off at your own leisure for all I care. After today, I understand that all you have known is the greedy, conniving side of life, so I'm not surprised to be greeted with this suspicion, but honestly, Verity, I have no intentions to use you, dupe you, or harm you. Now come. Let's get out of this warren." Turning around, he made for the mouth of the alley.

"You don't understand, you fool," she whispered after him. "I don't have anywhere to go."

"You're coming with me."

"Yes, I know." Skirts swished after him, her voice growing bitter. "I have to get your bloody Chalice back."

He turned and looked at her. Verity staggered to a halt, looking far too young, though there was a light of defiance in her eyes, the glint of someone who would and could survive anything this world could throw at her. He was suddenly furiously angry again, and half tempted to march back inside, but she needed more than that.

"I'm sorry if I haven't explained myself correctly. You're no longer beholden to the Hex. I'm not going to let you come back to this... ruin of hovels, regardless of whether we find the Chalice or not." Reaching out, he pressed his thumb against her forehead and gathered in his energy. "*Ladaskhe fortuna*," he spat, the power word flaring through his veins, hitting his thumb, and then leaping into her skin as he traced an invisible rune there. "I claim you for the Order, Verity Hawkins. By this mark, shall all sorcerers know who you belong to."

The sigil burned brightly against her skin, eliciting a gasp from her, and then faded. Bishop lowered his hand. "You belong to the Order now, as a free sorcerer of her own will. No sorcerer shall harm you, but only seek to guide you, and you have the offer of the Order's resources, including the offer of an apprenticeship in sorcery, should you will it. Until you have chosen your master and settled into your apprenticeship, you are welcome in my home and owe me no debt. If you choose to depart of your own terms and seek your own life in this world, then I shall not stop you. The choice," his voice lowered, "is yours. All I ask is that if you ever encounter a person in such need as yours was today, that you repay this kindness on to them."

Verity's mouth dropped open. Noises came out of it, but nothing coherent.

Grabbing her by the arm, he helped her to sit on the step. "Breathe. I know it's a shock."

Pressing her hands to her face, she sucked in a sharp breath. A breathless laugh burst out of her. "I don't even know if I can believe a word you say. Why would you do this? You don't even know me."

Imploring eyes looked up from beneath a thick row of dark lashes.

Bishop knelt in front of her. "My mother was raised in somewhat less than perfect circumstances. When she was sixteen...." His mouth twisted. "Well, she was beautiful. And there were openings in life available to beautiful girls, there still are. I hate to think that if someone had only helped her, then she would not have been forced to live the life she led." Only then was he able to meet those eyes. "I could never help my mother. When I was born, she'd been a kept woman for almost eight years, cycling through various protectors. It wasn't always a kind life for her, and I was too young to ever do anything about it. Well, this time I can do something. This time I *can* stop those people from forcing you into circumstances from which you cannot escape. Do you think I'm stupid? I know how those ledgers work, how those interest charges rack up. The Crows have no intention of ever seeing you free of this life. One day you'll find you owe too much and then that vile little bastard will say there's a way to help pay off your debt quicker, and all it will cost you is a brief tumble into bed."

Verity looked away. "I know how it works too."

Reaching out, he let his hand hover over hers, afraid in this moment to touch her. "You owe me nothing. Remember that."

"I've never met a man like you," she simply replied, and there were shadows in her eyes as if this was not entirely a good thing.

He stood and held out his hand to her. "Well. Now that that is clear, I think we'd best get going."

Verity bit her lip as she looked at his outstretched fingers. As if making a decision, she accepted his hand and he helped her to her feet. "At least we have a start to our investigation."

"Noah Guthrie. Know him?"

"He's Daniel's younger brother," she replied. "I haven't seen him of late as he was trying to steal from Murphy. Murphy didn't like that very much."

The thought that had been bothering him ever since the revelation in the study returned. "Was Noah the sort of man to consort with demons?"

"Ordinarily, no," Verity replied, still looking pale. "But then, who knows? They said he had some sort of mysterious new crew he was running with. I didn't pay it much mind."

Demons. His fingers twitched. There'd been a demon a month ago, when they'd confronted Morgana over the stolen relic, but he'd presumed that it had been beaten back into the Shadow Dimensions when the Blade of Altarrh was destroyed, and his half brother Lucien had denied the demon his body as a vessel.

Coincidence? Or had the demon somehow found another way back into the world? And if so, why had it gone after the Chalice? Without the Blade, the Chalice was no threat to it. Only with all three of the Relics Infernal could a demon be controlled, and one of the relics had been destroyed.

Something wasn't adding up right. He needed to speak to Drake.

"What was that look?" Verity asked.

He looked down at her. "I'm just thinking. A month ago, my father's ex-wife, Morgana, blackmailed his apprentice into stealing the Blade of Altarrh for her—the first relic in the set the Chalice belongs to. Morgana wanted Drake to suffer for the divorce and was planning on using the demon against him. She's... not a very nice woman. Or wasn't."

"Wasn't?"

"Long story," he muttered, "but the demon needed a vessel to hold it, and so Morgana was trying to sacrifice my half brother Lucien as the intended vessel. Drake and I tried to stop her and her son, Sebastian—my other brother—and were both crushed beneath the house when our magic brought it down."

Verity looked thoughtful. "You think the demon that killed Murphy was the same demon she was trying to summon?"

He frowned. "No. It couldn't be. She needed all three relics to summon and control it, and we destroyed the Blade. Plus, she didn't have the Chalice. I had it. But it just seems an awful amount of coincidence. Demons are... not the sort of thing you run into every day." His frown deepened. "Though my father's men have been working to clear the house site. There's been no sign of Morgana or Sebastian's bodies."

"Maybe they escaped?"

He saw the house collapse in on itself again, and the utter despair that had crossed his father's face. "It would have required a miracle for them to escape." They walked on for another half block before he blurted, "They were working with the Earl of Tremayne, however, and *he* escaped. He would have known about the Chalice's powers, and the demon. And he too wants my father dead."

"I don't think I've ever heard of the earl." Verity hastened to add, "In case you were wondering if there was any connection between him and Noah."

"Was Noah the sort who might have liked to earn a spare bit of coin by doing an earl's dirty work?"

"Of course he would have. But how would they have met?"

"Hmm." It wasn't much of a connection, but at least it gave him a few leads to track down. An icy sweat sprang down his spine. Tremayne and Agatha had bad blood between them, and Tremayne was both powerful and ruthless. He wouldn't think twice about unleashing a demon in this place, if he thought it might bring him the mantle of Prime, which Drake had recently abdicated.

Bishop had a very bad feeling. He didn't want it to be Tremayne.

Verity paused beside him, looking around with a faint frown darkening her brow. "There's something wrong."

Instantly he was on edge. "Why?"

"The streets are too quiet. It's never quiet here in Seven Dials. They say it never sleeps."

Fog had begun to creep in, anticipating evening. It was only four o'clock but darkness would descend quick as a flash in this late autumn. Pale yellow orbs of witch light gleamed from iron posts, replacing the gaslights in this section of the city. In the distance, he could see a woman draped in heavy shawls with a bowler hat on her head conjuring the orbs out of nothing and lighting the streets. One of the Crows, no doubt. How unusual this section of town was.

"Do you think the Crows plan retaliation?" Bishop glanced behind them, but only shadows loomed. Wisps of fog eddied as though something watched them from the shadows.

Verity's hand slipped inside her sleeve, withdrawing her small knife. "I wouldn't put it past them, though your position in the Order shall make them wary. You scared them in there."

Something about her voice drew his attention. He'd known what had happened; the feeling of those two lives quivering in his hand, just begging to be snuffed, had nearly overwhelmed him. That she had seen him like that— "And you?"

Verity met his gaze. "I am made of sterner stuff than that." A faint smile flickered over her lips. "Plus I've seen you shivering in a bath of ice, trying to burn off a Lover Boy curse rather than unleash yourself upon me." The smile died. "I know what type of man you are. A lesser man wouldn't have bothered to try."

A dark shape scuttled out of the shadows, vanishing in the fog.

"What was that?" Verity whispered, as they both spun to face it. She swallowed. "Didn't look human."

"Could be hell spawn." Bishop sniffed the air. "Doesn't smell like it though."

No, it smelled like... an open grave. The call of it whispered along his sorcerous senses, like calling to like. A sudden premonition turned his gut to ash.

"Oh, shit," he said, as he realized what they were facing. Only one thing called to the Grave Arts that he was cursed with.

"What?"

"Flesh constructs." Spitting a power word, he breathed life into the incandescent knife that formed in his hand—his etheric blade. It hummed in the darkness, gleaming gas-fire blue. "Some necromancer's poured Grave power into a dead body and raised it."

"But that's...."

"Highly illegal." Constructs could be formed of anything: earth, stone, statue, even leaves, like a Jewish rabbi breathing life into a golem. But flesh constructs.... The last time anyone had raised flesh constructs, it had taken over forty sorcerers to destroy them as they rampaged through the East End. "It also takes a lot of power, or a lot of sacrifices."

Or the Chalice. Bishop swallowed.

"How many constructs could a necromancer raise?"

He turned in small circles, his back pressed to hers. "Maybe ten if they were particularly strong." One of them lurched out of the shadows, its rib cage hollow and scraps of flesh clinging to its bones. Sinew worked in rotted flesh and hollows gaped where its cheeks had once been. A ravenous green light filled those empty eyes. "Stay behind me!"

Sorcery throbbed through him, all the hairs along the back of his neck lifting as he flung a weave toward it, flames spewing out from his fingers like the lash of a whip. "*Ignitious!*"

Not his forte, but flames crackled and burned in the creature's shaggy clothes, and it made a dry whimper of a scream in its throat as it went down. Clawing at the ground, it looked at him, wide mouth gasping as it dragged itself toward them.

"Bishop! Behind you!"

Verity vanished in a punch of power, and he spun, slashing his knife across the tendons of the wrist of the creature reaching for him. Where had it come from? Bishop ducked beneath its grasping hands, kicking it in the chest. It staggered back with a wet sloshing sound and Verity re-formed behind it, whipping her knife across its throat. Black ichor splashed, but it simply backhanded her toward him and kept jerking toward Bishop.

"Cut it to pieces! Or burn it!" Bishop shoved her out of the way, driving his etheric blade deep into the heart of the creature, where it crackled and spat electricity through the flesh construct's rotting body.

It shuddered, a rasp of fetid air emitting from its throat. Bishop turned the blade, using his strength to pin the creature to the wall while he boiled its heart in its chest.

He waited for the surge of power to sweep him up as death settled over it, waited hungrily....

A blow struck him in the throat and rough hands shoved him back. Bishop fell onto his ass, tripping over Verity's legs as the creature's eyes lit up with an eerie green light. And then it wrenched the dagger out of its chest, dropping it on the ground and started toward them.

"What the hell?" Verity demanded, backing away.

It didn't die. Etheric blades could sunder a soul from *any* flesh. Bishop had all of two seconds to consider this before he turned and scrambled into Verity, shoving her out of the way. "Get moving!"

If it couldn't die, then how were they going to stop it?

Icy little pinpricks lit all down his skin. "There are more coming," he yelled, and reached out with his senses toward them.

One, two, three... ten... twenty?

Death was his Art. Every sorcerer leaned toward one of the three Arts: Light, Gray or Dark. And he was Dark through and through. If someone thought to send these creatures against him, then they didn't know what they were dealing with. Bishop reached out and captured the darkening flicker of one of the constructs' minds with his power. There was a filmy barrier between him and the creature's soul; somehow he had to push through, but necromancy had never been something he dabbled with.

Bishop clenched his teeth, fighting to crush that bubble with his will, but it flared beneath his touch and just for a second he saw a startled face lift from a cauldron of immense darkness.

Then a punch of power sent him staggering back into the wall.

"Bishop!" Verity reappeared beside him with a gasp as she helped him to sink to the cobbles. The heat of her skin lured him, and he realized his own was as cold as death, his power reaching out to hers, tasting it, hungering for her life....

Bishop snatched his power back. "Someone's controlling them."

She gave him an odd look. "Well, yes, they didn't just rise from the grave of their own inclination."

"Yes, but... he's powerful." *More powerful than I am.* "And I think he has the Chalice."

Verity paled. "Right. Well, let's deal with the immediate problem first."

She vanished and reappeared behind a zombie, catching hold of the back of its coat, spinning it, and shoving it into the arms of one of its brethren. "Anytime you'd care to help, Mr. Bishop!"

Somehow he shoved himself to his feet, leaning heavily against the wall. *Just got to get my breath back.* Whatever the unknown sorcerer had hit him with, it had knocked his feet out from under him for a moment.

A sitting sorcerer is a dead one, Agatha's voice whispered and his training kicked in. Bishop spun and slammed a hand against a construct's chest, "*Ignitious!*"

Flinging her hand into the sky, Verity shot a flare of power from her fingertips. An explosion of white sparks erupted in the air, like Chinese fireworks. "Backup," she gasped, and he could see the strain on her face as she translocated out of the grasp of a pair of constructs.

Boots pounded on the cobblestones, Hex gang members flooding from every nook and cranny of the Dials. Some of them wore the white rabbit's foot on the back of their hand, others had four-leaf clovers, and one even wore a black cat.

"Threat to the Dials!" A huge man with a handlebar moustache bellowed, brandishing an axe, which he swung to decapitate one of the creatures. "All in, laddies!"

"The Hex!" a prostitute screamed, flinging a curse at one of the creatures that sent steam bubbling from its mouth as she boiled its insides. Somehow it kept going, crawling across the ground to latch a hand around her ankle. The woman fell with a shriek, and the construct ripped her leg clean out its socket.

More men fell on it, a woman stabbing it in the head, trying to get it off the fallen prostitute.

"Burn them!" Bishop yelled, and the older lady who'd been lighting the witch globes stepped forward, fire forming between her cupped hands.

Breathing over the smoldering flames sent them shooting toward the construct and the old lady cackled. But more of them were ambling out of the alleys, grabbing men and women from behind and tearing into them with blunt teeth.

"Burn them!" Verity yelled, vanishing and reappearing here and there as she launched a kick at one of the constructs' faces, then dragged a woman out of the way of another two seconds later.

She was fine on her own. Bishop forced himself to stop looking for her. The man with the handlebar moustache went down in front of him, screaming as the construct sank its dull teeth into his throat. His axe clattered to the cobbles at Bishop's feet.

Slowly, he bent and picked it up, still feeling the strain from the unknown sorcerer who controlled them. The axe was heavy but he forced his muscles to move, using his sorcerous power to send blood rushing through his veins in an attempt to fire his body with strength.

The axe whirred in his hands, striking into the creature's throat with a squishy *thunk*. Black ichor splashed up the walls. The creature staggered. Bishop swung again, this time decapitating it. The head tumbled to a halt in the alley and slowly, like a tree toppling, its knees gave way beneath its body, and it fell onto its front. A kind of blackened jelly oozed from the stump where its head had been.

As if drawn by some sense of knowing, he looked up as four of the constructs closed in on Verity, one of them wielding a club and another a knife.

Verity smiled. "Come on boys," she said, then vanished.

The manacle around his wrist gave a vicious tug and then she reappeared a foot away from where she'd vanished, falling forward. The club thumped down on her shoulder and she tumbled to her knees, just as the knife slid with sickening accuracy into her side.

"Verity!" Bishop bellowed. He didn't have her skills but it took barely a second to thunder through the fighting to her side, cutting down flesh constructs and shoving men and women out of the way.

One of the flesh constructs crouched over her, its teeth bared as it went for her throat, and his insides tightened in horror.

"*Absolemma hecratius!*" He flung his hand out and once again encountered that filmy wall surrounding the construct's life force. *Not this time.* Bishop slammed through it with all the finesse of a sledgehammer, and the flesh construct's soul glittered beneath his grip. Bishop crushed it, setting the soul free, heat and energy rushing through him and leaving him both giddy and dangerously overextended. He hadn't thought he'd have the power to get through that ward.

Breathing hard, Bishop lowered his hand. "Are you all right?"

"Smashing," Verity replied, though her face was pale and she couldn't take her eyes off the ripe body at her feet.

He staggered to his knees beside her. "What happened?" She was bleeding, one hand clapped around the wound as she gasped.

"Tried... to teleport." A quiver went through her, sweat dampening her hair. "Something happened. It stopped me from moving more than a foot."

The manacle. Guilt soured his mouth. "Let me see."

Crying out as he touched her shoulder, she shook her head. "Shoulder's fine. Just... bruised."

Which left the bloodied gash against her side. Bishop gingerly peeled away the black cambric. Verity paled as a wash of fresh blood wept from the slash along her side.

Wadding up his coat, he pressed it to her side. "Hold here."

"Bloody hell," she said, pressing against it and then swaying.

"Don't tell me you're squeamish." She'd cut through flesh constructs as though they were bags stuffed with straw, after all.

Verity cringed. "It's the blood. My blood."

Looking around revealed that most of the fight was done, the denizens of the Dials bellowing in victory as they raised pitchforks and bludgers in the air and danced around the greasy flames of the burning flesh constructs.

"Come on then, Miss Hawkins. This looks done and I'd best see to that wound." Reaching under her, he drew her lean frame into his arms, settling her there as he stood.

Verity squeezed the flex of his bicep through his coat. "I would say... 'my what big muscles you have,' but frankly... I think I'm going to... faint."

Which she did. Promptly.

CHAPTER SIX

"HOLD STILL," Bishop said, peeling back the rough linen bandage he'd administered in the carriage.

Verity winced, turning her head away so that she wouldn't have to see the cut. Light gleamed through the windows of his parlor. "I am."

"The bleeding's stopped, but the edges of this look raw and—"

"Stop!" she yelped, fanning her face.

"What's wrong? Are you feeling ill?"

"I don't particularly like to... talk about blood," she admitted, swallowing the lump of bile in her throat. "Or wounds."

"For all your bluster, I thought you were invincible. Well, I don't want you fainting on me again, what with all of your delicate sensibilities. I'll stop."

"Bishop," she growled, her cheeks heating. "If you ever mention this to anyone, I will personally find Zachariah and get him to hex you. Again."

Resting her skull against the daybed, she took low, steady breaths as Bishop examined her injury. She needed to take her mind off it. She was feeling that dizzy, breathless sensation again and fainting once was one thing. To do it twice was mortifying. "Do you think that our presence in the Dials had something to do with the flesh constructs attacking?"

Dark eyes flickered up, then returned to their purview of his work. "Perhaps. I'm fairly certain that the necromancer controlling them was using the Chalice to do so. Though I do wonder why they'd attack us?"

"Taking care of loose ends, perhaps." Which meant her. Verity frowned. "What if I know something important but I can't remember—" She hissed out a breath as he dabbed at the slash along her ribs with an alcohol-soaked cloth. "Hell, Bishop. Some warning next time."

"Sorry." He squeezed her hand as her back arched off the daybed. "Agatha's working on how to revoke your compulsion. If you do know something, she'll help you recall it."

"I hope so," she said, remembering the way those flesh constructs had torn their way through men and women she'd grown up with. Not all of them were friends, but when an outside threat attacked the Dials, the Hex banded together as one.

Was it her fault that those constructs had attacked in the first place? She felt ill again, and it had nothing to do with blood. "I wish I'd never gone along with this commission." Murphy dead, the Hex attacked, a demon on the loose....

"I know. Here, drink this." Bishop poured her a glass of something and set the cup into her hands.

"What is it?"

"Poison."

Verity paused with the glass at her lips.

"Brandy," he corrected dryly, rolling his eyes. "What type of man do you think I am?"

"Someone without a sense of humor to this point," she admitted, watching those dark brows draw together as he returned his attention to the second gash along her ribs. Emotions rarely plagued his expression, but his eyes... they told a thousand stories, always. And with the gentle manner in which he pried her dress out of the crusted wound, she could almost imagine that seeing her injured bothered him.

Which was a curious thing.

What type of man was Adrian Bishop? She couldn't figure him out and that was a frightful thing. She knew he wanted her. She'd seen the way he looked at her at times. But he insisted there was no debt between them, and that he would help her... out of the goodness of his heart?

She knew men. She knew the way of the world. Bishop must have some sort of angle, and until she found it she was determined not to let her guard down.

"Hold still. This one is a little deeper." Bishop pressed his fingers lightly to her inflamed skin. "I'm not much of a Healer, but I know the rudimentaries."

The fire in the hearth flickered as Bishop drew energy from its heat and from the room around him. Not a single chill dampened her skin, however, which betrayed considerable skill. One that she didn't own herself, if she were being honest. Verity simply pulled in energy from everything around her.

What would it have been like to be tutored the way he clearly was? To learn the deft weave of sorcery?

Daniel Guthrie wouldn't have laughed in her face then; she'd have smashed him flat in under a second. *Imagine the power....*

Breathing out a power word, Bishop flexed his fingers and tightly woven threads of sorcery sank into her skin, a cold effervescent sensation that made her breath catch.

Then it was over. No pain, no raw, burning sensation in her side.

"Where did you learn to heal?" A few of the Hex had the talent, but every practitioner she knew hoarded their secrets, and she'd never known how to do it herself.

Bishop busied himself tidying up the bloodied linens and the pan of water he'd used. "The first thing we learn as Sicarii is how the body works, how to stop a heart, how to cause a clot in the brain, how to bruise, how to sprain. Healing is simply a reversal of such."

"So you're a Healer?"

"I'm an assassin, Miss Hawkins."

"Verity," she corrected dryly. "I believe us familiar enough now to use our names. I have seen you naked, after all." And an excellent sight it had been.

"I'll do you a deal. I won't mention your fit of vapors, if you don't mention that ice bath again. Ever."

"Only if you say my name," she told him.

Bishop rolled the bloodied linen up carefully, considering her words. "Verity," he finally said, and the way he said it made something wary clench up tight inside her. The way it sounded on his tongue... it sent a shiver of something unfamiliar through her.

Longing?

Now she knew why he'd hesitated. A simple word, but it held within it a sense of familiarity, of connection, that she hadn't expected. Verity cleared her throat. "Well, now," she said, forcing herself to be cheerful. "That wasn't so hard after all, was it?"

Bishop sighed. "I'll fetch you some supper."

"Wait!" She held her wrist up to him with the golden cuff he'd locked around her. "I want this off."

His lips thinned, as if in protest.

"I want it off," she demanded, sitting up. "After today, is it not clear that I can be trusted?"

"It's not so much a matter of trust," Bishop replied, then paused again.

"Oh? Then it should be no trouble to remove it."

"Verity," he breathed. "The Chalice is an important relic. I cannot risk losing any chance I have at getting it back."

"What you're saying is that you *don't* trust me." And just when she'd been warming up to him. "I'm not going to run, Bishop. I have nowhere to go. I am not a slave, I am not a criminal, and I am *not* yours to command."

"This shackle only stops you—"

"From straying from your side?" Bloody hell, could he not understand? "It nearly killed me today! The only reason that *thing* cut me was because I reached the end of my tether, and the bracelet forced me directly into the path of creature's knife!"

His nostrils flared, but she latched on to the guilt she saw in his black eyes. "If you don't remove it right now, then you make it clear that I cannot trust you. Regardless of your actions today."

Their eyes met, and Verity stared him down. *Please.* She felt so lost today. She needed a victory. Bishop swore under his breath and reached for the chained links around her wrist. Light flared at his fingertips and Verity rubbed her wrist as the shackle fell into his hand.

"Thank you." It meant more to her than he could ever know. Today had cut most of the ties to her former life, but instead of feeling free, she had the odd sensation that she was now alone in the world. The Hex Society had been her prison, and yet familiar. If someone had ever tried to hurt her, the Crows would have stood at her back.

Not anymore.

What was her place in the world now? Did she even have one?

Bishop might have claimed her for the Order, but what did that mean? He and the former Prime were the only two sorcerers she'd ever met, but she'd heard far too many stories.

"Don't make me regret it, Verity." Bishop stepped toward the candle, lifting his hand to snuff it with his fingertips. "I don't give my trust so easily."

"That makes two of us," she admitted, drawing her knees up to her chest. "Today has been a strange day."

From adversaries to wary allies. She wasn't quite certain what to make of it.

Dark shadows highlighted his cheekbones as he tilted his head toward her. "I'll fetch you some dinner."

"Will... you stay with me?" The words leapt from her lips before she could restrain them.

Bishop paused by the door, the pan of bloodied linens in his hand. She could almost see the tension work its way through his shoulders.

"Just for... dinner." Goodness, why were her cheeks heating?

Perhaps because she couldn't pretend to be so flippant. Not at this moment.

"I'll assume you want your meat well-done?" He arched a brow, cutting the tension with the faintest of smiles. "Not... bloody."

Verity heaved one of the pillows at him. "As long as it's my favorite cut... a nice, lean... rump." She stuck her tongue out at him as he smiled.

"Fine. Let me fetch you something to eat."

CHAPTER SEVEN

"When the red comet rules the skies, the Prime shall fall. A new Prime shall ascend to the head of the Order. Three sons. Three relics. Three sacrifices. Only then can the Prime be torn down.

There is but one chance to save them. The Snake at the Breast shall cast the first roll of the die, setting the Game into motion, but might be all that holds back the pall of madness. The Thief shall wear a false face but wield a true heart; and only the Blind One can see how to save the heart of the Mirror."

-Prophecy of Drake de Wynter's downfall

HE STAYED FOR dinner, a largely informal affair.

Silverware clinked as they settled at the dining table together. Verity kept glancing up at him as she ate, and tried to mimic his fancy table manners. There'd evidently been a cook in today, but she'd left their meal in the oven, something that seemed a regular occurrence. It was delicious: roasted meat that almost fell off the bone, bonny potatoes roasted in goose fat, Yorkshire puddings, peas, and so much gravy Verity could barely fit it all in.

She was trying though. The Crows' table wasn't as lean as others in the Dials, but it certainly wasn't to this standard.

"So tell me about the Order," Verity said, swallowing a mouthful of beef and washing it down with a red wine that almost made her eyes cross with pleasure. "You seem to know so many different types of magic. I saw you using fire today, and healing, and stopping hearts in chests, and then there was that knife you created...."

Bishop set his knife and fork aside. "What do you know of sorcery?"

She shrugged. "If you want something bad enough, sometimes you can mentally force the world to adapt to your will."

"True enough. The mind is a powerful tool. The first time, it occurs when someone finds themselves in a situation where they want something so desperately that their mind forms... some sort of connection, and they force matter to rearrange itself around them. Usually it's something destructive and physical like burning down a house, or forcing floodwaters to part, which is what we call Telekinesis. But sometimes it's purely on the mental plane. Perhaps a girl's father beats her so often that she just wants him to stop, and so she forms a compulsion in his mind. He cannot hit her anymore. Or maybe there is a miner trapped underground and he wants his wife to find him, so he links to her, tells her where he is. This is Telepathy, and they are the two separate spheres of sorcery."

Fascination made her pause with her fork hovering. The most she knew of sorcery was curses and hexes, or tricks and strange talents. Everyone in the Hex had their own ability, perhaps a couple more, but that was usually it. "So... I'm Telekin...."

"Telekinetic," he replied, picking up his knife and fork again. "By natural inclination, yes, you are, but you could learn to control Telepathy if you apply yourself. I am Telekinetic by nature, but can do both. What was the first manipulation you formed?"

Verity shifted uneasily. "I translocated."

"Why?"

Of course he would pursue this. "I was twelve and coming home from my shift at the workhouse. We had to unpick ropes until our fingers bled, and our meals were small and infrequent. So... sometimes I would go home through the markets and steal food for Mercy and me. A bit of bread here and there. Maybe an apple." She stared into the distant past. "You don't know what it's like to be so hungry that you feel hollow all the way to your bones."

There was no condemnation in his expression, merely curiosity. "And?"

"One of the vendors caught me. He threatened to chop off my fingers or send me to Newgate, and I was so terrified that I just wanted to be home in my cot. Home, safe. And I don't know what happened, but when I came to... that's where I was. It sent me into a fever, and I shivered there for two days straight."

"It's a very rare talent, Verity. I'm not surprised." Bishop laced his hands over his middle. "I don't think you understand how truly difficult teleporting—or translocation, whatever you want to call it—is. The simple laws of physics that you break...."

Verity frowned. She had no idea what he was talking about and it rankled, because he was educated and she was not.

"I've only ever heard of it happening once, and Sir Edgar spent years studying the base knowledge of every cell in his body, of space, of time, of pure matter... and he was an eighth level sorcerer."

"Was?"

"Well," Bishop hesitated, "it didn't end well for him. He only made the jump twice, and then.... Nobody ever saw him again, but there were bits of him strewn through his house."

She pressed her fingertips to her lips. "Do you mind?"

"Sorry. You do it so easily that it must be your natural inclination."

"My what?"

"Our first impression always locks hold. Whatever we do first remains our natural inclination for the rest of our lives. Perhaps we learn other methods, but our strongest and easiest spell craft is what happened first."

That made sense.

"So after you did it once, how did you keep doing it? Sometimes people can never perform a sorcerous working ever again."

Picking up her fork, she chased a pair of peas across her plate. "The vendor worked for Murphy, and told him I'd vanished into thin air. Three days after it happened Murphy came looking for me. Offered me a place in the Crows if I worked for him. It was a good deal. Better than the workhouse, at any rate. I insisted that Mercy be included, and so we joined the Crows.

"He pushed me into... a sort of training. It took me a long time to be able to translocate again—I couldn't work out how to make that energy shift—but he locked me in a tank and started pouring water in. Said I needed to be desperate again. It was almost over my head before I managed to get out of there." Stabbing the peas, she popped them in her mouth, giving him a little shrug. "It became easier after that. Then he started giving me items, telling me to find where their owners were, or their matching pair. It was a trick he knew. He always had ways to make you desperate enough, and eventually I learned to pull it together myself at will. That's when he started me cracking houses. I've earned him a small fortune over the years."

"I'm sorry."

"For what?" She took a sip of the wine and swirled it around the bottom of the glass. "If he hadn't taught me I'd probably be dead by now. Or living in some hovel somewhere. Learning something new is the most valuable thing one can ever receive."

"Yes, but it seems a rather ruthless way of doing it." Bishop frowned.

"What was your natural inclination? Did you kill someone?"

That stopped the conversation in its tracks. "Yes," Bishop replied, and his tone was cool enough to make her consider other questions.

"Oh. I'm sorry." She searched for something else to say. "So what was your learning like? You said you're a seventh level sorcerer, was it? How many levels are there?"

Bishop relaxed, telling her all about the Order. Verity could scarcely hide her amazement. The Order not only shared their knowledge, but could learn all different kinds of tricks, like divination, wards, pyrokinetics, necromancy, healing. To advance to a different level they had to sit tests and prove that they'd conquered the steps of each level.

Once they'd finished dining, she glanced at the fireplace in the sitting room. "Could you... could you tell me more? In there?"

"You're cold?"

"A little."

Pouring her another glass of wine, he directed her through into the sitting room, leaving her alone to take the dishes down to the kitchen for the staff in the morning. Verity prowled the room, stopping before the fireplace and holding her hands out to warm them as she peered at the portrait above it.

The woman in the painting reclined upon a daybed, holding a rose to her lips as if to hide her faint smile. She was stunningly beautiful, with waves of golden curls flowing over her shoulders and dark eyes that seemed to hold a thousand mysteries. It was an intimate portrait, with the woman's gown slipping from her shoulder to reveal the faintest curve of her upper breast, and her expression seemed to belong to that of a lover.

The door clicked open behind her as Bishop returned. Verity jumped, feeling slightly nervous. Why would a man have such a portrait in his sitting room unless it belonged to someone he loved? All of a sudden she wondered if Bishop were unattached after all. His coolly reserved manner seemed aloof, all of a sudden. Perhaps he had a lover somewhere? Perhaps he was *in* love.

"Here," he said, bringing a book over from the bookshelf in the corner. "You can read, yes?"

"Slowly," she admitted, taking the book from his hands. "*A S-study of Sorcery, and the Dawning of the Order.*" Flipping the book over, she examined the back of its cloth cover. "What is it?"

"Some background on the Order, if you're interested? To get you started."

Started. She stroked her thumb over the cover. He was serious then, in teaching her more. Verity's gaze lifted to the portrait, and she flushed when he caught her. "Who is she?"

"My mother."

Verity blinked. "She's beautiful."

That earned a faint scowl, and a withdrawal as he turned toward the sofa. "She was, yes."

Which meant she was gone. Verity looked again. It was entirely easy to see how this woman would have captivated dozens of men, but Bishop obviously didn't like the reminder of his mother's days as a courtesan. "How did she meet your father?"

"A ball, I believe. Drake was in mourning for his nephew. Morgana had poisoned the boy, which led to the divorce, and so he withdrew from society and the world for almost a year. My mother needed a protector at the time and so they... formed a relationship." Bishop glanced at the sofa. "Do you mind?"

Verity stared at him.

"I cannot sit until you do."

Hastily she sank into the chair opposite him, collecting her glass of wine on the way. "You're not going to tell me some poppycock notion about ruining my reputation by sleeping under the same roof, are you?"

"No. The Order is somewhat more lax in social requirements than others. However, my mother raised me better than that."

"Did she love your father?"

"It was an arrangement, Verity. My father was grieving, yet he was kind. They became very good friends, until it became clear that I was... on the way."

"Oh."

Bishop raked a hand through his hair. "It wasn't like that. He didn't abandon her, or me. There's always been a prophecy stating that if Drake were to know his sons, then disaster would befall them. He thought it best to stay away, and watched from a distance. He settled a small inheritance upon my mother so she could live her life freely, and they corresponded regularly."

"But you didn't know him?"

"Not until I was older, no." He glanced up at the painting, his voice softening with some emotion she couldn't name. "I always knew he was my father, I just never knew that he was a sorcerer until it was too late. He wanted to keep me out of this world. Wanted to keep me safe."

Too late. What did that mean? "But if he knows you now, then aren't you frightened of the prophecy?"

Bishop stared into the crackling fire. "I think of it sometimes. Sebastian's death last month was an enormous blow to my father. He blames himself for coming into our lives, and sometimes I wonder if the prophecy is already claiming us."

"What does it say?"

"I'm not entirely certain. I don't hold much truck with prophecies. They're usually so opaque you can barely understand them until they come true, or so vague that anything can fit the words. Something to do with *'Three sons, three relics, three sacrifices.'*"

Relics? She felt ill. "Do you think—?"

"It doesn't matter, Miss Hawkins. I believe that destiny is a matter of taking your own fate into your hands and wielding it. If the Chalice is to be my undoing, then I will go down fighting."

"I should never have stolen it."

His lips quirked. "You seem the superstitious sort. Perhaps it was your destiny to do so? Perhaps we were always bound to cross paths?" His tone made it clear what he thought of that, but the words struck her.

She looked at him, a funny feeling tying up her insides. When she'd first met him, he'd been little more than a shadowy figure she'd swiftly grown curious about, watching as he went about his life for the last two weeks. But to actually come to know the man.... And to speak of destiny, which she *did* believe in.... "Are you mocking my poor superstitious ways?"

A smile softened his face. She'd thought him cold, at first, but she was gradually coming to see the warmth in him. He merely hid it, or no, not hid it, but guarded himself against getting too close to other people.

Verity looked down at her hands. Her heart was beating a little faster. Maybe it was because her life had turned topsy-turvy in the space of a day and she needed something to hold on to, but she was swiftly coming to recognize she quite liked him.

She'd never felt like this before.

Keep to the course, Verity Anne. Don't lose your head over a man, just because he was kind to you and has a nice smile. There has to be an angle here somewhere.

She needed to make him stop smiling, make that teasing tone of his vanish. "How many people have you killed?" she blurted, and drank most of her wine.

A quick flash of dark eyes speared through her. "Eighteen."

The way he said it was not a boast. No. He lost the smile, which was exactly what she'd hoped for. "I thought that those drawn to the Grave Arts relished the act of death."

Again she was the recipient of *that* look; the one that said he clearly would prefer to pull out his own fingernails rather than discuss this matter with her. "Have you ever killed someone?"

The heat drained from her face. "Once."

"I crave the power death brings," he admitted, in a slow, careful tone, as if feeling out his words. "But it's one thing to sink yourself into that blaze of power—where you feel on top of the world, invincible—quite another to watch someone's eyes cloud over, and realize they'll never take another breath again. Never see their families. Never laugh at something one of their friends said."

"A Sicarii with a conscience?" Until now, she'd not have believed such a thing existed. The sickles in the shadows were the bogeyman of the Order, used to cow such rebels as her into good behavior. *Keep your head down, or the Sicarii will come for you. They don't like them as uses uncontrolled magic, or don't toe the line. Their line.*

Bishop watched her. If his face remained expressionless, his eyes told a thousand stories. She could see him gathering his thoughts. "Verity, the Sicarii aren't monsters who hide in the dark. We're normal people—like you or your friends. We simply share a... duty."

"To kill those who stand in your way?"

"Those drawn to the Grave Arts naturally crave the power that comes from death, the same way others get energy from sex, or from cutting themselves. Some Grave Arts practitioners use their skills to ease the suffering of the dying, some turn to necromancy—though that is forbidden now—and some join the army, or become Servants of the Empire, to serve the Queen in her empire expansion. For others, like me, there's only one option left.

"I serve. That's all. The thought of sitting by someone's deathbed and trying to pretend that I'm not craving the rush of power that comes when they take their last breath sickens me. It makes me feel like a vulture. I'm no necromancer, and I've tried being a Servant of the Empire. It didn't work out well."

"Why didn't it work out?"

"It's a long story." Bishop took a sip of his wine.

Dragging her knees up in front of her, Verity hugged them, resting her chin on them. "Humor me. It's not as though I've much fight left in me tonight, and I know you're only going to spend half the night pacing through the house. So if you're not going to tell me why you can't sleep, you could at least tell me about the Sicarii. Convince me they're not evil."

"Far better if you never know of the Sicarii at all, Miss Hawkins." He stood then, peering down at his empty glass. "I think that you should find your bed, at least. We have a lot of work to do on the morrow."

She gaped at him. "What? Why?"

"Because not all Sicarii are like me, Miss Hawkins. Some of them like killing, and the less you know, the better."

Bishop tracked her footsteps upstairs as Verity readied herself for bed. Alone at last. Though the room felt oddly large and silent without her in it, and that troubled him a little. Dinner had been strangely comfortable. There'd been an intimacy about it, the small table gilded by the ring of light cast by a single candle. Verity's intrusion into his life and his household was quite obvious, but... he couldn't say that he disliked it.

God, he'd liked it far too much. Every time she glanced up at him from beneath those dark lashes, he'd had to shift in his seat, as if the Lover Boy hex still afflicted him. All he could think about was that kiss in that alley.

It was a distraction he didn't want and didn't need right now, and if he didn't get moving, he'd be facing another erection again.

Bishop snagged the whisky decanter with a sigh, and then pressed the indentation above the fireplace, heading for his secret study.

He hadn't been in here since the night she'd stolen the Chalice. The safe still hung open, useless now without anything to guard, and the walls were lined with books, candles, and the items he used for more complicated spell craft that required focus and ritual. There was a stand set with a half dozen globes, a thin glasslike substance along the wall, and it was to them that he turned.

He'd created them five years ago with his sorcery, by forming a mage globe of pale blue light and forcing it to change from light, to... whatever it was. Harder than diamond, but so transparent it looked like a bubble.

Setting the sphere on the table, he put the whisky bottle to his lips and swallowed raw fire.

It was nothing as to the heat inside his skin, the burning need he felt for her in his veins. Leaving her alone in there tonight was almost more than he could stomach, but it frightened him how much he longed to touch that smooth skin and to brush his lips against it. The only thing that had ever come close to this craving was the *maladroise*, the Curse of the Grave, that lethal, killing edge within him that hungered for death, for the power that spilled as blood did.

Bishop clenched his fingers into a fist. He needed to contact his father, but first he needed guidance.

"*Astaphor mercadi ethuselah...*," he breathed, spilling power across the globe with the personal ritual words he had trained himself to use to create this link. The words didn't matter; only the familiarity of them did. Some used Latin, some used ancient languages, some made up their own, like he had. A trick of the mind, to create a link for his spell craft to form a particular spell, so that his sorcery relied on control and force of will rather than rash emotion. Many in London thought power words held magic themselves, and he'd heard the norms on the streets throwing them at him—*abracadabra!, presto!*—but the truth was the words were merely keys to train the mind.

A spark of blue light formed in the heart of the ball and a ripple of chimes sounded in the distance.

"Adrian?" Agatha looked startled as her face swam into view. "What is it?"

Instantly, he realized it was night and this could have waited. "I'm sorry, Agatha. I wasn't thinking."

Shrewd eyes narrowed. "Wouldn't have anything to do with that girl, would it?"

"No. I'm just tired. And worried."

It was the first time he'd admitted that.

"Your father's going to be all right, boy," she said, her voice softening. "I'm watching over him."

"Thank you," he said, and he meant it.

"And how *is* the girl doing?" There was a wealth of meaning in those words.

No help for it. He wasn't fooling his old master. "Do you think she could stay with you?"

"What has she done?" Agatha gained that fire-breathing look around her eyes.

"Nothing." He scraped another hand through his hair, thinking of Verity in her chemise, upstairs, lying on the bed in his guest room. The hex might have worn off, but it lingered like a curse. "It's not right—a young woman staying beneath a bachelor's roof. She should stay with you, for her reputation's sake, if anything."

"Reputation?" Agatha snorted. "As if that's ever bothered you before. You kept Lady Ackerly locked in your cellar for a good month until I was through with her."

"Lady Ackerly was poisoning babies to feed off," he said in disgust.

"We weren't convinced," she reminded him. "Not at the start."

Bishop shrugged. He didn't like speaking of Lady Ackerly.

"Do you think that it started out this way?" the older woman had begged, ignoring Agatha and looking directly at him, dropping her sneering façade for the first time. *"Do you think I wanted this? It burns inside me, this craving. I've tried.... For so many years I tried. You know what I'm speaking of... you feel it, I know you do. You have to."*

Bishop scratched his left arm as the itch ignited. Power, bleeding through his veins like a supernova. Beyond any level of energy that a sorcerer could gather from the world around them. Only someone with an affinity for the Grave Arts knew what it felt like after a death, to walk around for days with blistering heat spilling through a man's body, all of his senses heightened, his cock hard and aching for release, and his body barely needing to sleep. One felt invincible; alive for the first time.

And then the dream would start to shatter and the energy lagged until it felt like he was sucked dry. Everything itched. His body would twitch for hours, wanting more, more power. Wanting to feel that current running through him again, until it was all he thought of....

"She appeals to you, doesn't she?" Agatha's voice cut through the distraction, and just like that, Bishop stilled.

He removed his fingers from his arm and the roughened graze there, where he'd been scratching of late. "She's a thief."

"And you're a young man who's never been in a woman's bed—"

"Christ, we're not discussing *that.*"

Those eyes narrowed. "It might be good for you. I know you've been feeling... tightly strung of late."

"I don't know what you're talking about."

"Adrian." This time she looked sad. "There are ways to ease the craving."

There was no point in denying it further. Agatha had a direct link to his mind, a bond between master and apprentice they'd never bothered to sever. "But no Grave Arts practitioner has ever managed to avoid it forever." Words he'd never dared admit before. "I've read the histories, Agatha. The only way to avoid it is to kill yourself."

"If you're thinking of doing something stupid—"

"I'm not." His voice softened. "I'm nowhere near that point. Yet. Lady Ackerly held out for almost forty years." He tried to smile. "I've got what? Another dozen years to go?"

"My dear, dear boy. I won't let you go so easily, you know? We will find a way to ease the ache of it so that you're not tempted." Squeezing the bridge of her nose, she clearly tried to think. "There has to be one practitioner of the Grave Arts who has managed to find relief before the craving grew too strong. I'll set Marie to digging through the histories I have."

"Thank you." He didn't bother to point out it would most likely be a waste of time. He'd been searching for something—anything—ever since he turned sixteen and discovered what he was.

"As for the girl... if her presence becomes too difficult for you to manage, she is most welcome in my home."

"That almost sounded as if you meant it."

Agatha screwed up her face. "Fine. I'll do it for you but I don't *have* to like it. It's taken me too many years to finally find peace, and I don't particularly care for any strangers to come peering into my personal life."

Guilt soured him. "Only if I cannot handle her. I'll try, Agatha." He paused. "Do you think you and Marie could find some clothes for her? She doesn't own very much, and none of it's suitable for this world. She'll need to blend in, if we're to find the Chalice."

"You think it's here? In the West End?"

"I don't know." He didn't tell her his theory about Tremayne. She'd be knocking on his doorstep with a pitchfork in hand if he did. "Possibly."

"I'll send Marie around in the morning with some dresses. Heavens knows Marie will probably never wear them, and they're much of a size. You owe me, Adrian."

"Mark it down on my slate," he replied with a faint smile.

A chime whispered from the communicator. Both of them heard it.

"Looks like you're a wanted man tonight." Her smile dawned. "Go. See who else is demanding your time. Then get some sleep. You look terrible."

"Thank you." With a frustrated half snarl, Bishop raked his hand through his hair and cut the connection. There were only two others who knew the link to his communication sphere. One of them was his father; the other...

"*Mercadi*," he whispered, circling his fingers over the globe to accept the link.

A cowled face swam into view. "Tomorrow. At ten. British Museum of Natural History."

Bishop stilled his frustration. He had a Chalice to hunt, and the Earl of Tremayne to find—and kill—before Tremayne became a threat to the Prime again. But this meeting was not something he could avoid. "I'll be there."

The communicator's glow died, and Bishop rubbed his hand over the stubble of his jaw. Just what complication was the Magister of the Sicarii going to throw into his life? A frisson of fear trembled down his spine. After all, the Sicarii served the Order and the Prime, and his father had stepped down from that position to care for his injured lover, Eleanor. Nobody had ever done such a thing before.

Which meant that Bishop's loyalties were now split.

What would happen if the Sicarii decided Drake was a threat to the stabilization of the Order, and the new Prime who would be elected at the end of the week during the Ascension Rites?

They'd kill Drake.

"Over my dead body," he whispered.

But he was only one man—one Sicarii—and there were four others.

Verity had a bag of tricks in her repertoire besides the ability to teleport.

Sorcery stirred somewhere in the house, a strange kind of spell craft that she'd never felt before, and curiosity finally got the better of her.

Wiggling her fingers in a complex pattern, she tore open a small rift between her room and the room where the spell was being cast, just big enough to listen and see—

An orb glowed and Bishop stared intently into it.

"Tomorrow. At ten," whispered a harsh voice. "British Museum of Natural History."

Bishop frowned, looking troubled. "I'll be there."

Then he waved a hand in a sharp gesture, dispersing the spell, and the orb's light vanished as he turned—

Verity flicked her fingers and the rift closed. Falling back onto her bed, she lay still and quiet, her heart pounding in her ears as she listened.

The house remained quiet. Nobody came to castigate her for listening to a private conversation.

Who had he been speaking to?

He'd promised that they would work together to recover the Chalice, but she wasn't entirely certain how far she could trust him. There had to be *some* angle. Didn't there?

Trust him? Or follow him?

Perhaps she could wait until breakfast to make that decision, depending upon whether he told her the truth about the meeting, or not.

Wait and see, she told herself, then let her body relax. *Let's give him one more chance.*

CHAPTER EIGHT

FREEDOM. IT HAD been a brief but sustaining dream.

Sebastian Montcalm stepped out of the hackney and stared up at the house on Banbury Square with a note in his fist. He limped a little as his boots crunched over the gravel drive, his side still aching from where his mother had buried a knife in it just over three weeks ago. The wound shouldn't have healed—no blow struck by the Blade of Altarrh could ever stop bleeding—but somehow it had.

Or no, not *somehow*....

He knew exactly why it had crusted over and begun to scab. The little knot of anticipation in his mind was linked directly to his wife. After years of loneliness, it was quite startling to feel the bond between them every time he woke up, a bond that she'd used to save his life. Cleo, the only person he had ever trusted, was wrapped so tightly around him that sometimes he woke and reached for her in the empty bed. But that too was a trick, a dream. For Cleo was missing, and he knew exactly who had her.

As the note in his hand, delivered just this morning, dictated.

Your freedom for hers, it promised.

He was a fool to even be standing here, staring at the front door. Morgana could never be trusted and he was finally free of her, but if he didn't come... then Cleo would suffer the consequences. Sebastian, who knew more about his mother's evil nature than anyone, knew precisely what would happen to her.

Damn him for a fool. Morgana had warned him after all; *"Never allow yourself attachments, Sebastian. They're only weaknesses that can be used against you."*

He'd never truly understood that sentiment until this moment.

The doorbell rang and dread shivered down his spine as he steeled himself. Every nerve in his body pushed at him to flee. This was wrong. So wrong. But it was either cast himself to the lions, or see harm done to the innocent young wife he'd known for only a matter of days.

And that could not be borne.

"Sir," the butler greeted, opening the door and gesturing him inside. "Madam is waiting in the library."

Wondering to whom his mother had attached herself now, Sebastian took that one fatal step inside.

"This way, sir," said the butler, and Sebastian followed him warily, raking the hallway with a glance.

He'd been expecting his mother. But as the butler ushered him into the library, he realized this was but one last sally against him, a way to twist the knife and put him off guard. For instead of his mother, a young woman clad in purest white stood there.

His wife.

"Sebastian?" Cleo whispered, blinded by the linen blindfold that kept her visions pure. She'd always owned fine senses, and now the bond between them flared bright gold at their proximity, she had to know who stood there.

He could feel that link between them, both a taunt and a hope. "What happened? How did they steal you away?"

The last time he'd seen her had been directly after he brought the house down on top of his mother and tried to destroy a demon. Of the man who called himself a father, there'd been no sign. Raw edges scraping his psychic abilities, he'd collapsed in the bed in the inn that Cleo had somehow managed to get him to, undone by the sheer amount of power he'd wielded that day.

By the time he woke, Cleo was gone.

"Your mother found me," she told him. "She threatened to kill you if I didn't come."

"Cleo." *Jesus.* "She wouldn't have killed me. I'm far too valuable a weapon against my father. You should have fought her."

"You weren't there! Morgana was wild, beside herself at the cost of her schemes. I think she *would* have tried to kill you if I hadn't said yes!" Cleo took a step toward him. Both fists were clenched at her sides, her chin quivering a little as she tried to be brave. He knew how much the world frightened her, and for those brief few moments when she'd been safe under his roof, she'd looked to him for guidance.

And more.

A temptation that had proven his downfall. He should have stayed away, just to prove to his mother that Cleo meant nothing to him and therefore couldn't be used.

"They haven't hurt you?" he asked gruffly.

"I'm fine. It's you I'm worried about. You shouldn't have come! It's a trap—"

"Do you think I don't know that?" He stared at her hungrily, remembering a night when he'd gathered all of his courage and reached out to stroke her spun moonlight hair. The urge to touch her was as strong as ever, but he forced his fingers into a fist. Far better if she never saw him again.

"What did they promise you?" Cleo whispered.

"I've spoken with the Earl of Tremayne this morning." She swallowed. "Father."

There was a moment of fear in her voice. Sebastian's heart hardened. He knew how beastly her father was to her. And he couldn't allow himself to care.

"The deal is already struck. Your freedom for mine."

"No!" She took another half step toward him. "You cannot do that! I know how much your freedom means to you. I know what your mother has done to you all these years!"

"Cleo." He looked away, feeling the icy burn of the controlling collar around his throat. "I've already put the *sclavus* collar on." Once upon a time he'd have done anything to get it off, but this time he had no choice. "As soon as my mother turns you free, safe and unharmed, I'll hand her the ring with which she may control me. Your father gave them to me, along with a choice."

"I'm not going to let you do that," Cleo said fiercely. "Please. Please don't do this."

She'd always been a warrior. His heart ached a little in that moment, but he forced himself to harden his voice. "How are you going to stop me?"

"They're going to hurt you. For betraying them and for destroying their plans. I can See it."

"I expected nothing less," he told her, though his body was restless, remembering the pain that his mother had dealt him through the collar in the past. A flinch reaction that he couldn't quite control. It would be worse now.

Sweat chilled his spine. "I've paid the hackney out front to take you anywhere you want to go. You just have to give him directions."

"Come with me," she begged. "We can run. We can go—"

"Where?" he asked brutally. "There's nobody to run to, nobody who can protect either of us."

"What about your father?" she blurted. "The Prime?"

"*No.*" The man was no father to him.

"Your brothers? Lord Rathbourne? And that other one... Mr. Bishop."

"They all left me to die," he said bluntly, seeing the look on his father's face again as Drake de Wynter chose the son he knew—Lord Rathbourne—over Sebastian. For a moment, as Sebastian lay on the floor bleeding, he'd seen the man who had sired him turn, a grief-stricken look on his face, as Drake took a half step toward him. And he'd lived that moment of hope, that moment of disbelief that the father he'd never known would save him—might *actually* care for him—only to have it turn to dust when the roof started to collapse and Drake was forced to make a choice. Rathbourne. Or Sebastian.

Never again would Sebastian hope for more. There were few things more painful than the crushing decay of a dream he'd never known even existed inside him. "What makes you think the Prime would even give a damn about us now? About me? It's not as though they've come looking for me."

"Well, I'm not going without you."

"Yes, you are." He stepped closer, almost close enough to touch her now. "Else I've given up my freedom for nothing."

"I don't deserve that," she whispered. "Please, Bastian...."

He did touch her then, capturing her upper arm and feeling the gauzy slip of her sleeve beneath his touch. "This way."

Cleo tripped and stumbled as he hauled her out of the library, toward the door. He didn't stop. A fall wouldn't hurt her. Staying here would.

"Stop it, damn you!" Cleo slapped at his arm, but he wrenched the door open.

Sunlight streamed in, gilding her white dress. That blindfold turned, unerringly, toward his face. Behind her, he could make out the hackney and the driver he'd already paid to take her to safety.

"Go."

"Where?"

"Anywhere. I don't know. Surely you have family?" Sebastian's grip on her arm softened. "Just not here."

With him.

"Bastian." She caught his other hand, and Sebastian hesitated.

"You gave me hope," he told her, his voice roughening, "when I needed it. Thank you."

Then he couldn't stop himself from touching her; just a pair of fingers brushing against her smooth cheek. The only thing that he could ever have of her; a memory to sustain him through the forthcoming torture. The bond flared to life between them and he could sense his own touch against her skin and her astonishment at it. Then something locked hold of her and she gasped, her body jerking as though some puppet master yanked on her strings.

Before he knew what he was doing, he caught her as she slumped against him. The tension suddenly dissolved from her body, leaving her panting.

"Cleo?" he whispered. "Was it a Vision? What did you see?"

Clapping her hands over her blindfold, she shook her head. "No! No, I won't let you suffer through that."

His torture, then. Sebastian clenched his jaw. "Yes, you will. You're the only thing that can ruin me. I want you to leave this house and never look back. Go and live your life, the way you were always intended to do. Be free. Of me. Of this wretched curse I'm stuck in."

"If you think I can just walk away–"

The sound of a jarring clap broke them both apart. The Earl of Tremayne—Cleo's father—sauntered into the hallway. "What dramatics, my dear. Leave the man in peace. My dear son-in-law has the right of it, you know."

"And I'm to believe you're just going to let me walk out of here freely?" Cleo snapped, her voice hardening as she faced her father. "I know you, after all. You've always craved my Visions, my power, and it wouldn't be the first time you've broken your word."

Tremayne's dark eyes locked on his daughter. "You've grown rather rebellious in the past month, Cleo. A young woman should be seen and not heard. Someone ought to remind you of your place. "

"You wouldn't dare," Sebastian murmured darkly.

Tremayne shot him a look of wild hatred, then turned back to his daughter. "Once upon a time you were a powerful tool, Cleo. But it's clear from your actions in the past month that you betrayed me to my enemies. I won't forget that. Ever."

Sebastian stepped between them, a threat in itself. Sorcery whispered through his skin. How much he wanted to simply obliterate this man, and never deal with him again....

But Tremayne was a powerful adversary, and Sebastian knew his sorcery was untrained and erratic. Doubt ate away at some of his strength.

"That's a good decision, boy," Tremayne whispered, satisfaction flavoring his dark eyes. "Step away from her and all will go well."

"You touch one hair on her head, and I'll destroy this entire house, with you in it." The world began to darken as shadows etched at his vision, daring him to do it.

"Sebastian," drawled a familiar voice, and instantly he was on edge. "My dear boy, you do like to bring the house down, don't you?"

The words were poison. "Morgana," he replied icily, turning to face his mother, and—

Freezing in surprise.

His mother had once been a vibrant woman with raven-dark hair and wicked green eyes. She'd stood tall, always adorning herself in the silks she demanded were due to her, but now she was confined to a wheeled chair, pushed by one of the servants. Dark shadows of pain hollowed the skin beneath her eyes, and there was more gray in her hair than there ever had been. But the most startling change were her legs, thin and faded beneath her skirts.

"Come to see your handiwork, my son?" Morgana spat, watching him with bitter eyes. She gestured to her legs. "When you brought the roof down upon me, it crushed my spine. This is entirely your fault. Tremayne and I have much to repay."

"I'd hoped you were dead," he told her coldly, stepping forward. She might hold Cleo as her pawn, but he'd wanted this chance all his life.

Morgana flung something from her fingers—a tangled knot of sorcery that darted straight past Sebastian. Cleo gasped behind him and tumbled to her knees. That alone halted the building power in its tracks, his vision clearing as he realized where he was.

"The next one goes straight through her heart," Morgana promised. "At least my sorcery seems to have survived the attack intact."

Damn her. His fist clenched. Just one strike. That was all it would take to destroy the bitch.

Cleo cried out behind him, and the breath went out of him. He didn't care if he died, as long as he took Tremayne and Morgana with him.

But Cleo was innocent, a light in a world of darkness. He couldn't force himself to bring any harm to her.

Sebastian slowly lowered his head and let go of the pulse of energy that whirled within him. Surrender. But what other option did he have? "Let her go."

Morgana wheeled herself forward, a smile on her full mouth. Her spell work faded, and Cleo pushed herself to her hands and knees.

He didn't go to her, or help her to her feet. Just watched as she struggled upright.

"Sebastian," his wife whispered, reaching for him.

"Get out of here," he told her coldly. "This is good-bye."

"I don't want you to do this!"

"Then you should never have involved yourself in my affairs."

"Hand me the ring, Sebastian," Morgana crooned.

"Just another minute," he told her. "The second she gets in the carriage."

"Don't trust me?"

"Not an inch," he said, casting her a dark look.

That all too-smug smile on her face threatened him. She was up to something.

"After all," he said, pushing her a little. "It's surprising to see you let her go. Cleo has a talent that far surpasses my own. She's either a useful ally or a dangerous enemy, and I know how you prefer your enemies."

"Oh, Sebastian." Here came the knife in the back, he just knew it. "Everybody has a weakness. You just have to know how to use it."

Cleo's cry of shock stole his breath. Sebastian spun toward her, power clenched in his fist.

But there was no enemy. Nothing to fight. Only Tremayne, brandishing the blindfold that he'd torn from his daughter's eyes.

Cleo blinked, crying out and clapping her hands to her eyes.

Her eyes were brown. The darkest kind, like molten chocolate... so pretty. But never meant to be seen.

"What did you do to her?" he demanded, staring at Cleo as Tremayne shoved her into the carriage.

"It was the first thing she ever Foretold as a little girl," Morgana gloated, watching Tremayne stride back across the lawn toward them. "If she ever saw the world again, her visions would vanish and she would be the all-knowing Cassandra no more. So you see," Morgana pushed on her wheels, guiding her chair back into the house. "Your pretty young wife is no longer a tool, or a weapon. Now, she's merely nothing."

"No," Sebastian whispered, but as he took a step toward his wife, hands caught at him, dragging him back. A ting sounded as the ring dropped from his lax hand and hit the tiles, rolling toward his mother's chair, where she bent and picked it up. The servants overwhelmed him with blank looks on their faces, as if they'd been spelled into submission. He was shoved inside the house.

And his mother slid the controlling ring on her finger with a smug look. "Now, Sebastian... it's time to repay your betrayal tenfold."

And he began to scream as pain obliterated his senses.

CHAPTER NINE

THE NEXT DAY Bishop left a disgruntled Verity at Lady Eberhardt's house for her dress fitting with Marie. She'd been particularly watchful of him all morning, and he had to concede that removing the bracelet from her gave him some measure of freedom, as well as her. If she'd still been linked to him, he'd have had to bring her with him, and he had no intentions of letting the bloody woman anywhere near the rest of the Sicarii.

For if his fellows considered her a threat to the Order, they'd kill her.

When the hackney pulled up at the British Museum's Natural History campus, Bishop alighted on Cromwell Road and paid the man before checking his pocket watch. A quarter to ten. Nearly time.

Taking the blank mask with its carved runes out of his coat pocket, Bishop slipped it over his face. "*Finersh*," he whispered, activating the runes on the Mirror Mask. Now none would know his true face. All they would see would be what they wanted to see: a handsome man, a young lad, an older gentleman... every person passing him would see something different.

Stepping into the pedestrian crowd, Bishop shoved his hands into his coat pockets and moved against the ebb and flow of foot traffic. Hackneys clopped past, jarring the tranquility, as well as the blare of a horn or two. Bishop darted across the road, fetching up at the grand doors to the British Museum.

Madrigal Brown waited for him by the arch to the Hintze Hall, wearing a white, frilled gown, with her silvery hair swept up into a neat chignon beneath the broad lilac-colored hat she wore. Bishop nodded to her, but didn't relax. A drape of arctic fox fur shielded her throat, and one of her gloved hands curled around the brass hilt of the cane she held. Though she had entered her sixth decade, she wasn't the type of woman one dismissed as weak or vulnerable.

Firstly, she was the only member of the Sicarii who had ever belonged to anything but the Dark discipline. The chip of pale marble in her prime ring betrayed her as a disciple of the Light, which made her targets never suspect her. When she'd first appeared at the Sicarii meeting, they'd all been shocked. To join the Sicarii, one had to kill your predecessor, and Baron Samedi had been the most dangerous man Bishop had ever met.

Secondly, she'd risen through the ranks within three years to become Magister of the Sicarii. To do so, she'd dueled the previous Magister, Wōden, a sorcerous duel Bishop had born witness to. Every time Wōden had flung a weave at her, Madrigal had the counter-weave ready, until Wōden finally made one mistake too many. She might lack the killing edge the others owned, but a man underestimated her at his own risk. For Madrigal had the powers of Foresight, finely honed over decades of diligence.

In a duel or a battle, she could Foresee the next move her opponent made, and possibly even further than that.

"Hades," she said, tilting her head in greeting, with an amused smile playing about her lips.

She was the only one of the Sicarii who did not disguise her identity. The rest he knew as Thanatos, Kali, and Osiris.

"Madrigal," he greeted, taking her hand and pressing a kiss to the back of her glove. Agatha always said he had a way with older ladies.

"Walk with me." She turned toward the stairs, her skirts sweeping over the terracotta tiles. "The others are already here."

"Something on your mind?"

"Someone, perhaps," she replied, capturing her skirts in one hand and swishing down the stairs as though it were a ball. She led him toward the East Wing, with its display of extinct creatures. Fitting perhaps, for those who were masters of death. "Osiris is planning to put through a motion that the Prime—the former Prime—be quietly dealt with, in order to ensure the succession." Green eyes slid toward him. "I don't think you want that."

Bishop clasped his hands behind his back, suppressing the urge to clench them. Madrigal must know who he was, and the connection between him and the Prime. "How do you think the others will vote?"

"Kali goes where Osiris wills, but Thanatos... I'm not certain." That mouth thinned a fraction. "He's obtained a crystal that wards him against my Foresight."

"And yourself?" he asked, for until she committed to one particular side, he wasn't fool enough to think her his ally.

Madrigal paused at the base of the stairs. "There are troubling times coming, and it's all connected to the ex-

Prime. I only see flashes of it, but... there is darkness ahead, Hades."

"Then you cannot be certain whether Drake is the cause of it," he told her, "or if his death will set off a chain of events that might lead to these times."

"True." She arched a brow. "But I must make a decision, without all of the information I would prefer. What do you think?

Glancing around, Bishop caught her wrist and swept her into an alcove beside a bronze cast of a pterodactyl. None of this was information he'd shared with the Sicarii, but he needed Madrigal on his side. The others... perhaps he could take them one by one, but she had always made him doubt the outcome of any duel between them. "It's not well-known," he murmured, "but a month ago, the Blade of Altarrh was stolen from Drake's mansion and turned up in his ex-wife Morgana's hands."

Madrigal's eyes sharpened. "I've seen nothing of this."

"You wouldn't. Drake's wards would hide it from even your eyes."

"And the rest of the Relics Infernal?"

"The Blade was destroyed when Drake confronted Morgana, but there's no sign of the Wand. It vanished the week before the Blade was stolen, leaving only its caretaker's body behind."

"Dead?" Madrigal demanded.

"As a doornail."

"And the Chalice?"

He hesitated. Verity belonged to him. "It *was* safe, but a thief of extraordinary skill managed to get their hands on it and pass it along to someone else. I'm currently tracking it."

Madrigal sucked in a breath. "All three of the Relics Infernal are missing? Why the hell wasn't I informed?"

"Drake commanded that the recovery be kept quiet. Only those who needed to know were aware of any of this."

"So he turned to you," she said, and he wasn't certain if she were pleased or not. "What are your orders, Hades?"

"Protect the Prime," he said swiftly. "Protect the Order."

"One would say that you have the order of that mixed up." Her voice dropped to a silky whisper. "You serve the Sicarii, who serve the Order. The Prime is a highly important playing piece, but not more important than the Order."

His voice roughened. "Understood."

"What efforts have been made to recover the relics? Even with the Blade destroyed, who knows what they could be used for? We could find ourselves battling a demon, even without the Blade. And what of Morgana?"

So he told her, leaving out certain details such as the fact that the thief was inconveniently lodged in his house right now. "Morgana was presumed dead in the collapse of the house, but the excavators have not yet discovered her body." Nor had they found the body of his half brother, Sebastian, which troubled him even more than Morgana's missing remains.

They couldn't have escaped, could they?

Some remains should have been found by now, instinct whispered.

"Does Drake's resignation have anything to do with his ex-wife?"

Of course it did. Bishop didn't understand his father's decision. Eleanor Ross might have been Drake's lover, and injured in the attempt to recover the Blade, but Drake had to have known the mess he'd leave if he resigned. Didn't he? He could have hired a nurse to care for Eleanor, but

Bishop's arguments had fallen on deaf ears. "He's tired of being pulled in both directions," he admitted. "The Order has always been his priority, but now others take its place."

Madrigal tapped her lips. "Troubling. Drake has left us in a fine mess."

"Or perhaps," he suggested softly, "Drake is the only one with the power to confront a demon and survive."

"That wasn't even subtle, Hades."

"I wasn't trying to be."

"No." She perused his face. "That's one of the things I like about you. At least it's good to know your feelings on the outcome of this vote. What would you do if it goes against Drake?"

Dangerous to let her know, but perhaps the thought of fighting amongst the Sicarii would give her pause. "The question isn't, what would I do? The question is," he suggested, stepping close to her, "what wouldn't I?"

As much as Verity found herself liking Marie Adams very much, the second the woman's back was turned as she looked for thread to take in the dress Verity wore, Verity vanished.

All it took to track Bishop was the lock of his hair that she'd stolen the first day. Verity could find anything, once she'd got a feel of it. Thus she found herself staring up at the British Museum, thankful that it was free to the general public as that lingering *tug* pulled her inside.

In the hall, she found her mark talking to a woman wearing white ruffles. Images shifted over his face, making it difficult to see it, but then it finally settled into his dark, watchful expression.

Bishop was a dark flame, the woman his opposite. Veering left, Verity meandered into the mammal chamber as if she were interested in the displays. Pausing in front of some sort of stuffed creature, Verity stared at the nameplate, pretending to read it as she eased out the faintest touches of power. This was her most complex weave and difficult to hold for long periods of time, but she was insanely curious about just what he was up to. Through the glass case she watched the older woman lead him into a smaller room filled with three others, whose faces shifted in and out of perception. Clearly some kind of spell work was involved, but she'd never seen the like.

The eavesdropping rift opened just near her ear as she watched them from a distance.

"—let us be blunt: We've never encountered a scenario like this in all the years of the Order's history," said a sneering male voice. "How is this going to affect the stability of the Order? There are those who might not care for the new Prime, who would look to Drake and see a figurehead to return to glory—"

"He's made it clear he doesn't ever intend to resume his mantle as Prime," Bishop cut in.

"Yes, but who knows what the future holds?" the man responded.

"If the new Prime cannot hold their position, then they're not qualified to lead," Bishop countered. "Unless you'd like to hold their hand, Osiris? Perhaps you can nursemaid an ineffective Prime through his leadership years."

A faint laugh greeted his words.

"The Sicarii remain apart," said the woman in white, who was the only one whose face didn't flicker and change. "Nobody's holding anybody's hand. We serve, we protect. That is all."

Sicarii. *Oh, hell.* Verity swallowed. This was clearly a meeting of the very people that she wanted to avoid.

"And one might argue that we cannot predict what will happen," Bishop responded. "Perhaps a new Prime will falter? Or perhaps a powerful new Prime steps into the chair and the Order happily continues its course? There's nothing to say that Drake's ongoing life will cause difficulties."

"I don't like it," the man he'd called Osiris said bluntly. "It's a potential threat."

"And I say it's not," Bishop countered, in a very soft, very dangerous voice.

"Shall we take a vote?" asked another woman, someone younger, wearing brown. "Who believes that Drake should be removed from the equation?"

Watching Bishop's face, Verity saw the strain there that he couldn't quite hide.

"I do," said the man named Osiris.

"I agree," muttered the woman in brown.

"I say nay," Bishop muttered, crossing his arms over his chest.

"Thanatos?" the older woman murmured.

Another man, one who'd remained silent, seemed to frown. "It's too early to commit to action," he finally said. "Do we snuff a candle flame because it *may* burn out of control and burn our house down? No. So I say no. For now."

"I agree with Thanatos," said the older woman. "It's too early to make predictions. Drake can be... removed later if he becomes a threat. For now we watch and wait, and prepare for Ascension."

Bishop let out the breath he'd been holding, but the older woman cocked her head on an angle and held out a hand to still him. "We're being watched."

Verity froze.

"Madrigal?" Bishop asked, looking around.

"Someone is watching this meeting."

Verity didn't wait around to see what the woman was up to. Cutting the connection, she watched the rift hiss closed, and then immediately slipped into the crowd of Londoners who were enjoying the exhibits. The rules of the chase were simple: don't get caught. Which meant that she forced herself to stop and peruse something called a hairy-nosed wombat, making her magic very small inside her, so small and hidden she was holding her breath.

They'd be looking for someone on the move, someone pushing against the tide of people, fighting for the exits.

Instead, Verity slowly edged toward the exit at the back, forcing herself not to fidget, nor to move from exhibit to exhibit too quickly. She was almost clear when someone grabbed her by the arm.

"What the hell are you doing here?" Bishop demanded, pressing her into an alcove with the hard flex of his body. "Are you insane? I told you to stay at Agatha's!"

The unyielding wall of his body hid the rest of the room from view. Verity tipped her chin up. "I didn't realize you were meeting with the rest of the Sicarii. Else I wouldn't be here."

"Then why did you come?" Those dark eyes narrowed in suspicion.

Verity glanced away. "I overheard your conversation last night, and wanted to see who you were meeting. I thought it might have something to do with the Chalice, and you were trying to keep me in the dark."

"*Overheard?*" His voice was soft with sarcasm.

"Very well, I eavesdropped," she bit out. "You were performing some sort of magic. I wanted to know what it was."

The tension in his shoulders lingered, but he wasn't looming so obviously at her now. "You don't trust me."

There wasn't much she could say to that. "It's not personal," she pointed out. "I grew up in the Hex, Bishop, and the only way to make sure you weren't going to be dragged under was to make sure you were informed."

"Did you spy on Murphy like this?"

"All the time."

Thought darkened his eyes. He pushed away from her and the wall she was pressed against before glancing around. "Well, as you can see," he bit out, glancing around, "I wasn't going behind your back. I didn't want you here for quite obvious reasons."

"They were planning to kill the Prime." She let herself touch his arm gently. It was his father, after all, and she'd heard his tone during the meeting. "Bishop—"

"They were thinking about it," he replied, jerking free as if he couldn't bear her touch. "And I convinced them otherwise. Now come. They should have gone by now. Keep your head down and in future, if I tell you not to follow me, *don't* follow me. You could have been killed."

"They'd have to catch me first."

That earned her a scoring look. "Verity, the Sicarii aren't ordinary sorcerers. Catching you wouldn't be a problem. And one of them wouldn't even have to try. All she'd need to do would be to click her fingers... and you'd be dead. No matter where you vanished to."

A chill ran through her. "I won't follow you in future then."

And she was going to stay as far away from the Sicarii as she could.

CHAPTER TEN

"SIT." LADY EBERHARDT pointed dramatically at the daybed in her sitting room.

Verity didn't bother to argue. Bishop shot her a look as though surprised at her compliance, but she'd had enough of arguing today.

Besides, she knew enough about Lady Eberhardt to recognize when such a thing would be a waste of breath.

"I'm so sorry," Marie said, wringing her hands. "I swear she was there one moment, then gone the next."

"It's not your fault, Marie." Bishop smiled at the secretary. "Verity has a problem with following orders and trusting others. You couldn't have stopped her."

Verity folded her hands in her lap and pressed her lips together. She was *not* going to bite.

"Meek does not become you," Lady Eberhardt grumbled under her breath as she circled the daybed.

"That's when she's at her most dangerous," Bishop agreed.

Verity couldn't help herself. "I am not!"

He crossed broad arms across his chest. "You are too."

"Adrian, don't you have somewhere to be?" Lady Eberhardt interrupted, which clearly surprised him. "I'm going to put Verity into a trance and try and see if I can break through the memory hex. You're only going to be a distraction. Clearly."

There was not quite a *harrumph* on the end of that.

"I was going to see Drake, and let him know of the circumstances."

"Now would be as good a time as any." Not quite a command, but then who would argue against Lady Eberhardt?

"I'll see him out." Marie tucked a hand through his arm. "We'll make sure Verity stays safely here this time."

"Good luck," he muttered as she tugged him through the door.

"I heard that!" Verity called.

Silence fell, broken only by his footsteps on the stairs. Verity turned her attention back to the dragon whose den she'd suddenly found herself in. Lady Eberhardt glared at her. "If you bother that boy...."

"Yes, yes," Verity sighed. "I know. You'll knot me into a quilt."

A beady eye glared back at her as the lady took a seat opposite her, one hand curled around the handle of an ebony cane. "Impertinence is most unbecoming in a young lady."

"I can only imagine you were the very essence of pertinence yourself in your youth," Verity replied.

"Are you giving me cheek?"

"Would I dare?"

They stared at each other. A muscle ticked in Lady Eberhardt's cheek.

"Lie down," Lady Eberhardt instructed. "And let's take a look at you. Memory hexes are very rare. Toying with someone's mind is quite forbidden as it tends to leave a mark on the person afflicted... which is good news for us. I'm going to see if I can find it and undo the spell craft."

Verity complied, a knot twisting in her abdomen. "Will it work?"

"If it doesn't, you'll never know."

"That is hardly reassuring," Verity protested.

Lady Eberhardt snorted. "I'm the best telepath the Order has at hand, apart from the Prime. If I cannot unknot this hex, then nobody can."

Verity let go of an unsteady breath. She hated the thought someone had been in her mind, twisting her thoughts, her memories. It left her feeling remarkably vulnerable.

Lady Eberhardt sank onto the daybed beside her waist, pressing a hand on her forehead. "Relax, Verity. I'm not going to let anything happen to you. Bishop would never forgive me."

"He might thank you."

"Then you don't know him very well," Lady Eberhardt murmured, and lit a stick of sage, which she placed in a bowl on the small table beside the daybed. "Breathe it in, Verity. Let yourself relax and listen to my voice. I'm going to guide you through this. Close your eyes."

Verity breathed in the sweet smoke. Lady Eberhardt's hand returned to her forehead, her palm blazingly warm as the old lady began to chant.

"*Azureh heh dimadi*," Lady Eberhardt muttered, and a golden web gleamed against the back of Verity's eyelids, like a fine tracery of spell craft. "*Hesta vi astura, drenath vi cura.*"

A sweeping lassitude swept through Verity. She felt like she wanted to open her eyes, but the scent of the burning sage seemed to tug her down, down, into a cloudy nothingness until she hovered there, unweighted by her body, amazingly light of spirit. It felt like that moment just before she punched into nothingness during her translocations, except it was drawn out.

"Verity, can you hear me?" came a voice from far, far away.

"Yes," she thought she said.

"I want you to think back to the moment when you accepted the commission to steal the Chalice. Can you remember it?"

She slowly came back to herself, standing in the cloudy nothingness. Or floating, to be more specific. Verity looked down. Cobbles began to appear beneath her bare feet. The cloud swirled, becoming a mottled green, like fog.

"Can you take me to that meeting?" Lady E's voice seemed to print itself directly in the air, the letters forming in bright gold, and then fading.

Verity looked around. The meeting. The Chalice. There was a pressure in her head, as though some weight settled on her sinuses. Gingerly, she touched her temples.

"There it is," Lady Eberhardt whispered, and a hand brushed over her forehead, scattering cobwebs.

Instantly, the world around her seemed to brighten and become startlingly vibrant. A man appeared out of nowhere, pushing a barrow piled high with an odd assortment of skulls, hourglasses, and books.

"Watch it, lady," he snapped at her, then paused when her gaze locked on him. "Want a timepiece?" He jerked his waistcoat open, revealing a half dozen pocket watches hanging there.

Verity shook her head, then staggered out of the way as he pushed past, her back meeting the wall. A crossroads formed around her, people everywhere. Noise sprang up, but she couldn't make out the words. Murphy swirled out of the fog at her side, checking his pocket watch. He looked up, saw a hooded figure striding toward them. "'Bout bloody time," he said, tucking his pocket watch away.

Verity felt like something tugged her forward, and when she looked down, there were two of her. The second she stopped fighting, she slammed into her body, and then she was walking after Murphy as he strode forward to clasp the stranger's hand.

"Tell me where you are," came that imperious voice.

Verity looked around. The walls were hazy. "I'm in a narrow passage. An... alley, perhaps." Ahead of her, Murphy stalked through the gloom, ignoring the hooded figure at his side. "Murphy's here. And someone else."

"Follow them."

Verity scurried after them. The brick walls seemed to shudder, as though they were inches from her in one second, then nearly a foot away the next. It made her feel slightly ill.

"Where are they going?"

The alley opened into a crossroads. A figure hunched over a barrow lurched toward her, thrusting a handful of threaded beads and dead mice hanging by their tails at her. No, not beads. Warded tokens. Verity hurried past into another labyrinthine twist. "I'm not certain. It's all crooked. Like a maze. There are people here selling magical items, I believe."

"Brick walls?"

"Yes." There were runes painted on them in places, and a painted eye glared at her as she slipped past it. She felt like it watched her. "What on earth is this place?"

"You're in Balthazar's Labyrinth, I believe. Keep going. Where are they taking you?"

The world bled around the edges. Verity's next step took her inside a building. When she looked around, the door was shut and locked behind her. Warded runes were painted over its timbers.

"Come, and sit," rasped a voice from behind her.

Verity spun around.

Murphy took a seat at the table, and Verity saw herself drag out a chair beside him. The movement jerked her incorporeal body forward into her memory body. Then she was sitting there too, looking out through her eyes.

"Well-met," said a cool voice. The man sitting opposite them wore a hooded cowl that covered every inch of his face. "Who's the girl?"

"Protection," Murphy replied, with a faint, mocking smile. "She's of no interest to you. Who's the slump in the corner?"

To her surprise, Verity realized there was another man standing there, one she hadn't noticed. His gingery hair was cropped short, with thin mutton chops at the sides, and one of his eyes didn't quite look straight.

"Protection," the cowled figure mocked, and for a second she thought she knew that voice.

"Who is it?" Lady Eberhardt asked.

"I-I don't know. But I swear I've met him before."

"Have you considered my little proposal?" the stranger asked, ignoring Verity and speaking directly to Murphy. Those crisp vowels.... Who *was* he?

Murphy leaned back in his chair and scowled, his waistcoat straining over his broad belly. He'd worn the green one with the gold embroidery, which meant he was trying to impress someone, and his curly hair was pomaded flat across his scalp. "I've considered it. Seems a heck of a lot of risk, for little reward."

The figure sat so still, she wondered if he was even breathing. "I'm not going to argue terms. The offer is the offer."

Murphy leaned his elbows on the table and clasped his hands, his eyes narrowing greedily. "Now the way I see it, you might not have a choice. I have something you want: the means to get inside a heavily warded house, break into a safe, and get out without being caught by a Sicarii assassin. There's not a lot of folk as can do that. In fact, there ain't nobody else, and I should know."

"How?" it asked flatly. "How do you get into the house?"

Murphy leaned back and tapped his nose. "That's for me to know and you to find out. *After* I get you this relic-thingy."

"Then what do you want in return?"

"Double or nothing."

"Double?" The creature slammed a hand onto the table, and she was relieved to see it was a human hand, gloved in tight black leather. "That's impossible. I don't have that kind of money."

"Then find it." Murphy didn't care.

Silence fell. The creature silently seethed as it watched him, but she could almost sense it making its choice. "Done." It stretched its hand across the table. "You have three weeks to bring the Chalice to me. I don't care how you do it. But if you don't deliver it... you will repay in a pound of flesh."

Murphy shook hands, though she saw the threat bothered him. The stranger tugged a money pouch from within its robe and tossed it on the table with a metallic clink. "Half now and half upon delivery."

It pushed away from the table and Verity tried to see within its hood. "Trask," it called. "Do your job."

The man in the corner muttered under his breath, and Verity blinked as time slipped away from her. A golden web struck her in the face and for a moment, she wasn't sure where she was or what she was doing.

"Can you see?" a woman's voice demanded. *"Verity, try harder!"*

"Who are you?" she asked.

The woman sucked in a sharp breath. *"Hell and ashes."* Something warm brushed against Verity's forehead. Then she could see again, and knew where she was. "Verity, hurry!"

She felt ill again. The cobwebs clung to her, but somehow Lady Eberhardt kept them away.

The cowled head turned her way. "What have we here?" it asked, but this time she was certain the words weren't memory. It seemed to step outside its body, the way she had. Then the image seemed to jerk toward her, and the hood fell back, and—

"Noah!" Verity sat upright with a scream, her heart racing as she tried to translocate.

"Stop!" Lady Eberhardt cried, and Verity slammed back into her body as a golden net of pure light hauled her back in, collapsing her back on the daybed.

She felt like she'd plummeted off a building and smashed into hard cobbles. She couldn't breathe. Couldn't speak. Surprisingly strong hands caught her by the shoulders and rolled her to her side, where Verity's lungs finally opened up with a sucking heave. Dizziness swam through her vision.

"Just breathe," Lady Eberhardt told her gruffly, rubbing her between the shoulder blades. "That was poorly done by me. I should have let you go. My apologies."

Verity shuddered. Her entire body ached. "W-what happened?"

"You tell me. Who's Noah?"

Noah. Verity squeezed her eyelids shut. "It was Noah Guthrie, a young curser who used to run with the One-Eyed Crows until Murphy threw him out of the gang. But at the same time, it wasn't Noah at all. It was...." She tried to drag herself upright, to recover her composure. It was long gone. All she could see was that horrible face leering at her, superimposed over Noah's, and when she tried to put it into words, she struggled to describe it. "What was it? A monster?"

"Monsters don't exist," Lady Eberhardt replied, turning to pour her a cup of tea from a setting that had appeared out of nowhere. "It could have been something straight out of the Shadow Dimensions. Sometimes they slip through and colonize a person."

"It saw me," she blurted, taking the cup gratefully and draining her tea in one large gulp.

Lady Eberhardt frowned. "What do you mean?"

"It looked right at me and asked me what I was doing there. It was as though it stepped outside of its body, the same way I did." Panic lit through her. "How could it do that? How could it know I was in some sort of trance, watching the scene? That would require slipping through time itself!"

"Not slipping through time," Lady Eberhardt corrected. "But there is one sort of creature who can see through it. Sometimes."

"What?" She felt like she knew the answer.

"A demon."

All of the blood drained from her face. Verity set down her teacup and hurried to the window, driving the sash up to let in some fresh air. She swallowed hard, just as she realized that the sun had reached its zenith and was beginning to head toward the horizon. "What time is it?"

"Late afternoon."

"We've been here for hours?"

"At least three." Lady Eberhardt sipped her tea, watching as Verity tried to compose herself. "And we were speaking of demons, not the time."

"I know." She closed her eyes. Demons were well outside her repertoire. She knew danger; she'd stared into its face far too many times. But a demon could steal your soul from your body and destroy the very essence of a person. That was an entirely different matter. "Just what have you gotten me involved in?"

"Me?" Lady Eberhardt pointed out, with one meticulous eyebrow. "Or your dear friend Murphy?"

Fair point. Verity looked away. "I cannot fight a demon."

"I can."

Verity stared at the old harridan. "You can?"

"The demon is in our world, not its own," Lady Eberhardt said with a shrug, as though she wasn't speaking of a hell dimension. "It needs permission to be in this Guthrie boy's body, and its powers are tied directly to his. Was he a talented sorcerer?"

"Noah?" Verity saw him again, laughing at her as he showed her some sleight-of-hand trick from years ago. "Noah was talented, but he struggled with opium. He began by smoking it in the opium dens, and then after a while he began to eat it. It destroyed him from within."

"Hmm." Lady Eberhardt's eyes grew distant. "That would explain how a demon managed to trick him into playing its host. It would look for weak-natured hosts, or those who had nothing to live for. It needs to make its offer sound appealing." She set down her tea with a sigh. "Well, at least I've solved the problem of the memory hex."

Verity touched her temples. "I cannot recall anything still."

"You most likely won't. It's meticulous work, and it might take more than one session to break through it."

"You recognize the work?"

"I should." Lady Eberhardt's lips thinned. "After all, I taught him."

"Who?"

"Phineas Trask. He was cast out of the Order over a decade ago. Makes his living in Balthazar's Labyrinth selling minor memory hexes, and odd bits and baubles he manages to find from somewhere. His sorcery was supposed to have been restricted the moment he went into exile."

"Supposed to?"

"I performed the warding myself." Lady Eberhardt pushed to her feet. "Looks like I'll have to flush the rat out of its den and see how it managed to slip my warding. This is troubling. It's not the first time someone has been restricted, and yet turns up with powers he shouldn't have. I need to meditate on this. Let's go get you freshened up while we wait for Adrian to return." The old harridan paused by the door and looked back almost reluctantly. "You did very well today, Verity."

Verity couldn't stop a smile. "Was that a compliment, Lady E?"

"Don't let it go to your head. And *don't* call me Lady E."

A quick visit to his father's led Bishop to telling the Prime about the Chalice, the flesh constructs, and the scent of demon in the One-Eyed Crows' house.

He was almost finished with his thoughts on Tremayne's involvement when he realized that his father was only half paying attention.

Drake gently picked up the fork and resettled it in Eleanor's fumbling hand. Bishop paced in front of the fireplace, watching them in frustration. He'd always cared for his father's lover; Eleanor might have been a sorceress, but her love for Drake had always come before any interest in advancing her own position in the Order. Or at least she *had* been a powerful sorceress, until she'd suffered some kind of apoplectic fit, brought on by her imprisonment by Drake's ex-wife, Morgana.

"The Sicarii held a vote," Bishop finally said, trying to get some sort of reaction.

"Ah," Drake murmured, helping guide Eleanor's hand toward the mush of potato on her plate. For some reason, she had eaten everything on the right side of her plate, but not the left.

"Don't you want to know how it went?"

"You're here, and none of them are. I know how it went."

Cursing under his breath, Bishop paced to the fire. "It was a narrow win," he told the fire, for at least it was listening to him. "I think the only thing that swung the vote was the fact that Madrigal fears I will fight my brethren and cause a mess among the ranks. She doesn't want any more chaos to the Order, not at the moment."

Matters, however, might change. He didn't need to say it.

"You're usually more careful than that," Drake said, looking up. His brow knotted. "Don't put yourself between them and me, if it comes to it."

"That's my choice to make, is it not? You're not the only one who can make"—eyes flickering to Eleanor—"sacrifices. And you're missing the point."

Drake stood, spoon in hand. "That's not what I wanted. You're my son. I don't want to see you hurt."

"And what did you think would happen when you resigned?" Bishop snapped. "It's never been done before. One Prime duels another. The winner remains alive. That's the way it works. The Winter Solstice is coming, and with it comes Ascendancy. There's talk that they're going to have to elect a Prime this weekend, or perhaps candidates will fight for the right to sit in your chair—"

"It's not my chair. Not anymore."

"If you rescinded your resignation, this entire mess would go away." The idea made sense. He stepped closer. "The Order and the councilors would allow it, I'm certain—"

"My role is here with Eleanor. My role is with my family. Do you know what I have given up in my lifetime, in order to protect the Order?"

Bishop looked away. One son had died in that house, and Drake was still in mourning. His... brother. Half brother.

"Everything," Drake answered, as if he had asked.

"Maybe it's for the best?" he suggested, and from the wounded flash of his father's eyes, he realized that they weren't talking about *everything* anymore, but about Sebastian. The son who was lost. "He was dangerous, out of control... It wasn't just the fact that he could only wield his sorcery through Expression, Drake, but who could stand up to him? You? Me? I felt his power, and it made me shiver."

"He never had a chance to cast aside Expression, and learn to harness his will," Drake replied. "Everyone deserves a chance."

"Not *everyone* has the strength to rip London apart at the seams either." How much power was too much?

"And if Madrigal had asked, would you have gone after him?"

If asked, Bishop knew the answer to that. Expression—the art of spontaneous acts of sorcery through emotion—was dangerous. Entire towns had been torn apart before. The Great London Fires had been caused by Expression. The Order had ruled that sorcery *must* be a rational act, stripped of emotion and guided by rituals, by careful meditation. Only then could the populace—and by extension sorcerers—be safe. Otherwise they would have been banned and hunted to extinction.

The Vigilance Against Sorcery Committee already wanted to do that. The Queen's use of sorcery in her empire expansion, however, meant that Sir Grant Martin's Law Against Devilment hadn't been pushed through parliament.

Yet.

"Yes," he said, into the stillness of the room. "Yes, I would have taken the commission to kill Sebastian. Out of duty for the blood we shared. If any of the Sicarii were going to kill him, it should have been me."

Drake's entire expression shuttered. "I would have stopped you."

"You couldn't have. I'm very good at what I do." Very good at killing. Perhaps it was the only thing he was good at? "I always find my target." The words were emotionless, which almost made him laugh. One son too given to emotion and one who could barely feel it. Which one was the monster?

Or had been.

"Eleanor wouldn't have wanted you to resign," he said quietly.

"Really?" His father's nostrils flared in rage. "Well, why don't you ask her? She's not dead. She can hear what we're saying."

Bishop glanced toward the woman, then away. She'd always been kind to him. The only one he'd been able to speak to of Mya, in fact. But was she still in there? How could she be?

"I'm sorry, Eleanor," he said, for he'd been rude, and if his father was correct, then he owed her more than that.

Eleanor stared at him, her right fist clenching and her eyes spitting sparks. "Mm-hmm... I'mmm...."

Drake strode to her side and fell to his knees. "Darling, it's all right. Here, have some water."

"What are we going to do about the demon?"

His father held a glass of water up to Eleanor's lips, murmuring something to her.

"Don't you care?" Bishop demanded. "If the demon has found a way back to our plane of existence, then it will be coming for revenge. You're the only person it fears, the only person who has some sort of chance of standing against it, and it won't let that sit idly."

"I'm aware of that." Silver eyes glinted in the firelight as Drake looked up. "I'm just not certain what I'm supposed to do about it. I'll alert Lucien, and let him know that there might be some more danger coming his way."

Lucien Devereux, Lord Rathbourne, was Bishop's other half brother, and had once been chosen by the demon as the perfect candidate for its vessel. After thwarting the demon's attempts to take him over, Rathbourne was enjoying a quiet month with his new wife and their child. He wouldn't welcome this news.

"You'll alert Lucien." He couldn't stop bitterness from seeping into his tone. "I'm sure that will do the world of good. He can barely use magic after the demon's psychic attack."

"He and I are working on that."

"Damn it, Drake," Bishop appealed directly to him. "We need leadership. Of all the times you could have chosen to step back from the Order, this was potentially the worst." And he knew why. It wasn't just Eleanor's state of being, but the loss of Sebastian, the son Drake had never known about.

"It will sort itself out—"

"That's the best you can offer?" he exploded. "What about all of the people who relied upon you? Those sorcerers who aren't strong enough to stand against this war that is coming?" *Me, damn you.* "How do we fight a demon without you? How do we—"

"Well, perhaps I don't have all of the answers anymore!" Drake slammed the spoon down, his eyes flashing silver lightning.

Finally. Bishop glared back.

And then Eleanor touched Drake's hand. Just that, a simple touch, a fumble, but the Prime turned back to her, bowing his head. Bishop couldn't quite meet her eyes as she glanced up at him above his father's head, as though trying to tell him something.

Drake's head sank, and Bishop felt ill at the sight. He wanted to apologize, but it was too late. "How do I save *them*?" Drake rasped hoarsely. "When I cannot even save those I love?"

"By trying. I don't know." Bishop swallowed hard. "The Order needs you. Lucien needs you. There's no way that he can stand against the demon a second time." Still no response. "*I* need you."

This time, those silvery eyes turned his way.

"I've never asked you for anything," Bishop blurted. "I know why you couldn't be in my life as a child. I know that prophecy dictated your presence would bring about the deaths of all your sons, and so you kept away. Well, it's too late. The prophecy is here. It's already stolen one of your sons. You have two left, and one of us is the next to die." Reaching for his hat, he swallowed hard. "If you sit here, then maybe it will be both of us next time."

Drake flinched. "Adrian—"

"No. I'm done. I've said my piece." He headed for the door. "The next move is yours."

"I worry about him," Drake said, gently wiping the mush of potato from the corners of Eleanor's mouth. "There's a darkness in his eyes that I haven't seen before. And I didn't notice it until tonight." Putting the plate aside, he looked down.

What was he doing? He'd lived as the Prime of the Order for over twenty years, confidently making decisions that he'd known might cost lives, and forcing himself to make them because the alternative was unforgivable, but... the loss of Sebastian had cost him more than he'd known, and the damage to Eleanor.... He would never forgive himself for not fighting her harder when she'd insisted on wading into deep waters in order to protect him.

"I don't know what to do," he admitted to her. "I love you so much, and yet this... all of this is my fault. And I cannot ask more of Lucien and Ianthe. They barely got out of the last assault with their lives. But every move I consider involves Adrian, and do I dare? After tonight? I couldn't lose him, Ellie. Not him. He's the one son I was ever allowed to watch over, and he's been through so much."

A hand brushed against his sleeve.

Drake's head shot up.

"Ellie," he whispered, capturing her wavering hand. The Healers that had treated her after the fatal showdown with Morgana came in every few days and worked their sorcery over her. She wouldn't have survived otherwise, one of them had told him bluntly, but she was improving and would continue to do so, though they couldn't say how much of her cognitive function she would retain.

There was a look of fierce determination on her face. "N-nnuh.... N-Nottt...." Frustration made her look away, shaking herself.

"Not?" He asked. She squeezed his hand with her good one, and Drake's mind raced. "Not my fault," he said, though he didn't believe it.

"F-froen...." Eleanor lurched into an excited babble of words that ran together, and Drake helplessly looked on. "You. You... choy...."

He tried, he really did, but he could see her frustration growing with his inability to understand her.

Reaching out, she tried to capture his hand and pressed it to her shoulder, then looked angry. Drake maneuvered it at her whim, until he finally realized where she wanted it. "Here?" he asked, pressing his palm flat over her heart. "What do you—?"

That fierce look told him everything. "Choy... choyz...."

"Choice?"

Relief showed in her face.

"Choice," he said again, then understood what she was trying to tell him. "By not making those choices, I'm frozen. Which is a choice of its own."

Drake let out a long-suffering sigh. There was a hole inside him that would never fill. He couldn't even remember the last time he'd stepped out of the house. Or bothered to discover what was going on in the world around him. Bishop's emergency call the night Verity showed up, perhaps. Sebastian's death had ripped his heart right out of his chest, and all he could see when he closed his eyes at night was his son desperately reaching for him... and then the look on the boy's face when Drake had to choose whether to save Lucien, who might have had a chance, versus the son who was already dying.

He'd never suffered such indecision before.

"M-move," Ellie told him.

"Make a move." Everyone wanted him to do so. How the bloody hell could he tell them that he didn't know which way to go? Standing, Drake paced. "I cannot accept the mantle of Prime again." He simply didn't have it in him. The others might think that it was a simple solution that would fix everything, but he wasn't that man anymore. "But there is another who can. I just have to convince her that she's right for the role."

Eleanor's eyes were wise.

"I'm a fool," he told her. "I cannot let everything that we've tried to build all these years fall to pieces. I cannot lose Lucien or Adrian as well."

Footsteps echoed in the hallway outside. What now?

"Sir," said the butler, rapping at the open door. He was drenched and trying to hold someone upright.

Drake stepped protectively between Eleanor and the door. "Yes?" he demanded, trying to see who leaned against the butler's side.

"There's a young woman here," Milton said apologetically. "She insisted that she see you. I wouldn't have let her in, it being so late and all, but...."

The young woman looked up, her bedraggled blonde hair clinging to her shoulders. Those dark brown eyes flinched away from the faint lantern light, and her aura was bleeding around the edges. "You're the Prime?" she whispered.

"Not anymore," he told her, a flash of uncertainty unknotting within him. He could sense sorcery leeching off her, like a faint mist. "Who are you? What are you doing here?"

He thought he knew most of those who belonged to the Order.

"I need help," she whispered, and her knees gave way as she tried to take a step toward him.

Both he and the butler caught her. A deeper glimpse at her aura showed that it was savaged almost beyond repair. Something had happened to her—something magical.

Drake set a hand to her face, caressing her clammy skin as he used his power to soothe her aura.

The girl wilted in his touch, pressing her forehead against his hand. "Thank you."

"What happened to you?"

"They took everything away from me. I was halfway through a Vision when my father removed my blindfold, and suddenly I could see everything...." She swallowed hard, forcing herself to calm. "My visions are gone now. It's the first thing that I ever predicted—that I would lose them the day I saw the world again."

Drake frowned. Visions? He felt a sudden clench of cold spear through him. There'd been a blindfolded girl in the house where his son died.

"My name is Miss Cleo... well, it was Sinclair, but now it is Montcalm." Then she said the words that rocked him to the core. "I'm your son Sebastian's wife, and he very much needs your help."

CHAPTER ELEVEN

"NOAH GUTHRIE USED to frequent Balthazar's Labyrinth," Verity said, peering at the Black Horse Pub, which was the entrance to the occult world they called the Labyrinth. The Portobello Road markets bustled around them, completely unaware of what dark secret was hidden nearby. "That's where he fell in with a bad crowd and turned to darker arts than what we're supposed to practice."

"Typical," Bishop murmured, flexing and unflexing his fist. "If you want to find the scum of the sorcery world, you look here."

"Why thank you," Verity announced. "I thought you'd have considered the Hex to fit that description."

"The Hex has its charms, surprisingly enough."

"Do you know, you can be almost charming when you set your mind to it?" Verity cleared her throat, flushing faintly.

He looked away.

"Lady E said that if we were looking for Phineas Trask, he'd be here too. And this is where Murphy and I met with the demon," Verity said. "It makes sense to start looking here."

"And all it costs to get in is a drop of your blood to pay the stone golem at the door."

Blood. Verity forced a smile. "I can cope with that, Bishop."

"Blood can be used in a lot of spells."

"You don't trust the Labyrinth, or its denizens? Everything I've ever heard about the Labyrinth says that it has rules and they're strictly enforced." Rather like the Hex, in a way.

"Fine," he muttered under his breath, shoving his hands in his coat as he stalked across the road toward the Black Horse. "Just don't say I didn't warn you."

The pub was nearly empty this early in the afternoon. The short man behind the bar jerked his head toward the steel vault door in the wall and continued polishing his glass as they entered. A chain manacled him to the bar.

"Odd little fellow, isn't he?" Verity murmured, glancing over her shoulder.

Bishop slashed his thumb with a blade he produced from somewhere inside his coat sleeve, and held it over the lead bowl in front of the altar. "Fellow may be somewhat imprecise. I'm not certain what he is, but it's not entirely human."

Verity echoed him and the ex-bank vault door swung open, revealing an enormous stone golem that guarded the entrance. She smiled at it uneasily as she stepped through. Constructs could be made of anything: blood, shadow, grass, stone.... But they remained inanimate objects, driven purely by their master's will, and rather difficult to destroy.

Then they were through into the narrowed streets and mishmash of alleys that formed the Labyrinth. Dirty glass panels far overhead kept the weather out and watchful eyes away. The street was lined with little shops tucked in against each other like little old ladies on a winter's day, and people hawked their wares from barrows in the square up ahead.

"This way," Bishop told her, directing her down a small laneway that appeared empty. Except for the shadows and gloom, of course.

Verity sighed. "Always the back alleys."

"Where else does scum hide?"

"You know where we're going?" She swept her skirts clear of a puddle of... something oily.

"I know where Trask resides." Bishop moved with predatory intent, those hawk-like eyes prowling every shadow. They turned down another street, and then another.

"Here it is." He pointed to a small shop with an Eye of Horus gilded into the brickwork.

Bishop glanced up toward the roof.

"What is—?" A whistle jerked her gaze up and a young lad scampered across the tiles, vanishing behind a chimney. Verity drew just enough power into herself to punch out of there, if need be.

"Trask's a collector of black occult items," Bishop muttered. "Some of them are deadly, some of them are worth a small fortune. He's got a half dozen lads working for him, no doubt, to make sure nobody steals into his shop."

"Can we handle them?"

"Yes." Bishop pushed the door open, and the bell tinkled.

She had a feeling that no matter whom he faced, Bishop would be able to handle them. He exuded a quiet sense of competence, and fear seemed to be a distant connection he barely knew of.

He stepped through the door, keeping his large body in front of her.

"You don't have to shield me," she pointed out.

That earned her a startled look, then he gave her a faint smile. "You're right. I learned that when Zachariah hexed me."

"At least you can smile about it now," she pointed out.

The jest killed that expression.

Sound skittered from the back room.

"Trask?" Bishop called, one hand near his belt as he took careful steps into the shadowy shop. "A word, if I might?"

The shelves were lined with all sorts of odd ends: mirrors that didn't seem quite like mirrors, books, amulets, a skull on the counter, and a half dozen opaque globes set on fine red velvet. There was a pair of sarcophagi looming near the door, and several fine scrolls on a shelf.

Shadows shifted as someone separated from the gloom. A fine cloud of red powder was blown toward them.

Bishop jerked her out of the way, shouldering her into the side of the gold-and-blue sarcophagus as he barreled past. Then he was leaping over the counter after the figure, a flare of white-hot blue gleaming to life in his hands as he vanished through the curtains.

Etheric blades. "Bishop!" she called, and went after him.

"This way!" Bishop yelled, thundering up a set of crooked steps. His footsteps were the only ones she heard.

Verity took a cautious step into the back room. A safe gleamed in the wall, the painting that hid it swinging wide open. A single candle fought the gloom, and there was a musty scent she couldn't quite place.

She couldn't see anyone, but she also didn't feel like she was alone. An empty room lacked a certain little something.

"I know you're there," she said softly, sliding a hand toward the pistol in her belt. Her indigo skirts swished around her ankles as she took another careful step forwards. "I assume Mr. Bishop is chasing shadows?"

Something moved behind her and yanked her back into his arms, jerking a blade to her throat.

Verity froze.

"Not another step, missy." Whoever it was smelled like stale cigars and burned cinnamon. Another flare of light swirled to life as he lit a pair of candles with his sorcery.

Bishop thundered back down the stairs, slamming to a halt as he saw her caught there.

"You," her attacker said. "Don't move. I know what you are."

"Trask," Bishop said flatly. He straightened, both hands held in front of him. "You don't have to do this."

"Put the blades away."

Bishop vanished them, and Verity's eyes burned with afterimage. She tried to catch his gaze, to tell him she could handle this herself, but he was focused purely on the man behind her. "Let her go."

"Or?" Trask sneered, jerking her backward.

Bishop froze again.

Look at me, damn you. She growled under her breath and he finally, finally glanced toward her.

I've got this, she tried to tell him. She wasn't telepathic, alas, but the tense muscles in his shoulders relaxed. Somehow he saw the message in her expression.

"We just wanted to ask you a few questions," Bishop said, watching only her.

"Aye." Trask shifted behind her, which made the knife prick her throat. "Course you did. That's why you come in here with them blades."

Bishop smiled. It wasn't very nice. "If I were here on a commission, then you wouldn't have seen me coming at all, Trask. Let her go."

"Why should I? Seems to me that this here"—Trask jerked her roughly—"is what we call insurance. Or perhaps... the spoils of war, I should say. What? What are you smiling about?"

"That was your last warning," Bishop told him. "Verity."

Verity let her breath out slowly then gathered in her power, a stealthy glide of pure heat through her veins.

"Don't you try nothin'," Trask snarled, and she knew he'd felt her blossoming with heat.

Verity vanished.

She slammed back into being just behind Trask as he stumbled forward, coming up with her pistol in hand. "I don't really want to hurt you," she said, drawing the hammer back as she pressed the muzzle of it against the back of his skull. "But I will, if need be."

Trask spun, and she punched through time and space again, slamming a fist into his side as she reappeared. Then she was gone again. A kick to the back of the knee. A knee to his groin when he bellowed and spun toward her. Then behind him again, where she shoved him through the curtain, onto the counter. Trask groaned.

Stepping through the door, she leveled the pistol in his face coolly. "Spoils of *war*?"

This... this was the memory worker and she felt a sudden intense fury. Who knew what he'd taken from her? She'd faced dangerous people before, stared death right in the eye—but the idea of losing bits and pieces of herself both had her back up and sent a shiver of fear down her spine. Imagine if he'd taken Mercy from her? Or even the few faint traces she could recall of her mother?

"Verity," Bishop warned. "Don't hurt him. We need answers."

She stared down the barrel of the pistol and almost wanted to pull the trigger. "And I *need* my memories back."

Trask panted, half curled over the counter. "You," he said, recognition gleaming in his eyes. "Murphy's little crow."

Verity hadn't missed those memories until now, but the thought of this man in her head.... It made her feel dirty. "Don't tempt me, you filth. I can run rings around you if I so desire, and Mr. Bishop already wants to knot your intestines together."

Trask laughed under his breath at her. "So that's how Murphy did it," he said, half to himself. His cock-eyed gaze slid over her shoulder as Bishop pushed through the curtain, pausing at her side like some lethal shadow. "Or did she fuck the Chalice out of you?"

Bishop moved, and somehow Verity caught his arm.

"I thought we didn't want to kill him?" she asked Bishop when he flexed beside her with fury. "Save your blows for later, if Mr. Trask grows somewhat recalcitrant with answers. His petty insults are simply not worth it."

Trask glared back at her. "I ain't talking."

Verity stepped to the side. "Oh, I think that you will. Mr. Bishop, he's all yours."

"Thank you," Bishop replied, faintly amused for some reason. He stripped off his coat and began to unbutton his sleeves at the wrists. "This won't take but a moment. Just make sure I don't get any blood on your skirts. I know how you feel about that."

"Isn't he thoughtful?" she asked Trask, who looked green.

"Here now," Trask muttered, his fingers curling into a fist. "No need for theatrics."

"Flex those fingers again and I'll cut them off." Bishop's voice was pure ice as the two of them locked eyes. "Like you said: we both know what the other is capable of."

Trask froze.

"And I didn't like you the moment Agatha told me about you. Being impolite to Miss Hawkins only exacerbates the intensity of such an emotion. *Don't* tempt me."

Verity didn't quite know when he'd appointed himself guardian of her reputation, but it was rather interesting to realize that Bishop didn't like hearing slurs against her. Interesting, and... surprising. She'd been alone for so long, just her and Mercy, fighting their own battles. The very idea of someone else trying to do it for her.... She didn't need him to—she could take care of herself—but... it gave her a strange sensation in her chest.

Bishop stripped off his waistcoat and folded it in a neat pile atop his coat. He rolled his sleeves up, and Verity couldn't stop her gaze from sliding over him like a caress. My, my. She hadn't truly realized how large he was. Muscle rippled in his shoulders, and the shirt strained over that well-indented chest. But it was the faint hint of scars up the inside of one forearm that caught her eye.

"Now, we know you were hired by a demon to wipe Verity's memories of a particular meeting away from her." Bishop turned his full attention to Trask, and Verity was suddenly very glad that he wasn't looking at *her* like that. An iceberg didn't seem as cold as Bishop right now.

"A demon?"

"Noah Guthrie," Bishop said, "who is currently serving as a vessel. Don't try and pretend you didn't know. Agatha's too good a teacher for you to have missed that particular lesson."

Trask ran his tongue over his teeth, thinking. "Aye. I knew. Could smell it on him. He paid well."

"What else did he want you to do?"

"Just wipe the lass's memory, and alter Murphy's once they brought us the Chalice."

"Murphy was killed," Bishop told him, "in a room that was locked, with a guard on the door. It's the one thing that's been bothering me for a while."

Trask's gaze sidled sideways.

"You were there," Bishop said, "weren't you? And you wiped the guard's memory."

Trask said nothing, his lips pressed firmly together. But Verity went very still. She'd not thought about it. But how, precisely, had the demon killed Murphy without Conrad realizing? She set her fingers to her temple, frowning at the slight ache that grew there.

"Trask, it's been a very vexing month for me," Bishop said, grabbing the fellow by his collar and squeezing. "Trust me when I say that I would really, *really* like to hit something right now. The only problem is that I'm not entirely certain I would stop if I were to begin."

"Fine!" Trask held up his hands, starting to look nervous. "I didn't know he were going to kill him."

"Who?"

"Noah Guthrie," Verity said, the details beginning to fill themselves in. "Murphy would have let him in. He always thought he could handle anything. And Conrad... he's the best of the Crows. Murphy would have been too confident."

"So Murphy hands over the Chalice, demands his coin, and then gets his throat cut?" Bishop asked.

She pressed a hand to her temples, which were suddenly aching. "No. Murphy wasn't a fool. He sent me off with the Chalice, to rendezvous with Noah once Noah paid him the second amount. That's when I was attacked."

It was starting to come back to her, in flashes that skewed her perception of the world around her. Nausea rose in her stomach. She felt that knife shove itself into her side as she'd stood there in the street, so cocky while she asked the demon's henchman for the code that Murphy had told her. The one that would have indicated the Crows had been paid, and hence she could hand over the Chalice.

"So Murphy tells the demon he doesn't have it, and the demon kills him. Trask wipes Conrad's memory, and then...." Bishop's head turned back to Trask. "Then he goes after Verity, with Trask by his side."

Trask swallowed. "Look. I just did as I were told. He had these... men... with him that weren't really men. They were all wearing—"

"Masks," Verity whispered, seeing it again. "One of them stabbed me when I demanded to know where Murphy was."

"Keep talking," Bishop suggested, a muscle in his jaw ticking as his fists curled in Trask's collar.

"We got the Chalice, but the girl vanished somehow, then ran. That's all I know, I swear it!"

Bishop let him go, and Trask touched his throat, swallowing hard.

"What happened to the Chalice?" Bishop demanded.

"Don't know. I was starting to get a bad feeling about all this, so I cut out of it. Didn't need the money that bad. The demon let me go."

"Let you go?" Bishop's gaze flattened. "That's why you have so many boys watching the shop. You think he's going to come after you?"

"Well—" Trask cleared his throat, cutting a glance toward Verity. "—he's tying up loose ends. I didn't want to be one of them 'ends.'"

Bishop stepped away from him. "So you have no idea where the Chalice is?"

"None...." There was a hesitation on the end of that though.

"You're lying," Verity said.

"Think about it," Trask said, swallowing visibly. "The Chalice needs someone from the Grave Arts to work it. The demon can't use it."

Thought clearly raced behind Bishop's dark eyes. "Who? Who's working with Guthrie?"

Trask shrugged. "Don't know. My part in this was done." His gaze slid sideways toward Verity. "But if it's a Grave sorcerer at his side, then it ain't one of the Order."

"Which leaves... five possibilities," Bishop muttered, half to himself.

That's when a flare of red magic spat into the sky outside.

CHAPTER TWELVE

"WHAT WAS THAT?"

Bishop strode to the window, glancing out into the Labyrinth. Dealing with Trask had all his nerves on edge, and the flare of sputtering sparks that slowly fell back into the Labyrinth's streets made his gut knot up tight.

"Jesus." Trask scrambled for the back door, but Verity blocked it and set her pistol right in his face. "Get out of the way, you daft woman! They're coming!"

"Who's coming?" Verity demanded.

"Something! I don't know! That's a warning sign from one of my boys." Trask shoved her aside, careless of the pistol. "I ain't staying around to find out what it is."

"Let him go," Bishop told her, and Trask snatched a carpetbag off the floor and bolted toward the back.

"He wiped my memories," Verity said, glaring after him.

"Did you want him to dabble in your head again and bring them back?" Her expression said it all. "I thought not.

Trask is a coward, and he'll meet a bad end one day. But not at our hands. Let's get out of here."

"Exactly what I was thinking," Verity replied.

They were halfway to the door when a second flare of magic went up. It burst just below the glass panes above that shielded the quarter from normal eyes.

"Get moving," Bishop barked, pushing her through the door and out into the streets.

People screamed from the direction in which they'd come. Magic washed the walls and cast a bluish glow over the entrance to the Labyrinth.

"How do we get out?" Verity gasped.

"This way." He shoved her toward the right, and the back of the cramped quarter. They started running, Verity cursing her skirts under her breath as he tugged her along.

Arum. The guttural cry didn't come from any throat he'd ever heard.

"What the hell is that?" Verity cried, glancing over her shoulder.

His skin was crawling along his arms, sorcery thrilling through his veins and stirring the dark pulse that lay at the heart of him. "Grave magic."

Verity shot him a sharp look, her green eyes meeting his. "The Chalice?"

"Possibly," he said, and ducked to the left, down a narrow alley where the walls brushed against his shoulders. "We're not prepared to face it right now. Not if some Grave Arts sorcerer is wielding the Chalice."

The memory of coming up against that mind in the Seven Dials stirred within him. Whoever it was, they'd blocked Bishop's thrust with ease, threatening to roll his mind over like a bug and squash it. A nervous sweat broke out along his lip. He wasn't used to meeting his match. The vulnerability unnerved him.

"There!" he said, pushing her toward an apothecary. Slamming both hands into the double doors, he strode inside.

Three men turned, icy-blue mage globes springing into form just above their hands.

"Stand down," he told them, flashing his Order rings.

One of them paled.

"I just want passage out of the Labyrinth," he added, ushering Verity inside at his heels.

The leader vanished his mage globes, and the other followed him, thank goodness. "How much is it worth to you?" the man asked, his eyes glinting with sudden avarice.

"The question is: how much is it worth to *you*?" Bishop replied coolly, staring the bearded man down.

He could have heard a pin drop in the sudden silence.

"Creedy," one of the fellows muttered, the white of his eyes showing as he tried to peer past Bishop. "Probably ain't the time for it. He's Order, man."

Creedy scratched at his beard, then sighed. "What's out there?"

"Flesh constructs. The streets are crawling with them."

That earned another breath-catching silence.

"Jesus," a smaller lad blurted. "What are we going to do?"

"Let me and my companion out, and they'll most likely go away," Bishop replied, moving fast toward the back of the shop. "It's this way?"

"Where are we going?" Verity muttered, following on his heels.

"Aye." Creedy scrambled after them. "How'd you know I got passage out?"

Because it's how I get into the Labyrinth when I don't want to be seen.

Bishop merely shot him a bland look. "The Order knows everything." And then he jerked the wardrobe in the back room open and gestured Verity inside. "After you."

Her nose wrinkled. "It stinks of mothballs."

"Trust me," he said, stepping inside after her. "It could be worse."

Much worse.

The press of her body was distracting.

Bishop hunched inside the wardrobe, waiting for Creedy to fire the runes that linked the wardrobe with a locker in Marylebone Station. The other half of the wardrobe was filled with boxes, and he was forced to rest his elbows on the timbers on either side of her head, even as he tried not to sink into the warmth of her embrace.

Soft breasts pressed against his chest. His vision was slowly becoming accustomed to the dark, and he could almost see the tip of her nose thanks to the light gleaming through the cracks in the door. It was a pert little nose, much like her.

And right below it was her mouth.

Bishop swallowed. He could hear her heartbeat, whispering in conjunction with the call of his power. He was always acutely aware of others and their bodies, but this was the first time that he'd felt the stir of his own in response.

Her breath whispered against his mouth. "What are we waiting for?"

A shiver of power stirred over his skin, as Creedy chanted outside. "That," Bishop said softly, as golden lines streamed suddenly all over the interior of the wardrobe.

The pair of them slammed together as the golden lines suddenly collapsed over them like a net. He wrapped his arms around her, driving her head into the protective curl of his chest and arms, as the world spun out of alignment.

—falling, tumbling, head over heels, his stomach punching up through his throat, and then back down again, as if it rebounded into his lower abdomen—

—and then they became solid again, Bishop shaking with the force of the translocation as he landed hard, slamming back into his body.

There was even less room in here, in the locker. He was practically wrapped around Verity, and the air was still and humid, tasting of old socks.

"I think I'm going to be ill," Verity said with a gasp, trying to push away from him.

He slammed the locker door open with his shoulder, the pair of them tripping as they tumbled out. Verity fell to her knees, pressing her hands to her mouth.

"Sorry, I should have warned you." He felt like joining her on his knees, but this wasn't his first trip. He just needed... a moment. "I thought you'd know what to expect."

Verity looked up after a long moment, shuddering as a train whistle echoed through the corridor. "That," she said, "was nothing like what I do. I feel like I've been pulled apart and then put back together again, but not quite properly."

He offered her a hand. "But... no flesh constructs here."

Verity dragged herself to her feet, and shuddered. "Small gains."

Bishop slammed the journal down on the reading table and flipped it open.

"What are you reading?" Verity murmured, rubbing her wet hair with a towel. She'd taken a bath to try and wash off the slimy feeling that coated her skin from the translocation, whilst he'd been hunting through his library.

He couldn't help noticing that the midnight blue robe she wore was extremely thin, and molded to her body. What was Agatha thinking, to give her that? "*Relics of the Order*, a compilation by Josiah Whitmore."

He ran his finger down the contents page, trying to find the chapter he needed. It was the third time he'd done it since she'd entered the room.

"Why?" Verity tossed the towel aside, sitting on the edge of one of his stuffed armchairs near the fire and withdrawing an ivory-backed brush from her pocket.

"Because it has occurred to me that we need to know precisely what we're dealing with, and what the Chalice can do.

"Together the three Relics Infernal can be used to summon a demon through into this world in the flesh. They can also vanquish one. However, separately they all have powerful properties of their own. My father created them, along with his ex-wife, Morgana, and the Earl of Tremayne. I didn't have much time to study the Chalice when it was in my possession." He swallowed, remembering the smoky lure of it, the way it called to him. Perhaps it hadn't been lack of time, but fear in the strength of his own willpower. "I was too busy trying to help recover the Blade of Altarrh. The Blade was destroyed when we sought to recover it, which makes the other two unable to control a demon, though they still have mysterious powers on their own. I think we need to know precisely what the Chalice is capable of so that we can work out who wants it, and why."

He found what he was looking for and flipped forward to the twelfth chapter while she brushed out her hair. Steam lifted off the ends of it as the fire set to work drying it, and he was surprised to realize it curled at the ends. "There's a treatise on the Grave Arts on the third shelf. Once you're finished, do you think you could look through it?"

He looked down at the book. "The Ankh of Set," the chapter headline read. Clearly not what he needed. Bishop flipped back to the start. His mind was all over the place.

Most notably on the way her breasts shifted behind the robe as she reached up to knot her hair into a tight chignon, and then stabbed a pin through it.

Hell.

He was rock-hard, his cock straining against his breeches. Anyone would be able to see it. Thank God for the reading table.

"Third shelf?" Verity asked, setting the brush aside and circling the library. "Which one?"

He pointed to her left. "No. Next one, and another shelf up... there. Yes."

Verity reached up, and he cursed under his breath. Her robe clung to the rounded contours of her breasts as she tugged the thick treatise off the shelf. And despite the fact that he knew better, he couldn't look away. "We know the Chalice can raise the dead," she said. "In vast quantities, if today was any indication."

"I also believe it exacerbates the power of the sorcerer connected to it." At least, that was the only explanation he could find for how strong that other sorcerer had felt when they'd clashed, mind to mind. He was no slouch himself, but that other mind had rolled him under like an ant beneath its heel.

"How do you use it?"

"You use your own blood to empower it, and link it to yourself," Bishop replied. He looked up from the book he was staring uselessly at. "All three relics require a sacrifice to work."

"What sort of sacrifice?"

"Well, Drake helped create them, and he said that they worked when fuelled by blood. But he also said that they were hungry relics. They wanted more. He could hear them whispering in his head when he used them. And when Tremayne had his hands on them it is suspected that he sacrificed someone to the Chalice's cause, but he always denied it."

"Your father created them." She sounded dubious.

"It was in his youth, when he fell in with Tremayne and Morgana. He said he was curious, that he dabbled in the dark arts and became fascinated with demons and what they could teach us."

"That does not sound reassuring."

Bishop frowned. Talk of demons and sacrifices had managed what control alone could not: his cock had begun to flag. "He realized what he had helped create was dangerous, and that's when he and Morgana stole them off Tremayne and hid them. He couldn't destroy them, but he never used them again."

She gave a noncommittal murmur. "Found something." Lifting the book up, she read, "The Chalice has the power to negate, as well, that which rides a necromancer and hounds him to the grave. A sacrifice is required, but neither blood nor death will do. The sacrifice is required within. A personal sacrifice of great value." Verity frowned. "What does that mean?"

"I have no idea."

"Hmm." Verity took slow steps as she quietly read.

It was a comfortable silence. Bishop stared at the way the strands of hair that had escaped her chignon were beginning to curl.

He'd thought having her here would be a distraction and a nuisance. He liked his solitude.

Well, she was a distraction, all right. But he was startled to discover that far from irritating him, her presence made him feel calm. He... liked it.

What would it be like to have a wife? Or a lover? To sit in companionable silences as they read after dinner, or to curl up on the sofa together, her feet tucked in his lap. He looked at Verity and realized he couldn't think of anyone else in that role. He wanted her.

And he couldn't have her. To take that step forward would be to cause them both unimaginable grief in the future, when the *maladroise* began to haunt him. Better just to enjoy her company now, before she found a master who would teach her and moved on.

"Bishop?" she said, and it sounded as though she'd repeated the word. "Did you hear what I said?"

"Chalice," he repeated, dropping his gaze to the book he carried, as he sat on the sofa. "Both negates and enhances the swell of a Grave Arts sorcerer's power. I was correct. Whoever Noah Guthrie has on his leash is using the Chalice to improve the amount of power that he can draw."

Verity sighed.

Focus, damn you. Bishop cursed, and turned the pages of the book. He'd lost all trace of the thought that he'd been following. Something about there being only five Grave Arts sorcerers who didn't belong to the Order. "I've been trying to think of the names of those Grave Arts sorcerers who were cast from the Order."

"And?"

"There is one who... would no doubt like to get his hands on the Chalice. One who wouldn't bat an eyelid at the thought of unleashing flesh constructs in London. Elijah Horroway."

"So what's the problem?"

He glanced at her, then glanced again. "I—um, just have to find him."

"So that's our next lead?"

Bishop nodded.

"Good, then we can focus on that. Tomorrow." Verity sighed and crossed the room toward him, closing the book and setting it on the small book table beside the sofa. She sat at his feet, resting her cheek and arm atop the sofa beside his hip as she looked up at him. "I know when a man is looking at me, Bishop. I know when he wants me."

Christ. He set his own book aside and prepared to move, but her hand on his thigh stopped him. Bishop looked down, and suddenly he didn't think he could move. He didn't want to push her away.

Why could he not have just one bloody minute with her in his arms? One minute of sheer physical enjoyment?

Because you know what happened the last time you tried....

"Verity." His throat was dry. "We can't."

Her hand slid up his thigh. Verity glanced up at him from beneath a fan of thick dark lashes.

He couldn't breathe.

He knew what she was doing: knew that the question in her pretty green eyes was very much focused on him and what his answer would be.

"Why not?" she whispered, sliding into his lap, the rounded press of her arse settling tauntingly close to his aching cock. Clever hands began to toy with his collar. "You want it. I want it."

Somehow he caught her wrist. His mind was scalded blank with the sheer sensation of her body pressed against his. "I w-would be taking advantage of you."

A mysterious smile curled over her mouth, and then she turned and straddled him, pressing him back into the sofa. His traitorous body went willingly enough.

Leaning close to him, she whispered in his ear. "Maybe it is I who would be taking advantage of you?"

Bishop's mouth went dry. Her robe gaped, revealing a hint of her nightgown beneath it and the shallow valley of her small breasts. Hell. He could almost make out the indentation of her nipple, and her hand was making small strokes up his thigh now, almost like a cat flexing the pads of its feet against his skin.

He was lost. Balanced on a fine edge of pure need that knotted him up tight. His cock hardened again, flooding with heat and blood until he couldn't think straight.

"You want me," Verity whispered, and leaned her weight on his thigh as she reached up to brush those damning lips against his. She had the sweetest mouth in all creation.

Verity teased his lips open with her own, her tongue darting against his. Bishop's hand slid up her back and he pressed her against him, his erection riding against the smooth slope of her inner thigh. Good God. His eyes widened, and some sort of noise came from his throat, then she was parting his shirt collar, pushing her hands inside. Skin on skin. There was no teasing now. No gentle seduction. Verity plundered his mouth, and fuck it, but he didn't even remember why he'd thought to deny them both anymore.

It felt so good.

Verity sucked his tongue into her mouth, and Bishop nearly lost all of his composure. He curled his arms around her lithe body, grinding her against him. The silk robe slipped and slid around her, and suddenly it wasn't enough to merely hold her like this. He wanted more. He wanted skin.

Hands delving beneath her robe, he parted it, and she gave a soft sigh, tilting her head back to allow him access to her throat. "*Yes.*"

Bishop tasted her jaw, then lower, his lips brushing over her pulse as his hands explored beneath her robe. Up her thighs, so smooth and soft. His thumbs dug in a little as his breathing harshened. What would it feel like to part her thighs and touch the wetness there? *Yes.* Every single inch of his body came alive in a way he'd never felt before. "Verity. Verity." The words came in harsh, ragged whispers as he kissed her collarbone and slid the robe from her shoulder.

Something pounded in his ears. Verity's heartbeat. He bit her throat, felt her pulse kick there, and suddenly he wasn't in the room anymore. A flash of Mya's face sprang to mind, her eyes wide with shock after he finally got her heart beating again, begging her for forgiveness, telling her that he hadn't meant to.... She'd looked at him as though he was a monster, and she was right to do so—

Bishop spilled out from under Verity, taking three long strides across the room as he tried to push the past away. Mya. *Jesus.* Verity. He couldn't allow what had happened before to happen again. It was long moments before he thought himself contained enough to face her.

Verity had tumbled onto his recently vacated cushions with a small squeak, her robe slipping off her shoulder.

He was wrong. He was nowhere near contained enough.

"It's been a long day." He meant the words as an explanation. Instead they came out hard and curt, and he knew it. Bishop winced. "Perhaps some sleep will serve to clear our heads so we can focus on this problem?"

From the look on her face, he was only digging himself deeper. Bishop stared at her helplessly. He had nothing to say. Nothing that could satisfactorily explain his problem. How to tell her he worried that he would kill her? That he'd lose control in the moment again, and start listening to her heartbeat the way he had before? Start stealing little pieces of her breath as his magic called at him.

"Good night," he said, and turned to flee.

CHAPTER THIRTEEN

"WHAT'S WRONG?"

Bishop looked up from the map table he was toying with, one brow lifted as though in enquiry. "Wrong?"

No sign of the disheveled man who'd fled from her in the sitting room. There had been secrets in his eyes then, and something terrified, but he hadn't told her the truth. Bishop was keeping secrets, and it vexed her.

The way he'd leapt away from her earlier still smarted, but he was no longer stiff and tense with distaste. An hour's grace had given him his composure back. "I thought you went to bed after dinner." That disastrous dinner—or the end of it, at least. "What are you doing?"

"I did go to bed," he said, his chest straining beneath his shirt as he tried to lift the map table and shift it slightly to the left. "Then I got up again." He sighed. "I couldn't stop my mind from working."

"I know the feeling," Verity muttered.

"Can't sleep?" he asked, tracing another golden sigil into the map table's silver casing with his finger. It flared bright, then sank into the metal, etching the rune as he withdrew his finger—and his sorcery.

"Not really." The sight distracted her. Power and the use of it were instinct to her; a gathering of that rush of power that bled through her, a simple thought, or a flick of her wrist, and then she was leaping through space and time. Other skills came harder to her: she could barely light a candle flame out of thin air, even as she could touch an object and track its owner across London.

What he did was another thing altogether. So complicated, with clearly defined rituals and runes to force its user into controlling their magic, rather than emoting it. It fascinated her, the things he could do.

The things he might be able to teach her.

That alone made her hungrier for the knowledge. Imagine what she could do—what choices she could make—if she wielded her sorcery expertly?

"Don't worry, Verity. We'll get the Chalice back. We just have to be patient." He seared another rune into the metal surrounding the table.

The Chalice was the least of her concerns. She shot him a glance, but his attention was purely focused on his work.

And not even remotely upon her.

Verity dragged her night-robe tighter around her thin shoulders. Obviously, she was the only one who felt this horrid yearning. She felt so very alone tonight. It wasn't so bad during the day when they were busy, but at night she had time to dwell on the loss of the Crows and her place in the world, and most of all, Mercy. She very much wanted to ask him to just hold her, but that would clearly be crossing a boundary, judging by the way he'd leapt from her touch like a scalded cat earlier.

Verity sighed. She was on her own, and it was clear she would have to learn to accept that.

The map table was a curious piece; a detailed map of nearly every street in inner London, rolled out upon what looked like a silver stand. "What does it do?"

"Through this, I can locate every practitioner of the Grave Arts in London, if I set up the spell work properly," he told her, stepping back and pouring fine metal filings across the map of London. Once they lay in an inert powder, he gently eased a glass cover over the top, settling it into the grooves were it clearly belonged. "I was thinking about what Trask said about our mysterious Grave Arts sorcerer not belonging to the Order. Using this, I might be able to track them. The runes trace Grave magic."

"Like you?"

"Like me." He stood back, splaying his hands over the table. His rings spat silver sparks as he began to draw in energy from the world around them. The fire flickered a little, and grew low. "Watch. *Hestula vi anti, mi agra despulic hedora.*"

Silvery lines of power flowed through the silver engravings around the edge of the glass, lighting up each rune that it hit. Bishop held his breath, leaning closer as the air within the glass case seemed to crackle with static.

The little iron filings quivered.

"It's working," Verity whispered. The iron filings began to tremble and jerk as they slid across the map.

A pile of them grew on the street where his house lay. "There's me," Bishop murmured.

A thin thread of iron tracked their journey that day, from the Natural History museum to Lady Eberhardt's, and then to the Labyrinth, where it grew a little thicker.

"Why is it doing that?" she whispered.

"I think I've been leaving small amounts of power wherever I go," he murmured, closing his eyes as he manipulated the threads of sorcery. "Sort of like a scent trail that gradually fades."

Another small pile began to grow, this time at the East London Docks. Its trail was thick and strong, and jagged all over the place. Then three other piles. Each thinner and wispier than the last. She could almost make out where they were forming. The thicker trail was heading toward Cheapside. Another wisped off toward Greenwich, and the Natural History Museum lit up like a beacon.

"There are at least seven sorcerers we're looking at here," she said, leaning closer. Bishop's hands trembled. "Hold still," she said, watching the trail of filings march like ants to where they grew thickest. "It's nearly—"

A spark, a small cough of smoke, and Bishop yanked his hands off the glass. "Bloody hell," he cursed, grounding the energy he'd been utilizing.

All of it ground to a halt.

"What happened?" The iron filings collapsed on the map inertly, like puppets with their strings cut. Some of them circled certain places, but others lay in a scattered sprawl that meant nothing.

From the clenching of his fists, Bishop was tempted to kick the chair in front of him out of the way, but he swallowed hard, let his hands relax, and then collapsed into the chair, sinking his head into his hands. "I don't know. Obviously I didn't set some of the runes correctly. It's a complicated setup. Or perhaps... I'm tired. I lost control of the threads."

He looked exhausted, not just tired. Hollows pooled beneath his eyes, and there was weariness in the set of his shoulders that she hadn't seen before.

Verity pushed away all of her rejected feelings and crossed toward the liquor decanter to pour them both a brandy.

"Here," she said, kneeling in front of him and offering him the glass. If he didn't let go of some of this nervous energy, then something inside him was going to shatter.

"I'm fine," he told her, looking up. His eyes were black pools. "I'll get the map spell working before dawn. We can—"

"You're exhausted," she pointed out. "You should take the time to rest. The map table will wait. The Chalice will wait."

"I don't *have* time to rest." There was the muscle clenching in his jaw. "There's so much to bloody do, and...." He ground his teeth together.

Verity arched a brow. "And?"

"Nothing." His head collapsed into his hands again.

Nothing, my Aunt Betsy. "People make mistakes when they're tired. A mistake in this situation might get both of us killed." She settled on the seat beside him gingerly, tugging her night-robe away from his thigh. "Something's bothering you. And I thought we were to work together. We can hardly do that if one of us is keeping secrets."

"A lot of things are bothering me. To begin with: I can't find the Chalice, and... I'm not sure that I can devote all of my time to the search for it."

"I thought finding the Chalice was all important. Hordes of flesh constructs being dragged out of the ground, London burning, demons gallivanting about. That sort of thing."

"It is." He pushed away from the chair and paced to the small grate.

"Then what else could be so distracting?"

Bishop rested one hand against the mantelpiece, looking into the embers in the grate. His shoulders were stiff.

Frustration burned through her. "You don't want to tell me. It's fine for me to place my trust in you the other day, when you ruined my place in the Hex, and it's fine for you to tell me not to worry, because you're not the type of man who would misuse that trust, but it's not fine for me to expect the same in return?"

"Verity...." His voice roughened.

"It's not as though I have anyone to tell," she pointed out, "and nor am I likely to. I've kept your other secrets."

"It's not that," he said roughly. "I'm just... used to keeping my cards close to my chest."

Her eyes narrowed. *Go on*, they said.

He gestured at the room in general, his brandy slopping out of the glass. "I'm Sicarii. Everything we do is shrouded in secrecy and I made oaths to that point. I don't even tell my father most of what I learn in those meetings."

Dragging her knees up in front of her chest, Verity rested her chin on top of them. She could take this small concession. Even she understood that sometimes it was best to keep things close, but... trust was something she always found difficult to give. And she'd given it to him. Something inside her ached that she couldn't be found worthy of the same consideration. "Sounds lonely."

"Lonely? No, it's... complicated. It's...."

"You're tired, you're plagued by problems, and you're not thinking clearly," she pointed out. "Sometimes just talking through your problems with another person helps."

Something like consideration twisted his mouth. Then he sighed. "I don't see how you're going to help."

Verity said nothing. Her old life suddenly felt like a lifetime ago, though the wounds were still raw. She looked away. *Where do I stand now?*

With a sigh, he crossed to pour himself another brandy. "Stop looking at me like that."

"I'm not looking at you," she muttered into the silk that covered her knees.

"Fine. Promise me you won't breathe a word of this to anyone?"

Verity slowly looked up. "You have my word."

"The Chalice needs to be recovered. That's a priority. But... there are a few problems in the Order at the moment."

"Does it have anything to do with your father's resignation?"

He looked at her.

"I'm not stupid," she pointed out. "Agatha and Marie were dancing around the topic, and you get this constipated look on your face whenever it's mentioned. I would almost say that you're worried about him."

Sinking into the armchair again, he rested his brandy on the armrest, staring into space. "The Sicarii held a vote—that's the meeting you witnessed. They were deciding whether to assassinate Drake."

Verity sucked in a sharp breath. No wonder he was out of sorts. "Why?"

"Problems with the succession; fear of the future; concern that him staying alive while a new Prime is elected will split the Order in half." He shrugged, his face darkening. "A little bit of everything."

"But the vote went against this idea, didn't it?" she asked, slipping off the sofa and crossing to sit in the chair opposite him. "You wouldn't be this calm if it didn't."

"Three to two," he admitted. "For now. They're going to wait and see what happens. Ascension is on Sunday at the Winter Solstice, where the decision of who will sit in the Prime's chair will be answered. But I'm concerned the two Sicarii who voted against him might take matters into their own hands. Or...."

"Or?" Verity whispered, reaching over to lay her hand on top of his.

Bishop sucked in a sharp breath, looking down at her pale hand laid over his tanned one. Yet he didn't ask her to remove it. "I made it clear I would stand against it if the vote went the other way. If they decide they're going to remove him as a threat, then it's likely I won't be invited to that meeting. They'll make a move without me. I won't even bloody well know. I'm an idiot."

"I might not know a great deal about sorcery in all of its forms, but even to me the Prime looked like he could handle himself."

"His wards are ridiculously strong, but there are ways through them."

"You tested them?"

"It's the way my mind works. I like to solve problems, and I wasn't really paying attention one day, just opened my Sight up, and by the time the half hour was up, I'd managed to work out the flaws in his wards. If *I* can do it...."

Well. She'd never been one for false comfort. *Solve the problem*, Murphy had always said. "Who else can you trust to protect him?"

Bishop stared at her.

"You cannot do it all alone," Verity pointed out. "You're only one man. Which means you must either turn your entire focus upon the Chalice, if we're to make headway there, or give up that quest to another and guard your father. Could Lady Eberhardt do either of the tasks?"

Those dark eyes were dangerous when they were thinking. "Could she protect him? Yes. Perhaps. But that means she'll be standing between Drake and a Sicarii assassin or two, and we're good at what we do, Verity. Besides, she's getting older, and as much as I want to think she's invincible...."

"She's not," Verity murmured, remembering the odd bond between this man and the older woman. "Even if I *would* hate to earn her wrath. So who else do you trust?"

"And therein lies the problem."

"Surely you have someone else whom you can turn to." After all, he was part of the Order, surrounded by sorcerers. Even the members of the Hex had a network of people they could turn to.

Bishop shook his head. Then paused, his eyes firing with some thought, some light. They were so damned expressive at times. "There is someone."

"Who?"

"It's not so much someone I trust, so much as someone who Drake trusts. My brother, Lucien Devereaux, the Earl of Rathbourne, and his new wife, Ianthe. She served as Drake's seneschal throughout the last decade, until she married Lucien last month."

"And they can protect the Prime?"

"Ianthe can. Lucien's still recovering from the demon's psychic attack, but they are bound together by a soul-bond," he replied. "Ianthe can use Lucien's power as a well, from which to draw. And they both want him alive, just as much as I do."

Verity offered him a smile. "There. Problem solved."

"Thank you," he murmured.

"You're welcome," Verity replied, just as softly, and with that, he turned back to the map table.

She was snoring.

Slightly.

Bishop looked up from the chisel that he was using to remove the defective rune, and cursed under his breath. He needed all of his concentration for this delicate work, but somehow she stole every wit he owned, even it was simply by breathing.

Across the room, Verity had gradually slumped into the armchair, her chin resting uncomfortably on her shoulder.

He stared at her for three long seconds, then looked away. Christ, he shouldn't even have allowed her in here tonight, not with him so on edge, but something about what she'd said had struck a chord with him. He *was* lonely. And her company was both pleasant, and disruptive.

"Verity?" he whispered, crossing on cat-silent feet toward her.

Nothing.

Dragging a blanket over her, he sat down beside her, pressing his hand against his head. So bloody tired. But the map needed work, and he had too many things on his mind. Still, it was pleasant to sit here beside her. Even asleep, somehow she made him feel not so alone.

Bishop blinked, and realized that his head had nodded.

How many nights since he'd slept properly?

Two... three... four?

He couldn't... remember.

CHAPTER FOURTEEN

"TO WHAT DO we owe this pleasure?"

Lady Rathbourne was refreshingly direct, pouring both him and Verity a cup of tea as they sat in her and her husband's home.

"A concern we both share," Bishop told her.

"Oh?" Ianthe Devereaux arched one delicate black brow as she dunked lemon in all four cups of tea. "Last time we met, you wanted nothing to do with my husband. Or myself." That last was added with a discreet glance to his left to where Verity sat, but he knew what she meant.

My husband. It might as well have meant "your brother." But Bishop was still coming to terms with the shock of discovering that he and Lord Rathbourne shared the same father. Both of them were bastards, but Rathbourne had only recently discovered he was no true Rathbourne, after all.

"I have nothing against Lucien," he argued mildly. "But Drake saw us kept separate for a reason. Prophecy dictates trouble, should we cross paths."

"I believe in regards to the prophecy there's also an old saying, something about spilled milk."

How careful they were being. "You may speak plainly in front of Miss Hawkins. She's aware of a great deal of the subtler nuances of the Order."

"Now who's speaking obliquely?" Ianthe challenged, taking her cup and sitting back in her seat with those witchy eyes locked on him.

"Fine." Damn her. "Verity is helping me recover the Chalice. She knows Lucien and I are related, and she knows about the prophecy, and the demon and Morgana."

"In short, everything," Ianthe replied.

Verity sipped her tea, then her face brightened. "Oh, this is lovely."

Ianthe's face warmed. "A special brew I purchase, all the way from India."

As if he couldn't taste the familiar leaves, a ghost of memory that momentarily took him back to darker times. "Lady Rathbourne, is he coming or not?"

Both women looked at him and he cursed his blunt manners, but time was of the essence and he didn't particularly want to stir those memories.

"See for yourself." Ianthe tilted her head behind him.

Lord Rathbourne was strolling up to the French doors from the outside, his breath steaming in the cold morning air and his hand curled around a little girl's hand as she pointed birds out to him excitedly. Lady Rathbourne had sent a servant for him, but it was clear from the way his eyes locked on Bishop's through the glass that he knew exactly who was sitting in his parlor.

After all, the second Bishop had set foot in the house, he'd felt the quiver of prophetic warning shiver down his spine as he and Lord Rathbourne came in close proximity.

The first time they'd walked into the same room, the sensation had nearly knocked him off his feet.

"Bishop," Rathbourne greeted, dusting his feet off on the rug. Curious eyes flickered to Verity, but the little girl stole Bishop's attention as she peered at them from around her father's leg.

Not that Rathbourne was officially the girl's father—not on her birth certificate anyway—but anyone with eyes could see that she bore his resemblance, and Bishop could feel the affinity in both their auras. He'd known Ianthe for years, but clearly she'd been keeping secrets.

Which meant he had a niece. He didn't quite know what to think of that.

"Rathbourne," he replied solemnly, gesturing to Verity. "This is Miss Hawkins, who is assisting me with the Chalice's recovery."

Rathbourne perused them curiously. "Louisa, this is Mr. Bishop, and his friend. Say how do you do."

"How do you do?" Louisa peered directly at Bishop. "What is wrong with his aura?"

Both Ianthe and her husband looked sharply at the little girl. "Louisa," Ianthe admonished, crossing to her and giving her a kiss on the cheek. "Remember your manners," she whispered, then gestured to the door. "And why don't you run upstairs and see what Thea is doing?"

Louisa's shoulders slumped. "But Father promised we could have tea."

"Tea, and all the biscuits you can eat," Ianthe murmured, ruffling her hair. "But upstairs. Your father and I have business with Mr. Bishop."

Verity picked up a biscuit, as the little girl darted upstairs. "Aura?" she mouthed.

He shook his head. Not something he wanted to discuss. Ever.

"Louisa didn't mean anything by it," Lucien assured him, sinking into the chair directly opposite him. "She experienced her Awakening last month, and since then her powers have been coming in."

"I understand." Bishop stared at his brother, at the way they both sat with their hands curled over the ends of the armchair. "Let us cut to the chase; I'm here because I have a problem, and I need help."

"And you helped us last month when Louisa was kidnapped," Lucien murmured, tipping his chin up with a steely gleam in his eyes. "So you want the favor returned."

"It's not a favor for me, so much as...." He looked toward Ianthe, who was the more receptive of the two. Lucien had been working with Drake in the last month on healing some aspects of his sorcery-scarred soul, but they'd had their problems before then. There was no reason to believe his brother would care if Drake died or not. "It's Drake. I have reason to believe that one of the Sicarii *might* make an attempt on his life."

Ianthe paled, and her teacup chinked as she set it on its saucer. "Might? Or will?"

"Might," he emphasized, because as Drake's seneschal and right hand all these years, she knew what he was. "They've decided to let him live. For now."

"But nothing is certain," Lucien said, in his soft, gravelly voice. "You know them. I presume you could fend off an attack?"

"I could," Bishop replied, feeling the tension ease out of him. At least he had some allies in this. "But I need to find the Chalice. Whoever stole it is using it to raise flesh constructs, and I cannot afford to split my concentration."

"Constructs?" Ianthe's voice hardened. "Bloody hell, what kind of fool thinks they can control them forever? They might be able to raise them with the Chalice, but

London doesn't exactly need another case of flesh constructs running amok. The Vigilance Against Sorcery Committee would have a field day with such a disaster, and relationships with the Queen and the government are already tentative."

"Hence my concern," he agreed. It wasn't the first time a necromancer had lost control. It would be the last, however, if the VASC had anything to do with it. The last of sorcery and the Order, too. "Can you protect him?"

The pair of them shared a look, and for a moment it felt as though he and Verity existed outside a bubble, looking in. Something was communicated, because Ianthe arched a brow, but let her husband speak. Clearly telepathy was at play.

"Ianthe can," Lucien said. "As Drake's apprentice, she's more than a match for one of the Sicarii. We'll go visit with Drake, and I can look after Louisa and Thea should an attack appear."

"I assume, since you're here, that Drake is unaware of what's going on?" Ianthe took up her teacup again.

"Aware, but unconcerned," Bishop replied, and this time he let his frustration show. "He's still grieving the loss of Sebastian."

Silence fell. Rathbourne looked ill, but then it had been his life that Drake had spared at the cost of Sebastian's. "One brother down," Rathbourne murmured.

"Two to go," Bishop repeated, feeling the shivering grasp of prophecy lock its chill fingers around his spine.

Their eyes met.

"That's enough of such talk," Ianthe said with a scowl. "Prophecy predicted disaster *might* befall the Order and Drake, not that it will. Prophecies are twisty words. And if you think"—Ianthe met his gaze with a firm tilt of her chin—"for one second that I'm going to let my husband go so easily, then you might think again. The demon will have to go through me first. The prophecy will have to go through me first. Hell and ashes, I will deal with the plague itself if it rears a head."

"Ianthe." Rathbourne rested his hand on her knee.

"No," she replied, peering down her nose at her husband. "We are not discussing this. I will not just stand aside if danger comes lurking. No matter what happens."

The room fell into a strained silence.

Ianthe broke it, pouring herself another cup of tea. "Well. Now that we've shelved that discussion, we should move on to other matters. Bishop, concentrate on the Chalice. The Order cannot afford to have Britain—or the Queen—turn against it, and who knows just what precisely the Chalice is capable of. Lucien and I will handle Drake, and perhaps pull him out of this melancholy. Ascension is coming and like it or not, someone has to deal with this mess that Drake has left us in. We cannot just allow anyone to become Prime."

"Any potential candidates that we could back?" Bishop was grateful for the change in topic, though fully aware that Verity remained all ears.

Rathbourne exchanged a glance with his wife, who stared back at him over the top of the teacup. Another conversation that Bishop felt like he was on the verge of understanding.

"Perhaps Lady Eberhardt?" Ianthe turned to him.

Rathbourne smiled faintly into his cup

"I doubt it." Bishop watched his half brother. Something was going on. "She claims she's too old, and dealing with that rabble will drive her into an early grave."

"She's a Triad Councilor," Ianthe pointed out, "one step below Drake directly. If anyone has the experience to step into his shoes and adequately fill them, she would be the one. Everybody's half afraid of her."

"I can't imagine why," Verity muttered.

"I doubt it will happen." Agatha wouldn't volunteer, not with the level of scrutiny into her private life that such a position would bring.

"Mmm, what a shame," Rathbourne murmured. "Whomever could we turn to?"

"You're not helping," Ianthe shot back.

"Is there something I should be aware of?" Bishop asked.

"Absolutely not," Ianthe replied.

"Yes," Rathbourne added. "I couldn't imagine who would have the power to deal with Drake's position, or who has the experience, what with running the day-to-day minutiae and handling unruly sorcerers?"

Bishop was starting to understand. His gaze slid to Ianthe and the seven rings she wore on her hands. She'd recently passed her seventh level tests and could face down practically any sorcerer in the Order. "You know that's not a bad—"

"Not another word," she said crisply. "I hear enough of it from your father."

So this was Drake's solution? That was interesting and, the more he thought of it, the more he liked the idea. Ianthe *had* been Drake's right hand for nearly seven years. She'd taken care of more than enough dirty business, stood at his side, held her own in the rare Solstice meetings that drew the entire Order together....

"You'd have my vote," he replied.

Ianthe rolled her eyes, a sigh escaping her. "I don't know which one of you is worse. I have enough on my plate." She turned to Rathbourne, her gaze turning pleading. "I've only just brought my daughter into my home after all of these years *and* found you. Can we not have a moment to enjoy that? I have Thea to teach, and my responsibilities are already numerous. And you know what people think...."

Rathbourne shrugged. "I'm the mad, bad Earl of Rathbourne, darling. I've long grown weary of worrying what people think."

Bishop was struck anew by the camaraderie they shared. He glanced toward Verity, who seemed just as out of place as he did.

"Well," he said, standing and picking up his hat. "Now that is settled, I think Verity and I had best be on our way."

"If you need anything else, let us know," Rathbourne murmured, seeing them to the door. "We both share the same interests."

"Do we?" Bishop asked, accepting his coat and hat from the butler. "I didn't think you cared for the Prime."

The other man was of the same height, but considerably broader through the shoulders, and wore the power of an earl well. Their eyes met. "We are making peace," Rathbourne finally admitted.

CHAPTER FIFTEEN

NO SIGN OF Grave sorcerers the next day, or any clue that might lead to Elijah Horroway. Just mud and filth, and when the heavens opened up, Bishop had been forced to retreat home as curtains of rain blanketed the city.

Nothing would be moving out there tonight. And as much as he wanted to get his hands on the Chalice as soon as possible, the second Verity had started shivering, he'd had to concede defeat.

She'd headed for her private bathing chambers the moment they entered his house, and Bishop had gone to find her some bath towels, trailing water through the house. He'd even warmed them for her, which made him feel a little uncertain.

Curse you. Taking the stairs two at a time, he strode along the hallway with them. *You know you can't have her.*

Temptation, however, knew no boundaries. At least not when it came to her.

Juggling the towels in his arms, he'd paused to rap on the half-cracked door, when water shifted, as if someone stirred their hand through it. Through the inch-wide slit in the door, he caught a hint of movement. "Verity?"

"Yes?"

Bishop shoved the door open with his shoulder and strode inside. "I brought you some towe—"

He froze.

Verity glanced up from the bath, the tips of her knees peeping through a froth of bubbles and her arms resting along the edges of the porcelain tub. Tendrils of wet hair curled over her bare shoulders, though the rest of it was knotted on top of her head to keep it dry. The upper slopes of her breasts gleamed wetly as her breath caught.

"You..." *are naked*, supplied the very helpful part of his brain that could still function. He slammed his eyes shut, but the image of her was painted on the insides of his eyeballs. "Why the hell didn't you warn me?"

"I forget how prudish you are." Humor warmed her voice and water stirred as she splashed. "I'm all covered up, Bishop. All of these bubbles...." The way her voice dropped, all smoky and hot, shivered through him. "You won't see a thing, I promise."

Too late for that. "This is indecent."

Turning around, he blindly reached for the vanity, groping nothing but air.

Water swirled, as though she stirred her legs through it. "You barely batted an eyelid when you were in the bath," she pointed out.

"That was different." His hand found the counter and he set the towels down. "I was distracted with other problems at the time. I'll... get supper warmed."

"You could stay. Maybe wash my back, Bishop?"

"That would be highly inappropriate." He headed for the door, but caught a glimpse of her in the mirror.

Verity laughed as their eyes met, and reached for the soap, her breasts—

Bishop slammed out of the room, pressing his back to the wall and shoving his closed fists against his eyes. Hell. He couldn't unsee it, however. Verity. Naked. All smooth, gleaming skin covered in suds, with her damp hair gathered up in a knot on top of her head, tendrils falling around her bare shoulders.

She was enough to drive any man to distraction.

Damn her.

His cock surged against the tented pants of his trousers, and he looked down in disgust, as if it had betrayed him.

Might as well fix that map table after supper. Maybe play a round of billiards with himself. There would be no sleep for him, after all.

Not tonight.

Verity found him in the billiards room, setting up impossible shots as he prowled around the table. It wasn't difficult to track him; the cracking ricochet of balls had lured her all the way from her bedroom.

What she had expected, however, was to catch him unawares, as she'd been tiptoeing so carefully, trying to avoid the squeaky timbers she'd begun to identify in the house.

"Are you going to hover out there all night?" Bishop called, bending over the table and hammering a red ball into the far pocket. "Or is there something in particular that you want?"

Caught. Verity slipped into the room, smiling faintly. His lack of composure in her bathing chamber earlier had surprised her. You'd have thought she'd offered to lie with him right then and there. How could a man so dangerous seem so flustered at times?

"How do you always know where I am in the house?" She sniffed her sleeve. "I'm not wearing any perfume, and I'm as silent as a mouse when I want to be."

"You've walked through four of my wards to get here," he replied, darting a glance at her, freezing, and then turning back to the table in a very deliberate action.

Apparently, Bishop approved of the pretty green gown that Marie had sent around for her. Hiding a smile, Verity circled the table, rolling the green ball that he was intent on setting up beneath her palm.

Bent over the table, Bishop narrowed an intense glare upon her. "Do you mind?"

Holding her hands in the air, Verity gave him her most innocent look. "Not at all."

A crack sounded, and the white ball smashed the green into the side pocket. The move was ruthlessly efficient, Bishop standing and prowling around the corner of the table with the cue in his hands like a weapon. He'd never looked more like an assassin.

Intense.

"Something bothering you, Bishop?"

"Not at all," he growled, glaring at the balls on the table as though they were at fault.

"It wouldn't have anything to do with you walking in upon me?"

Those knuckles whitened around the cue. "Miss Hawkins—"

"Verity."

He swore under his breath, losing all sense of that cold distance he'd been striving to maintain. "That won't happen again. I apologize, I—"

"Pity," she murmured under her breath.

Their eyes met.

"It *cannot* happen again," he said firmly.

She didn't quite know what to make of that statement. Who was he trying to convince? For his eyes very clearly told a different tale as he watched her glide around the table.

This dangerous man with his polite manners and aloof behavior fascinated her. He looked at her sometimes as though he were undressing her with his eyes, but anytime they strayed into what could be construed as dangerous territory, he backed away. She'd very clearly hinted she would not be averse to extending their friendship, an offer most men she knew would not hesitate to accept, but Bishop looked as though he were fighting a battle with himself in regards to her.

What did any of it mean? Did he want her? Or not?

And what did she want?

Time to find out. Verity changed tactics. "May I play?"

"I was almost finished." He bent, his back a smooth line, the cue a dangerous weapon as he sighted along it.

"Liar." She snorted, causing his ball to misfire dangerously. "You're going to be stalking the house all night. It's not as though you're going to sleep."

Bishop swore under his breath as the white ricocheted around the table. "Don't you have anything better to do?"

"Like what?" She offered him a faint smile. "All of my friends threw me out of the Hex, an anonymous group of masked men are trying to kill me, and someone's trying to bring the dead to life. It's not as though I can leave the house without you, and your library is boring enough to put anyone to sleep. Don't you have any scandalous novels at all?"

"So you're lonely?" He chalked the cue.

"I do actually enjoy your company," she pointed out.

Which made him glance toward her, nostrils flaring. Ever since they'd woken yesterday morning on the sofa in his laboratory, her head resting on his lap, he'd been avoiding her.

"Though I'm not certain whether you enjoy mine or not." This was said a little quieter. All teasing aside, she wasn't quite certain where she stood with him. Sometimes she thought he might like to kiss her. At others, he couldn't get away from her quickly enough.

"Verity." His voice came softly. "I don't dislike your company. I-I—" Hesitation caught his tongue.

And she waited. God help her, but her treacherous heart beat a little harder in anticipation, her tongue locking up in her mouth.

For an answer that was not to come. Wariness filled his dark eyes and they stared at each other, as if the answer were too complex to give voice to.

"Well," she said, breathing out a false little laugh. "I guess that answers that."

If he thought she was going to stay there, then he was quite mistaken. Swallowing her disappointment, Verity gathered her skirts and turned to flee, but he caught her by the door, one hard hand locking around her wrist. "I enjoy your company," he murmured, the caress of his breath stirring the curls at her nape. "Sometimes I wish I didn't."

Verity turned to face him again, their bodies pressed closely together, with but an inch separating them... even if it felt like miles.

"Stay," he said roughly, then cleared his throat, and repeated, "Stay, and play with me."

Verity took the stick. She didn't have any other option as it was thrust toward her, but she couldn't quite decipher what she saw on his face. He didn't seem happy, and yet he didn't seem to want her to go.

"Do you know how to play?" he asked, and a faint red tint stained his cheeks as he looked down at the cue.

"It's not as though Murphy kept a billiards room," she pointed out, but that wasn't a no. A plan had formed; a means of finding out whether he wanted to kiss her or whether he didn't.

"Do you want me to teach you?"

Verity smiled shyly. "That would be lovely."

"Have a try," he said, offering her the cue.

Verity took it, then leaned over the table, eyeing the green baize and the scattering of balls. It felt nice to be doing something other than talking of the thrice-cursed Chalice for once, though she knew he was restless.

"Is this right?" she asked, and tried to nestle the cue in her hands.

Bishop stared at her, trying to gauge her sincerity, but he grudgingly stepped up behind her, resettling the cue in her hands as his body surrounded hers. His warmth was tangible, his thighs brushing against her bottom. "You hold it like this."

Verity bit her lip, glancing over her shoulder at him. His dark, slightly-too-long hair tumbled forward, obscuring part of his face as he eyed the table.

"Aim for the green ball," he said.

It nestled close enough to the far pocket to make it a moderately easy shot.

"If I sink this ball"—she peered down the line of the cue—"what will you give me?"

"Give you?"

"Well, there has to be some sort of challenge to make it interesting."

"Do you gamble frequently?"

"Sometimes. I like the thrill of it." She smiled. "Don't ever sit down to cards with me, however, or you'll end up handing over the deed to everything you own."

Bishop leaned against the table, watching her set herself up. "One could say you're already halfway there," he murmured, just loudly enough for her to hear it.

Her heart leapt. Verity hit the white ball, and it careened wildly across the table, a miscue. "Damn it." She stared at him. "You did that on purpose."

"Did what?" This was an entirely different side to him tonight. Almost playful. She wasn't certain whether he was teasing her or not.

Bishop folded his arms across his chest, frowning at the table. "I suspected you were gaming me, and were about to sink that."

"Who? Me?" She sauntered around the table, determination lighting through her. If he wanted to play games, then she was quite happy to take him up on that. And she wasn't going to lose.

He snorted. "Yes, you. Little Miss Innocent over there."

"Play a game with me?" Chalking the tip of the cue, she practically dared him with her eyes to say yes.

Bishop rubbed at his face, then sighed. "It's not as though I'm going to get any sleep tonight anyway, is it?"

"If I win, will you tell me why?"

"If you win, I'll tell you anything you want."

That intrigued her. There were so many mysteries about him that she wanted to solve. "Done."

Bishop set up the table, then glanced at her. "Do you wish to break?"

"No. You do it. You're so much stronger than I."

He sent the balls flying around the table, then shot her an are-you-serious look. The sound of clacking balls broke the gentle patter of rain that wet the windows. Verity smiled at him obliquely and swept around the table toward him, adding an extra swish to her stride.

Verity took a step closer, but he withdrew almost fractionally. "The stick?" she murmured, reaching toward it.

Bishop let it go, but he watched her.

Let him watch. She smiled again, then considered the spread with a ruthless eye. Her previous miscue had worked in her favor. Bishop might be worldly, but he knew nothing of being gulled if he thought one broke the trick as early as that.

Verity eyed the nearest green ball. Time to play dirty.

She punched it into the pocket, then turned and considered her next move. Bishop folded his arms across his chest. "Nice shot."

"Thank you."

This time she potted the orange.

His eyes narrowed.

Verity nibbled on her lip, and deliberately missed the next shot. She handed over the cue as he stalked past her.

Circling the table, she rested on the far edge, leaning forward as if to survey what he was doing. Bishop looked down the length of the cue, then noticed her. His gaze dipped toward her bodice and he swallowed.

"Verity, sometimes I wonder if you are pure evil."

That sent her into a gale of laughter.

"You're deliberately trying to torture me," he muttered, and sank the blue.

Toying with a strand of hair, she nibbled at it. "I could only torture you if you actually wanted me."

"Of course I want you," he muttered, a soft sigh escaping him. "You're a beautiful young woman. Too young."

"I'm nineteen," she replied, rolling her eyes. She suspected he'd have a long list of excuses to throw at her, and this was the first. "I'm hardly a child." Her voice softened a fraction, thinking back through the years. "I don't think I've been a child for a very long time."

Sympathy gleamed in his eyes. "You missed out on a lot."

She shrugged.

As he set up his next shot, he asked, "What happened to your mother? I know your father left, but... you don't speak of her."

Well now. Verity glanced down at her folded hands. She never spoke of her mother, not even to Mercy. The pain in her chest was as sharp as the day she'd found her mother's pale, still body. "My mother was the most beautiful woman," she said quietly. "She used to work as a maid in a fancy house, until the owner's son tried to take advantage of her. She had to leave, but the owner refused to give her a reference. Said she was telling lies about her son. So mother married my father, and they moved into St. Giles. Not near the slum then, but on the edge of it. And she had work in a match factory until she started getting sick from the phosphorus. It scared her, for I was a little girl then and some of her friends had died, or suffered phossy-jaw. So she gave it up.

"And when my father walked out on us, well, she needed the money, didn't she? Hex Perkins, the leader of the Black Cats, saw her one day and decided he wanted her. That's how we moved into the Dials. But he grew tired of her after a while and she was forced to do other work to survive. I remember long hours of mending, of laundry, of cleaning in other people's houses. She... took on men sometimes, when the money was tight. And one of them beat her very badly one night. She didn't recover well. The

Healers said he'd made her bleed inside, but... there was no money to pay a hearth witch to heal her." Verity let out a long breath, seeing the bloodied linens all over again. "She died very quickly. I wasn't expecting it. When I came home with her mending, there she was... she... she was...."

A hand brushed her chin, and Verity realized she could barely see through her watery eyes. She blinked and a single tear ran down her cheek, another clinging to her lashes. "I'm sorry." She pushed past him, brushing at her cheeks and dashing her tears away. "I don't cry. I *never* cry. I don't know what's—"

Strong arms drew her against a warm chest. Verity hiccupped, and a fresh wave of tears overwhelmed her. Feeling mortified, she tried to stop herself but a sob erupted, and then she was undone.

"It's all right to cry," Bishop murmured, the rumble of his voice vibrating through his chest. He cupped the back of her head, pressing her sobbing face into his shoulder. "You loved your mother. You miss her." His voice roughened. "I understand that."

The storm of weeping left her hot-faced and swollen. But Verity had to admit it was nice to be held, nice to be in his arms. She'd wanted sex with him, but this... this affection was something she hadn't known she hungered for. It was dangerous in a way that bedding him wouldn't have been.

And she couldn't stop herself from wanting more.

Bishop rocked her slowly, rubbing her back as she collected herself. Verity closed her eyes.

When she and Mercy had been younger, they'd played a game once, lying in their beds and daydreaming about a future that would never exist for them. A game of what-if that was as inconsequential as the spider silk lacing the beams above them:

"What would you do if there was no debt over your head?" she'd asked Mercy.

"Steal a ship," Mercy had replied promptly. "Become a pirate."

Verity burst into laughter. "Should I call you Anne Bonny?"

And Mercy had thrown a pillow at her.

After the fight died down, which Verity had won using her translocation skills to pin her sister-of-the-heart to her mattress, Mercy had whispered. "What would you do?"

Verity had barely dared to put it into words, for if you said your wish out loud it would never come true. "I would steal a man's heart," she'd whispered. "Have my own children, my own family." One that couldn't be taken away from her, the way hers had been. "A home of my own, where I didn't have to steal or beg just to keep my head above water."

But what was the point in wishing, for a pair of girls from Seven Dials who knew better than to believe?

Here, now, she felt that same urge expand her chest. Her arms slipped around his waist, and Verity looked up, her cheeks tight and dry. Dark lashes shuttered his eyes as he glanced down. He must have seen the need in her eyes, for he slowly, slowly lowered his face to hers. Verity's heart erupted in a series of flutters, like someone had trapped a butterfly inside her rib cage.

Lips brushed against her own. Then back again. A light caress that spoke of so much more than desire.

A wave of nervousness swept through her. It was easy to smile and flirt, especially with Bishop, because he always made her feel safe. Sometimes her smiles were little more than a means to protect herself, because if she controlled the interaction, then she was the one in control. She couldn't get hurt, because she wouldn't allow it.

But she didn't feel safe at all tonight.

She felt like her eyes had just opened to a terrifying truth: this man could break her. Crack her heart right open and obliterate her. She was vulnerable to him in a way that she'd never felt vulnerable before.

Verity pushed away, clearing her throat. "You do know how to take all of the fun out of the room, don't you?"

Bishop offered her the cue, but she shook her head, gathering her thoughts.

"Your game," she told him, and smiled fleetingly before she wished him a good night and fled the room.

CHAPTER SIXTEEN

THE CHAINS HELD him.

Blinded by a strip of tight linen, Sebastian hung against the wall, trying to focus on his breathing. Something was broken. His ribs, perhaps. It didn't matter. Pain was an old friend and if his mother thought that would chain him down, then she didn't know him very well.

Despair came close to filling him. He'd been so close to escaping Morgana forever. He'd thought her dead after he and Cleo fled the collapsing house.

You knew it was too good to be true.

Days passed. His body ached, and the silence became deafening. Nobody had been to feed him, or to clean the filth from his body. His knees were shaking now, desperate for respite, but the chains forced him to stand. Either that, or tear his shoulders from their joints.

Alone. Alone, and trapped, and full of despair. Sebastian clenched both his fists, trying to force heat and circulation back into starved extremities. It was starting to get to him.

But somehow, on the third day, there was a whisper in the dark, a brush of something against his psychic senses.

"There you are...." It felt like a hand reached out toward him in the darkness, though it was only a psychic touch.

Sebastian instantly jerked away from the reach, not trusting it. Sweat sprang up against his spine and he thought that he'd imagined it, but almost a minute later, it came again.

"Please. I've been searching for you for days."

Sebastian hesitated. Why would someone search for him? Nobody knew he was here, rotting in this dungeon, nobody except Cleo. Had she found someone to help him? Hope made his breath catch, but then he shook it away. Maybe that was what this stranger wanted him to think?

Don't be a fool.

Nobody cared about him. Nobody ever had. Except perhaps Cleo, and his mother had shown him that caring for his wife only gave him one more weakness she could exploit.

"Sebastian...." A man. It was definitely a male, and a powerful telepath at that. The urging whisper filled his mind. *"Open up to me."*

If he wasn't so alone, then he might have held back, but even this brief encounter made him hunger for contact. Something. Anything. Tentatively, he reached back, not quite certain what he was doing, but brushing up against that dark whisper in his head. The touch firmed, but he was fairly certain that was due to the other entity's grip on him. "Who are you? What do you want?"

"I want to help you."

"Why?"

"Because I'm your father."

Sebastian severed the connection. Drake de Wynter, the Prime. In his head he saw the man's face again as Drake reached out toward him, then glanced back at his other son.

And chose to save Rathbourne.

He was no friend to Sebastian.

This time, when the touch trailed fingertips down his mind, Sebastian held himself firmly walled away. His mother had taught him the value of trust when he was a child. He wasn't about to repeat the experience.

The door to the cell opened.

Sebastian turned his head toward the sound, sweat rolling down his spine. So... she'd finally come.

What was it to be today? More pain? More blood? He almost didn't care. He was so hungry and thirsty he felt stretched to breaking point.

A hand reached out to rip his blindfold down and light suddenly burst into being, making Sebastian cringe. Days.... Days since he'd been able to see. Of the slow, silent torment of hanging here, the lack of sight had perhaps been the worst, for it made him feel alone in a way that he'd never experienced before.

How did Cleo do it, all those years?

That stopped him in his tracks. *Don't think of her. You can't afford a weakness. Not now.*

When he'd finally blinked away the light flares that had initially blinded him, Sebastian realized that Noah Guthrie was the one who'd torn his blindfold away.

The young man's hair had been cropped into a stylish man-about-town haircut, and the scruff along his jaw was gone, revealing smooth, lean cheeks.

Sebastian eyed him. Something felt wrong. Noah had been a street lad plucked out of the Hex by his mother. Noah had always been nervous, and though they'd had little to do with each other, he nevertheless knew the man.

This wasn't Noah Guthrie, even though they looked the same. Whoever this was they showed none of Noah's tics and nerves, nor the faint blurred haze of an opium addiction that had made Noah stare into space for long hours. No. These green eyes were cool, calculating.

And frighteningly unemotional.

"Who are you?" Illusion was one of his mother's greatest abilities, but Sebastian didn't think that was the case here, and he'd never heard of anyone able to shift into someone else's skin.

Not-Noah's head tilted to the side as the stranger considered him. There was a rash ringing the stranger's throat, barely hidden by his collar. "Perhaps a friend." Those shrewd eyes thinned. "How did you know I was not Noah?"

Sebastian's skin cringed. Wrong. This all felt wrong. "Noah was never in control of himself. He always looked distracted, or nervous."

Not-Noah didn't blink, and a knot began to tighten in Sebastian's stomach.

"*What* are you?" Sebastian asked quietly, and a cold pit of fear began to grow within his belly as suspicion took hold.

There was one way another being could assume someone's shape—or perhaps the correct word was to *possess* another's shape. His mother had been trying to control a demon, after all, when she stole the Blade of Altarrh a month ago, and despite the fact he'd dropped a house on top of her, she'd somehow survived.

Morgana was a well-trained sorceress, but even she would have had to have help to survive that. "Is Noah still in there?"

"You're cleverer than she suspected."

"Who? My mother?"

The demon who wore Noah smiled, a thin, faintly menacing shape. With his hands clasped behind his back, he paced, eyeing Sebastian like a tasty morsel. "Noah's inside me, locked up nice and tight. I'm kind to him, Sebastian. He graciously agreed to host me in his body and such can be rewarded."

"I'll bet."

The demon cocked its head again. "What reason do I have to lie?"

"What reason do you have to tell the truth?"

Those eyes were frighteningly intelligent. "Ah," Not-Noah said. "It's like that, is it?" With an odd blink, his expression shifted. Noah swam to the surface in bits and pieces, his brow slackening and his mouth softening. That hazy look was back—perhaps it had never been the opium, but the man itself.

"It's all right, Bastian," Noah said, smiling his slightly crooked grin. "It's not like I'm locked in here. And he takes the cravings away, makes it a little easier to deal with. Let's me out whenever I want a girl, or an ale, or a night on the town."

The face shifted sideways. That was the only way to explain it. Not-Noah was back, and Sebastian felt ill.

"What do you want with me?" he rasped.

An eyebrow cocked, but it almost seemed as though the gesture was a deliberate act: like the demon knew how it should react and produced the motion, but didn't precisely feel it. "I'll speak plainly then, as you're clearly a man who cannot be fooled. I want the same thing that you want."

"My mother dead?" he sneered.

"Precisely."

Sebastian froze, his heartbeat ticking in the silence. "I thought she was working for you?"

"She does," the demon replied, pacing slowly in front of him. "I need her services for a little longer, whilst I deal with... a slight problem."

A problem? Sebastian's mind raced, then the answer appeared. What else could his mother want but to cast down the Prime? "You want my father killed."

"Did you know that they once thought to control me?" The demon mused. "The Prime, his friend Tremayne, and your mother. They made relics to bind me tight and force me to their will. And then when your father realized how dangerous I was, he forced me back into another world. I have been waiting a long time to have my revenge on them."

"You're working with Tremayne and my mother," he pointed out.

"Drake's powerful," the demon admitted, its lids obscuring its eyes thoughtfully. "When I tried to come back last year, he trapped me within the recesses of the Earl of Rathbourne's mind. There is a possibility that I could defeat Drake—not in this body, certainly—but perhaps...." The way the demon was looking at him made him feel ill again.

"Over my dead body." It was the only thing that had ever, in some ways, belonged to him, and even then, not often. Not with the controlling sclavus collar around his throat.

But the idea of giving himself up completely....

"No. Not you. You and I do not match very well. It pleases me to take another."

"What about Noah? And who?"

"Noah is weak. His body can scarcely hold me and my presence is... eating him up from the inside. That's not fair to poor Noah, and nor does it suit me either. I want what was promised to me."

"Rathbourne?"

The demon smiled. "We are already linked, he and I, and he holds the power to sustain me. Kill his soul-bound companion, and he is putty in my hands."

"What happens to Noah?"

"He gets his body back, without the issue of the addiction. It has paled by now."

"Then why do you need me?"

Blink. "Because you are powerful, Sebastian. You are the one person who can go up against your father and survive, because he does not care to kill one of his sons."

Sebastian wasn't entirely certain about that. The Prime had chosen Rathbourne over him as the house collapsed, and left him bleeding on the floor.

"Think about it," the demon mused. "I bear no grudge against you. Indeed, we could find ourselves allies, if you wanted to accept my bargain." It smiled. "Neither your mother nor your father have done very well by you either, after all."

Sebastian's mouth felt dry.

"I'll come again," the demon said, and reached for the door. "When you've had time to think."

CHAPTER SEVENTEEN

FINDING ELIJAH HORROWAY was easier said than done.

The necromancer wasn't at Balthazar's Labyrinth, where he could usually be found. Indeed, Marius Hastings, Horroway's one true friend, hadn't seen him in over two weeks.

But he did have something that belonged to Horroway; a ring that he'd once given to a long-ago lover, according to Marius.

"And with this," Verity announced, as she and Bishop left the Labyrinth, "I can find him anywhere." She twirled in a circle, dancing a little jig. "We're getting closer! Now we have the means to track him."

"Is it more difficult to find people rather than things?" Bishop asked, using his body to protect her from the onslaught of a herd of tweed-bedecked businessmen trotting to work on the pavement.

Verity grew a little nervous at the proximity of his body. Neither of them had mentioned last night, or the way she'd taken flight. *And I'm certainly not going to bring it up.* She shot him a meaningless smile. "Sometimes. People change all the time, whereas objects don't. Sometimes people change enough that they no longer 'match' the psychic imprint that they've left on the object."

"A little like how the police are using fingerprints these days to identify criminals," he mused. "Every person has their own 'imprint.'"

"Somewhat. I don't think I could prove the ring belongs to a specific someone in a court of law, however."

"I'm certain if you put your mind to it, you should stand a fair chance."

Verity paused and looked up at the stern line of his jaw and those firm lips. "Was that a compliment? Or a critique of my tenacious nature?"

Lazy brown eyes twinkled as he glanced down. His voice softened. "Merely a comment that you *can* be a force of nature when you wish to be. Now stop stalling. Find me Elijah Horroway."

"As my master commands, I serve and obey." She rolled her eyes, but obliged.

Tucked against his shoulder, Verity let her vision glaze and her senses lock around the ring. It was faint, but it was there. A tingle pulled her to the east. "This way," she said, darting past him and waving a hand at a hackney that was clopping along. "I've got him now."

The bewildered hackney driver agreed to ferry them, though the lack of a firm direction made one of his eyebrows arch. "Quid's on you," he finally said with a shrug, and Bishop handed her up into the hackney.

"What did you use to track me?" Bishop asked, settling in across the carriage from her, his long legs eating up the space.

"Some of your hair."

"My hair?" He touched his skull. "How on earth did you...?"

Verity arched a brow. "You probably don't want to know."

"Try me."

"You were on Bond Street, arguing with another sorcerer about a book you wanted to buy. You didn't even see me in the crowd." Flipping her knife out of her sleeve, she made a quick slashing movement, then vanished the knife and grinned. "So much for your impressive powers of observation."

Bishop scowled.

"You get very focused when it comes to books," she mused. "For someone who thinks his only talent is killing, you have a very strong interest in reading, and in creating strange magical inventions. One would almost suspect you had scientific leanings."

"I'm only curious, and I like books." He glanced out the window. "After my mother died and I was sent to Burma, they were the only things I had to console me for a long time."

Curiosity itched at her. "What was it like to travel the world?"

His face closed over. "I was no explorer, Verity. I had a particular talent and the Order saw a use for it. They saddled me with Major Richard Winthrop for a master, and he was a Servant of the Empire who knew the Grave Arts. I'm sure it made sense at the time, but the second we were on the ship I learned he wasn't the type of man he portrayed in Society, or in the Order. He cared nothing for my grief, nor for teaching me. I'm certain the only reason he accepted my apprenticeship was because he knew who'd fathered me and hoped to ingratiate himself there.

"Winthrop was the only Servant of the Empire sent in with the British Imperial forces in Burma. His major gift was the art of illusions, and the official company line went that we were removing the Burmese king, Thibaw, in favor of his elder half-brother, Nyaungyan, who had escaped Thibaw's earlier massacre of his brothers and sisters when he inherited the crown. The problem was that Nyaungyan—who had lived in British India in exile—was dead. So Winthrop was called upon to disguise a young man as the king's brother, to present to the locals on the way to Mandalay. Some of them even cheered when they saw him, as the king was not well liked in some circles. We weren't to occupy the country for very long... it was all a bunch of lies concocted to make the occupation run smoothly." Bishop drew a breath. "Ugly times. It certainly opened my eyes to the world, and to human nature."

"What happened?"

"There was something Winthrop wanted me to do. I refused."

Verity curled her knees up to her chest as the carriage rocked. "He wanted you to kill someone," she said, with some certainty.

"Some locals who were protesting British rule." Bishop's shrug was loose and uncaring, but she saw the tension about his eyes. "They were just... trying to protect their homes, and he wanted me to obliterate them like they were naught more than insects. And the last thing I needed at the time was to kill someone else. I'm sure Winthrop would have killed me if we didn't have witnesses—if my father wasn't who he was—but instead he shipped me back home in disgrace, where I was brought before the Order Triad Council for blatant refusal to do my duties and endangering the cause of the Empire. And Agatha was one of the Councilors."

Someone else.... Verity was dangerously curious about his first kill but to satisfy her curiosity right now would only come with the cost of his grief. Instead, she simply reached out and held his hand, giving it a small squeeze. "You're no killer, are you?"

"I'm an assassin." He looked down.

"Yes, but at heart, if you had the choice, you'd never take another life again, would you?"

"Verity...." He let go of her hand and turned his face away from her, revealing the scars that lined his jaw and temple. He was usually more careful than that. "Sometimes we don't get that choice. I know I will kill again. I know... that a part of me will like it."

She nibbled on her nail. The steady tug of the leash was veering to her right. "Give me a moment. The location's changing. Horroway's on the move." Sticking her head through the window, she pointed out the new direction to the driver, who shook his head but turned the carriage.

By the time she'd found her seat again, Bishop had regained his composure and clearly didn't want to speak anymore on the topic. Verity took pity on him. "Goodness," she muttered, tapping her nails on the carriage door. "Could we be going any slower?"

Bishop arched a brow, his arms crossed. "Impatient little chit, aren't you?"

"Well, technically you're the one slowing me down. I could be halfway there already."

Bishop's arms sprawled along the back of the seat. "Am I?" he drawled. "I assume you can simply hop across the city, and catch our erstwhile necromancer before I have time to scratch my nose?"

"I could, but it can be dangerous. I don't like making blind leaps. So I'd have to move from place to place."

"Blind leaps?"

She dragged her sleeve off her shoulder, revealing the scar there. Bishop's brown eyes locked on it. "This happened when I was younger. Took a blind jump into a White Rabbits warehouse and skewered myself on a hook. It's best if I can see the area first to prepare myself for a landing. I prefer at least knowing the layout." Memory resurfaced. "Trapped myself in a wall once too." And hadn't that been humiliating?

"Younger?" he asked. "It looks like it's barely faded."

"Oh, all right, I was sixteen, so only a couple of years ago."

That tightened the line of his mouth.

"My age bothers you, doesn't it?" she asked innocently.

"I don't see why it should," Bishop replied, but he looked away.

Verity examined him, then bit her lip with a smile. A second later she was perched on his knee, and Bishop's arms wrapped around her in surprise as she re-formed.

"Jesus." He stiffened.

"I'm a grown woman, Adrian," she whispered, stroking a finger down his collar. The hard flex of his chest filled out his coat quite nicely. "One doesn't maintain their innocence very long in Seven Dials, and besides that, I'll be all of twenty in a month. And look...." She cupped her breasts, the fabric and her hands molding to the soft flesh. "I think this means that I'm definitely a woman."

"Verity!" He caught her wrists, drawing them away from her breasts, his nostrils flaring. "Verity, we're in public."

"A closed carriage is hardly public," she whispered in his ear, earning another flinch from him. Her fingers went to the buttons on his coat. "In fact it's very, very private indeed. I wonder just what we could do to pass the time?"

"I think we could talk. About what happened last night."

Verity stilled, shooting him a look. "That was a low blow. I was embarrassed. That's why I fled."

"I think it's more than that."

"And I think that you are wearing entirely too many clothes." She shook off his attempts to make this deeper than it was. A good night's sleep had assuaged the doubt she'd felt last night. She liked him, and she liked his company. She didn't have to fall for him though. She was far too clever for that. Biting her lip, Verity slid his coat off his shoulders. "That's better."

Bishop captured her wrists. Interest flared in his eyes, but he shook his head. "No."

Verity groaned in frustration. "I'm not an innocent, Bishop! And I'm not a little girl! If you wanted to do some naughty, wicked things to me, I truly wouldn't mind. And I know you're not averse either." She could feel the press of his blatant enthusiasm all too well beneath her bottom.

"It's not your age that bothers me," he replied, still trying to hold her still, though he'd given up on her wrists by now.

"Oh?" Verity cupped his jaw with her hand, her thumb stroking the rasp of his stubble. Touching him like this meant that he couldn't look away from her. "We've already ascertained that you like kissing me. So if it's not my age, and it's not me, then what is it?"

The carriage rolled to a halt. "Which way, sir?" bellowed the coach driver.

"Left!" Verity called, then lowered her voice. "We're nearly there. Tick, tock, Bishop...."

"It's not you," he blurted, straightening his coat, and setting her aside. "I can't be with a woman."

A suspicion began to gnaw at her. Verity straightened, her eyes widening in pure shock as memories intruded upon her: the hesitant way he'd kissed her that first time, the somewhat fumbling attempts to caress her. She'd thought his hesitation was due to her. But.... "Bishop, are you trying to tell me that you've *never* been with a woman?"

All of her suspicions were confirmed by the look in his eyes. Verity gaped. "You're a virgin?" she blurted. "But how?"

"I'm going to sit up top," he replied, his cheeks red.

Then Bishop slipped out of the door and vanished, leaving her sitting on the spring seat with her skirts awry and her mouth gaping open.

Of all the reasons for him to push her away, she had never, ever expected this one.

"Why are you a virgin?"

"Can we concentrate on the matter at hand?" Bishop growled, eyeing the white brick building ahead of them and ignoring her. "If Horroway's inside that house, then this might be dangerous."

Verity shot him a long, slow look. "I will temporarily refrain from this line of conversation, but don't think it's over."

It was definitely over. He didn't want to think about his reasons, or how explaining them to Verity would make him feel. He liked the way she looked at him, her flirtatious attempts to seduce him. He didn't want to see her smile fade off her face when she learned the truth of what type of man he was.

You're no killer, are you?

God. If only she knew.

He swallowed hard and pushed aside those thoughts. Horroway was close, Verity was certain of it. And that meant the Chalice might be at hand.

Bishop focused on the house.

"Something's not right," he murmured, his hard body held defensively in front of her. "This place looks like a well-to-do nabob owns it. Not a shabby necromancer without a shilling to his name. Last time I saw him he could barely even afford a bloody coat."

"Maybe someone's paying him?" Verity murmured.

Tremayne. "That bodes ill," Bishop muttered, striding along the pavement beside the garden walls. "I'd prefer a single target, not an entire conspiracy of allies."

Though it would mean this could be all done and dusted within the hour.

It also meant more potential danger that he was pushing Verity into. Bishop scowled.

The gardens surrounding the home were lush and sprawling, ringed by a black wrought-iron fence. A flock of crows fluffed themselves on the front lawn, eyeing the pair of them with beady black eyes, and he had the uncomfortable feeling someone else was watching them. Verity tucked her hand through the crook of his arm as he slowly led her past. They might look like any other couple out for a stroll, if not for the fact that nobody would mistake him for simply a well-to-do gentleman.

"It's well warded," he noted quietly, seeing the shimmering traces of ward work stretched over the gardens. "Exceptionally well warded."

"Which means someone's trying to stop others from getting inside. I wonder...." Verity peered at the top floor, where a shadow flitted past a window. "I could translocate inside, get a closer look—"

"Not on your life," Bishop replied, and trapped her against the fence. He towered over her, a knot of hard worry choking him. "You're too rash and careless with yourself."

"I was stealing when I was thirteen, Bishop, from dangerous people who wouldn't have thought twice about cutting my throat. If you think I cannot handle myself—"

That wasn't it, at all. "I know you can handle yourself, but Elijah Horroway is a powerful and dangerous necromancer, and we don't know if he's allied himself with anyone else. You're not invincible, Verity. And Horroway could do things to you—horrible, horrible things—that you might never escape from."

"You almost sound as if you care," she whispered, glancing up, and Bishop wavered.

"Of course I care, Verity," he told her, his expression turning to stone again. "I'm not completely heartless. Just don't mistake compassion for something else. This... us... nothing will come of it. Nothing *can* come of it." He said the words firmly, as if trying to convince her. Or perhaps it was himself who wavered.

We'll see. This man, with his heart of stone, was so fascinating to her. A temptation indeed, and sometimes she didn't know if it were just the passion that flared between them she wanted to explore, or... something more. Something like what she'd felt last night, when he held her in his arms.

That thought startled her.

Life in Seven Dials wasn't the sort of rosy existence where one dreamed of love. The type of relationships she'd seen existed of power exchanges between pimps and their whores, or even Murphy and his mistress, Betsy, who didn't seem to have shed any tears following his death. She couldn't think of one marriage that had been happy.

So what did this yearning inside her mean? Why did she want him to kiss her so much? It was just a kiss. Just a romp in the sheets. Wasn't it?

"Verity?" His palm settled on her waist, his thumb rasping against the material there. For a moment he looked down, as if distracted by the sensation of her dress beneath his hand. "Penny for your thoughts?"

She wasn't that brave. Verity wet her lips and glanced to the side. They were momentarily shielded from the house. "How would you care to play it then, my lord?"

A small silence.

"A little surveillance, before we think of breaking and entering. Take my arm. Consider us just out for a stroll in the gloomy afternoon."

She slipped her hand through the crook of his elbow and he rested his gloved hand upon it, his beaver hat pulled low over his face. Suddenly, he wasn't some prowling assassin, but a jaunty young fellow out for a walk with his woman. Everything about his posture and stance shifted.

"You do that very well," she whispered.

"Years of practice." He shot her a glance beneath the brim of his hat. "This way. Pretend I'm saying terribly witty things, and laugh a little. The best way to go about subterfuge is to pretend you're not really hiding at all, I've found."

She patted his arm and laughed, leaning against him. "How's this?"

"Excellent. Anyone would think you're used to covert operations."

"I did pluck the hair right from your head," she pointed out. "You didn't even notice me."

Bishop's gaze dipped briefly to her mouth. "I cannot quite figure out how. You're not the type of woman one doesn't notice."

Her heart gave a little flutter.

"Here," he murmured, pulling her into the small park across the street from the back garden of the mansion they were watching and putting his back to the house. He positioned her against a tree, watching over his shoulder. "Still feel that pull?"

"It's stronger now," she admitted, feeling the tense knot in her core jerk her toward the house. A glimpse of red caught her eyes through the French doors at the back of the house. "I think Horroway's about to come out into the garden."

Bishop reached past her to press his palm against the trunk, capturing her hand lightly in his other hand as if he were courting. "Tell me what you see."

"He's... he's...." Her brows drew together. "A woman. How does that work?"

A woman in a wheeled chair pushed herself out onto the back terrace, wearing a fetching gown of pure scarlet. Her hair was dark—or had been—but now streaks of gray marred it.

"Oh, hell," she whispered, looking down at the ring. "I haven't brought us to Horroway at all. I've brought us to the woman to whom he tried to give the ring." Verity frowned, trying to *taste* the ring again. "There is no other corresponding imprint."

"I'm an idiot. Of course not." Bishop cursed under his breath. "You're trying to find a man, but rumor says that Elijah Horroway is neither dead, nor alive, but caught in some state in-between. Would that affect your attempts at finding him?"

"Significantly," she said, pocketing the ring.

"Damn it." He shot a glance over his shoulder toward the house. "All of that for nothing."

"Well," she said with a sigh. "Perhaps we can go back to your map table? Track him by magic."

Bishop wasn't paying her the slightest bit of attention. His gaze locked on the woman in the garden and stillness slid through him, the muscle of his arm tensing beneath her touch.

"Bishop?" she asked. "What's wrong?"

"Verity, do you know that woman?"

Verity examined the woman again, darting her glance between them. "Well... no. I don't think I've ever seen her before, why?"

Every inch of him was still. He had that "hunting" expression on his face, and tension etched his muscles. "Because that's Morgana de Wynter, my father's ex-wife. I'm certain of it."

Verity's voice dropped. "I thought she was dead."

"So did I," he breathed, fading back into the bushes in the park, drawing her with him. "Don't move. Don't make a sound. And *don't* use your sorcery, or she'll sense it."

Pressed against him from breast to thigh, Verity caught hold of his coat, the screen of overgrown shrubbery enveloping them. His wariness was contagious. Her lungs tightened. "What are you going to do?" She caught his sleeve as he shifted minutely. She'd never seen that sort of intensity in his dark eyes. They looked almost black in the shadows. "Bishop. You can't kill her. Not here."

He finally looked at her, and she saw how much he wanted to. "Everything that has been done to my father can be laid at that woman's feet. *Everything.*"

"Who knows what is in that house," she pointed out. "And if she survived what you threw at her last month, then what tricks does she have up her sleeve?"

"You're right." He swore. "I'm not usually this careless."

"You're angry, and you're not thinking." Verity took a wary step backward. There was something about him in this moment that seemed quite dangerous. "Perhaps we should tell your father. I assume he would want to know?"

Bishop nodded. He looked back at the house just as a young man strolled out onto the back porch, his hands in his pockets and his hair neatly pomaded.

Verity's jaw dropped again. *Oh, no.*

"What?" Bishop breathed in her ear.

"That's Noah Guthrie."

Bishop froze. "Verity, I'm fairly certain that's not Noah anymore. I think we've just found the demon."

"What are we going to do?" she mouthed.

"*We're* not. You're going. I can move silently without you by my side, and I need to find out more."

"I'm not leaving you here alone," she pointed out.

"Someone needs to let Drake know." He took her chin firmly between his palms. "Verity, matters just took a turn for the worse. That woman wants to destroy my father, and the demon is her means of doing so. We need to know who else is in that house, and Drake and Ianthe need to be alerted." He shook her a little. "Promise me you'll go to Drake. Get as far away from here as possible."

"And you?" she asked in a small voice.

"It would take more than Morgana has to kill me," he said, turning his gaze toward the house. "Go on now, Ver. I'll catch up with you at my father's house."

CHAPTER EIGHTEEN

VERITY TRANSLOCATED BACK to Bishop's house, where she picked up a book she'd seen in the library with a scrawled note from Drake in it to Bishop, and then punched across the city, using it to track Drake down.

Finally, she fetched up outside a manor on the outskirts of Kensington. The door opened the second she went to knock, and Verity started, staring at a young woman in a pale pink gown with a wealth of golden ringlets curling down her back.

The young woman blinked. She had the thickest, darkest lashes Verity had ever seen, and her eyes were so dark a brown that she almost looked as though she bore some faint resemblance to Bishop. "Oh," she said, clearly taking Verity's appraisal just as much as Verity took in the stranger's. "I knew something was coming—something momentous. I didn't realize it would be you."

Verity stood there rather stupidly, holding Drake's book. "Is, ah, the duke at home?"

The woman smiled, and her entire face softened. "Come in, come in," she said, gesturing her inside. "I've been expecting you."

Which was a rather strange thing to say. Verity glanced at her sidelong as the stranger closed the door behind her. "You were?"

"My thief," the stranger said proudly. "I'm so relieved to see you. This has been a horrendous week, but at least your appearance gives me hope." She saw Verity's expression and her cheeks flushed. "Oh, I'm so sorry. I'm babbling. My name is Cleo. I used to be the Cassandra."

"I see."

She didn't, at all.

"I Saw the future," Cleo added, accurately reading her. "I saw you," she corrected, "plucking the eyes from a blind crow in order to save a man dressed all in black who was being crucified."

A cane clicked on the marble floor and the duke appeared, wings of silver highlighting his dark hair. He looked nothing like his son, Bishop, except for the sensation of absolute power and competence that he exuded. His gaze dipped to the book in her hands, then back again. "Adrian?" Those knuckles tightened on the handle of his silver-topped cane.

"He's well." She knew Bishop was worried about his father, but the opposite appeared to be true as well. "He saw something he thought you needed to know, and he's investigating further. So he sent me to tell you about it."

Drake's gaze swept over the pair of them, then he gestured her inside, just as Lucien appeared in the shadows, like a concerned wraith. "I'll send for some tea," Drake said. "Come. And tell me everything."

"You knew Morgana was still alive and you didn't tell?" Bishop demanded ten minutes after he'd arrived at his father's house. "Why? Why would you do that?"

The rest of the room remained very still. Verity looked like she'd spent the afternoon stuffing teacakes in her mouth with the girl his father had introduced as Cleo, Tremayne's daughter. Both of them watched with wide eyes.

"I...." Drake paused, then glanced toward Cleo uncomfortably.

"I've spent days traipsing all over this city." Worrying about his father, worrying about Verity and who had threatened her life. "Why would you keep this—" His expression cleared as his thoughts raced ahead. "You thought I'd go after Sebastian, didn't you? You thought I'd carry out the threat I made against him."

Turning around, Bishop shoved his hands through his hair, tension screaming through him. He didn't know what to think. Morgana and Sebastian still alive after all this time, and living with the demon. Now he knew who had commissioned the theft of the Chalice. Morgana. And Tremayne. Everything was intertwined, and the threat against his father had just tripled. It was no longer merely the Sicarii Bishop had to worry about, but the demon as well, and Horroway, who must have the Chalice.

"I just wanted a chance to reach him," Drake replied. "I'm nearly there."

Always this cursed brother of his. Bishop curled up his lip. "So you can do what? Rescue him? What price will Morgana demand from you? You know what she'll want. You. Dead. Is he worth that to you? Christ, he tore that house apart last month as though he was ripping paper! You can't stop him. *I* can't stop him! He is dangerous!"

"Everyone deserves a chance," Drake replied, his face paling. "If he can be shown another way, taught to control his powers—"

"Maybe he cannot be saved?" Bishop yelled.

"You don't know what she's done to him!" This was the first time he'd ever seen his father lose his temper. "Cleo tells me there's been torture, sexual abuse, possibly worse. How can I leave him to that?"

"How can you save someone who's so badly wounded?" The breath exploded out of him. "He knows nothing but Expression, and if he's been tortured, if...." His stomach curdled. He couldn't truly understand what Sebastian had been through, but he knew that coming back from that would be virtually impossible. "How does a man so wounded set aside his emotions and learn control? I know you've seen what happened to others we've tried to rehabilitate."

"You're asking me to leave him there? To abandon him?" Drake snapped. "The same way I abandoned you when you came home from Burma?"

"It wasn't the same." He turned on his heel, remembering all that his father had done to see his trial set aside and to help him find a mentor in Agatha. Those had been dark days. But not this dark.

"If someone like *you* can learn control," Drake said coldly, "then so can he. I've never—" He broke off as if biting his tongue, then turned back to Bishop as if he simply couldn't stop the words. "I've never been so disappointed in you in my entire life as I am in this moment. Yes, I kept the truth from you. For precisely this reason!"

The words blinded him. Bishop turned away, the world washing out around him. God. It hurt. He had to get out of there. "I'm done," he said blankly. "I cannot... cannot watch you sacrifice yourself for a lost cause."

Then he was out of the room and staggering down the stairs, the numbness sweeping up to lock him in a cold, dark place.

CHAPTER NINETEEN

"WELL," VERITY WHISPERED, finally locating him on the terrace on his rooftop. The afternoon sun peeped through the clouds, highlighting the man on the daybed, his knees drawn up to his chest and his eyes on the sky. "Here you are."

It felt like it should be raining, after such a brutal confrontation.

Bishop glanced her way, then sank his head onto his palm. "How is he?" he asked quietly.

Verity sat on the daybed beside him, seeing the hurt in his eyes. She gently touched his back. "About as glum as you," she murmured, her heart aching for him. "But trying to hold it together. Cleo said that she would watch over him tonight, and Ianthe came home from that meeting in time. He'll be fine."

"I'm so sorry," he rasped, his eyes blank and staring into the distance. "I shouldn't have said what I said. I know how much it hurt Drake to think that Sebastian was dead. But... it would have been easier."

Verity pressed her cheek against his arm, biting her lip. "Why does Sebastian scare you so much?"

"Because I know who's going to have to deal with him if he explodes out of control." Bishop swallowed. "Drake will never forgive me for it, but it's a duty nobody else can do."

And he would lose his father.

That was what was really plaguing him.

Seeing the wet shine in his eyes, Verity dragged him into her arms, desperately wishing that she could take that hurt away. Having lost her mother—and her father—she knew exactly how he felt. Bishop sucked in a sharp breath, then let her hold him. His arms slowly came up and curled around her back, his face burying itself against her shoulder.

No time for pretense now. She was falling far too fast for this man. It physically hurt her to see him in pain. She would do anything to stop that pain.

Anything.

If she could.

"None of us know what the future holds," she whispered. "But you'll never be alone, Bishop. Even if the worst comes to pass, then... you'll always have me."

He lifted his head, stroking her hips. "Ver?" There was a faint frown on his face.

Her heart started beating a little faster. "I think I'm starting to fall in love with you," she whispered, and that stab of terror came sharply again, threatening to overwhelm her. "A little. And... I don't care if you don't feel the same way." A blatant lie. "I don't expect that. I don't. But I wanted you to know that I care for you. I wanted you to know that you're not alone. Not tonight. Not tomorrow. Not ever. If you wish it." Her courage was starting to waver now. He hadn't said a thing, merely gaped at her. "I would like to kiss you," Verity whispered. "But I think if I try, you'll push me away again and I don't know why."

"Verity—"

"So I won't," she said softly, pushing herself upright. "If you wanted me, then I wouldn't say no. But I think it's time that I stopped chasing after you. I'm tired of being pushed away. So if you want me, Adrian, then you must make your move. Not I." Taking a step back, she swallowed hard. "I-I'll... I'll give you a moment alone, and just go see to dinner, shall I? That will make you feel a little better, and then we can talk about what is to be done."

Bishop lasted all of a minute, his heart beginning to thump harder and harder in his chest as her words kept playing around his mind. *I think I'm starting to fall in love with you.* He'd never expected such a thing. Never dared dream of it. And yet, as the words filled his chest, made something inside him swell, he realized a tiny part of him *had* dreamed that dream. A little part that he'd never dared examine. And it filled him with both fear and a desperate, desperate longing to go to her and tell her she was not alone. He felt it too.

He was on his feet before he knew it, the blood pounding through his veins as he slipped down the stairs and went after her. He couldn't afford to think, to rationalize all of the ways this could go wrong. The confrontation with his father had scoured him dry, and yet, in a way it had stripped away all of the worry that plagued him. Stripped him back to bare, back to pure primal need and hunger.

And what he needed was ghosting along in front of him through the halls, the whisper of her pale pink skirts floating behind her.

He could move silently when he wanted to, and the first she knew of his presence was when he caught her hand in his.

"Adrian—"

He caught her gasp with his mouth, strong hands catching her by the hips and pressing her back against the Chinese wallpaper. Lust slammed through him. Need. The urge to claim her as his. Verity's fists curled in his collar, as she was wont to do, and their mouths met in a desperate surge. This was what he'd dreamed of. It filled him all the way up inside, as if his body had been hollow somehow and she was a vital piece that had always been missing.

To free himself of all his self-imposed constraints left him breathless and trembling. He'd been so careful for so long that unleashing himself left his head spinning. "Ver," he breathed, tasting her hot little mouth. "Ver, oh God. I want you."

He might as well have set her alight. Greedy little hands tugged at his coat, slipping inside. They darted up his chest, touching him as if he were something precious, when he knew he was not. The kiss deepened, as she devoured him. It was a moment of such pure, utter perfection that he wished it could last forever.

Drawing back, he barely managed to catch his breath. Trembling fingers stroked a lock of hair behind her ear. Soft. So soft. Like silk. And her mouth was swollen and quivering, her green eyes asking a dozen questions.

Bishop cupped her face with his hand and pressed his forehead to hers. Anything to still the raging thunder of his heart and the fierce desire that flushed through his veins. Power tempted him, beyond that of any he'd known, but he wasn't certain if it had anything to do with the Grave Arts or whether she was simply flush with sexual energy.

And it was that uncertainty that made him draw back. He wasn't going to live the same hell as he had with Mya.

"Take me to bed," Verity whispered, her hands pressing flat against his chest beneath his coat. Exploring. Tempting him.

He shook his head.

"You want to. I want to."

Bishop caught her wrists and drew back just enough to meet her eyes. Forcing the words to his lips almost hurt, for somewhere in the deep dark heart of him, kissing her had become part of his own forbidden dreams of the future. "If I hurt you, then I would never forgive myself."

She was breathing hard, but she wouldn't let him look away from her, capturing his face in her hands and turning hers to place it in front of him as he tried to pull free of her. "What do you mean?"

He swallowed, his heart in his throat. "I want you, Verity. I want to do things to you that I've never dreamed of doing to any other woman." He bared his teeth. Hell. "And I can hear your heart racing, hear the blood slipping through your veins in anticipation. You want it too. You want this." Taking her hand, he cupped it against the full, straining length of his erection, earning a groan from himself and a gasp from her before her fingers closed around his cock, rasping against the material of his trousers.

It was the first time someone else's hand had ever touched him there. He almost came on the spot.

Somehow he forced himself to continue. "But I'm dangerous, Verity. I don't want to hurt you."

There were those questions in her eyes again, but he thought somehow, she'd begun to realize what haunted him. "You don't want to lose control," she whispered.

"I *can't* lose control." Bishop swallowed as her hand shifted on his cock. "I want to. I do. I want it so badly it hurts."

"We don't have to do everything," she replied thoughtfully. "We could take it slow. The second you feel yourself slipping, you tell me."

And here was where the danger lay, because he wanted to agree. "Slowly?" It was both an answer and a question.

A brilliant smile lit her face. "So slowly that you'll beg me for more."

Velvety lips caressed his throat, sharp little teeth nipping at him. Somehow he found himself pressing her back against the wall, thrusting into the heat of her hand.

A hand that began to stealthily unbutton his trousers, to part the buckskin there and sneak inside. He couldn't have stopped her if he wanted to. "Verity, *Jesus.*" Skin found skin, and then she was exploring the silk-slick length of him. It was all he could do not to lift her, shove her skirts out of the way, and bury himself inside her in some age-old instinct he'd never felt before.

"Tell me what you want to do to me," she whispered in his ear, her soft lips nuzzling his earlobe as her hand worked his cock. A thumb rasped over the molten head of his erection, rubbing the slickness there across the head.

"Fuck. *Fuck.*" He ground closer, drowning in her perfume, in the spicy heat of her skin. The rasp of his stubble against her throat earned a gasp from her lips, and he licked her there, tasted her. Bit her. "I want to... fuck you. But I can't. I don't... Oh, shit." She was squeezing him hard. He couldn't stop himself from thrusting. Fucking his way into her hand.

It felt amazing.

"This is not going to end slowly," he gasped.

Verity laughed, and squeezed again.

Somehow they were sliding to the floor. She pressed him flat onto his back, straddling his thighs. All he could see when he looked down was his straining cock quivering in her pale hand. Their eyes met.

"You'll like this," Verity whispered, giving him a secret smile that clenched inside his chest, as though she'd wrapped that hand around his heart instead. Then she lowered her head and licked the crown of his cock.

Bishop jerked, his back arching. *Fucking Jesus.* Somehow his hands were in her hair, and that hot little mouth swallowed him down. Took nearly all of him. And he was pushing her down more, thrusting his hips up, trying to get more. Trying to push himself over the edge that was building.

She glided up with a wet little pop and worked him with her hand. "Look at you." Those green eyes were alight. "You're right. This is not going to be slow at all."

Then she devoured his cock as though she'd never wanted anything more in her life.

"Ver," he gasped. "Ver, I'm going to...." His hands started shaking.

She lifted up just enough to blow across the top of his cock, and his eyes nearly rolled back in his head.

"Let yourself go," she whispered. "I want this to be the best moment of your life."

More heat. More sweet caresses with her tongue.

He came, a blinding wave of heat that started in the back of his balls and exploded into her mouth. And she was right.

It was perfect.

Somehow he'd made his way into the sitting room carrying Verity in his arms. Then he collapsed there, completely undone, while she curled in his arms and rested her head on his chest.

"I can hear your heart beating," Verity murmured, caressing his chest.

Bishop lifted his head off the cushions. "It's beating there for you."

Verity smiled. "My virgin assassin with his gentle heart. Who knew?"

Bishop glanced down. He felt like a weight had been lifted from his shoulders. "I am never going to live this down, am I?"

"Never," she replied cheerfully. "But I must admit the idea intrigues me. Exploring uncharted terrain and all. I could quite happily plant a flag in your pants. 'Property of Verity Hawkins.'"

Bishop rolled until she was trapped between his body and the back of the sofa. He traced his fingers down her side, feeling the graze of the embroidery on her dress. Their eyes met. The idea intrigued him too.

"I thought we were going to take this slowly?" Verity arched a brow. Sometimes he forgot how pretty she was, and then when he saw her anew, she took his breath away.

"We are," he breathed, slipping her sleeve off her shoulder. "But it seems remiss of me to keep all of the pleasure for myself. That would not be very gentlemanly of me."

"Well, we cannot have that," she whispered back, cupping her breast through the silk of her dress. "Though this lady can take care of her own pleasure when she needs to."

The thought of that made him hard again. "Show me," he breathed, kissing her lips.

Verity glanced up at him, as if gauging whether to be shy or not. Gathering a fistful of skirts, she drew them up, revealing her pale stockings and the lean length of her legs. There were so many petticoats and layers in the way that frustration danced through her eyes, and then she finally bunched them out of the way.

Bishop's lips followed her hand as she cupped her breast, her fingers rasping over the faint outline of her nipple. He kissed her there through the dress, then teased her bodice lower until her stays were revealed. Pale pink lace. Smooth skin the color of cream. And then her nipple revealed itself, as brown as a pale nut.

Bishop's lips swallowed it whole. Verity sucked in a small breath. Flicking her nipple with his tongue, he shifted until she lay flat in the space where he'd been. Verity spread her thighs wide, her other hand sliding down between them.

"Like this," she whispered, stroking herself there.

He couldn't see a thing with her skirts all crushed between them, but the thought made him burn hotter. "Do you do it often?"

"Sometimes." She bit her lip, her eyes glazing a little, as though she were focusing on the feeling. "Here." She took his hand and guided it up her thigh. "Have you ever...?"

"Let's not talk of the past," he replied, and rolled her nipple between his teeth. "Let's just focus on the here and now."

There was a dark knowing in her pretty green eyes, but she let him divert the topic. Her thighs parted as he stroked the soft skin there, feeling her tremble beneath him. Every moment was wondrous. Verity took his hand and pressed his fingers through the slit in her drawers.

Wet. Slick. Flushed with heat. He caught her gaze again as she bit her lip. "Inside me," she whispered.

He stroked the smooth bud between her legs that she'd been playing with, then started to slip a finger inside her silken sheath. Everything in him wanted that to be his cock. The sheer thought of it nearly made him come again. But this was Verity's turn. Not his. Verity bit her lip, her hips arching, and he had the flushed remembrance of what it had felt like when she put her mouth on him.

He wasn't entirely innocent. There had been those books, after all. He had ideas, and now, with a very willing woman beneath him, he wanted to test some of those ideas.

Sliding a second finger within her, he stroked up, feeling her muscles clench around him as the thickness doubled.

"Yes," she gasped. "Curl them a little."

He complied, and a shiver ran through her. It wasn't enough. He wanted to please her as much as she'd pleased him.

And he wanted to taste her.

Pushing lower, he buried his face in between her thighs, nuzzling through the slit in her drawers. Verity stiffened. "Bishop!"

Then he licked her. It was incredibly intimate, as though he had full control over her body right now. The taste of her was faintly musky, and he swirled his tongue around that little bud she'd been playing with. Verity nearly shot out of her skin. She liked it, clearly.

Withdrawing his fingers, Bishop pushed her thighs open wider and kissed her deeply, tasting and suckling. Verity made little incoherent sounds above him, wriggling uncontrollably. Gasping. Begging him for more.

He wasn't satisfied until she was screaming his name, and then he smiled faintly as he kissed her thigh and crawled back up into her arms.

I think I might be falling a little in love with you, *Verity Hawkins.*

The sky was a blaze of diamond pinprick stars, strewn across a velvet background. Sebastian stumbled into a world he didn't know with black-and-white checkerboard tiles beneath his feet.

The pain was gone; all of the strain in his shoulders, the dehydration, the ache of hunger.... Instead, he stood alone in a world crisp with possibility.

Boot heels echoed on the tiles. Sebastian spun around, trying to work out where he was.

"*Over here.*"

He turned and there stood a man, his hands clasped behind his back and his face turned away as he examined the horizon.

"Who are you? Where am I? What have you done to me?"

"I have pulled you into a dream. I wish that I could do more." The man turned around, the moonlight gilding his dark features—the same features that Sebastian saw in the mirror every morning. "I wish that you would let me."

Sebastian backed away, but there was nowhere to go, nowhere to run. "What do you want?" he demanded as the Prime drank in the sight of him. *Stop looking at me like that....*

"To free you," his father replied.

Sebastian breathed out a laugh. *Don't believe him. He's lying. He wants something....*

But what?

Perhaps if he played this game, he would manage to discover what it was. "Why?"

The Prime stared at him. "What do you mean, why? I thought you dead until your wife appeared at my doorstep—"

"Cleo's with you?" Sebastian took a half step toward the man, then forced himself to still. Of course she would be. The foolish bloody woman! "I want her kept out of this."

"If you cannot manage it, then how do you presume that I can? It is her link to you that allows me to do this— she's lying right here, beside me, in a meditative trance." Reaching out, Drake pressed his thumb to Sebastian's forehead and an image of his wife sprang to mind, peaceful as she lay on the floor beside his father's body in a gleaming circle of silver light.

Sebastian hovered over the pair of them. There was another woman in the room, sitting outside the circle as if on guard. Ianthe Martin, if he wasn't mistaken. He'd helped kidnap her daughter a month ago, and forced her to steal the Blade of Altarrh, at his mother's request.

"She looks... better than I'd have expected considering her loss," he said quietly, returning his gaze to Cleo. It seemed strange to see her without her ever-present blindfold. The flutter of dark lashes against her pale cheeks was new to him. And so too the way she dressed in a vibrant gown of green that dipped shockingly low—to his mind, at least—in front. All this time he'd only ever seen her gowned in virginal white lace, but that had been her father's influence, clearly. "They took her visions from her."

"Did they? Or is it a self-fulfilling prophecy? She believes that the moment she loses her blindfold is the moment she loses her Foresight, and so she perhaps places a block in her own mind. We will see. It is rare to lose a talent like that." A hazy image of Drake formed beside him, surrounded by a pale nimbus of light. "There's so much more to the Divination Arts than Foresight, and she has the ability to learn so perhaps it is not such a loss, after all? Tremayne was remiss in teaching her how to control her sorcery. He wanted to use her Visions, but he never explained to her that she could do so much more."

Sebastian's mother shared Tremayne's prejudices. "He feared her power."

"Yes."

"Do you?" Sebastian demanded, and this time they were not speaking of Cleo.

"I fear... a great many things. But not another's power. Every man and woman should have the opportunity to stretch themselves to the extent of their abilities. Especially you."

He wasn't sure if he believed the words. "What is this?" Sebastian asked, staring at his transparent hands.

"It's a form of astral projection."

He knew so little. "I'm not the one doing it, am I?"

"No, you needed my guidance."

In another world he might have asked this man to teach him. He looked again at his wife. One would have thought her pure and pristine, but he'd seen the fire within her, the passion. Cleo demanded to be loved and she wanted a place in this world that was safe and welcoming. He could give her that, at least. "What will it cost me," he asked, "to see her kept safe from my mother?"

His father frowned. "There is no cost—"

Sebastian laughed under his breath. "There's got to be something you want."

"Ah, my son," the man breathed, looking sad. "I hoped.... But it seems your mother has dealt you a poor hand. She hasn't been kind, has she?"

"If she had been I would not have trusted it," Sebastian replied. "Don't pretend to know me."

"The problem is that your mother never understood what power is. She craved it—a by-product of her own tortured adolescence—but she never truly knew what it meant to be powerful."

"And you do?"

"Sebastian, I have the power to bring London to its knees. But power is not about what you have the means to do, it is about what you could do, but don't. Power is responsibility to those you serve. That is what it means to be Prime to the Order of the Dawn Star. I've never been its ruler, but its servant." Drake tilted his head. "And whilst I could make London tremble, you yourself have the power to destroy it. So you must ask yourself this question: what does power mean to you?"

Freedom. His nostrils flared. "I don't know."

"I felt the tremor of your Expression a month ago. You were spiraling in on yourself. You should have obliterated the city, the way you were going. What stopped you?"

A little girl crying in a room next to him.... Sebastian looked away. "I didn't want to harm anyone."

"Ah."

That irritated him, as though his father presumed to know the man he was from the answer to a single question. "You didn't come here to lecture me on sorcery, did you? What do you want? To show me you have my wife? Then have her, keep her safe. Just keep her away from me."

And then he cut the connection between, slamming a wall up that the man couldn't breach.

Sebastian awoke with a gasp, curled on the cold stone floors of his mother's cellars.

There was always a price, and he would pay it.

The knock at the door drew Bishop away from bed and the warm peaceful slumber he'd known wrapped in Verity's arms.

Bishop slid through the early dawn, tugging his night-robe's ties tight at his hips before pausing at the door. If the visitor had malevolent intentions his wards would have made them wary, but there was only one, and not a single trace of power whispered through the night. Bishop let the etheric blade form in his palm, warm and faintly pulsing, as he tugged the front door open.

A man stood there wearing the livery of Drake's household. He flinched when he met Bishop's gaze, and there were singe marks on the collar of his coat. "My lord." The stranger nodded. "I've just come from the Prime's home. Lady Rathbourne requested your presence, if you please? There's been an attack. "

CHAPTER TWENTY

BISHOP LEFT VERITY with Lady Eberhardt whilst he went to visit his father.

Verity complied with his directions, as the expression on his face resembled a cell door slamming shut. Not so much a sign of a lack of emotion when it came to Bishop, but perhaps too much of it. She'd much rather be at his side to offer comfort, if nothing else, but he'd muttered something about it not being safe with Sicarii assassins on the loose.

And she didn't want to distract him. Not now, when his heart was in his eyes.

Which left breakfast with Lady E, a nerve-racking proposition at the best of times.

"Look at this," Lady E muttered to Marie, scowling down at a letter that had earned her wrath. "Lord Dinklage presumes to cast his hat in the ring for the seat of Prime, but *he is concerned* that the Triad Council is favorably disposed toward another candidate. And though he doesn't mention her by name it's quite clear whom he's talking about. *Hmph*. As if I've ever been less than partisan in my life! Besides, she hasn't even applied yet."

"And she is?" Verity asked politely.

"Lady Rathbourne," Lady E bit off. "I'm not quite certain whether Drake is setting those rumor mills into motion, or whether people are presuming."

"She does have the qualifications," Marie pointed out.

"But does she have the desire?" Lady E countered. "I've been waiting all month and still no sign of her intentions. If she intends to make her move, she's leaving it late. Ascendancy occurs this Sunday!"

"How does one become Prime?" Verity asked. "Do they have to apply?"

"To be quite honest, we're making it all up as we go along," Lady E admitted. "In the past, one candidate dueled the reigning Prime and whoever was left standing either ascended to the seat, or remained in it. It's the way it has always been. Until Drake decided to stir this hornets' nest." That earned a scowl. "Fool man. Could he not have waited until we've buried this demon threat to suffer this crisis of conscience, or whatever is plaguing him?"

Verity nibbled at her coddled eggs. "So why don't you do it? Become Prime? You're powerful, and you seem to know everyone in the Order and everything about it. You're also quite adept at, ah, suggesting what people should do."

"Bossing people around, do you mean?" Marie shared a conspiratorial smile with her.

Lady E's wrinkled lips feathered and she flexed her left hand subconsciously. "I quite like my privacy as it is, thank you very much. And I'm too old to step up into that seat. No. I'd prefer to pull the strings in the background. Far less taxing."

"And then you can sit back and critique whoever *does* get the job," Marie added with a faint smile. The secretary's gray hair was pulled back in a rather severe knot this morning, highlighting the fine bones of her face.

"Precisely," Lady E nodded.

There came a faint scratch at the door, and Lady E's butler cleared his throat. "This just arrived, my lady." He offered a letter to her on a silver salver, then crept out quietly.

"One of your little pigeons by the look of it," Marie noted.

Lady E flicked the letter open and scowled down at it. When she looked up her gaze speared Verity, who set her spoonful of coddled eggs down.

"What is it?" Verity asked, a nervous flutter starting in her chest. Not the Prime, please no. She barely knew the man, but Bishop's heart would break if his father died, and he already carried far too much on his shoulders as it was.

"Drake is fine," Lady E assured her, reading it on her face, and Marie patted Verity's hand. "Driving his son halfway to Bedlam with his insistence that he doesn't need any help at the moment. Bishop is most vexed."

Bishop's telepathic bond with his mentor made Verity feel a little left out, but at least it seemed as though he and his father had made amends.

"This is a report from someone I know in East London. I asked him to watch the docks for me, following Bishop's little tip-off that someone there was wielding the Grave Arts."

"And?"

"He's spotted something he thinks I should know about. Foxby swears he saw a dead man walking last night, heading toward Dock Number Five."

"A flesh construct?"

"Indeed." Lady E tapped the letter against her lips. "What say you? Do you want to join me in a little exploration of the docks?"

"What about Bishop?"

"He's arguing with his father right now. Let's not distract him. Besides, we don't know if this is actually a sighting, or someone imagining things. You can pop in and out at whim, and I've got the magical wherewithal to back you up should push come to shove." Lady E's chair scraped back as she stood.

The decision had clearly been made.

Verity exchanged a glance with Marie. "Can you let Bishop know when he gets back here?"

"Of course she will," Lady E interrupted. "Now step lively, gel. Let's go ferret out this flesh construct."

The coach disbursed them near the docks, and Verity helped Lady E down from the step as she looked around. Fog filled the nearby streets and the sun had long since vanished behind dark clouds. It was only midday but it felt like night in some respects. A nearby lamp had even been lit.

"Perfect place for an ambush," Verity pointed out, her background in the Dials making her wary.

"Perfect place to hide something you don't want others seeing," Lady E countered, brushing out her skirts as the coach turned around. John Coachman would meet them in an hour back by the Pig and Thistle pub they'd spotted up the road. "And if it is an ambush, well... this old dame has a few tricks up her sleeves yet. Come along."

In the distance, sailors and dockhands shouted as they used cranes to haul heavy crates off a docked ship. Ships lined the docks, and they bustled with activity. Verity focused on making herself very small and unnoticeable as she trotted at Lady E's side, far too used to the rough sort of men that lived and worked in these areas. Nobody would give a damn about the crow tattooed on the back of her hand here. Most of these workers were completely non-magical, and a woman alone—or perhaps even two of them—might look like easy pickings to the wrong type of man.

Several of the dockworkers glanced in their direction, but a single fearsome glance from Lady E served to send most of them scurrying back to their duties. "Amateurs." Lady E sniffed.

Verity decided she'd have to learn to mimic that precise expression. It could be useful in future should men ever give her grief in the streets. "You managed that well."

Lady E hauled out what looked like a compass as they left the main thoroughfare and wandered further along the foggy docks. The fog distorted the sound of men shouting, until it seemed as though they were miles away. "I spent a year in Cairo tracking a demon through its slums. The London docks pale in comparison."

"What are you doing?"

Lady E unwound the directional hands of the compass, revealing a hole inside. She poured a small handful of dirt into it from a pouch she'd been carrying. "There," Lady E said, winding the device back together. Tiny little runes gleamed golden as she breathed power words under her breath, and Verity felt the stir of sorcery as the compass hands began spinning.

"What is it?" Most of the hexes or spells she'd seen cast in the Dials were simple things, but this looked like a knot work of spells, all combining to perform something quite complex.

Lady E turned as the spinner came to a rest. "Grave dirt," she said, staring down the docks toward the hulking warehouse at the end as the compass jerked her toward it. "The compass is keyed to pick up trace amounts of Grave magic through the link with the dirt. The dirt has absorbed the trace amounts of power that leave a body following death. You can use anything: ground-up bone, blood from a dead man's body, chips of headstone... they all contain trace residue of the power spike preceding death. And right now, my compass is quite strongly convinced we need to go this way."

The compass pulled Lady E toward the warehouse like iron toward a magnet. Verity scrambled along in her wake, her skirts fluttering about her boots. She'd worn Marie's sensible charcoal cambric dress today, thank goodness, so at least any dirt wouldn't show.

Ahead of them, a shadowed flickered.

"There's something moving," she hissed, dragging Lady E behind a pile of crates.

The pair of them peered over the top. Lady E's compass was still tugging at her.

"We need to get closer," Lady E muttered, shaking out her hand as if a nerve was pinching.

"Are you certain you're all right?" Lady E's skin had paled.

"Right as rain." Lady E spat a couple of power words and a shiver went through Verity's bones as some sort of cloud settled over the pair of them. "It's a Veil," Lady E explained. "It will disguise us to most eyes, though if someone is looking directly at us they might pierce it. Make sure you don't move too fast. A stroll is about the most it can cloak."

Walking out into clear view was quite nerve-racking. The pair of them strode unhurriedly, and Verity began to notice other signs that they weren't alone. There was a man in a hooded cloak standing guard at the entrance to the dock that led to the warehouse they were interested in viewing, but it wasn't until they were right upon him that she noticed him, and that was odd.

Or perhaps not.

Closer inspection showed he didn't move, not even a single fidget. Most people couldn't hold a still position like that for so long. Lady E's compass jerked toward him as they slipped past, and she met the older woman's eyes as she huddled in close to her.

Lady E nodded. A flesh construct, standing guard. They were definitely in the right place.

Verity swallowed. This was outside her realm of experience. And though she could simply punch out of there, Lady E couldn't.

This way, the older woman mouthed.

All of the hairs along Verity's arms began to stand on end. Inside the warehouse there seemed to be some sort of green glow. Another construct stood on duty at the other end, and she and Lady E tiptoed past. The compass was pulling quite steadily on Lady E now, jerking toward the green glow inside the warehouse.

Lady E ground her teeth together and then the compass simply jerked out of her grasp, sailing through the air and straight through one of the windows up high.

Glass shattered. A pair of doves suddenly broke from nowhere, their wings thundering in the still silence of the fog.

Verity drove Lady E sideways, behind an old crate. "Jaysus," she swore, pressing her back against the crate.

The doors to the warehouse ground open. A man stepped out, his lanky form limping slightly. At least he was alive. Or more alive than the pair of constructs who followed woodenly on his heels.

"...*eleven, twelve... fourteen...*," Lady E muttered, craning her head to peer inside the warehouse. Her face paled. "He's insane. Nobody can control that many constructs at once."

Verity stared at the hypnotic green glow and the shadowy figures surrounding it. "Could he do it using the Chalice?"

Lady E's lips thinned. *Yes.* Potentially.

Through the fog and the green glow, Verity began to make out a golden object sitting on top of a single crate in the middle of the warehouse. Definitely a trap for the unwary. But also definitely the Chalice they were after. If it were her, she'd have planted a fake, but then that meant there would be no flesh constructs to guard the place.

The man leading them turned in circles, peering into the gloom. But whatever spell work Lady E was casting, he didn't seem to be able to peer through it.

"What do we do?" Verity whispered. "I can see the Chalice."

This might be their one chance to get it back.

"It's definitely a trap though," she added.

Lady E peered along the docks. "What we need is a distraction. If we can get that necromancer moving, then we might be able to get past the constructs. They're simply dead bodies, fuelled by power and capable of performing only simple tasks. Like killing or maiming anything that comes near it. They might even follow us if they see us, but we can outwit them easily." Her gimlet gaze narrowed on the necromancer. "It's him I'm curious about. I'd love to see his face."

Lady E gathered in power, and Verity felt it like little ants marching across her skin. It was done so slowly and so smoothly she was impressed. "*Forshuva di asko,*" the older lady whispered, letting it go in such fine tendrils that Verity could almost see the spell forming.

A sudden wind whispered over the dock, and sweat gleamed on Lady E's brow. No small feat, manipulating weather.

But the man's hood slithered back from his brow and he cursed under his breath as the wind died down.

Lady E froze and knelt back down behind the crate. She clearly knew him.

Who? Verity mouthed.

"It's definitely Horroway," Lady E breathed back.

Bishop had been right.

Lady E held out her hand and gestured for her to take it. Verity accepted it, and suddenly Lady E was pushing inside her head.

It was instinctive to push back: Verity had never felt like this before, but she held herself back and allowed the psychic touch.

"*Horroway's dead himself,*" Lady E told her. "*Uses some sort of elixir to keep his soul tied to the flesh, and he jumps from body to body every month or two. I can never forget those eyes, that aura.... He's been banned from the Order for over ten years, and there's a warrant on his head. Sometimes the bodies he takes are not empty before he commandeers them. Nobody has ever caught him, however.*"

She didn't know how to link back, so she mouthed, "Dangerous?"

Lady E nodded. "*Unknown range of skill, which makes anyone dangerous. Linked to the Chalice? Extremely dangerous. I was hoping it wouldn't be him.*"

"Now what?" Verity whispered.

Lady E shot another glance over the crates. "*Let's see if I can distract him.*"

With a whisk of power, a sudden clatter sprang up toward the entrance to the dock. Horroway turned that way, body erect like a hound on the scent. Verity could see shadows rippling: three of them. They looked like they were running. The only giveaway was the fact they didn't stir the fog, but in the heat of the moment she thought that might have been missed.

With a snap of the fingers, Horroway strode toward the shadows as they ducked into an alley, taking five of the flesh constructs with him. They lumbered after him steadily, focused on the shadows in an eerie, one-track way.

"This way, child." Lady Eberhardt's grip was like a manacle, so it wasn't really as though Verity had any choice in the matter.

"What are we going to do?" she whispered to the old woman. "There are dozens of them inside that place!"

"Yes." Lady Eberhardt looked grim as they scurried behind another section of crates at the back of the building. "That mewling, piss-poor excuse for a sorc—" She blanched all of a sudden, sucking in a sharp breath and pressing her hand to her chest.

"Are you all right?" Lady Eberhardt didn't look it. "Perhaps we should return to the house? I'll come back later, and—"

Stubbornness etched its mark on the older woman's face. She flexed her left arm several times, shaking her hand. "I'm fine. It will take more than a little pain to stop me in my tracks. Now stop your dillydallying and strap on your breeches, girl. There's too much to be done, and not enough people to do it. If we deal with Horroway and the Chalice now...."

Verity bit her lip. Lady Eberhardt was still far too pale for her liking, but what could she do? The old battle-axe would simply ignore her advice and tow her into battle.

Peering over the crates, they watched the ring of flesh constructs guarding the Chalice before bobbing back down. It was easier to see from here, as the doors hung halfway open.

"Stealth," Lady Eberhardt said, "is preferable to direct confrontation in this circumstance."

"Agreed."

"And we have only moments before Horroway comes back. Can you get in and steal the Chalice before they notice?"

Verity glanced over the crates once more. "I could get in and out easy enough, but what concerns me is what I might not be seeing. I usually prefer a little more reconnaissance before I infiltrate a potential trap."

"I can deal with any wards that Horroway might have set," Lady E told her, and began rolling up her sleeves. "Quickly, Verity. If anything goes wrong, you make your way back to my house. Can you do that?"

Verity nodded.

"Off you go then."

The Veil dropped from around them and Verity tore through time and space, the world rushing back into being as she landed in the building directly in front of the Chalice.

The relic gleamed bronze, standing about a foot high where it rested on a crate. There was something not quite right about it.

A ring of flesh constructs stood around her, but they all had their backs to her, as though they were expecting the threat to come from without.

Verity circled the Chalice. Nothing that she could see. Not directly. Biting her lip, she reached out, grabbed the Chalice, and then translocated out of there.

Or at least, that had been her intention.

Something hooked at her, like a magical hand grasping the collar of her dress, and she slammed back into real time and space, directly into the back of one of the constructs.

A spark of green light appeared above the crate and a shimmering dome of vivid green formed, trapping her on the inside and the flesh constructs on the outside. The one she'd crashed into turned and looked at her but it couldn't push through the shimmering ward. Thank goodness for small mercies.

So far the ward wasn't doing anything. Just keeping her inside. Testing the ward again earned her nothing more than an abrupt slam back into her body. Damn it.

What the hell was Lady E doing? She'd promised to deal with the wards!

Sorcery crackled. Red light shimmered into a dome around her and then a ring of gold sparks began eating away at the bottom of the dome, slowly lifting—

"Come on!" Verity whispered, eyeing the flesh constructs that circled the dome. The second it was gone she was out of there.

"Who's there?" called a hollow, cadaverous voice.

Verity ducked low, her heart rabbiting in her chest. Horroway had returned, no doubt sensing the ignition of his ward.

The constructs moved aside for him, barely paying her any attention at all. Horroway paused in front of her, his mouth slightly slack and his eyebrows drawing together.

"Who the hell are you?" he demanded. "You ain't who I were expectin'."

Anytime you'd care to intervene, Lady E.... Verity steeled herself. "Would you believe I belong to Dock Security Authority?"

His gaze dropped to the Chalice tucked under her arm. "You stink of sorcery, my dear. One o' the Prime's little rats?" He chuckled, glancing down at the ward that was slowly lifting. "Certainly trapped like one. The second that lifts, they're comin' in."

Verity swallowed, glancing at the decaying constructs around her. The odor was definitely starting to penetrate now the ward was halfway to her shoulders. One of them moaned, pushing against the ward. She drew in power, waiting for the moment the magic keeping her trapped failed. "Well, they can come in. I'm certainly not hanging around to wait for them."

With a crackle and a fizz, the ward evaporated.

Verity punched through time and space, taking the Chalice with her. Landing lightly on her toes, she caught Lady E's hand. "Come on! They won't take long to realize what happened!"

She turned, but there was a gasp behind her and a heavy weight pulled at her.

"Lady E?" Verity turned back to the woman.

The old woman really did look quite dreadful, clutching a hand to her chest, her face bearing the strain. "Go!" Lady E gasped. "Get the Chalice... to Bishop." With a low moan, she bent over, shaking as she caught at a crate to hold herself up.

"I'm not leaving you here!" The flesh constructs would be on them at any moment. "What's wrong?"

"I'm having a bloody angina attack," the woman shot back, clutching her wrist with an iron claw hold. "Leave me here. The Chalice is more important." Some emotion tore at her expression. "Give my love to Adrian. And Marie."

Verity didn't know what to do. This was all going wrong. "If you think that I'm going to return to Adrian without you—"

"You'll do what you're bloody well told—" Lady E gasped again, sinking lower to the ground.

Bloody rotting hells! Verity knelt beside her. This was outside her realm of experience. She was a thief, not a Healer. And Horroway wouldn't take long to come looking for them. She stared at the Chalice. Even now, its magic churned green, wisps of hazy fog crawling over its bronze lip and creeping toward the warehouse. Horroway would track them for sure.

But how could she leave Lady E? What would Bishop do if she returned without his beloved mentor? And how could she leave a friend here to suffer the fate that terrified Verity to her very bones?

No.

"I'm not leaving you here," she told the woman, her resolve firming. "And you can curse me the entire time, but I think it best if you just focus on breathing."

"You bloody—"

"Breathe, Agatha," Verity insisted. "And shut up and let me concentrate!"

She'd never translocated someone else with her. Only objects.

You can do it. Come on. But her heart knew the risk. What if she made a mistake, and Lady E arrived... in two separate pieces?

Well, the only other option is to leave her here to be devoured. Which was not an option at all, not with that low moan growing louder as the flesh constructs shuffled toward them.

But neither was getting the woman to Bishop. Verity needed a Healer, and she needed to go somewhere she knew well, to increase the chances of this working. By herself she might risk a blind jump, but not whilst carrying someone else.

The image of her room at the Crows formed in her mind. It was her base location, the one place she could always find, ingrained as it was in her consciousness, in her body. Power tingled through her as she drew in as much as she could handle, and locked her arms around the older woman in preparation.

She just hoped that Mercy was there.

And that Daniel Guthrie wasn't.

Verity hit the floor hard, her entire body stretched and raw in places. She felt certain someone had punched her in the sternum, driving the breath out of her, and the very thought of summoning her powers at the moment made her want to retch.

But it had worked. Hadn't it? She'd carried Lady E's weight the entire time, feeling it pulling at her, growing heavier with every microsecond.

A gasping wheeze brought her back to herself. Verity scrambled to Lady E's side, the Chalice tumbling abandoned to the timber floors that she knew so well. Its magic had cut off abruptly during the leap, the link to Horroway vanishing. "Lady E?"

The woman couldn't answer. Sweat soured her hair and she gasped faintly, her fist clenched against her chest.

No time to lose then.

Verity dragged a pillow off her bed and stuffed it under Lady E's head. "I'm going to get help. I promise I won't be long."

She dragged herself to her feet and nearly went top over toes as her knees quivered. That had taken more out of her than she'd imagined.

Steps echoed in the hallway outside the bedchamber she used to share with Mercy. Verity froze, slipping the small knife she kept up her sleeve into her palm.

The door opened—

And Mercy slipped inside, shutting it behind her so swiftly that the light barely penetrated.

"Sweet Jesus, Verity, what are you doing here?" Mercy hissed, wearing her familiar boots and trousers. "If Daniel realizes you're here...."

He'd have her right where he wanted her.

Verity shook the thought away. "You felt me?"

"I do ward our rooms," Mercy replied, then her gaze fell on Lady E's crumpled form and she strode warily to the fallen woman's side. "What happened? Who is she?"

"Angina, I think. Can you heal her? Can you stop the attack?" Verity hovered over the pair of them as Mercy reached out and pressed her fingertips to Lady E's chest. A faint blue glow surrounded her hand.

"Verity, she's dying." Mercy withdrew her touch with a flinch.

"No. No, she can't." Bishop would be devastated and God blast the old harridan, but Verity had begun to like her. "Can't you do something? You can heal. I know you can heal—"

"I can heal cuts, scrapes and broken bones," Mercy shot back, "but not this." Her eyes grew vague as she lost herself in the inner workings of Lady E's heart. "It's so complicated and I'm not entirely certain what to do. There's... some kind of blockage and it's stopping the heart from pumping blood through it. Plus, there's some bleeding there, as though the muscle has torn."

Lady E gasped, her face turning a most alarming shade of gray. But somehow she managed to lash out and catch Mercy's wrist. "Patch it... up." Those dark eyes flickered toward Verity. "Get me... Bishop."

"Can you do that?" Verity asked, taking a step back and hovering indecisively. With the lock of hair that she carried she could find him and travel there, now that she wasn't burdened with another.

If she had enough strength left in her.

Mercy frowned, that blue glow widening around her hand. Lady E sucked in a sharp breath as Mercy set to work. "I'm trying to stop the bleeding," Mercy muttered. "Stop pacing. You're distracting me."

"I'm—"

The door thumped open. "What have we here?" Betsy demanded, backlit by the light in the hallway. The old procuress's eyes narrowed with triumph as they locked on Verity. "Trespassers by the look of it."

Darting a glance at the forsaken Chalice, Verity took a step toward it just as Betsy lashed out with the braided whip she carried at her side. Verity flickered out of the way, landing near the window, but Betsy was ready for her and the whip cracked across her cheek with a brutal lash of fire.

Damn it. Her gaze landed on the Chalice again, which was a mistake. Betsy flicked the whip, wrapping the end around the Chalice and then jerking it toward her. The old bawd held it up triumphantly. "Looking for this, Verity?"

"That's mine!"

"We shall see." Betsy smirked, and her attention shifted as footsteps thundered in the hallway behind her. The Crows, no doubt, alert to strange sorcery in their domain.

Verity was outnumbered and outpowered, but for the first time in her life she had allies. The Crows might have been a place where she could blend in and hide, but they'd never been family. Not truly.

Verity exchanged a look with Mercy, wary but not defeated. "Keep her alive." And then she sucked in her power, stuttering faintly as weariness pulled at her bones, and vanished.

CHAPTER TWENTY-ONE

"DRAKE'S ALIVE AND well," Ianthe murmured, seeing Bishop to the door. "And I intend to keep it that way. I'm sorry that I called you out of bed. In the panic I wasn't certain if it was just the one person attempting to breach the wards, or whether there were more and they were simply testing our defenses."

"Don't apologize. We're in this together," Bishop replied. "And you have your daughter to worry about now, as well as Rathbourne."

"Lucien," she insisted.

He still felt uncomfortable referring to his half-brother by his given name. "I'll do one last check of the grounds before I leave, but don't hesitate to call upon me if anything else happens."

Bishop slid his hands into his pockets as he stepped out onto the front porch. A failed attempt at getting through Drake's wards, but an attempt nonetheless. He stared into the gardens, hunting through the shadows. *I know you're out there*. But who? Kali? Or Thanatos? Or Osiris?

Ianthe followed on his heels, closing the door gently behind her. "Any sign of the Chalice?"

He knew what stirred her concern. The demon had intended to possess her husband as its vessel, and came very close to it. *Your brother*. "No sign as of yet, but I feel like our web is tightening. Horroway's our main suspect. We'll find him."

"Do you have any idea why he would want it?" Ianthe drew her shawl tight around her shoulders. "We might have destroyed the Blade of Altarrh, but if Morgana is involved with the Chalice's theft, then what, precisely, is she up to now?"

"Hell if I know. Unless she plans to unleash an army of flesh constructs upon London? Force the government and the Queen to turn their backs upon the Order? Disgrace us? Or send them to destroy us?"

"She's never wanted the Order's destruction before," Ianthe said. "She's always wanted to rule it and destroy Drake."

"Plans change. We *did* drop a house on her head. Maybe she's peeved?"

"Maybe." Ianthe didn't look convinced. "I can't help thinking that Ascension is only a few days away now. If she wanted a chance at the seat of the Prime, then it's virtually hers for the taking."

Bishop glanced sideways. He knew what Agatha thought should happen in regards to the mantle of Prime, but he wasn't certain what Ianthe thought. Hell. Perhaps now was not the time for politeness if Morgana was alive and the demon was still out there. Perhaps now they all needed to begin working together. "Are you going to take a tilt at it?"

Ianthe scowled. "Not you too."

"You *are* the perfect candidate," he pointed out. "You have Drake behind you, and years of experience as his seneschal, dealing with all his dirty work. You know the Order inside and out—"

"Are you going to do anything about your attraction to young Verity?" Ianthe countered.

Bishop fell silent. It... bothered him a little that matters were so transparent. "That's really none of your business."

"My point precisely."

"It's not the same." He held a hand up when she moved to argue. "We're on the same team. You, me, and... Lucien. Right now Drake's barely any help at all, as inclined as he is to stick his head in the sand. And if the three of us cannot join forces, then what happens to the Order? You want me to be blunt, Ianthe? Ascension is three days away, as you say. Someone's going to end up sitting on the Prime's chair at the end of it. Now whether that someone is Morgana and her puppet, you, or one of a half dozen other candidates, is up to you. Your husband seems reluctant to put his hand up and I'm fairly certain I know why." He'd seen the ruin of his brother's aura a month ago, after all. It was healing slowly, but a Prime needed to be invulnerable. "I'm an assassin and I don't have the experience, the skill set, or the aptitude to rule. Which leaves you. Could you sit back and watch Morgana rule? Could you sit back and watch the Earl of Tremayne rule? He's still out there, after all. And he's no friend to either of us. If someone else sits on that chair, then Drake's life remains at stake, and you will no longer have any say in the running of the Order. Can you do that?"

Frustration sparked in Ianthe's blue eyes. "What about Lady Eberhardt?"

"Not interested," he replied, "and quite frankly, her health worries me."

Silence settled over the pair of them.

"I know you've only just gotten your daughter back in your life," he continued. "I know you nearly lost her and Lucien. I also know that you're the best option—the only option—that we've got."

At that her shoulders slumped. "You sound remarkably like your brother at times."

Hope flared. "Lucien thinks you should do this too?"

Ianthe rubbed at her temples, her skirts swishing as she rested her hip against the balcony. "He thinks everything we risked our lives to achieve last month will be destroyed if I don't."

"Then you have Drake on your side, your husband, Lady Eberhardt... and me."

Ianthe smiled sadly. "Thank you."

"But...?" He could sense that she still held reservations.

"If I do this," she whispered, "then a great deal of scrutiny will fall upon me and my past. Upon Louisa."

Ah. That was what was holding her back. Louisa might have been Lucien's, but there would always be whispers about her birth. "Your husband has formally adopted her as his own. She has both of you to fight at her side. And we're sorcerers, Ianthe. Her illegitimacy is never going to go away, but we accept all as equal within the Order. After all, I'm a bastard too. It's never stopped me."

"That's not all. If I do this," she continued, and he realized that this last confession was the true crux of the problem, "then I'm going to end up facing my father head-on."

Bishop racked his brain. Nothing came to mind. "And your father is—?"

"Sir Grant Martin."

Hell. He suddenly understood her reluctance. "The Head of the Vigilance Against Sorcery Committee."

"The very same."

They stared at each other.

"He despises me for what I am," Ianthe pointed out. "If I do this, then VASC will come after us with everything they have. He won't rest until the Order—and I—are destroyed."

Sir Grant Martin had been lobbying parliament for over a decade to see sorcery declared illegal, and in the past few years had taken his cause to the streets to rouse the common people. Parliament held firm. After all, the sorcerers who served as Servants to the Empire were too important to the crown and its expansion plans. But the people....

When things went wrong in the lives of the poor and uneducated—mysterious accidents, illnesses, houses catching fire—most people needed to point the finger somewhere. Martin had been very successful in using that superstition and ill will to make headway among the populace. Some even suspected his handful of loyal followers set fires themselves.

Bishop frowned. It *was* a problem. One that might affect them all. "He's already working against us."

"If I become Prime, I can guarantee that those efforts will triple, at the very least."

"Do you want me to take care of the situation?" It wasn't an option lightly offered.

Ianthe stared at him, hunger lighting her blue eyes momentarily before she shook her head. "Good God, listen to us. Plotting murder. I'm not even in the chair yet."

"Yet."

Ianthe pushed away from the balcony. "That's enough. The Sicarii were formed to protect the Order, mostly from threats within. Not to annihilate those who *might* become a problem. If we take that step, then where does it end?"

Bishop scrubbed at his mouth. She was right. And he wasn't entirely certain if the offer had come from pure cold-blooded practicality, or from that never-ending itch that shifted beneath his skin. *Death*, the *maladroise* whispered. *Power*. He could practically feel the rush of that assassination whispering at him, like some devil breathing temptation.

"I'll consider what you've said, and... think about the VASC problem," Ianthe finally said. "I don't think it needs to—"

Something slammed into the house wards.

Bishop stepped in front of Ianthe, his etheric blades springing to life in his hands.

A flicker, then a woman fell onto the lawn. A tumble of skirts. Chestnut hair. Pale skin. His heart kicked inside his chest. "Verity?"

He vanished the blades as he sprinted toward her. She moved with a groggy groan, and relief flowed through him. Why was she here? What had happened? He glanced around, but nothing seemed to have followed her.

And what was wrong with her? Why wasn't she getting up?

"Verity?" he demanded, sliding to his knees beside her in the gravel. "What's wrong? What happened?"

Lady Rathbourne was but a second behind him.

"Oh, God." Verity lifted her head, saw him, then collapsed back down weakly. "Those are very strong wards. I slammed right into them."

Bishop helped her to sit up, fussing with her skirts and brushing strands of honey-brown hair out of her eyes. There was a smudge of dirt on her cheek. "Why are you here? Where's Agatha?"

She swayed alarmingly. "I'm—"

"Here," Ianthe murmured, catching Verity's face in both her hands. A soft glow warmed her fingertips, and then Verity managed to straighten as Ianthe fed her some of her own vitality. "You've burned too much energy. Didn't you feel the warning signs?"

"She's Hex," he muttered to Ianthe. "Self-taught, mostly."

They shared a look.

"That's better," Verity said, touching her head. Color washed back into her cheeks. "Thank you."

He helped her to her feet, still fussing. Verity was so self-assured, so strong and confident. He didn't like seeing her like this.

"Bishop, we need to get to Seven Dials as soon as we can! Lady E's heart is giving her problems. I think I can take you with me."

"Agatha's what?" he demanded, snuffing out the magic that she tried to weave around him. "And stop that, you've barely gotten your feet back under you again. You're not ready to make another jump so soon!"

"She's dying!" For the first time he saw fear in her eyes, and then they glistened with tears. "I have to get you there right now, or it might be too late!"

No matter how deeply he felt those words, he clasped hands with her. "Not by yourself," he said, pushing aside all of the fear he felt for his mentor. "Link with me. You use my energy and all of the power I can draw into myself while I act as a wellspring."

A single tear slid down her cheek, but she nodded and swallowed hard. "How?"

Bishop reached out toward her psychically. "Can you feel me reaching for you?" Verity nodded, and he opened up to her. "Accept the link. Let me in."

There was a fumbling touch against his psychic offering. Verity tried, but her shields were fully engaged, her mind locked down so tightly that he could see years of abuse behind it. Years of mistrust.

"Do you trust me, Ver?" he whispered.

"Y-yes. Of course I do."

That inner core of protection remained, however. He knew not to take it personally. From the little she'd told him, and from what he'd seen, she'd led a tough life. Opening herself up to trust was difficult, and went against every instinct she most likely owned.

"Then accept the bond." He leaned down and brushed his lips against hers, the faintest of touches. "Let me in, so that I can help you."

Her breath caught and she kissed him back. Her last remaining shields fell, one by one, until she bloomed suddenly within him, her mind brushing up against his.

For a moment he was lost in the exhilarating feel of her as they linked. Verity didn't have the experience to shield her thoughts here, and he caught the edge of some of them. She was pure hope, despite the fact that she'd been beaten down so many times. Fear for Agatha danced through her veins; curiosity about this new type of spell craft; a hunger for learning; and... a throat-filling, tremulous desire for him that extended beyond simple lust.

He almost broke the kiss at the shock of that realization.

In those odd moments at night when he'd wondered what sex would be like, he'd thought of this. Of two people merging, their breaths and dreams filling each other, until each body was but an extension of the other, each soul just another missing piece that finally fit together.

It was breathtaking to experience it. To understand his wildest imaginings could not even come close to the reality of the experience. Simply stunning to conceive that in this moment he was not alone, that the *maladroise* had no hold on him—none at all—and that the possibility of forever stretched ahead of them.

Them. Not just him. He didn't think he could ever think of himself separately anymore.

"Like that?" Verity breathed, withdrawing from their kiss, her eyes shining with surprise and delight.

"Just like that," he said, and smiled at her, feeling like they were alone in the world. "Now, use my strength and take us to Agatha."

The landing was smoother this time. He knew this, because some part of her noted it as they sprang back into being in a small bedroom with a pair of beds. No stomach-jarring jolt like when they'd escaped from Balthazar's Labyrinth.

One of the beds had a crocheted pink blanket laid lovingly across the bottom half, and there was a well-used toy cat stuffed with wool. Gifts from Maggie Henderson, who'd had the keeping of her in the workhouse. Her thought, not his. And sent only because she'd noticed the direction his gaze turned.

She was picking up thoughts from him, and he from her.

Bishop cleared his throat as he caught flashes of memory from her: a dark, grimy workhouse; hundreds of ill-washed bodies; cold, always cold; and a pit of hunger so deep in his stomach that he feared he'd never fill it. A little girl cried out, *"Mama, please!"* as she tried to shake the cold, still body of a woman in a narrow bed. *"Please wake up!"*

Jesus. He clutched at her shoulder, feeling her grief inside him like a fist of cold in his gut. Orphaned early, the pair of them. Only he had discovered a father much later, a strange gift that he'd never fully embraced.

They stared at each other. "I'm sorry," he said, feeling her loneliness and knowing it intimately.

Verity shrugged sadly. "So am I."

And he dulled the brief glimpses she'd caught of his thoughts of Drake.

It would be difficult to concentrate when they were linked so explicitly. "I can keep the line between us open," he said, "but I need to withdraw. I'm getting tangled in your thoughts."

"Probably a good idea," she replied.

The pair of them withdrew to a respectable distance, though he could still feel her on the edges of his consciousness.

"Guthrie's room is this way," she said, and strode for the door. "He has the Chalice."

"What?"

Verity hurried to explain, detailing her little side excursion with Agatha. He could have wrung both their necks. What had Agatha been thinking?

"I managed to get her back here, but only because this place is so ingrained in my consciousness. I can't quite explain it. I can leap blindly as far as I can see, or within a certain distance, but I have to know a place intimately to make a massive leap. I don't think I've spent enough time at your house, and I worried that I'd leave part of her behind if I tried."

He sensed the worry in her voice, and the guilt. "It's fine, Ver. You did better than expected considering the circumstances. We'll get her back."

And the Chalice.

"So how do we play this?" he asked.

"What do you want more? The Chalice? Or Agatha?"

"That's not even a question."

She nodded, looking relieved. "Agatha then. Guthrie will make us pay dearly if he can, but he won't give us both. Not yet. If we get Agatha to safety, I might be able to come back and steal the Chalice."

"We," he corrected.

She blinked, then nodded. "We. Here we are."

Rapping on the door earned swift attention. The tall, dark-skinned man opened the door, his eyes carefully narrowed when he saw who was there.

"Why, it's our Ver and her... friend," Conrad muttered back into the room.

"By all means," called Daniel Guthrie, "send them in."

Bishop was swiftly starting to despise the owner of that voice. The coursing chill of the *maladroise* slid through his veins like a lover's call: *Kill him now and you get both Agatha* and *the Chalice.*

Common sense said that they'd be prepared for him now. And Bishop had two potential casualties standing nearby. If he were in their shoes, he'd strike at Agatha or Verity first. Possibly both. And not even Bishop could cast wards to protect all three of them at the same time.

"Ah, my sweet Verity, returned to the fold," Guthrie mocked.

"You have something we want," Verity said.

Bishop's gaze went directly to Agatha, who lay recumbent on the daybed in the far corner of the room with the assassin girl sitting by her side, holding her hand. Fear shook him. Agatha had always seemed invincible. He simply couldn't comprehend what life would be like if she... wasn't.

Bishop took three steps toward her then froze as Conrad pushed away from the wall, stepping between them.

"Uh, uh, uh," Guthrie called, sinking into the chair behind his desk. "A sorceress of the Order stepped onto our turf, which means she belongs to me now."

Agatha? He sent the psychic touch toward her but she only flinched and waved him off with a hand, the other pressed over her eyes.

"I've done what I can," said the assassin girl. "It's not much but she'll survive another hour or two."

"Which gives us plenty of time to negotiate her release... or not." Guthrie smiled pleasantly.

"You little pissant, Guthrie." Verity snarled. "There are rules! We don't go up against the Order."

"Rules change," Guthrie said flatly. "Murphy's no longer in charge here and I think the Crows deserve to have a little bigger slice of the pie."

"You're making a mistake," Bishop told him.

Daniel Guthrie laced his fingers together, looking triumphant as the old procuress beside him settled the Chalice on the desk on front of Guthrie. It gleamed, but Bishop tore his gaze off it as it began whispering to him. Hell. They had no idea what they held in their midst.

"Magical object like that.... Oh, it looks like it'll fetch a good pound or two on the black market," Guthrie said.

"You don't know what kind of forces you're dealing with." Bishop ground his teeth together.

"The Order's been breathing down our necks for years," Guthrie shot back. "I think I know what they can do. And what they can pay."

"I wasn't talking about the Order." Bishop took a threatening step forward but Guthrie clicked his fingers.

Everybody in the room turned stiff with anticipation.

"If he twitches one finger in my direction, Mercy-lass, then you sink one of your magical shivs straight through the old broad's heart." Guthrie's shark smile stretched as he looked back at Bishop. "Do you understand?"

Bishop had never felt so helpless. He could snuff the young assassin in an instant, but she was both innocent and Verity's friend. Verity would never forgive him and Bishop didn't kill women unless he couldn't avoid it.

"Understood," she replied in a flat, distant voice.

"Then it seems you're at somewhat of a disadvantage." Guthrie was thrilled by this, and barely managing to contain it. "I have something you want—two somethings, by the way—and you have something I want." His gaze slithered past Bishop and alighted on Verity.

"No." Not her. She belonged to him.

Kill him, the *maladroise* whispered. *Squeeze his heart in his chest and drink in the power of his death.* It wouldn't even be that difficult. He wanted it. The *maladroise* wanted it. He could almost imagine the power of that death exploding through his body, igniting every one of his nerves, and leaving him a veritable God. Invincible. Unstoppable.

"Actually, I think we have two things you want," Verity said, stepping past him to lean on the desk. "And they're not the ones you think."

Thank God. Bishop was sweating with the need to destroy this gnat. It was all he could do to rein it in.

"Pray tell, Verity-lass." Guthrie smiled, toying with a pair of coins on his desk. "I always did like your brash heart, but I know when you're bluffing."

"The problem, you see, is that what you're holding in your hand is a very powerful object and unfortunately we're not the only ones who want it."

"Sounds like we've got a couple of buyers then. You're not convincing me, Ver."

"You're still thinking of this in terms of coin, Guthrie, but those who want this item don't think like that." Verity settled on the edge of the desk. "They had it in their hands and I stole it right out from under their noses." She tugged the edge of her sleeve back, revealing the crow tattooed on the back of her hand. "And I made sure that they saw this."

"We're surrounded by Hex witches. If someone wants it back then they'll doff their caps and come in all polite like."

"You're surrounded by flesh and blood, Guthrie. I wonder how long that can hold up against a wave of flesh constructs, the like of which attacked the Dials the other day, hmm?"

Bishop shook off the lingering effects of the *maladroise*. "And I wonder what the rest of the Seven Dials would think of that? You, playing so callously with their lives."

Verity shot him a brilliant smile. "Why don't we ask them, Bishop? I wonder what the faction leaders would think of Guthrie's play then? And his deliberate disregard of the Code."

Leather strained as Guthrie half stood. "You little bitch. You'd have to get to them first." He snapped a finger, and both Conrad and Betsy brandished weapons. Conrad slid a crackling glove of shimmering light over his fist, and Betsy snapped a whip that lashed with power.

Verity planted herself in the middle of the room, her arms crossed. "And just how do you think you're going to contain me?"

"Merce," Guthrie said flatly.

There was a tense moment. "No," Mercy said, uncoiling her lanky frame from the corner. "I'll do a lot of things, Daniel, but I won't lift a hand against Ver."

Guthrie's expression of disbelief collided with anger. "You'll bloody do what you're told to do, or—"

"Or what?" Mercy faced him down, then held up a hand and clenched her fingers. Guthrie gasped, hunching over himself with his eyes bulging. "I had the means to watch Mr. Bishop here the other day... and it seems I've managed to add to my repertoire. The Crows have always done all right by me and I'll do my best by them, but don't you think that you can force me to betray my heart-sister."

She suddenly released Guthrie, and the man's knees hit the floor.

"You little bitch," Guthrie breathed.

"So it seems we're at an impasse," Bishop told him. "You have something I want, and you can't stop me from taking it."

"I presume you mean the old sorceress," Mercy interrupted, flashing those vivid green eyes at him. "Because while I might not kill Verity, I never said anything about you."

He looked at her, but Verity grabbed his arm and stepped between them. "Don't you dare!"

"I wouldn't," he murmured. "I know she means a great deal to you."

Verity's shoulders relaxed, and she faced her friend. "Mercy, I never wanted it to come to this."

"Me either." The girl smiled faintly. "But we've both got our paths in life to tread. You're always welcome in my room."

"You can't keep Lady E," Verity said. "She's not an object, and we need to heal her."

"And you can't take this little antique," Guthrie snapped, sliding the Chalice closer to himself, his gaze taking a slow trip over Verity's body. "Not without meeting my price."

Over my dead body.

She must have heard it through the link. Verity rested her hand on his wrist.

"That's not an option either, Daniel," she said firmly. "So until you can work out another price, the Chalice remains here. Do try not to get eaten by flesh constructs before we can retrieve it."

She crossed to Agatha's side and gestured for Bishop to pick her up. "Be gentle."

Guthrie didn't like it. But he said nothing as Bishop swung Agatha up into his arms. She was more skirts than body at this moment. He hadn't realized how thin she'd become.

"I've got you," he whispered.

Agatha rested her head on his shoulder, and just like that, relief flooded through him. He didn't dare reach out to her through their apprentice-mentor link, but he could feel her.

"This way," Verity said, opening the door for him.

He swung Agatha through gently as Verity glared over his shoulder. "We'll be back, Guthrie."

"I'm counting on it." The Hex leader smirked.

"Knock, knock," Verity called, rapping on the open door to Lady Eberhardt's room.

The old woman looked frail against the sheets of her bed, her long gray hair laid across her pillows where Marie was brushing it. With a frustrated grimace, Lady Eberhardt waved her secretary away and tried to drag herself into a seated position.

"Adrian said you mustn't exert yourself," Marie chastised, discarding the brush as she rushed to help her employer.

"If I can't bloody well sit myself up in bed, then I may as well be dead," Lady Eberhardt snapped. "God's blood,

I'm not an invalid. I spent over three hundred days tracking that demon through the Cairo slums! I've been thrown into prisons, barely escaped a bloody harem, and survived three husbands! I'm a sorcerer of the eighth bloody level! A little heart murmur isn't going to stop me."

"A little heart *murmur*? Adrian said you'd nearly ruptured your coronary artery. And you've aged since then! That all happened years ago!" Marie shot back.

"I'm no less of a woman for the fact that there's forty years added to the tally. Enough of this mollycoddling. I've had enough!"

Marie's lips thinned and she stepped back, shoulders squared. "Then go ahead, and see yourself into an early grave. It's not as though I should care, is it?" Tears gleamed in her eyes, but she spun toward the door, trying to hide them. "I shall send Maxwell up with some nice chamomile tea for poor Verity. She, at least, has earned it."

She didn't quite slam the door after her.

Lady Eberhardt stared at the shut door, mouth agape and her hand outstretched before realizing. Spearing Verity with a gimlet eye, she fussed with her blankets, muttering under her breath whilst trying to pretend that she wasn't staring after Marie.

"It's all right," Verity said, taking the old woman's hand and sitting on the edge of the bed. Certain relationships were becoming quite clear to her. "Adrian's the same. Spitting like a tomcat backed into an alley whilst proclaiming that he hasn't a worry in the world." Her tone softened, and she stroked the paper-thin skin on the back of Lady Eberhardt's hand. "You gave everyone quite a fright. They're only worried about you."

Including me. It was only afterwards, when the excitement of the action wore off, that Verity had collapsed in tears. Not only had she lost the Chalice, but she'd nearly killed Adrian's beloved master.

"Where is he?" Lady E asked.

"Resting. Healing you took quite a bit out of him." Verity bit her lip. Their link had faded now, but she still remembered traces of what she'd felt. While Bishop held himself walled back, odd impressions had leeched through when he was concentrating more on healing Lady E rather than keeping her out.

He'd been scared while he'd healed his mentor. Not scared of losing Lady E, but scared of pushing too much, of taking too much.

Verity didn't know what to think about it.

Lady Eberhardt stared into space. "I'm getting old," she whispered. "And there's so much still to do, but here I am, helpless as a newborn babe."

"Nonsense." Verity pushed her dark thoughts aside. "If I'm as spry and hearty at your age as you are, then I'll be considerably pleased with myself. You might have aged, but you're not old, my lady. And perhaps you should stop thinking of yourself as Hercules, facing the tasks all by himself. A wise general commands his troops and sets them to running to and fro. He doesn't do all of the work himself."

Lady Eberhardt harrumphed. "Don't think I can't see right through you. You're trying to manage me, missy. I can still give you a thump around the ears if I want to."

"We'll see." Verity teleported across the room, landing by the window. "I can translocate and you can't."

Lady Eberhardt shimmered with power and then something invisible swatted Verity across the fleshy pad of her ear. "Ow!"

The other woman arched a supercilious brow.

Rubbing her ear, Verity crossed to the bed. "Well, it's good to see some things haven't changed."

"Are you referring to a certain young man I might know?" Lady E settled back against her pillows like a demanding pasha.

"Perhaps." Clearly Lady E wanted to forget about her own problems, and for once Verity was happy to allow her probing. "Bishop's... struggling."

"In what way?"

"I felt something strange when we were linked." Verity frowned. "It was a horrible feeling, like dark clouds hanging over the pair of us, threatening to consume us at any chance. But it felt heavy too. Like a weight on our shoulders."

"Have you spoken to him about it?"

Verity lowered her gaze. "He won't let me in." Not fully. As soon as he'd felt her wondering about his feelings earlier, he'd cut off their link sharply.

"He's afraid," Lady Eberhardt admitted, patting her hand as if she were the one comforting Verity. "You remind him very much of Mya and all that he's lost. But don't think you're not important to him. I'm neither blind, nor a fool. Adrian likes you very much."

Verity stared at Lady E. "Mya?"

Lady E's face froze.

And suddenly it all made sense. "There was a woman he loved, wasn't there?" Verity breathed. "And he hurt her."

"Damn it," Lady E cursed. "Yes. Though she wasn't a woman. Barely a girl. Her name was Mya, and she was Burmese. I'd assumed he'd told you."

"Did he love her?" Verity asked, swallowing hard.

"I'm not certain if it ever blossomed into love." Lady E's eyes watched her cannily. "He was fifteen and there was an entire Empire between them. But... it could have become more," Lady E conceded. "If Adrian weren't so afraid to let himself be with her."

"What happened?"

"Is he afraid to touch you, Verity?"

Heat speared through her cheeks, but she hadn't been raised in the Dials for nothing. "Sometimes he forgets himself, but... yes. He's very concerned about losing control of his power. I thought he didn't approve of me at first."

That eyebrow arched again. "Oh, he approves of you. That was evident from the start. In fact, I think he's moved past approval and straight into yearning. But there are complications for Adrian, some of them ones that he's forced upon himself. Verity, what do you know of the Grave Arts?"

"There are sorcerers who are drawn to the darker aspects of life," she replied promptly. "My friend Mercy. And Bishop, and clearly this Horroway man."

"Who's the oldest Grave Arts sorcerer that you've ever encountered?"

"It's—" She racked her brain. "I don't know. Probably Horroway."

"Who's been dead for almost seven years."

A little tingle of nervousness latched on to her stomach. "What are you trying to say?"

"Every time Adrian kills, he feels the full force of the death blow rush through him. He thrives on it, lives for it, yearns for it. And with every kill, the rush becomes sweeter and the yearning stronger. That's the heavy sensation you felt hovering over him. Most Grave sorcerers only last forty or fifty years before the yearning becomes too strong and they start to kill too often, or even resort to murder. Some find respite by helping the dying to their rest. Sometimes it's enough to stave it off a few more years."

"But Adrian can't do that," Verity whispered. "He hates the idea of sitting like a vulture at someone's bedside."

Lady Eberhardt's expression grew carefully neutral. "Did he ever tell you why?"

"I suspect it has something to do with his mother's death."

"Partly. Amelia Bishop was his first encounter with sorcery. She was tending to the grate one night when Adrian was ill with the sweats. He was cold and his mother would have done anything to make him more comfortable, but on this particular night, a spark leapt from the grate and caught fire in her dress. By the time she and Adrian beat the flames out she was very badly burned. Adrian still bears the burn scars on his hands and face." Lady Eberhardt looked inwards again. "This was before either of them knew anything of sorcery. There was no way to heal her and the pain she was in... it was quite unendurable, I'm told. She survived. That's the best that can be said of the whole matter. But sometimes death is a kinder mistress than bearing that kind of pain, and when she turned to opium she grew quite melancholic and began to beg Adrian to end it all for her. That poor boy endured four months of her misery. She would have done it herself but he was determined to keep her alive, until one night... neither of them could bear it anymore. She'd tried to take too much opium but something dragged her back. In hindsight, it was probably his burgeoning powers, not quite ready to let her go. Indeed, Adrian's powers were the only way she'd survived in the first place, something he began to suspect."

"Oh, my goodness," Verity whispered, seeing it in her mind. "He killed her."

"He let her rest," Lady Eberhardt corrected. "He let her go and it was the bravest, hardest thing he's ever done.

A nearby sorcerer caught the edges of it and arrived to find the boy weeping over her body, with no idea of his powers or what he could do. He thought himself cursed."

"Why didn't his father school him?"

"He needed a master of the Grave Arts to show him how to work his sorcery, and he couldn't bear to remain in England so it was deemed appropriate to give his apprenticeship over to Colonel Winthrop." Lady Eberhardt's voice dropped into a sneer. "Winthrop had recently signed on as a Servant of the Empire and was off to seek his fortune in Burma."

"With nobody the wiser about Winthrop's temperament."

"Precisely," Lady Eberhardt replied. "Winthrop was a terrible choice. He barely taught Adrian to control himself, given as he was to gaming and drinking, and once clear of England Winthrop was more interested in conquest and gaining a knighthood.

"And Burma is where Adrian met young Mya," Lady Eberhardt continued, "And therein lies our problem. True love ran its usual course with all the youthful problems of heated passions and tempestuous decisions. Romeo and Juliet didn't know how lucky they were with only two feuding families to deal with. Imagine two feuding Empires with assassinations, political gambits, lies, and broken truces on each side? And of course it all came to a head one night when she snuck into his tent."

"What happened?" This... this was the heart of it, and Verity desperately needed to know.

Lady Eberhardt plucked at the coverlet. "What do you think happened?"

Verity's heart raced.

"Two young sorcerers, one with the gift of the Grave.... Barely taught, trying desperately not to give himself over to emotions and the dangers of Expression, and thrust headlong into an act which is rarely ruled by rational thinking."

"He lost control," Verity breathed.

"He lost control." Lady E sighed. "He nearly killed the girl. Not intentionally of course, but in the throes of attempted passion the darker part of him started to listen to the rapid beat of her heart, the rush of her blood. Even as he kissed her, a part of him was lost in trying to seize that power, to drink in the last gasp of her breath. He didn't even know he was doing it until it was almost too late."

Verity's own breath caught. "But he didn't kill her, did he? He speaks of her as though she's still alive."

"Oh, she lived. He managed to draw back—just in time, mind you—and was forced to restart her heart with his healing gifts. And when Mya started to breathe again the full weight of the horror crashed in upon him. That was the last time he saw her. The last time he let himself see her. Instead, he threw himself into his studies, trying desperately to learn the meager scraps of control that he needed, whilst Winthrop set about creating havoc in the newly formed Burmese commonwealth. It wasn't until Adrian clashed with Winthrop about his callous treatment of the locals that Adrian was sent home in chains with a letter suggesting his gifts be extinguished by the Order. I was one of the councilors who sat in on his trial."

Verity sat back in shock. At first, all she'd seen had been his fancy clothes and the luxury of his home, and dismissed him as just another Order sorcerer, living large. She'd grudgingly adjusted her view of him, day by day, as he revealed his true self, but she'd never thought that he had survived worse things than she had.

Perhaps that was why she'd always felt an odd sense of kinship with him? And why he'd set about trying to help her escape the Crows? Bishop knew what it was like to be helpless, and he knew what it was like to have just one kind gesture set you on the right path in life. None of his actions had ever been driven by pity, but by understanding.

"And here you are," the older woman said, with another arch of the brow. "Temptation indeed, if I'm reading matters correctly. He's never looked at another woman the way he looks at you. Never even wanted one."

The thought both warmed her heart and made her feel remarkably vulnerable. "I don't know what to do."

"I'm sure you'll think of something," Lady E said dryly.

There was a pause in the conversation, leaving Verity deep in thought. She'd lost the Crows. Lost Mercy, in a way. Lost everything that had ever grounded her after her mother's death threw her into the workhouse as a little girl.

What did she want now?

A future in the Order? To learn her sorcery, so that she'd never be captive to anyone's manipulations again? Yes to both. But more than that, she wanted something else. Something more.

She thought of her old dreams, of a house and a family all her own. And it was Bishop's broad form that stood beside her. His child in her arms.

Verity sucked in a breath.

It had always been an abstract dream, but this time it had form and shape and it had a name. She wanted him. She wanted him to want her. Everything else could fall into place. Her lessons, her power. Her future as a sorceress. But most importantly, she realized it was Bishop that she loved.

Lady E cleared her throat, as though she too had fallen into certain recollections. "I wanted to say thank you. I know I don't say it enough."

"For?"

"For your actions today."

"I lost the Chalice," Verity admitted, her shoulders slumping. "Nearly got you killed, and then handed you directly to your enemies."

"I'm here, aren't I?" Lady E's stare was hard to meet. "When you get as old as I am, you realize that sometimes a campaign suffers small setbacks, but as long as you keep your chin up and keep wading through the dross, eventually you might find yourself the victor. I'm alive, thanks to your swift actions, and the Chalice is out of Elijah Horroway's hands, which can be considered a small win."

"And straight into the hands of the Crows," Verity reminded her. "You don't know them the way that I do."

Lady E snorted. "Perhaps. It's still safer than if it remained with that two-bit necromancer. And now Horroway and Tremayne have to wade through half of Seven Dials before they can get it back. No, my girl, it's not a complete shambles. Just a poorly dealt hand with one or two trump cards left to play, if you're smart."

"You're going to play them off against each other?" Verity asked, slightly impressed.

"Of course. That's what a wise general does. In the meantime, we have an Ascension to deal with. We know that Morgana is still alive. Her plans concern me, and with Drake out of action, we need to deal with that. If the relic is secure, if not quite safe, then we can turn our attention to getting a new Prime, one who sees eye to eye with our plans."

"You need to rest," she told the older woman.

Who snorted.

"I mean it," Verity told her. She tucked the covers up around Lady E's chin. "It took a great deal out of Adrian to heal you, and he cannot afford to be distracted by your health right now. He has enough to worry about with his father and the Chalice."

"Where are you going?"

Verity smiled and headed for the door. "To smooth things over with Marie, and bring you up some nice chamomile tea. Then I'll check on Bishop."

"Are you going to bring him tea too?" Lady E asked with an arched brow.

Verity blushed. "Maybe I'll just tuck him into bed. We can discuss this Ascension tomorrow, when we're all rested."

"Verity?"

"Yes," she replied, pausing at the door.

"You have won my vote. Go and seduce that boy and show him what's he's missing out on. A little rush of blood might be just what he needs."

Verity's eyebrows shot halfway to her hairline. "Lady E, what a thing to suggest!"

"Please." Lady E snorted. "Let's not pretend that you don't know precisely what I'm talking about."

With a grin, Verity slipped through the door, though she was more pleased than she let on. The old harridan had clearly just given her permission, and hence, approval.

Which made her feel almost like she had a new family of her own.

CHAPTER
TWENTY-TWO

AFTER HER BATH, Verity found Bishop in his workroom in the cellars. A row of windows along the top of the far wall gave just a hint of starlight, and the fire was dying low in the grate. It made him seem like a man wrought of shadows, the firelight gilding the harsh cut of his cheekbones and that temptingly full mouth.

Bishop sensed her coming, of course, his head tilting toward her even as his hands worked some sort of mechanical object. He was always working at something.

"How was your bath?" he murmured.

"Just what I needed." Verity shuddered. She'd been covered in muck and grime, and something that smelled suspiciously like rot. "And you?"

His dark hair was still wet. "Likewise."

The fire crackled as he fell silent. Verity gazed at his broad back, then crossed to the fireplace. "What are you working on?"

"A warded necklace," he murmured, holding up the pretty gold chain. Small sigils hung from it at certain points. "For you."

"For me?"

He shrugged. "Just in case Agatha convinces you to join her on some other foolhardy quest and you get trapped again. I'll tune it to your presence and teach you what to say to activate the wards. Only use it when you're in trouble."

"It wasn't foolhardy," she argued. "We found the Chalice and we recovered it."

"Agatha nearly died, you were nearly trapped in a circle of flesh constructs, and you barely escaped from the Crows without signing your life away."

"Nearly, nearly, and barely." Verity crossed her arms. "Are you bothered more by the fact that you were completely oblivious to events, or the fact that we didn't need you?"

That earned her a dark-eyed look. "Didn't need—"

"You *were* very helpful this afternoon with Agatha," she said in a softer tone. "But if you think that I can't handle myself...."

Bishop scowled and dropped the necklace on the bench. He ran his hands through his hair, cupping them behind his head. "You should have warned me of what you were doing."

Verity stoked the fire, her bare toes curling in the fur rug that lay before it. "You're right. We should have."

He shot her a startled look.

"I'm not used to having someone watch my back," she admitted. "And Lady E seems invincible at times. It made sense to go after the lead, even without my big surly assassin protector."

His brows drew together in a scowl, but she could tell that he was trying not to smile at the same time. "You're incorrigible."

Verity bit her lip as she set the poker aside, and crossed to stand in front of him. "Were you worried about me?"

"Of course I was." A pause. "Verity. I wouldn't like it if anything happened to you. You know that?"

She leaned up on her toes to press a kiss to his cheek. "I think I'm starting to. Thank you. For worrying. And for making me a necklace to guard me in future reckless endeavors."

The stubble of his jaw tickled her sensitive lips. Verity sank back down, but she kept her hand on the lapel of his coat. His skin smelled like lemon verbena soap. She wanted to inhale more of it.

"Are there going to *be* future reckless endeavors?"

"Probably. I have this habit of leaping in feet first whenever someone I care for is in danger. That list used to contain only one name—"

"Mercy," he guessed.

Verity smiled a little sadly. "Now it has three... no, four names. I'm forgetting Marie, but she's lovely too. And considering that life is growing dangerous, I'm bound to do something reckless if someone assaults those I consider mine."

Fingers stroking his coat, she looked up, meeting that dark gaze. This man. He was all she'd ever wanted.

Go and seduce that boy, Lady E had said. Well, she was going to give it her best shot. Verity's fingers flexed against his waistcoat and she brushed the backs of them down, down, just low enough to make his breath catch.

Dangerous silky-lashed eyes caught hers. "I can't be what you want, Verity."

This time she heard the regret in his voice, and realized it for what it was. Not rejection. But an intense yearning for something he thought he couldn't have.

Now that she knew what haunted him, she could see it written all over his face. Her heart ached for this lonely, lonely man.

"And what do you think I want, Bishop?" she whispered, sliding her hands up beneath his coat and over the smooth silk of his waistcoat.

He shut his eyes. Breathed deep. The muscles beneath her hands tensed. Trembled. "Forever."

Another raw whisper.

The loss in his voice ached deep in her chest. Verity brushed a lock of dark hair out of his eyes. She leaned forward, rising on her toes as she sought his mouth. "Maybe we should stop thinking about the future. Maybe we should just think about tonight. I want you, Bishop. And I know you want me. Love me. Just for tonight. Stop worrying about the future."

She didn't wait for his answer. She took it from his lips.

The kiss started out gentle. A sweet exploration of each other. Verity's hands slid under his coat again, tracing the flat planes of his abdomen and the heavy muscle of his chest. Bishop made a faint sound in his throat, his hands dropping to her waist. Tentative. But not pushing her away.

Nipples hardening, she pressed closer, her tongue lashing against his. It took little coaxing for his tongue to dart against hers. Verity moaned, her body melting against his.

This. Him. Now. It was all she'd ever wanted. And if they couldn't have forever, then she would take tonight.

"Verity." He drew back, his cheeks flushed with color and his eyes slightly glazed. "Ver, I'm not sure...."

"You won't hurt me," she told him, and kissed him again.

"You don't know that." A tremor ran through him, and she knew that he was remembering another night, one filled with fear and despair.

She cupped his chin. "Yes, I do. Trust me, Adrian. We agreed to take this slowly, remember?"

He looked at her and she saw all the hope in the world in his dark eyes.

"If you start to lose your focus, then we stop the second you start to lose control." Practical arguments would work better with him. He liked rational. She slid her hand along that scar-slicked jaw, staring into his gorgeous brown eyes. "But if you do, then I'm clearly not doing a good enough job of keeping your thoughts on sex."

Bishop shook his head, his eyes haunted. "How did you—"

"Agatha explained it to me," she said, stopping him in his tracks. "She told me all about the *maladroise* and what you fear. I know what happened with Mya. But it seems to me that you were young and inexperienced, and unable to control yourself." She caught his hands in hers. "You're no longer that boy, Adrian. And you've learnt how to control your power. Oh, and look at these...." Verity hooked her finger in the spelled manacles on the bench behind him that she recognized from the first night. "A means to stop any sorcerer from using their magic, right in front of us."

Bishop stared at the manacles, then back at her. His nostrils flared.

"Do you trust me?" she whispered, taking a step backward, toward the fur in front of the fireplace.

"With my life." He swallowed hard. Followed her.

"And do you want me, Adrian?" Casting a lash-lowered look over her shoulder, she circled him, trailing a finger across his flank.

Bishop turned, drinking in the sight of her. "More than I've ever wanted anything in the world."

Verity smiled, dropping the manacles to the rug. "You do say the sweetest things sometimes." Reaching up, she tugged her hair from its restraining pins, letting it spiral down over her shoulders.

He watched, lips parting as if he wanted to say something, but still restraining himself. Still clenching every muscle in his body, as though he fought some kind of internal war. "I haven't tested the manacles yet."

"Then consider me your willing test subject." One last pin dropped to the ground with a tinny clang. Verity's hands dropped to the silk night-robe she wore, and with a little shimmy of her shoulders, she let it slide to the floor.

Bishop inhaled sharply. Though she still wore her cotton nightgown, she knew that the fire backlit her—indeed, she'd deliberately placed herself in front of it. Cotton draped over her bottom and wisped between her thighs. Every nerve in her body was suddenly alight, her nipples pebbling behind the thin material.

"Verity." He took a step toward her. "Move away from the grate."

And she realized that he was not entirely overcome with lust, but assaulted by dark memories from the past.

She'd planned a slow seduction, a delicate unveiling, button by button. But now she wouldn't have that chance, for his gaze had turned to the treacherous grate, the crackle of the logs there. Bending over, Verity caught the bottom of her nightgown and whipped it over her head.

Then she tossed it at his chest.

The fabric slapped against his shirt, and Bishop caught her nightgown, but she was fairly certain that reaction was thanks to pure instinct. He slammed to a halt, his jaw dropping as she stood there in all of her naked glory.

With but a single action, she, Verity Hawkins, had reduced him to a statue. One with at least something in common with Priapus.

She smiled.

The heavy pendant she'd stolen three years ago hung between her naked breasts, firelight warming her skin. Verity turned so that he could see all of her, a proud pirouette, glancing over her shoulder to absorb his reaction as she flaunted herself. His gaze roved over her skin, a heated flush darkening his cheeks, and his cock hard and proud behind the restraining tent of his trousers.

Bishop barely dared breathe. "You look.... You—" He cleared his throat. "I'm...."

Entirely satisfactory. The man had lost all of his wits. Verity crooked a finger at him. "Now it's your turn, my lord," she all but purred.

He clutched her nightgown to his chest.

Swallowed.

"Don't be shy," Verity teased. Bishop's gaze dropped. To her breasts, then the small thatch of hair between her thighs. There was no doubt on his face anymore.

"I'm not shy." He tossed her nightgown aside and caught her wrist, dragging her into his arms.

Hot hands slid down her body, pressing her against his firm frame. Verity plucked at his shirt as he kissed her, tugging the buttons open impatiently. She'd caught glimpses of his magnificent body on display in that ice bath, but she'd never gotten a chance to explore it in detail.

Shoving his shirt off his shoulders, she moaned into his mouth. "You're getting very good at this kissing," she whispered, and then squealed as he lifted her up into his arms and laid her on the fur in front of the fire.

Verity laughed as he curled over her, kissing her again.

Bishop lifted his head, breathing hard. Muscle strained in his biceps. She could spend all day looking at him. Touching him.

"What's wrong?" she whispered.

Bishop closed his eyes. "I think I'm dreaming."

"Not yet, you're not." She plucked at the buttons on his pants, tugging them down his lean hips. Shoving a hand to his shoulder, she sent him sprawling flat on his back, and then cast his pants aside.

"Tell me, if this were your dream, what would you want me to do?" Verity asked, sliding her hands up the flat planes of his abdomen.

"I would tell you not to stop. Never to stop." Capturing her body in his arms, he hauled her atop him until she straddled his thighs. "Ver." His expression turned serious as he brushed a strand of hair off her shoulder, revealing the smooth slope of her breast. "I'm glad it's you."

One taste of her would never be enough.

It was that truth that consumed him as Verity laid waste to every inch of control he owned.

Just one night. That was all he allowed himself to focus on.

So he kissed her in the way that he'd always wanted to, tasting the salt of his body on her lips and feeling the slick skin of her sweet curves pressed against his flesh. He was drowning in the need for her, his cock hardening even as the sweet wetness between her thighs pressed against him.

He rolled her until she was beneath him, her thighs parting as he settled between them, the firelight gilding every single line of her limbs. Verity watched him with sparkling starlit eyes full of warm humor and cheerful lust.

"Now, sir," she whispered, "what do you want to do?"

"This," he breathed, leaning forward to capture the tip of her breast in his mouth.

She moaned a little, arching beneath him, and somehow the move brought his cock flush against her, slipping in the heated wetness between her thighs. No matter how many times he'd thought of this instant, of what it would be like, his imagination had never been able to quite do it justice. There was an earthiness to this moment he hadn't expected, a connection, as if both of them were stripped utterly bare.

Verity was lushness, and life, wanton and abandoned to her need. "Like this," she whispered, and took his hand, guiding it between her legs.

"Christ." He looked down, resting on one elbow above her. "You're so wet."

"That's because I want you."

"Wet and hot," he wondered, then she was undulating against his touch and two of his fingers slid inside her.

"Yes," she whispered, lying back and parting her thighs. "Just like that."

He fucked her slowly with his fingers, marveling at the sensation. Lust punched through his veins, his cock raging to get inside her.

"Here." Verity took his thumb and settled it over the fleshy pad of her clitoris. The second he thrust inside her again with his fingers, she moaned, her body clenching around him. Pressing her hands to her face, she rocked against him, unabashed in her pursuit of pleasure.

He loved watching her like this. There was no shame here, no fear. Just her parted mouth and closed eyes, and the way she chased something that somehow eluded her.

Every twist of his fingers showed in her expression, and so he learned what she liked as the tension in her body ratcheted tighter.

"Harder," she whispered, sinking her teeth into her fleshy lower lip. "*Please.* Harder."

He wanted to taste her. And so he did, bending down to kiss her swollen mouth. Verity jerked beneath him, her passage clenching around his fingers as her hips bucked. "Adrian!"

Collapsing onto the rug, she stared through glazed eyes at him as she panted. Bishop kissed her shoulder. It was impossible not to be aware of the way her heartbeat pounded, or the blood rushing through her veins. Indeed, what she'd gone through reminded him somewhat of what it felt like that moment when his powers went supernova.

Could he use his powers to bring her to the edge of pleasure again? The idea was somewhat fascinating, yet he instantly shied away, not quite as certain of himself as he'd hoped.

She vanished from his arms, and Bishop fell forward, turning, only for her to translocate into his arms again with the manacles. Straddling his thighs with hers, she pressed a hand flat to his chest and he fell back, pliant beneath her touch.

"Link with me," she whispered, locking her fingers through his. "I liked the way it felt."

Bishop opened himself up immediately, his psychic senses brushing against hers. Verity bloomed within his mind, all soft pleasure, curiosity, and naughtiness.

The sensory overload was significant. Suddenly, he was not one body, but two. He could feel his hands brushing over her skin. Feel the aching heat in her abdomen, and the streak of liquid lightning that ran through her as he touched her breasts, her nipples.

Then her hand curled around his cock, and Bishop lost all sense of her body, until only his remained.

The tip of his shaft dipped into her sweet cunny, and it was all wet, and hot, and tight. Bishop breathed out explosively, their eyes meeting as Verity smiled down at him. "Just like this," she whispered, and rocked against him.

His cock began to part her, all of that delicious tightness enveloping him like a firm hand. It was like nothing he'd ever experienced before. Verity gasped, and he sensed it wasn't quite hurting her, but that she was having difficulty mounting him.

"Are you all right?" He brushed her hair from her face, tension filling him. He wanted her to enjoy this, and didn't think he could do so himself without it.

She worked him deeper, biting her lip and focusing on relaxing her inner muscles. "I will be," she admitted, that faint, half-crooked Verity smile twisting her lips. "Don't worry about pleasing me, Adrian. You already have. It's just... been a long time, and you're... rather well-endowed."

This time she slid further. And as much as he wanted to see to her, he couldn't stop himself from gasping. Another slow rock of her hips took another inch of his cock, until he was fairly certain he couldn't get any deeper.

No more pain. No more tension. He felt her relaxing, felt her easing around him.

"Touch me," she whispered, riding him slowly. Her fingers curled into his chest hair, her eyes closed as she focused on her body.

He cupped her breasts. Small, perfect breasts, just enough to fill his palms with. Jesus. All of the nights he'd imagined this... and the reality was breathtaking. Nothing like his dreams. More. Intense. Like a world saturated in sudden color, heat, and sweat. Like every nerve ending in his body springing to stark relief.

"Ver." He lifted his head off the fur and kissed her breasts. Licked at those pale brown nipples.

"Yes." Her arms curled around him, her head thrown back. Something in the way she moved sent a shiver through her. Through him. She rocked again, and there it was, the base of her clitoris rasping against the base of his cock.

Faster and faster she moved. Bishop struggled not to lose himself in pleasure. It felt so fucking amazing.

He added his fingers to the mix, stroking her gently between the thighs. Verity quivered, unable to fully ride him, as though her body was threatening to betray itself. Her head rested on his shoulder, her breath wet against his throat.

"Adrian." She dug her nails into his upper arms. "Oh. Oh, there! Yes."

Then she was tipping over some edge and taking him with her.

They plunged. It felt like the world dropped out from under his feet, like lightning.

Couldn't stop. Couldn't contain himself. He arched beneath her, hands clenching her hips. More. Please more—

He fucked his way up into her, pleasure exploding through his veins like a supernova. And she squeezed, her inner muscles locking around him. *Like that?* she whispered in his mind.

The rush of power filled his veins, like a shot of pure life injected into him. He'd never felt anything like it. Never. Not even the *maladroise* came close.

Bishop came, white-hot fire blazing through his cock and balls. And he knew she followed him again, their minds so closely linked that he no longer knew where he ended and where she began.

When he collapsed onto the fur with her curled in his arms, sweat-slick body still engulfing his, he knew he'd never come closer to heaven, even if he tried.

Verity twitched against him with a laugh. "I guess that means that you liked it?" she purred, and then curled her finger in his chest hair and relaxed back atop him.

CHAPTER TWENTY-THREE

"YOU DO REALIZE that you're taking all of the fun out of this," Verity said with a sigh.

"What? You mean you'd rather steal the Chalice out from beneath Guthrie's nose to spite him?" Bishop arched a brow.

Verity peered out through the carriage window, tapping her fingers on the window ledge. Clearly nervous. "Of course I would. Just to prove that I can."

"But how much more enjoyable will it be if he's *forced* to hand it back himself?"

That earned him a sidelong glance from those glorious eyes. A warm smile curled over her mouth. There was a light about her this morning that he couldn't miss. He felt it burning in his chest too. A half dozen emotions he couldn't quite name, but some that he could. Intimacy. Happiness. Hope.

For a moment he felt like he could defeat anything the world could throw at him, with her by his side.

And then he felt the dark whisper of the *maladroise*.

Bishop sobered. It was one thing to finally take her to bed and enjoy the here and now. Quite another to pretend the dream was never going to fade. Never going to turn into a nightmare.

Verity saw his smile fade. Hers echoed it. She twitched her skirts into place. "Let's go beard the dragon in its den."

"Rat," he corrected as the carriage pulled up. "Let's not give Guthrie any more grace than he's due."

He stepped down from the carriage. How easily they could both pretend that there was no ghost in the room.

Focus on the here and now. Bishop turned to offer his hand to her.

Lord Rathbourne waited by the entrance to Seven Dials with Ianthe. Bishop handed Verity down from the carriage, his good mood evaporating entirely. This wasn't his idea, but as Ianthe had said when she'd called around that morning, he could only blame himself.

After all, if he expected Ianthe to make a bid for the mantle of Prime, then he would just have to grow used to obeying her orders. And Ianthe had decided that, while she wasn't entirely convinced she was going to put herself forward, she might as well finish cleaning up the mess she'd set in place a month ago, when she'd been forced to steal the first relic for Morgana.

Which meant dealing with the Chalice.

"Ready?"

"Not really." Verity shot him a tremulous smile. "But I don't have much of a choice."

"They can't hurt you now."

She glanced down. "It's not really me that I'm worried about."

Bishop tilted her chin up. "Don't hide those beautiful eyes." All he could see was green, and the nervousness within them. "And don't worry about me either, Ver. I'm not an easy target to take down."

"I'll stop worrying on one condition."

"Name it."

"That you don't try to protect me in here," she said, and her lips firmed in determination. "Focus on yourself, and I'll take care of me."

She was right, damn her. Verity was his one weakness, which he'd already proven to the Hex. And every time he'd tried to protect *her*, he was the one who'd been bitten on the ass.

"Duly noted. Anything else, my love?"

Verity studied him. Then smiled. "No. You can call me that again though. I like the sound of it on your tongue."

He liked it too.

"Rathbourne," he greeted, steering Verity closer to his half-brother and the others.

"Bishop." Their eyes met, and once again Bishop could feel that shiver of portent through his veins as he and Rathbourne came into close proximity.

"Well-met," Ianthe said, peering around at the seven roads that spiraled out from the sundial. There were no watchers sitting on their corners today, indeed no sign of anyone to be found.

He could feel eyes on him, however. Bishop traced out, his psychic senses rippling across five auras in the nearby vicinity. "Five of them."

"We're not here to fight," Ianthe told him, resting a hand on his wrist. "Please lead on, Miss Hawkins. I've had a message saying that they'll meet with us at midday, no earlier, no later."

"Do you think there will be any traps?" Rathbourne asked Verity.

Verity hesitated. "Maybe, though I doubt it. The Hex Council will be more curious in what you have to say first."

"So any ambushes will come after the meeting," Bishop said.

"Unless they come from the One-Eyed Crows," she pointed out. "Guthrie won't want this meeting. He's the only one who might know what it entails, and the last thing he wants is the council getting involved."

"Noted." He and Rathbourne exchanged a glance. Both of them had people they wished to protect.

Ianthe glanced at her pocket watch. "Let's get under way. They'll be waiting for us."

Verity and Bishop led the way, with Rathbourne guiding both of the other women.

The Dials were quiet. Here and there he saw movement from the shadows of a roof, and fog curled in wisps as it slithered down shingles and smoked its way out of narrow alleys.

"We're being watched," he murmured.

"Of course we are," Verity replied.

"One-Eyed Crows?"

"Not in this street. This territory belongs to the White Rabbits, and not even Guthrie would cross Queen Mab. She runs most of the brothels here, and it's said anyone who looks sideways at her ends up hexed with syphilis." She tucked her collar up against the chill and leaned in closer to him.

It wasn't the first time she'd subconsciously sought him for protection. Bishop rested a hand in the small of her back. Verity was starting to look at him with eyes filled with wonder. He hadn't missed what it meant. After all, they'd been as close as two souls could be last night. He knew what she thought of him.

It scared the hell out of him, even as a part of him yearned for it.

Even now, with his gaze roving the shadows and nooks of the rooftops, he couldn't help caressing the taffeta of her gown. A part of him felt the same way as she did. She was his.

Just as a part of him knew that he couldn't have her. Not forever. After all, how long did he have? The restless hunger of the *maladroise* ached in his bones. It had been too long between kills. Too long since he'd felt that rush. He yearned for it, ached for it... almost as much as he ached for Verity. If there was one hint of light in his dark world, it was her.

But how long would that last against the onslaught of the *maladroise*?

Here and now, he told himself again. *Just focus on now.* But was that fair to Verity? Especially when it was her heart he would break when he was forced to sever all ties with her.

They finally came to an old theatre. Guards lined the entrance, but one of them tipped their head in a gesture to enter. Verity strode calmly through, and the theatre opened into a wide room with no roof. It resembled an ancient Roman amphitheater, with rows of stone stands built around a central stage.

The seven leaders of the Hex gangs sat in a semicircle waiting for them.

"Madame Noir." The enormous man in the front leaned forward, resting his elbows on his knees as he locked gazes with Verity. "Kindly explain, if you will."

His hair and beard were both long and dense, and while streaks of gray silvered his temples, Bishop could sense the power in the fellow. Tattoos scrawled up the backs of his hands and throat, though the heavy oilskin coat he wore obscured most of his body.

This one was dangerous.

Verity gave a brief bow of her head. "Mr. Perkins. Forgive the intrusion. May I present Ianthe Devereaux, Lady Rathbourne, Seneschal of the Order—"

"We know who she is," said the woman at Perkins's side, with her blind eyes locked on Ianthe.

"Her husband, Lord Rathbourne," Verity continued, as if nobody had said a word. "This is Mr. Adrian Bishop, ah—"

"Seventh level sorcerer," Bishop interrupted smoothly, seeing her hesitation. How did one introduce an assassin?

Verity looked at him gratefully. "May I introduce Hex Perkins of the Black Cats; Paddy O'Reilly of the Clover Lads;"—the redheaded fellow beside Perkins—"Queen Mab of the White Rabbits;"—an old broad wearing a tricorne hat pulled low over her matted hair—"Jordy Lewis and his sister, Hesther, who lead the Nameless;"—a man with a shaved head and hex marks tattooed all over his scalp, and the blind woman at his side—"Gionni Sabatini of the Incubo Boys; and Madame Rose of the Reaper crew."

Sabatini stroked his thin mustache, a gold ring glinting at his ear. "You forgot one, Madame Noir."

Daniel Guthrie stalked onstage, smirking at her as he sank into the chair left vacant for the One-Eyed Crows.

"We've already met," Bishop replied coolly, and the Lewis siblings shifted as though he'd drawn a knife.

Silence fell.

"Well, that's all good an' all," Paddy O'Reilly muttered. "But you broke Code, Verity."

"Let no sorcerer walk among us," Madame Rose added, curling her gnarled fingers over the ends of her chair.

Ianthe stepped up beside Verity, her skirts rustling. "Then I believe it is we who broke the Code," she stated clearly, her voice ringing through the rafters of the burned-out building. "Or perhaps, we should say one of your own stole something that belongs to us, hence drawing us to the Dials."

Guthrie's lip curled up. "Verity brought it directly into my house. That means it belongs to me."

Six sets of eyes slid toward him. Bishop smiled, enjoying watching the man sweat.

"Did you take something that belonged to the Order?" Hex Perkins drawled, and there was a flash of anger in his eyes. "Knowing you risked the lives of the Hex?"

"That's bullshit," Guthrie snapped, gesturing at Bishop. "She brought him into the Dials days ago, claiming she were working for him now. That's a direct violation of our laws. You don't bring sorcerers sniffing around the Dials."

Bishop had had enough. He stepped forward, toying with the tip of his leather glove. "Let's get the details straight. Ten days ago, Verity appeared in my house to steal an item belonging to the Order, on the command of Colin Murphy." He tilted a head toward Guthrie. "Your predecessor. When Murphy went to complete the handover of the item to the person who'd commissioned the theft, he was killed and Verity knifed. Since she was in the vicinity of my house, she fled there for protection and she and I have worked out a deal. Verity was to find and return the object to me in order to keep relations between the Hex Society and the Order cordial. She found the relic, but in the process was forced to return to the One-Eyed Crows, where you took the relic off her."

"This is a very important relic," Ianthe pointed out, "used to summon and control a greater demon from the Shadow Dimensions. Verity was doing us a great favor in assisting with its recovery. If there is any blame to be laid here, I lay it at the feet of Colin Murphy, who perhaps overstepped his grounds, and"—her gaze shifted toward Guthrie—"Mr. Guthrie here, who believes in the rule of finders, keepers."

The other gang heads eyed each other.

Then Hex Perkins scowled at Guthrie. "You brought a *demonic* relic into the Dials?"

"She did," Guthrie snarled, stabbing a finger in Verity's direction.

"I was going to take it straight out of the Dials," Verity shot back. "You didn't give me a chance."

"You also threatened to keep my mentor here," Bishop added, "when she was gravely wounded. Lady Eberhardt is one of the councilors who sits on the Triad." He nodded respectfully at the gang heads. "Much in the same position as any of you."

Verity had explained how the Hex worked. If Guthrie had pulled this off, then not a single one them would bat an eyelid. Some of them would even congratulate him for pulling the wool over the Order's eyes. But now he was caught with his hand in the till, it was Guthrie who would bear the punishment, and with his reign so newly welded, he'd be furious.

"It seems the One-Eyed Crows have overstepped themselves," Queen Mab called with a vicious smile. "Significantly."

"And I say they haven't," said Jordy Lewis, striking a pose. "Who does the Order think it is? Their rules ain't ours."

"Shall we take a vote?" Hex Perkins demanded, and all of the assembled Hex leaders shifted to look at each other. "For those who think we should return the relic to the Order, raise your hand."

Relief slid through Bishop as four hands shot into the sky. Jordy Lewis, Madame Rose, and Guthrie were the only ones who abstained. Lewis shrugged at Guthrie, as though to tell him that he'd tried.

Perkins lifted the judge's gavel that he owned and brought it down with a thundering crash. "Hex has voted. Guthrie broke the Code. Go," he told Guthrie, as though he were an errand boy. "Fetch them this relic, and we'll have no more talk of it."

Bishop shared a smile with Verity. They'd finally gotten their hands on the Chalice, and all without a scrap of bloodshed.

"Get your house in order," Sabatini snarled as Guthrie passed his chair. "And get this mess off our doorstep."

There was nothing Bishop enjoyed more than seeing the stony look on Guthrie's face when he returned with the Chalice in hand.

"This isn't over," Guthrie snarled.

"You should learn when to accept defeat," Bishop murmured so only Guthrie could hear him.

"A pleasure doing business with you, Mr. Perkins," Ianthe said, bowing her head politely.

Perkins spat in his hand and offered it to her, and to Ianthe's virtue, she accepted it. "Seems to me the Order and the Hex could do some business in future."

"Maybe," Ianthe replied. "Perhaps I'll be in touch."

Morgana sipped a fine brandy as the dinner party bustled around her with enthusiasm. A success. She couldn't quite join in, as her back was aching so badly she wanted to sit. But she'd been stuck in that damned chair most of the day and the last thing she wanted was to see others aware of her downfall. Rubbing at her lower back, she eyed the Earl of Tremayne across the table and they shared a brief glance, a conspiratorial smile. The gathering of powerful sorcerers they'd reached out to was lapping up every word Tremayne could offer. It almost made the pain worth it.

So much for Drake's hold over them.

Reaching for her cheroot case, she slid from the table and turned toward the balcony of the house Tremayne was renting. Drake's insistence upon stepping back from the position of Prime both exhilarated and alarmed her. She knew she'd struck her ex-husband a blow last month, but she wasn't quite certain how. And she needed to know exactly how far he'd sunk before she could truly enjoy the moment.

Movement shifted at the corner of her eye, all of the hairs on her arms standing on edge as the demon who wore Noah Guthrie's body appeared out of nowhere and caught her wrist.

He leaned in close to her, far too close. "A word, if I might?"

"What are you doing?" Morgana whispered hoarsely. If any of the sorcerers inside saw him, they might realize exactly what was lurking beneath that human skin.

The demon merely looked at her, shockingly devoid of any of those human tics that made a person what they were.

He didn't have to say a thing. He owned her. Every damned inch. Morgana wiped all of the expressions off her face—especially her distaste—then dragged him out onto the balcony, where she lit her cheroot from the Döbereiner's lamp out there.

"What is so important you had to drag me out of there? Tremayne's about to put forth our candidacy for the seat of Prime." She cast a glance over the dozen Order sorcerers inside the dining room. Drake might think he ruled the Order, but there were always those dissatisfied with the restraining yoke of power and how tightly it rubbed. Those who didn't like all of the rules or restrictions, or those who simply hungered for more power. "And some of them might realize what you are."

Not every sorcerer worth his salt knew what a demon felt like, but just enough to make her wary.

"If they do, then I'll take care of it," he replied simply. Human speech patterns were starting to come more easily to it. Three weeks ago a mere sibilant hiss from its throat had been enough to make ice trickle down her spine; a constant reminder of the debt she owed. Without it, she would no longer have her legs, but with it...

Damned to hell.

"If you kill them all," she pointed out dryly, "then we don't have anyone to vouch for us when we take over the Ascension. Do you know how long it's taken Tremayne and me to cultivate them?"

"Who said anything about killing?" it asked. "Kill your tools and you can never use them again."

Morgana swallowed a mouthful of bitter saliva at the thought. It was something she might have said, but hearing it from a demon's mouth....

He has you on a string, after all. Just how long would it be until she was no longer useful?

"So what's the problem?" she asked. There was nothing she could do about its hold over her. At the moment.

"There's a slight problem," it told her, leaning against the balustrade in its suit.

"Oh?"

"Your son is listening to me, but last night I felt another presence in there with him."

Morgana nearly dropped her cheroot. "How the hell did anything get into that cellar—"

"Not physically."

Psychically. She felt ill. There was only one person she knew who had the strength or the inclination to do so. "Drake." Turning around, she sucked down on her cheroot, resting her hand on the marble balustrade as she saw red, just for a moment. All her life Drake had tried to take what was hers from her. And although Sebastian had been forged purely as a weapon against him, a part of her hated that her son leaned toward his father more than he ever had to her. "What are we going to do?"

"We need to isolate him," the demon mused. "Sebastian is beginning to listen to me and might come around to the plan, but he won't consider it if he thinks there's another option."

"Drake's offering to help him?"

"I barely dared listen in, but I caught enough of it. He's trying to get Sebastian to listen to him, and offering to help him escape."

"And we can't have that," she said bitterly. Her son might be her most perfect weapon against her ex-husband, but he was also the dog that bit the hand that fed it. Dangerous. Unpredictable. *Untrusting.* Her thoughts coalesced as she blew out a perfect ring of smoke. Yes. That was it. "What else did they speak of?"

"Drake promised to return tomorrow. He has the girl at his side." A twist of the demon's mouth showed some small hint of displeasure. It didn't like Cleo—or her gifts. Perhaps it was even scared of them. "It gives him a benefit in swaying your son's mind, and I need Sebastian for my plans."

"Our plans," she corrected, though a part of her wondered. The demon had promised her the position of

Prime during the Ascension in two days. It said it merely wanted Drake's head on a platter—which suited her perfectly—but she wondered.

Drake was the greater threat at the moment, however. Morgana turned in a swirl of flounced skirts and paced along the balcony, staring through the greenery. "Sebastian might want his father to rescue him, but I doubt he truly believes Drake will come. All we have to do is feed that doubt. Make him feel abandoned. Alone. Actually, this might work in our favor." She turned, gesturing with her cheroot. "There was never any guarantee that Sebastian would fall for your lies in time, but if he thinks his father reached out to him, then abandoned him...."

The demon cocked its head. "Yes," it said. "He wants his father's love. That much is clear. But he does not believe in it. Not deep inside. It might push him into my hands."

"Can we stop Drake from contacting him again?"

Those eyes narrowed. "I can ward the house. Stop him from getting through. Then the boy will think himself abandoned."

"Do it then." She didn't particularly care whether Sebastian broke or not. He'd betrayed her, his actions crushing her spine and costing her everything. All he was to her right now was simply a tool to be used.

The demon narrowed its eyes. "The other problem to consider is this: Could Drake use his link with Sebastian to find us?"

Morgana breathed out a gust of smoke as panic lit along her nerves. "We have to move."

"Yes. As soon as the guests depart."

Morgana peered impatiently inside then crushed the cheroot beneath her heel. "I'll get rid of them. You see to Sebastian."

The demon watched her go.

Patience, it told itself, peering out over the gardens and drumming its fingers on the balustrade, imagining her throat beneath its hands instead. Little pits formed in the marble beneath its fingertips. The demon stopped. As much as it wanted to snuff her life from her veins, Morgana's arrogance and determination to thwart her ex-husband played directly into its hands.

As soon as Drake was his, then he could remind her of what the consequences were when a sorcerer tried to dabble with a demon and control it. In fact, it would take great pleasure in doing so.

"No," said Noah, swimming up inside him. *"You promised—no more killing if I helped you."*

The demon made its body blink. It quite liked being alive. This plane of existence had so many possibilities. *"Be quiet,"* it said, and crushed Noah down inside the little dark box inside it. *"Or you'll never be free of me."*

CHAPTER
TWENTY-FOUR

"YOU'RE AVOIDING ME," Verity murmured, watching as Bishop paced around the billiards table.

He chalked the cue mechanically, his face expressionless and closed off. "I'm... tired, Verity. There's a lot on my mind."

"We have the Chalice back," she pointed out, resting her hip against the edge of the table. "Which means Morgana can't use it for any more mischief. Lady E is safe and whole, and bossing poor Marie around like she can't wait to get back on her feet. I'm alive. You're alive. We should be celebrating."

She made the mistake of reaching for his hand where it rested on the mahogany frame.

Bishop stared at it for a second, then subtly removed his hand from beneath hers. "Ascension is two days away. We still don't know what Morgana and Tremayne are up to, though if it involves Sebastian we're in trouble. Horroway is still out there somewhere...."

Verity curled the offending limb in against her chest. There was a pit opening up inside her chest. What she wouldn't give for him to open his arms wide and curl her up within them right now. "Can't we deal with all of that tomorrow? Can't we just have tonight?"

Her skirts brushed against his shoes as she followed him, but Bishop turned. Every line of his body told her to back away.

The pit in her chest became an endless gaping chasm that threatened to swallow her whole. She came to an abrupt stop. "Please don't," she whispered.

"I just want to play a round of billiards," he replied. "It helps to clear my mind. If you want, I'll wake you early enough for us to get a head start on Morgana's plans. Now that we know you can find her, thanks to Horroway's ring...." He leaned over and set the balls up properly.

Reaching out, Verity set her hand on the white ball. "No, I don't want you to send me off to bed like a good little girl, waiting for you to pay me some small scrap of attention. I want to talk about this now. I want.... I want you to hold me."

She held his startled gaze. He looked younger in that moment. Perhaps it was the way his hair desperately needed a trim, the sun-bleached tips of it brushed behind his ears.

"Ver." His mouth twisted in a scowl as he stared down at her hand and the captured ball. "You have to know what the future holds. I know you felt it."

She shivered a little. How could she not have felt it? How could he live with it? A dark mantle that threatened to smother him at any turn. "There has to be something you can do," she protested, forcing away the feeling. "I won't believe that this is inevitable."

Bishop set the cue down, staring blankly at the table. Even before he murmured, "Ver," in a hopeless tone, she knew the answer to her question.

"I'm not going to let you face this alone."

That roused the ire in him. "You don't have a choice." Bishop straightened.

"So you'll make my decision for me?" she replied tartly. "Like Murphy did? Like Guthrie wants to?"

He looked confronted. "Verity—"

"Why can't I make my own choices?" Taking a step toward him, she fixed the collar on his coat. "You promised me that when you offered me a new path, a place inside this Order of yours. Please don't take that away from me."

Bishop set the cue down on the table. "I just... I don't want to hurt you."

Swallowing hard, Verity reached out for his hand. "I want you. I... I love you." She knew now why he secluded himself. Why he roamed these halls at night, unable to sleep. "You don't have to be alone. Not tonight."

His breath punched out of him on a loud exhale. "Jesus. Do you think I don't want this?" His hand lifted, hovering in the air between them. "I'm trying to do the right thing."

"You're trying to protect me from a broken heart," she whispered. "Well, that's just too bad. My heart broke long ago." *With her mother's death. Her father leaving.* "I didn't let that destroy me then, and no matter what happens between us, I won't let it destroy me now. Do you know what got me through the bad moments when I was a little girl?"

His eyes met hers.

"The small moments," she admitted with a wistful smile. "The day after my mother died, I found a kitten in the workhouse. I stayed in bed all day with him tucked in against me. Two orphans in the world, both of us half starved, bedraggled little fighters. But together... we were no longer alone. And every time I thought of my mother, I could feel him purring against my throat, because he was happy to simply be warm and held, nice and safe. And it was a nice feeling, that moment, without all of the weight of the world against me. So I focused on that.

"And then I met Mercy, and she didn't have any parents either, so we decided we were going to be sisters. And we would share a bed, and I was never alone then. Sometimes she would bring me presents. She had a thing for little glittering scraps of metal. The first time I translocated; that breathless rush of landing. The first meal at Murphy's, when he tried to lure me to the Crows. It was the best thing I'd ever eaten in all my life." Verity bit her lip. "The other night, when you let me love you. That's what gets me through dark days. Because I know there is another moment of joy somewhere in my future, just waiting to be lived. I'm not afraid of the dark times. I can survive them, Bishop. I can survive anything. But I need these small moments to get through them."

He swallowed.

"Give me another moment," she whispered, leaning against him. "Give me an hour of happiness. That's all I ask."

Bishop cupped her face, tilting his forehead down to hers. The move was oddly intimate. "I can't promise you forever," he said bluntly.

"Who said that I asked for forever?" she whispered, tilting her face up toward him. "Small moments. Day to day. That's all I ask for: the here and now."

He shut his eyes. A look of pure thwarted need crossed his stark face. "Ver. I felt it. I know what you want. There's no hiding anything from me when we're linked."

He might not have been able to promise her a future, but he wanted it just as much as she did. The thought softened the blow of rejection. He wasn't doing this because he didn't want her; he was trying to soften the eventual blow.

And maybe he was telling the truth. Maybe there could never be a *them*. She'd felt the dark that haunted him, those demons that lurked within his soul.

And she didn't care.

Perhaps taking this step would have scared her a year ago. She knew now what she had to lose in life, but not daring to live it would be a greater tragedy. "Be here with me," she whispered, reaching up to brush her lips against his. "In the here and now. We'll let the future sort itself out."

Hands slid up and down her side, so gently he might have been calming a flighty horse. His eyes were closed, as if he drank in the sensation. Verity kissed him again and slowly closed her own eyes.

Capturing her hands in his, he tugged her firmly against him, the hard press of his erection digging into her stomach. Verity moaned, then drew back. She caught a glimpse of his dark, serious eyes, then she slid her hand behind his neck and dragged him back down for another kiss.

His lips were so soft. He kissed as though he had all of the time in the world, as if just tasting her was pleasure enough. "God. I want to take you again, and never stop."

She smiled into his mouth as she slid a hand down his waistcoat. "That sounds more like it. Please ravish me." Her hand dipped between them, cupping the bulge in his pants. "Most thoroughly, if you would."

Hands caught her up under the bottom, lifting her into his arms. Verity flung her arms around his shoulders, meeting his heated kiss with a muffled laugh.

Balls scattered as he shoved at them impatiently. Then she was sitting on the billiards table as Bishop slid his hands up beneath her skirts.

He never broke the kiss. It was as if he drowned himself in the sensation, as if he needed this so desperately, needed to cling to her like a life raft to stop himself from going under.

And she held him back.

She wanted this man. Wanted him now. Forever. Dreams were always risky, but she had finally come to realize that this one was worth going after.

And Verity had always been a fighter.

One step at a time, however.

Verity tugged at the buttons of his trousers. The firm length of his erection strained behind the buckskin flap, and then the flap gaped. Verity dove her greedy little hand inside, fisting the length of him, pumping his cock in small motions. "Yes," she gasped as he bit her throat in reaction. "Yes!"

Her back would have hit the green felt of the tabletop if she didn't have such a stranglehold on his coat collar. Bishop's mouth grazed her chin, then slid down her throat. Suddenly, her breasts were under siege. All she wanted to do was get out of this dress. Out of her corset. Too many cursed ribbons and ties. Verity gasped and fisted his cock again.

"I don't want to wait," she gasped as teeth nipped at the slope of her breasts. Grabbing a fistful of his hair, she dragged his face up to hers. "Now. Take me. Please."

Those dark eyes glimmered with heat. She'd thought them cold once upon a time, but the obsidian depths of his irises were like banked hearths, embers smoldering just beneath the surface.

He didn't offer to link with her. Not this time. And she didn't ask for it. The last thing she wanted was for him to know what she was planning.

Instead, she slid his cock through the slit of her drawers, rubbing the head of it through her wetness. A shiver ran through her at the sensation. Her skin drank in the feel of him; the rasp of his trousers against her inner thighs where her stockings ended; the blunt tip of his cock gently parting her; the abrasion of his coat against her fingertips.

Verity let her head sink back as Bishop half thrust. What she wouldn't do to have this man forever.

However, she'd settle for tonight.

"Do you like that?" he breathed, thrusting again as his cock slowly filled her.

"You know I do." Verity slid her hand through the silky hair at the back of his skull. Their eyes met. "No talking. Not tonight."

And then she kissed him again as he finally sank home within her, obliterating every other thought of the world around her.

He'd dreamed of fucking his way inside her. Dreamed of the trace of her skin under his hands, and the silk of her gown abrading his fingertips.

Those dreams paled in comparison to reality.

Bishop couldn't get enough of her. He lost himself in the wet-slick thrust and glide of this ancient dance as she ate at his mouth. There was a wildness about her tonight, as if she clung to him with every inch of her being.

Everything was that thrust and pull. He groaned as his hand found her breast and his tongue tangled with hers. Why had he ever waited for this? Sexual energy danced over his skin, almost as tempting as the *maladroise*. There was no psychic connection between them tonight, but he felt as though their bodies joined, becoming one. Tugging at her ribbons, he pulled her bodice loose enough to reveal the creamy slopes of her upper breasts, and then his mouth was there. Licking. Nibbling. Jesus. Why had he waited for so long? This was intense. Amazing. The best bloody thing ever.

But it wouldn't have been the same if it were not with her.

Bishop curled his fists in her skirts. What a truth to behold, but it struck him straight through the heart.

Every moment of waiting had been worth it. For her. For this. Every aching moment of loneliness had led him along this path, and now he couldn't dream of anything else.

He wanted to please her. Wanted to hear her scream his name on her lips. The heat flushing through his cock and balls, however, promised that his pleasure would come before hers.

Grasping her by the hips, he withdrew briefly and turned her over.

"What are you—" Her words turned into a moan into the green baize as he slid his hand beneath her mound, cupping her through all the layers of silk.

"Did you know that in the Orient, there is a book called the *Kama Sutra*, full of all of the philosophy and theory of love and what triggers desire."

Verity's nails dug into the green baize as he finally found the wet heat of her through all of that silk. "Is there?" she gasped as his fingers slid wetly through those delicate folds.

"Mmm." He slid her skirts up and tugged her drawers down, revealing the smooth white globe of her bottom. "I studied it most assiduously as a young man. There were some quite detailed drawings about what a man can do to a woman in there. I always wondered what this... would feel like."

Parting her thighs with his knee, he returned to his task, teasing lightly at her clitoris even as he pressed his cock against her opening.

"I think—" He breathed heavily as he thrust slowly back inside her. "—that I would like to study it again, now that an English translation has been made by Sir Richard Burton."

"I think"—Verity arched her hips becomingly—"that I would like to see this naughty book too."

"Would you?" He felt her tighten as he swirled a small circle over that little bud. The angle of this position drove him deep inside her. Both the depth and the tight fist of her sheath were doing terrible things to his self-control. Sweat dampened his temples.

"Y-yes," she gasped. "Yes, oh, my goodness."

Bishop ground his teeth together, and thrust a little harder. He felt her tremble, her fingers forming small claws in the green baize. *That's it. Come on, darling.*

"More," Verity gasped. "Harder."

Another thrust set off the quake inside her. Verity cried out, and he felt her come, felt every exquisite tremor, and it terrified him.

Yes, he was scared. Of losing this, losing her. Of never getting the chance to try for anything more. And maybe that was why he'd turned her away from him, so she wouldn't see it on his face.

He wanted a chance with her more than anything, but that was foolish. Adrian Bishop had never asked for anything in his life. All he'd ever wanted was to stop *hurting others*. To stop wanting to hurt them. To burn this thrice-cursed haunting ache out of his blood.

But he wanted her.

Small moments. Day to day. That's all I ask for; the here and now.... That's what he wanted too. If he couldn't fix everything else, then at least he could have this. One small moment of pure happiness.

He lost himself in her, lost himself to the world around him, fucking and thrusting inside her. Tuning everything else out but the feel of her melting beneath him. And it was bliss.

He looked at her beneath him, at the way her spine bowed in submission, her hand flung out across the baize as though reaching for a lifeline, something to hold on to as he poured himself within her. Her chignon was a mess again, and as she tilted her face to the side, the breath exploding out of her, he saw the expression on her face. Saw that precious profile tilted toward the light, lips parted as though she'd throw herself quite happily off a cliff, content, as long as she was with him.

His heart couldn't take it anymore. Neither could his body.

They were both falling, and damn him, as he caught her hand in his and gripped it tight as he came, a part of him couldn't let her go.

"You've quite ruined billiards for me," Bishop admitted as he straightened her skirts and brushed himself down.

"Oh?" Verity looked entirely too innocent as she glanced up at him from beneath her dark lashes. Her cheeks were flushed, and he could see the devil in her eyes.

"I don't think I'm ever going to be able to concentrate on the game again," he growled, "without thinking of you and getting a bloody erection."

Verity smiled, toying with his waistcoat. "Good. I promise by the time we're through, Adrian Bishop, you won't be able to think of anything *other* than me ever again."

Far too bloody late for that. He was already wrapped around her bloody finger.

And a part of him liked it far too much.

CHAPTER TWENTY-FIVE

AFTER VERITY FELL asleep, Bishop went hunting.

Verity wasn't the only one who could find people. And while she might have had misgivings about him going off alone, she was asleep now. She wouldn't know.

And despite the fact that tonight had been the best night of his life, the itch had started again sometime after midnight. Lying in her arms, half dozing, half-awake, he'd tried to dismiss it at first. Why couldn't it leave him alone, especially tonight of all nights? But the *maladroise* didn't work like that. The second things stopped moving and the stillness of night crept over the world, it came to pay him a visit like some jealous mistress he could never escape.

Verity's heartbeat began to radiate through his ears, and Bishop had slid from the bed before his mind could turn to darker things.

Like just how long he could escape his destiny.

Bishop paused by the corner of St. Michael's cemetery, feeling the tracking spell tug him toward the middle. He'd finally gotten that blasted map table working, and pinpointed toward where Horroway was hiding. If he was going to be awake half the night, he might as bloody well do something. And now that he'd found Verity, he wasn't going to allow anything to threaten her. Not Tremayne. Not Morgana. And certainly not the necromancer who'd seen her face when she stole the chalice back from him.

Grunting sounds drew him to the left. Bishop crept through a tangle of ivy and vines that snaked over the ground. Fog whispered between gravestones, hovering thickly on the ground. There was no breeze tonight. Just silence and moonlight, preferred themes for an assassination.

A lean figure materialized out of the shadows. Kicking at something, the man straightened, then sighed and cast aside his shovel. From the pile of dirt, it appeared he was robbing a grave, though Bishop didn't know what he wanted. Necromancy might be a talent he was capable of, but he'd never dabbled enough to know more than the basics.

Bishop sucked shadows around himself with his power, sliding from tree to tree. Horroway froze, resting against the headstone, and Bishop waited patiently, his heartbeat ticking along loudly in his ears as he waited for his prey to relax again.

"Wondered when you'd come for me." Horroway spat into the dirt of the grave he'd been digging.

Bishop paused as Horroway reached inside his haggard coat and withdrew a flask. Inside it was some type of liquor that helped anchor Horroway's soul to the flesh he'd robbed.

"You gonna just stand there watchin', or you gonna come out and face me like a man?" Horroway upended the flask, making a horrid gurgling sound in his throat.

Which presented Bishop with a chance. It would be incredibly easy to throw his etheric blade into Horroway's back, cutting the ties of soul to flesh. Instead, he vanished it. There were questions to be asked and Horroway sounded as though he wanted to talk. "How did you know?"

"Felt you comin'." Horroway looked up, one of his eyes beginning to rot in his face. He screwed the lid of his flask back in place. "Same way you tracked me, I'll bet."

They faced each other. Bishop found himself in somewhat of a quandary. He'd meant this to be a quiet assassination, a removal of one of Morgana's threads, but the scene didn't feel right. Horroway looked neither afraid, nor cunning. Just quietly resigned.

Prepared for anything, Bishop let himself relax, his power dissolving. One couldn't hold it indefinitely, though the second it was gone he felt the ache of the *maladroise* upon him again, sinking its hungry claws into his chest. It would take but an instant to re-form the blade.

"Look at you," Horroway whispered. "Feelin' that itch, ain't you?"

He tensed. "What itch?"

Sinking down onto a nearby headstone, Horroway scratched at his jaw. "Boy, give me some credit. I spent thirty years with that bitch at my heels. I know what it looks like. I know what it feels like."

No point in hiding it. Bishop glanced away. "It's our cross to bear, thanks to our calling. Nobody escapes it."

"There's one way," Horroway suggested, and Bishop's head jerked up.

How? He realized what Horroway meant. "This?" he said incredulously, gesturing toward the mottled body Horroway wore. "You did *this* to escape the *maladroise*?"

Horroway's fleshy lips thinned. "Seemed a good idea at the time, and I were desperate." Sorrow filled his eyes.

"You're the only one who can understand that. There's a point... where you can't take it anymore, and you know you're going to give in to it, and take what shouldn't be taken." Holloway studied him quietly, a sense of connection seeming to form between them. "We've all got someone we don't want to take," he said. "Even me. My little girl might be a bastard, but she's all I've ever had. Couldn't do it. Couldn't stay there anymore, watching over her and feeling like a vulture for the life force that filled her. This were the only way I could see, to slip from flesh to flesh so that the *maladroise* couldn't gain hold anymore."

"Did it work?" He couldn't hide the hunger in his voice.

Horroway laughed, a dry, rasping sound. "Aye. When I woke that first time in a new body, that crushing weight was finally gone. It worked. *Maladroise* don't have time to build before I've got to skip to the next body." The humor faded from his face. "But you don't ever forget that feeling."

"Is that what you're doing now? Preparing to skip bodies?" Bishop circled the half-empty grave at their feet. The scent hit his nostrils like a fist.

"Fresh three days ago." Horroway smiled bitterly. "This one's half worn out. Got to get meself a fresh body every month or two."

It was horrible in a way that Bishop had never thought of before. Horroway was legendary within the Order. A menace, a sniveling coward, a traitor, a necromantic wretch.... But Bishop alone knew what the man had gone through. Or part of it.

He couldn't do this. It disgusted him on every level but he *could* understand the desperation that could drive a man to these lengths. He himself searched for that freedom, just not like this.

"The question you need to ask yourself is: was it worth it?" Horroway continued, as though Bishop saw it as the answer to his own illness. "To have those you love turn away from you in horror? To never have a woman look you in the eye with longing ever again? To find yourself with but one friend left, a friend who could sell you out for a rare copy of a book."

Guilt tasted bitter in his mouth. "Marius didn't want to sell you out. I threatened him and threw in the book as a deal."

Horroway shrugged. "All the same from this end of the spectrum." He looked weary as he surveyed the night. "I didn't want to die," he whispered. "I didn't want to kill meself, but Becky.... I couldn't do that to her. I just wanted to be free of it."

"I cannot let you walk away," Bishop told him.

Horroway unscrewed his flask again. "I know." He took another mouthful, his eyes watering. "I don't want to die. I still don't... but...." His knuckles flared white around the flask. "There ain't nothing left for me but this. I'm so fucking tired, boy. And alone. The betrayals just don't ever stop, do they?"

Bishop stared at the grave. "You'll barely feel it," he whispered.

"What?" Horroway started.

"I can give you what you crave," he said. "Freedom."

Horroway's face twisted in fear but he forced himself to sit still. The pulse in his throat was racing, a beckoning lure that Bishop looked away from. "In exchange for?"

"In exchange for the hope that someday there will be someone to guide me into the long, lonely dark."

"I'm afraid," Horroway whispered. "What if there's nothing there? What if the Christians' beliefs are true, and I wake up in hell? Or the Egyptians.... What if...."

"We cannot know," Bishop replied, clasping his hands behind his back. "None of us really do, not until we face such a challenge ourselves. But you will have peace. I promise you that. And I can make sure it doesn't hurt."

Horroway looked down at his flask, a look of determination crossing his face. "Me little girl, her name's Becky Whitshaw. Married to some tanner in Bethlem Green. She's got the gift, but I didn't dare bring her into this world."

"I'll see that she's taken care of."

"You know, I almost believe you." Horroway shook his head. "You. My killer."

"I keep my word."

Upending the flask, Horroway poured its green bubbling liquid onto the mound of grave dirt. Hissing and bubbling continued as the liquid ate away at the stone and pebbles. "Then do it. Do it fast." His voice broke. "Before I change me mind."

Bishop moved before Horroway could blink, the etheric blade forming in his fist and sinking into Horroway's back, angled up under the ribs.

Horroway gasped, catching at his sleeve, but Bishop held him through the first spasm. Distilling his power through the man, he forced the body to shut down quietly, each organ going to "sleep" as his sorcery worked through Horroway's veins. "You're not alone," he told the man, for that was the one thing he feared himself. "I don't know what comes next, but you're not alone now."

"Thank you," Horroway whispered, clutching his coat. His chest gave a wracking heave. "You ought to know.... There might be a way to avoid it.... The Chalice... is the key. And there's... a book. Almay's *Theory on the Grave Arts*. Got the info you need to work... Chalice. Won't be easy... Takes a sacrifice of some sort." He coughed and looked down at the blackened ichor weeping from his chest. "Irony is... it takes... l-life to be able to use it.... That's one thing that bitch lied... to me about."

"Morgana?" He didn't dare hope but it stole through his veins, a tingly warmth that rushed straight to his head.

"Never should've trusted... her again. But she promised... me the Chalice. Promised me... an end to this." Horroway's strength was fading, his grip on Bishop's collar loosening. "Morgana has the Blade of Altarrh. It weren't... destroyed... last month like she claimed. Has all three... relics. Or had 'em. Don't know... where the Chalice... is now. I were meant to give it back to her, but some bitch stole it, and then Morgana tole me I didn't have... no more use... for her."

Why was he telling Bishop this? Bishop lowered him to the ground.

"Kill that bitch," Horroway rasped, his skin paling and the light fading in his eyes. "Kill 'er... for me. And burn this... body."

And then his soul extinguished from the body, floating like a hot white spark above the rotten flesh. Bishop reached out and closed his fist around it, setting Horroway free.

It wasn't the supernova that he'd been expecting. Bishop still felt power flame through his veins and clenched his eyes shut to hold on to the feeling. So quickly burned out... it left him gasping, but there was nothing else. Horroway had been more dead than alive and so his death was but a trickle of what Bishop craved.

He stayed there for long minutes, trying to fight the hunger. *More.* He needed more. It made his hands ache and his jaw clench as he fought through it. Every little death was but a step in the wrong direction, and the more he took the less it satisfied him.

No. No more.

Kneeling in the grave dirt, he slowly lifted his head, panting. There were years of this ahead of him. And he suddenly couldn't stand it anymore. He wanted more than this hollow ache that gripped him so fiercely that he could barely think of anything else. He wanted what Verity offered; her warm smile, the feel of her hand in his, the taste of her mouth.... He wanted a future where he no longer stood alone, locked in his house at night for fear that he'd inadvertently reach to snuff a life in his sleep.

If what Horroway told him was true, then there might be a way to save himself.

If he could work out how to use the Chalice.

CHAPTER
TWENTY-SIX

A WARM BODY slid into bed beside her and Verity froze, then relaxed when she smelled the familiar lemon verbena of Bishop's soap.

"Adrian?" she whispered, blinking sleepy eyes as she turned into his embrace. "Where have you been?"

He kissed her, his skin wet from the bath, and the towel he wore around his waist the only barrier between their bodies. A deep, hungry kiss that had her melting beneath him, her arms sliding around his broad shoulders as he rolled her onto her back. There was something wild about him tonight, almost as if emotion roiled through him.

No chance to give voice to her thoughts. No chance to do anything other than kiss him back, her body warming beneath his as he slid into the welcoming vee of her thighs. He ate at her mouth. Pure dominance. Pushing and taking what she wanted to give, and so hungry that though she'd been asleep mere seconds before, now she felt vibrantly awake.

She'd dreamed sometimes, of being taken like this by him.

Every last line of hesitance vanished from his body and he became someone else. An Adrian Bishop who knew exactly what he wanted and was determined to have it.

Verity's hands slid up his quivering flanks. There hadn't been a great deal of time to explore before. The hunger and eagerness they'd both felt had obliterated any chance at taking their time. But now she had all the time in the world.

"Ver," he whispered, breaking the kiss and rasping his stubbled cheeks against her throat. The way he said her name made her heart catch fire in her chest, but she was too busy trying to catch her breath. A shudder racked through him. "Ver, there might be a chance for me."

As her eyes grew accustomed to the dim light, she saw the earnestness in his face. An expression she'd never have thought to see there: hope. Her heart started to beat a little faster. "A chance?"

It made him look so much younger, sloughing off the weight she realized that he'd been carrying with him ever since she'd known him. "Horroway said that there's a way to burn away the grip of the *maladroise*. All I need is the Chalice, and the means to do so. He said there's some kind of book. And I'd have to make some sort of sacrifice."

It froze her. She'd been trying not to dream of the future. Trying to leave what lay between them as it was, but her heart swelled with joy at the thought of it. "What type of sacrifice?"

Bishop shrugged. "I don't know." He saw the expression on her face. "Nothing like that," he assured her. "That's black magic, sacrificing a being's life. It's used in demon summoning, that type of thing. No, maybe I have to... make some sort of sacrifice myself?"

"I don't like the sound of that."

"Believe me," he said, with a faint laugh that swiftly died. "I don't like the sound of it either. I've had enough to do in my life with talk of sacrifices."

She knew he was speaking of the prophecy that hung over his head. And she wasn't quite brave enough to ask him more about it. She'd never felt more at peace than she did now. Being here in his arms was like belonging in some bizarre way that she'd never even known she craved. She just wanted this peaceful moment to drag out. To live in it forever, far away from the Hex and demons and sacrifices.

"Then we find the book," she said, threading her arms around his neck. "Use the Chalice, and get rid of this dark curse on your soul forever."

Bishop's expression became intense. He said nothing, merely captured her lips again, throwing everything he felt into the kiss. A kiss that consumed her soul. She'd have sold herself to the Devil for another second of it.

"You're not too sore?" he murmured, thrusting a little against her. The towel tented over his cock, but she could feel him against her despite the layers between them.

Her entire body heated. Melted. Somehow she hooked her finger in the edge of the towel, and then it was slithering free, the hairs on his upper thigh brushing against the sensitive skin of her inner thighs. "No." She was a little sore, but the ache felt nice. Like fulfillment. "Not for this."

It was as if her words had unleashed a fury within him she'd never witnessed before. Bishop was violence and passion carefully contained beneath the smooth veneer of his skin, but not now. He kissed her again. Stole the breath from her lungs, his hands sliding beneath her nightgown and sliding it up until his erection fell heavily across her mons.

That set her off. How she wanted this man. In every way. Nails raking into his biceps, she flexed her fingers into his skin, reveling in the feel of the power in his body. He was so much bigger than her. Stronger. Yet amazingly, she was the one who felt like she had all of the power in this moment.

Fingers slid down between them and danced between her thighs, hesitant at first, then gaining confidence as she moaned a little and arched into his touch. The first streak of pleasure shot through her nerves as he hit the exact spot she needed. Bittersweet and aching. Stealing her breath. "Yes," she gasped, sinking her teeth into her lower lip. "Yes... there... right there.... Oh, Adrian...."

Somehow her fist was in his hair, clenching violently with her need. It was nearly embarrassing how wet she was, as if her body betrayed secrets she'd tried to keep hidden in her heart. She'd never told him. The thought flashed through her mind as he worked those fingers inside her, those inner muscles tightening around him like a glove. Verity grabbed his head in both hands, desperate in some way she couldn't describe. Their eyes met, a secret little moment in which he saw everything that she knew was in her heart, in her throat, in her chest.

I love you.

He bit her throat. Then her cheek. Back to her mouth. God, the taste of his tongue was faintly smoky, like fine brandy. She was lost in the moment. All of the need and desperate desire she'd felt for him spilled out of her. Maybe she didn't have him, not truly? Maybe there was no future between them? She didn't know. But in this moment she felt like she did. There were no words in her head. Only gasps. Only a *please*, and maybe a *yes, please, please*, desperate begging sounds as every muscle in her body wound tighter than a corkscrew. Couldn't think when he kept kissing her like that, like a drowning man trying to steal the oxygen from her lungs.

Verity lost herself with a shattering wave of pleasure. She didn't know if that was her voice calling out, but she clung to him as spasms racked her. Nails digging into his back and shoulders, no doubt leaving little pale half-moons there, as his fingers fucked their way inside her.

Too much. Too much sensation, oh, God....

"No more!" Verity begged, shoving his hand away as she came crashing down, her entire body jumpy with nerves, with pleasure. Senses heightened. Practically leaping out of her skin. She'd seen men and women blissed out post-orgasm. She'd never truly felt it before, not like this. She felt boneless. Weightless. Both locked in and out of her body, as if she were floating. Power surged through her, temping her to try and shift the very world in its gravitational spin. She probably could right now.

That lifted his head, his voice raw with a question: "I didn't hurt you?"

Verity laughed. She couldn't help herself. God, she felt amazing. Locking her arms around his neck, she drew him back against her, skin against skin, even as another flinch of stimulation made her jump. "It was just too much," she whispered against his lips, pulling him in for another kiss. "In a good way."

He drew back to look at her, a faint, curling smile stealing over his lips. A secret smile, just for her. "Well, look at you," he said. "All flush with power. Guess we know what your natural inclination is."

Some sorcerers could draw power from blood. Some from death. Some from sex. He'd told her that once. She met his eyes. He'd also told her what it felt like when he stole another life. If this was even half what he felt, then she didn't know if she could blame him for wanting more. The pure rush of energy through her veins—

Her smile died, and he saw it. "Ad—"

His mouth stole her own, cutting off the words.

The kiss was long and slow, drowning out the rest of the world. She fought it for all of a second, then softened in defeat. Later. Definitely later. Her body began relaxing beneath him, her thighs parting as she cradled him back into her grasp. The insistent press of his erection made her sleepy eyes open wide, and she saw the smoldering heat in his own pupils as they stared into each other's eyes.

The hard thick tip of his cock brushed against her entrance. Bishop half turned his head to the side, his lashes lowering over smoldering eyes as if he were concentrating. Verity arched her hips a little. Then he was almost breaching her, the blunt head of his cock sliding where his fingers had been and setting her alight. A faint hiss went through him. Dragging her nails up his side, she rolled her hips, and he sank deeper within her.

Inch by inch. Bishop's lips parted, his eyes slamming shut as he slid home. She loved watching the amazement dance over his face. Loved being the first one to show him this, how good it felt. Kissing his throat, she made a weird purring sound of contentment in her chest.

Verity arched her hips, her body taking him whole. She ached a little, but it was a well-earned ache of overuse that would soon soften. Sliding a hand down his spine, she wrapped her legs around his hips, digging her heels into the hard flex of his bottom to drive him deeper.

"Fuck," he breathed, his whole body moving in a smooth glide that filled her. His lip curled. "Fuck, Verity. You feel.... You're amazing."

She glowed deep within. "You've barely felt anything yet."

Clenching her inner muscles, she set him into a faster pace, losing herself to the push and pull of smooth skin and the satiny glide of muscle. Pleasure shivered through her, that little edge building within her again. So close. So... now.... Her mind went white-hot.

"Adrian," she gasped into his mouth as she half turned her head to the side to gain a moment to breathe.

Bishop groaned against her shoulder. "Getting close," he whispered.

She didn't care. "Then come with me."

"Wanted... to make this... last."

Verity giggled and he groaned again as her body tightened around him. This man.... This man lost all sense of control when he was in her bed, and she loved it.

"Wench," he growled, slapping the side of her bottom.

Then he was withdrawing between one thrust and the next, grabbing her hips and rolling her onto her elbows and knees. She had just a second to grasp his intentions before he thrust inside her again, this time from behind.

Thoughts scattered. He was so deep inside her that she couldn't think.

"Je-sus," he hissed, and the next thrust slowed.

A warm hand slid down her spine, his fingers curling in the mess of her braid. That insistent tug forced her head back, forced her spine to arch until his cock was riding over something deep within her. Something that beckoned another quake. She let it ripple through her, crying out loudly as his thrusts sped up, and then he buried himself in her for a long, heart-stopping moment, before withdrawing swiftly.

Hot seed spilled over her back. Verity collapsed into the pillow, resting her forehead on her wrists. Her entire body shook and quivered from the aftermath, and then something rough wiped over her back—his towel maybe—

and he spilled them both into the sheets, breathing hard as he tossed it aside. Somehow Verity found herself sprawled in his arms, her cheek resting on his shoulder. Strong arms wrapped around her, his hand cupping the base of her skull as if he held something precious. Verity snuggled in against him, more content than she'd ever been.

Until she remembered what he'd said about sex giving her energy. Her eyes blinked open, her hand pausing on his chest, mid-contented-rub.

Bishop's abdominals flexed as he lifted his head to look down at her, no doubt sensing the sudden reticence in her body. "I pulled out in time, Ver."

There was a little pang in her chest, even though she knew he meant to protect her. Meant it for her own good. A little part of her, however, wondered what it would be like to hold a baby in her arms. A baby with his eyes.

She didn't dwell on that thought for long. Just a second before she set it aside. Bishop wouldn't want to bring a bastard into the world, not when he'd been born one himself. He'd been fairly closed off to her when they were linked, but she'd caught just enough of his secret thoughts to know that illegitimacy bit at him. And he would never do that to her, leave her alone to raise a baby like his mother had been.

So she set it aside and didn't look back.

"What was all that about?" she whispered, glancing up into his eyes. The coals in the grate had long since died down to a muted glow, but her vision had adjusted to the dark. She could make out the curve of shadows across his cheekbones and the faint dip above his well-formed mouth.

"I'm fairly certain that was obvious," he said, smiling as he kissed the tip of her nose.

"Ha, ha," she replied drolly and smacked his arm. Settling down again, she couldn't resist stroking his arm, touching him... little signs of affection. "You know what I mean. That was... fairly intense, even for you. Where did you go? What happened?"

"I couldn't sleep," Bishop admitted, and she rubbed his chest as her heart ached for him. "Thought I might as well take care of Horroway. Make sure he won't come looking for you."

"Did you find him?"

Bishop shifted. "Aye. I killed him."

So that was what drove him tonight; the power and energy of Horroway's death. Verity kissed his pectoral, then snuggled back in against him, anxiety making itself felt inside her. Of all the things that she'd suspected she might lose him to, this was the one she felt like she didn't have a chance at fighting back against. His own demons. His own craving.

Stronger than what he felt for her.

She swallowed the lump in her throat. "So Horroway's dead. Good riddance."

"I felt... sorry for him in the end."

She glanced up.

"He's vile, and a sniveling coward—he always has been," Bishop's voice lowered, as though he spoke through a mouth of gravel. "But he knew what it felt like. To live like this."

She saw the doubt in him. "You did the right thing. Who knows what trouble he could have caused?"

"I didn't do it because of that." Bishop sighed, then kissed her fingers. "He wanted me to do it. God, he was so tired, so.... And I felt sorry for him in a way, because Morgana played him. She promised him the Chalice and the power of it, and then she discarded him when he lost it. Jesus." His eyes stared into the distance, seeing something else.

Verity wanted to rub the loneliness and ache she saw from his expression, but settled for kissing his shoulder again. "Did he say anything about them? About Morgana? And Tremayne?"

"No." Bishop sighed, turning on his side to face her, those talented hands stroking her face, her cheek, the hair off her brow. It was as though he couldn't stay still.

"So what do we do now?" she whispered.

"Now? I was thinking about sleep," he grumbled.

Verity smiled. "But tomorrow?"

"Find Morgana. Kill her. Tremayne too, if possible," he muttered, resting one hand behind his head as he sank back into the pillow. He glanced at her. "Kiss you as often as I can."

Verity nestled against his side. "That sounds promising."

"You bloodthirsty little thing...."

Verity poked him when he laughed. "I was talking about the kissing part. You do need the practice."

Dark eyes slid her way. "Practice, huh?"

"Or maybe that's just an excuse," she whispered, lowering her face and tracing her tongue along his lower lip.

Bishop's hand slid through her tangled hair as he drew her down against his mouth. This time it was sweet. Gentle. A kiss to steal her heart, not just her breath. Verity felt a bittersweet twinge in her chest as she broke away from him. Who would have guessed this taciturn, scowling assassin would be everything she'd ever turned out to want?

But he hadn't said a word about her in return, or about how he felt.

"Mmm," she said, drawing back and catching her breath. "I do think you're beginning to get the hang of it."

Bishop trailed the backs of his fingers down the slope of her naked breast and she shivered, then shook her head.

"Not again. Not tonight. Or I swear I won't be able to sit at all tomorrow."

Instantly, he was all contrition. "You said I didn't hurt you."

Verity sank into his arms. "You didn't. But you have ridden a horse before, yes? It's like when you haven't ridden for months, then suddenly think you can handle eight hours in the saddle."

A faint smile traced his mouth. A somewhat smug smile that was infinitely male.

"Oh, shut up," she said, slapping his shoulder.

He caught her hand and dragged her around until she was curled in his embrace, his breath blowing over the back of her neck. "Tomorrow," he murmured, curving a hand around her breast and snuggling her in, "I am going to claim all of those kisses you're promising. Which means you should definitely get some more sleep."

I love you. Verity rested her head on the pillow and bit her lip as the blatant truth streaked through her. *And I won't let you go. No matter what this prophecy says, or how much the* maladroise *pulls at you.*

The world had tried to take everything she loved away from her: her father, when he walked out on them; her mother; her home; even Mercy....

This time, Verity was going to fight back.

CHAPTER
TWENTY-SEVEN

SEBASTIAN WAITED.

Perhaps that was the worst part, for he truly had begun to believe that the man who had sired him wanted to be his father.

"I'll return," Drake had promised him. *"Tomorrow at the latest. Then we can begin to work out where you are, and get you out of there."*

Hollow promises. *Jesus.* He should have known better, but even though Morgana had done her best to stamp hope out of him during his youth, that little boy inside him still remained.

Maybe Drake had tried? Maybe the fact that his mother had moved them in the middle of the night to another house had thwarted Drake's efforts?

"You idiot," he whispered to himself with dried, cracked lips. If Drake had Cleo at his side, then it wouldn't matter where Morgana moved them. All he had to do was follow that link between Cleo and Sebastian, that bond.

Even now it stretched away into the distance if Sebastian closed his eyes and imagined a golden rope tied between them. West. Cleo dwelled somewhere in the west.

He hoped she stayed there.

Cleo. He didn't know why the memory of her would haunt him so often. She might be his wife, but he'd only known her less than a week before all had gone to rack and ruin.

Still... those brief meetings had been more than enough to tell him that she came from a different world than the one he lived in.

Cleo. With her blonde, silky hair, and her endless kindnesses and soft voice. He couldn't forget the one night when they'd shared a bed for almost a half hour—their wedding night—before he'd fled from the bed in shame.

Sex held no interest for him. All it had ever been was forced and shameful. He was beautiful. He knew that. Women told him all the time, with their hungry eyes and their incessant need to own him for the night. His mother had allowed it, handing over the ring that controlled his *sclavus* collar—and hence him—for the night to entertain them, in an effort to convince them to join her in her revenge schemes. He'd hated every second of it. Sometimes his body obeyed him, leaving them unfulfilled, but there had been some who had worked his body like a well-oiled machine until it no longer obeyed his command, but theirs. It left him feeling violently ill and desperate to scrub their perfume off him. If he had a choice, he never wanted to touch another woman again.

But for a moment, when Cleo had lain beside him in that bed, he'd almost... wondered about it. Cleo smelled like apricot soap, with her hair spread across the pillow as she waited for him to touch her. Silvery hair in the moonlight.

She'd barely been breathing, as if waiting for him to lay a hand on her.

And he'd wanted to. For just a moment. Wanted to pretend that he wasn't what he was, and that the filth of his past, of what he'd done, of what he'd been forced to do, couldn't contaminate her purity if he touched her.

"You are what you are," Morgana whispered in his memory, *"You are my son. Mine."*

And it was true. There was a darkness in him that he couldn't deny.

He had no place dreaming of someone like Cleo.

Sebastian clenched his eyes tightly, banishing thoughts of her before he could truly lose himself to despair. His father was another hope, another dream, he couldn't have. This cold cellar around him—stinking of rotten onions— was the cold, hard truth of his life.

Footsteps echoed in the hallway outside. Letting out a hopeless breath, Sebastian flexed his wrists against the manacles that bound him. At least they were no longer held high above his head. The demon had made good on that promise at least. He prepared himself for anything.

A clank, the sound of a lock being turned, and then it opened and light flooded inside. Sebastian straightened, his head turning toward the door even as his eyes flinched shut against the light.

The long moment of silence stretched out, then boots stepped down into his makeshift cell. "Here," said the demon wearing Noah Guthrie's body. It set something down—a tray covered in a small towel—and the scent of food made his stomach ache.

Holding the cup to his lips, it poured water into his mouth. Sebastian drank greedily, though a part of him hoped the water was pure and not drugged. He was too thirsty to pay the proper caution.

Finally, the demon lowered the cup. "I brought food."

It had been two days since he'd last eaten. The demon unfastened his manacles, and Sebastian knelt on the ground, flipping aside the warm linen cloth. Bread. *Jesus.* And soup. His mouth watered and he set to with a vengeance, breaking apart the bread with his bare hands and stuffing it in his mouth ravenously.

"I am sorry I did not come earlier," the demon said. "The human processes elude me sometimes. I did not think to feed you until your mother and Tremayne sat down to dine."

Sebastian tilted the bowl to his lips and drained the salty broth, washing down the bread that stuck in his throat. His stomach gave a warning lurch, but he couldn't have stopped himself if he tried. Using the last bit of bread to mop up the barley and dregs of meaty liquid in the bottom of the bowl, he looked up, gauging the demon's cool expression before he set the bowl aside. His stomach rumbled. More. He wanted more.

He was probably lucky to get what he had.

"What do you want?" he demanded.

One of the demon's eyebrows arched. It tilted its head. "You are angry."

Better that than the despondency that had filled him during the last twenty-four hours. His hands curled into fists. He glanced toward the door.

"You wouldn't get far," the demon said. "Your mother is upstairs and she's wearing the ring."

As if to punctuate the words, the collar at his throat throbbed. Sebastian slumped back against the wall. Hopeless.

"What do you want?" he repeated, and this time the words echoed emotionlessly.

"I have a proposition for you," the demon said.

I'll bet. Everybody wanted something from him. But perhaps he could play it both ways? Tit for tat. Every muscle in his body locked tight. "I'm listening."

It cocked its head to the side, idly stroking the rash at its collar. "I have promised Noah that I will give him back his body, which means I have need of another."

It looked at him—looked through him—and sheer terror obliterated his senses.

"*No way in hell,*" he breathed. It was the only thing that had ever been his, and even then others had abused it, and done what they wished with it. But this....

"Oh, I don't want you," the demon said. "Not for very long, anyway. But there is a very important meeting to be held tomorrow. You're the ace up my sleeve. The last gambit I can play. And we share similar aims. You want revenge. So do I."

That soothed his terror for a second. Sebastian rested his wrists on his knees and stared at the creature, starting to think. What did he have to lose? Really? What would it be like to be trapped inside his own body, no longer in control of it?

Something rather like this, he imagined.

He couldn't escape on his own. He'd tried. And his father wasn't going to ride to his rescue. That hope had been brief, a fantasy he flirted with more than anything else, but there'd been no sign of his father.

Revenge.

If there was one thing that he lived for, that might just be it.

"I only want you for twenty-four hours. That's all I'll need."

He thought about it. Could it do anything that was worse than what had already been done to him?

The demon knelt, his arms resting loosely on his upper thighs. "This is what I want, Sebastian, and in exchange I swear that I will set you free and help you to snuff your mother's life out."

That thought pushed him over the edge, convincing him like none other. Demons couldn't lie, after all. "What do I have to do?"

"This way," Verity said, holding the ring in her hand as she walked through Berkley Square. She'd woken that morning feeling quite determined to see an end to this. As soon as Morgana was found and the Ascension sorted, she and Bishop could begin moving forward in their lives. Or working out where they both stood.

Verity paused at the next intersection, hackneys clopping past. She stared at the ring in her hand, feeling it tug her back in the opposite direction. What on earth?

Bishop paused by her side, glancing around. Always on guard, as though he couldn't relax whenever he was outside the safety of his own home. Assured that there was nothing of concern in the immediate vicinity, he looked down

"Bloody cock-swiving piece of—" She looked up, sensing eyes upon her.

The corners of Bishop's mouth had crooked up, though he tried to straighten them when he saw her looking. "Go on. I'm trying to increase my vocabulary."

That was the Dials showing in her. Verity colored up, feeling the heat flush through her cheeks. She shook the ring, but the directional tug changed again, leaving her quite perplexed. The pull of the ring seemed to be leaping all over the city. One moment it was north of her, the next south-east, and now it was tugging her toward the west. "I'm not certain...."

Bishop's hard body shielded her from the wind. "What's wrong?"

Verity hated to admit failure, but from what her magic was telling her, Morgana had now leapt to the far east of the city. "It's not working. I can't.... It feels like she's moving. Or like something's preventing me from getting a lock on her."

Bishop tipped her chin up. "Tune everything out. Close your eyes. And trust your instincts."

Easy for him to say. She'd never had to force her talents before. They came to her as easily as breathing. And now.... Verity opened her eyes and shook her head, finally admitting the blatant truth. "I can't find her."

"She must have realized that somebody was watching her."

"This always works!"

"Not if Morgana's somehow managed to ward her presence from you. If she's working with Noah Guthrie and the demon, then it's possible she knows the extent of your talents."

"The demon never knew what I could do," she pointed out. "Murphy made sure of that."

"Verity—"

"No! This is not right!" She brushed off his hand and took two steps toward the south and the magical leash that drew her in that direction. She'd never failed before, damn it! And she couldn't do it right now, not when Bishop needed her so badly.

But the direction had changed again. Verity's shoulders slumped in defeat. "Son of a bitch," she swore, ignoring a startled passerby, who looked at her disapprovingly.

Firm hands slid over her shoulders. "Patience, Verity. Have faith."

"I wanted to help you," she said, glancing over her shoulder.

Those warm brown eyes met hers. She'd never seen such beautiful eyes on a man before. "You are helping me," he pointed out. "But I'm an assassin, Ver. Hunts don't always end so quickly. I didn't expect it to be this easy."

"So what now?"

Bishop scrubbed at his mouth. "Now I think we need to go see my father. Turn our attentions to the Ascension and prepare to bait that particular trap."

"You think she'll be there?"

"All Morgana has ever wanted is power, and to pay my father back for the divorce. A chance to sit someone on the seat of the Prime?" He smiled, and it wasn't very nice. "She'll be there. She won't be able to resist."

CHAPTER
TWENTY-EIGHT

THE TRIP to Willoughby Hollow proved uneventful. Snow was beginning to fall as Bishop and Verity exited the carriage they'd shared with Drake and Eleanor. Ascension had finally arrived and all of the sorcerers of the Order would be travelling here to bear witness.

Including the one who formed the greatest threat to his father: the son who mirrored him.

Bishop's half brother.

If there was one weakness that Drake owned, it was the thought of Sebastian.

The horses stamped with sweat-slicked flanks as the carriage rocked to the side, disbursing its contents. Their steamy breath fogged the air. Bishop fidgeted as he helped Verity down and looked around. He'd barely been able to sleep the night before, too many possibilities of what could happen today running through his mind. Though he wanted Verity at his side, it scared him a little, especially after holding her in his arms for the last two nights. She'd become precious to him in a way that he still didn't think he could quite accept, and the thought of her life being snatched away.... It terrified him.

According to Cleo Montcalm, Sebastian was still out there with his wild, impossible power; and the Earl of Tremayne, the demon, and Morgana were still at large. Horroway had been an important thread, but still only a thread. It would all come down to today.

"Still no change of heart?" Bishop asked his father lightly as Drake stepped down from the carriage. The forest around them was so still, with soft drifts of snowflakes blanketing the firs and beeches.

Drake glanced around. He looked like he'd aged ten years in a month, frost-bitten streaks stealing through his dark hair. Finally, he looked back at Bishop. "No change of heart." He hesitated. "I've been given a second chance with Sebastian. I don't intend to lose it. I can't lead the Order anymore, Adrian. I just can't."

It was a hard medicine to swallow, but Bishop felt like he finally understood his father's need to save this son. Drake had made a choice last month: Lucien's life in exchange for losing the chance to save Sebastian. He still wore the weight of that choice, and knowing now there was a chance to make amends for it.... The weight was lifting, and Bishop could see a spark of the man he'd once known as a father returning. How could he want his father to lose that spark? That hope?

Because the practical side of him also saw the future unfolding in front of them. Chaos, instability, an inside war that might tear the Order apart if the wrong person became Prime.

And Madrigal Brown, the Sicarii leader, with her knife poised over his father's throat.

"I thought Sebastian wasn't responding to you anymore?" Bishop asked, his breath fogging in the chill air.

"I'll keep trying."

Of course he would. "Do we even know if he's still alive?"

"Cleo knows. She's linked to him, and she tells me he's still there."

"So he's shut you out?" Bishop asked. Eleanor hovered on the top step of the carriage and Bishop reached up to help her down. The left side of her face was still faintly lax, but healers had been in to work on her again this week and Bishop could see a spark of her old self in her eyes.

"Maybe. If I could reach him once, then I can do so again," Drake told him.

If only it were that simple. Sebastian represented danger to his mind. A threat. Bishop didn't like the idea of that, however, as Verity had politely pointed out, not everything in the world should be seen as a threat. It was the assassin in him; looking at the reality of the situation rather than seeing it through the rose-colored glasses of familial affection, as Drake did.

This will only cause trouble. He knew that. And he was helpless to turn his father aside from this quest. A part of him wanted Drake to succeed. He loved his father. He'd do anything for him.

Even stand by and watch as Drake committed to this path that might damn them all.

Snow crunched under his boots and at his side, Eleanor lurched as she staggered on uneven ground.

Bishop caught her other hand as she staggered on the gravel. "Here. Easy, Eleanor. You don't want to fall."

She patted his hand gratefully, then limped forward to Verity's side.

Bishop watched them step toward the forest. "You can't save everyone," he said, turning back to his father.

"Just remember that. If Sebastian's blocked you out, then maybe he'll never listen to you. Don't throw everything away on a hope that might never come true. There has to be a point where you let go."

Drake gave him a sadly bemused smile. "If it were your mother, would you let her go so easily?"

God. The words were a knife to the chest. He stared his father in the eye. "Don't forget... once upon a time I had to make that choice and I *did* let go."

Turning around, he walked away, bitterly swallowing the lump in his throat. He knew it had been for the best. The pain was too great and his mother had pleaded with him—*begged* him—to let her go. Memory slashed through him, twisting his innards into knots. So much damage. So much pain. Christ save him, she'd been drowning in it. The peace on her face when he slowly, gently eased her over the threshold of death had been the only thing capable of saving his sanity at the thought of what he'd done.

Bishop clenched his gloved fingers into a fist, forcing the tension within him to dissolve.

He'd not known much about his power then.

If you had the chance now, knowing that you might be able to save her, would you still do it?

Would you risk everything, try anything to save her?

The answer to that held no other options. *Yes,* a thousand times over.

His shoulders sank. Maybe this would bring disaster to the Order, but he could no longer fault his father for his choices. Bishop paused and waited for Drake to fall into place beside him.

"If you need my help with him...." His voice came out dry as they set after the ladies. He couldn't feign excitement at the thought, no matter how hard he tried. "Then just tell me what to do. I'll respect your choice, even if I don't agree with it."

Drake limped along beside him, his cane sinking into the powdery snow that had fallen overnight. He silently clasped a hand on Bishop's shoulder. "Thank you."

Lights bobbed through the forest ahead of them as sorcerers streamed through the trees. Dusk was falling and the lights soon began to resemble those of will o' the wisp. Some were mage globes, hovering balls of pale white light that bobbed ahead of their owners. Others were merely lanterns.

Bishop tucked Verity's hand in the crook of his arm and nodded at a sorcerer he knew as the man ushered his two sisters through the snow. A buzz of nervous excitement lit through his veins. Too many trees. Too many people in hoods. The rest of the *Sicarii* could be anywhere.

All it would take would be one of them.

"This is amazing," Verity whispered, looking around. "Where are we going?"

"Willoughby Hollow," he replied, seeing it anew through her eyes. To someone who had known nothing of the Order he supposed that this was probably quite astounding.

A quick sideways glance showed her pert nose and upturned profile. There was something about Verity that was pure innocence. A joy in life that she couldn't hide, and one that beckoned him along with it. Being with her was like experiencing the world without the gloom and shadows that accompanied his version of it. Or perhaps, like stopping and actually seeing what was around him for the first time in years.

He wanted to show her more of the amazing things that filled his life; things he rarely even gave thought to anymore. Imagine what she'd think of the Samhain or Beltane rites? And the dancing then.

"The Hollow's a sacred place that the Order used when it was first established. The owner of the land was a sorceress named Amelia Kane. Upon her death she deeded the land to the Order. There's an enormous ley line running beneath it, that you might be able to feel when we get closer. Only sorcerers are welcome, and we celebrate the equinoxes here."

They were getting closer. More and more sorcerers streamed out of the trees, wearing red velvet capes. It was quite ethereal, if one looked at it in whimsical fashion.

Lucien, Ianthe, and Cleo Montcalm waited at an intersection of birches ahead of them. Trembling snowflakes quivered through the air, as if almost hesitant to touch the ground. He looked up, but the clouded skies promised only a light flutter of snow.

A flash of movement made him glance to the side. A sorcerer in a red cloak nodded at him, and unease skittered down Bishop's spine as the stranger slipped away through the trees. If he weren't imagining things, the man had been watching him.

There went the wonder. The sense of enjoyment.

He couldn't forget what else this was; a chance at power for a lot of people.

"Be on your guard," Bishop told Verity, looking around at the shadowy forest. Snow crunched underfoot and the scarlet robe that he wore dragged in it. Only Verity wore a robe of black velvet; the rest were adorned in red, like he, to indicate their status in the Order. "The grotto is a half mile away and if anyone is going to try something, it will be here. Once we're at the grotto, it's too late. Too many witnesses."

"Well-met," Ianthe called, stepping forward and greeting Eleanor, then kissing Drake on both cheeks. Her eyes met Drake's and Bishop wondered what they were both thinking.

Ianthe hadn't yet committed to throw her hat in the ring. As Bishop glanced past her, toward his half brother, he saw no sign of the answer there either.

"You expect trouble?" Lucien asked, stepping forward to clasp his hand. His half brother bore the rings of a sorcerer of the seventh level, and power spilled through his body to an immense degree. Bishop might not be able to match him in raw strength, but was certain his control and finesse with weaving sorcery granted him equal status.

He met his half brother's eyes. They were an unusual amber color, but Bishop saw perhaps a little similarity between them around the nose and the shape of the mouth. Disconcerting, to say the least. As was the tremor of power running between them as their hands linked. Bishop pulled his hand away. "I always expect trouble, but at this moment, I consider it a foregone conclusion."

Lucien's gaze shifted to his wife, and it was easy to see the emotions that flickered there.

"If anything happens, I'll protect Drake," he told his brother, to assuage his concerns. "You keep an eye on the ladies."

Ianthe overheard and arched a black brow. "Yes, do be a dear, darling, and make sure I'm safe."

Lucien held his hands up in surrender. "I didn't say it."

Ianthe snorted, and very deliberately rolled her eyes in Bishop's direction. "Is he always like this?" she asked Verity, tucking an arm through Verity's elbow in a conspiratorial manner. "Paranoid, controlling, and grim?"

Verity considered him, then smiled. "Only until you get to know him. He's not half as grim underneath and I prefer to think of him as practical, rather than controlling. He wouldn't be so stupid as to tell me he'd protect me. The last time that happened he ended up in an icy bath."

"What is wrong with wanting to protect you?" he countered, ignoring her reference to the bath.

That smile softened in mysterious ways, and Verity patted his hand. "There's nothing wrong with wanting to protect me. It shows you care. But keeping me out of harm's way while you try to save the day...."

"Would be a waste of breath," Ianthe added. "You're not the only dangerous one here."

Bishop shook his head. Outnumbered. "In hindsight it was a stupid thing to say. I meant only to set Lucien's mind at ease. Not to doubt anyone's abilities. Are we all satisfied?"

"Nice save," Lucien murmured, coughing into his hand.

Drake sighed. "Behave, children. Now let's get moving." He took Eleanor and Cleo by the arms and set out toward the grove, as if there could be nothing threatening out there.

Another flash of movement had Bishop turning, his attention locked on the trees. A clump of snow dumped off a heavily laden fir, as if something had brushed it. Bishop placed a hand in the small of Verity's back and directed her onto the boot-trampled path on his father's heels. "Perhaps I should take the lead?"

"Relax," Drake murmured back over his shoulder. "They'd be fool to make a tilt at us now. There are four sorcerers here wearing seven rings, and there's nobody alive who can get past my wards."

Nervousness inched down his spine like icy fingertips marching over his skin. He could get past his father's wards, but he'd never told Drake that. Maybe he should have? "That's precisely why I expect it. Because nobody with any common sense would dare, and our guard will be lowered. Perfect time. Perfect place."

Drake looked at him, shaking his head, and he knew that his father didn't quite understand the way he thought. He'd never had to.

Cleo's head shot up, a gasp coming from her lips. "Drake!"

A flash of movement—

"Get down!" Bishop barked, leaping forward and slamming his shoulder into Drake's back. He locked his arms around his father's waist as they both went down, Bishop rolling them in the snow until his father was beneath him. The blaze of an etheric blade flew through the air above him, exploding against the tree behind them. A punch of fear slammed through him. "Verity?"

She had a hand on Cleo's head, forcing the young woman into a crouch behind a tree. "I'm fine."

Another glance raked the clearing. Lucien had Ianthe and Eleanor. And Drake's wards shimmered to life around them like a soap bubble. Almost transparent, with the oil-slick gleam of a rainbow painted over its surface. Tree branches rustled as the assailant darted back through them. All he saw was the flutter of a red cloak, and then it was gone, vanishing into the shadows.

"Stay down," he told his father, his etheric blade forming in his hand with an electric buzz of energy. "Don't any of you leave Drake's wards."

Then he was running, the ward shivering over his skin like a cool glove before vanishing the second he was through it.

Bursting through the interlocked branches of a pair of firs, he sent snow flying. A flash of red taunted him, and he staggered in a deceptive hole beneath the snow before twisting and ducking after the assailant.

Slamming through clearing after clearing, he finally paused, his breath coming in great heaving exhales that fogged in the air in front of him.

Nothing.

Footsteps crunching through snow. Bishop tilted his head, narrowing his focus down to his hearing, forcing out everything else around him except for those footsteps. Left. He turned his head, tracking the assailant, and then, crouching low, he slipped through the trees after the fellow. He'd been expecting Sicarii, but the sheer blundering missteps the idiot was making argued against it.

The assassin threw a glance back over his shoulder— just a glimpse of a pale, face, eyes widening as the fellow saw him.

Bishop leapt over a log, blood thumping through his veins as he poured on speed. He wanted answers. But the violent urge of the *maladroise* began to whisper to him, sweet, sweet lures of *how good it would feel*, and *how hungry Horroway's pitiful spark had left it.*

The assassin ducked and wove with Bishop barely ten feet behind him. Another glance over his shoulder, and then an etheric blade was flipping end over end toward Bishop.

Bishop threw himself beneath it, coming up in a roll, only to face another shimmering blade of pure power. He slammed both wrists together and a ward shimmered to life just in time. Power lashed through his ward as the knife collided with it, setting off a showering shimmer of sparks. The energy grounded itself in the earth beneath his feet, leaving him kneeling in a perfect circle of pure snowmelt.

Son of a bitch. Bishop didn't think. Just flipped his wrist forward and threw as his ward flickered out.

The etheric blade flew straight and true, even as instant regret soured his mouth. It buried itself in the middle of that red cloak, and the would-be assassin staggered a step, then plummeted face-first into the snow.

And didn't move.

A small, pale spark floated above the body, beckoning just for a moment. *Yes. God, yes— No!* Bishop curled his fists into his body, fighting against the pull of the *maladroise.* His jaw ached as he ground his teeth together, and he shook and shivered, blinded to the world around him for the few seconds it took to fight his way through it. Before his eyes, the soul-spark slowly vanished.

It took longer than he'd expected to find his feet. Damn it. If he'd waited he might have some answers by now. A part of him wondered whether he'd reacted merely on instinct, or whether that thrice-cursed hunger had taken over for a second.

Bishop rolled the body over.

It was nobody he knew.

And that was when he heard the scream.

Verity had spent a lot of time on the streets, working as a dipper and a spotter, or even running rackets.

She recognized a con when she saw one. The second Bishop slammed into the forest after the would-be assassin, Verity suddenly realized what a target they all made, sitting there. For an outsider looking in, all they'd see would be two male sorcerers, one whose doubt had cost him the mantle of Prime, and another still wounded by some mysterious assault on his aura; a woman who might be able to match them but couldn't protect all of them; a young woman with no training; the still-crippled Eleanor; and herself, an unknown, but certainly not a threat to watching eyes.

Bishop was the most dangerous one out of all of them. And now he was gone.

"Damn it!" Drake cursed, rolling to his feet and reaching for his cane. He glanced toward Eleanor, hesitation marking his face, before he turned toward the silent forest. "We have to go after him."

Which would play directly into someone's plans.

"Wait!" Verity darted forward and grabbed his arm. "There's a con we run in the Dials—when we're trying to steal from someone rich, we send in a decoy. He's cocky, draws attention, makes the con focus on him, because he looks exactly like what a thief looks like and the noble doesn't want him anywhere near him. That's when I show up dressed in silk and bump into the con. Within two seconds I've got his purse and I'm away, stammering apologies and pretending to be all virtuous and embarrassed. He never thinks I'm the thief because he's too busy watching the decoy."

"So what you're saying is that this was a distraction?" Drake's eyes narrowed.

"That's how I'd play it. Bishop's not in danger," Verity breathed, looking around the suddenly still forest. "They've drawn him away. If we separate, we play directly into their hands."

Drake met her eyes and she saw the moment he realized the truth. The only person who could match a Sicarii assassin was another one. "Don't move out of the ward," he said, and sudden tension suffused the group as they all looked into the darkened trees.

"Lucien, could you see to Eleanor and Cleo?" Ianthe asked, settling herself in the middle of the group.

"Got them," he replied, tugging the pair of women into the space around him. A second ward crackled down over them, which made Drake sigh with relief and turn his gaze outwards.

Ianthe's blue eyes lit on Verity. "Drake and I will protect you—"

"It's not necessary," Drake cut in, nodding at her. "Verity's our secret weapon."

Ianthe looked at him sharply, then nodded. She put her back to Drake's and the pair of them stared out into the forest.

A tall figure dressed in a red velvet cape stepped out of the trees, wearing a blank silver mask that hid his or her features. Another joined them. Then another. And another, until finally there were seven sorcerers in all locking them in.

"You would be wise not to do this," Drake called, and Verity startled at the powerful sound of his voice. She'd grown quite used to the soft-spoken man with his sad eyes and gentle nature.

The circle began to draw in power and the hairs on Verity's arms lifted as they all joined hands.

"Not even you can challenge a full circle of seven," one of the masked figures sneered. "We've grown weary of your puppet strings. This time we're going to take back what we're owed."

Drake's eyes narrowed. "Tremayne."

The stranger lifted his hand to the mask and cast it aside, an ugly smirk splitting his face. They were of an age, but from the intensity in both their eyes, Verity guessed that these two men held bad blood between them.

Cleo screamed, taking a half step forward. "Father!" Cleo begged, stepping out from under Lucien's wards. "Don't do this."

Tremayne barely glanced her way. "You're not my daughter anymore. The second you cast your allegiance in with him was the second we stopped being blood."

Cleo swallowed and tilted her chin up. "This won't end well for you."

"You think I believe that you've Seen it?" Emotion turned his expression ugly. "I took your blindfold away, you little bitch. And with it your gifts."

"Not all of them," Drake replied, stepping between father and daughter, faint power blurring the air around his hands. Where Tremayne flaunted his sorcerous strength, Drake didn't bother. Verity would have bet money on the outcome of this battle based purely on that fact alone. She'd seen enough posturing in the Dials, and the mere fact that Tremayne doubted the outcome enough to bring six others with him....

Tremayne shook his head. "You couldn't remain content with merely destroying our friendship, could you, Drake? You had to steal everything—Morgana, my relics, the mantle of Prime... and now my daughter."

"The problem with you, Tremayne, is that you think you own everything and that the world owes you a favor. Perhaps it was you who drove your daughter away from your side?"

An immense wave of power flung directly toward them. Verity was a microsecond away from getting the hell out of there when Drake merely brushed it aside.

One of the masked sorcerers trembled, as if hit by the backlash. Their cloaks blew backwards with the impact, then fell still.

"Stand straight, you weakling," Tremayne snapped at the swaying sorcerer, and the circle around him buoyed him with new strength. "This has been a long time coming, old *friend.*"

A dozen vicious red battle globes sprang to life in the air around Tremayne's head. Whoa. Verity stepped back, retreating to Ianthe's side. She didn't know how to make them—none of the Hex did—but she knew what mage globes could do. She'd heard more than enough stories, and red were the strongest.

"Stay out of it," Ianthe warned, capturing her upper arm.

"Quite happily," Verity replied. This was well outside her boundaries.

Power flowed through Ianthe and directly into Drake, as though they were linked. It made Verity dizzy to realize how much raw energy the duke was manipulating.

Drake took a step forward and battered Tremayne with a wave of sorcery. Tremayne countered it, and sparks flew as the two waves of energy met. One of Tremayne's linked sorcerers—the one who'd wavered before—collapsed backward into the snow. The others stepped closer, joining hands again to make up for the break.

"Fight me," Tremayne snarled, and sent two of his mage globes flying toward Drake.

They shattered against Drake's invisible wards, the explosion making Verity cry out and clap her hands over her eyes. Two more explosions sounded, and a pair of whizzing hisses, like fireworks. Scrambling behind Ianthe, she peered over the other woman's shoulder.

Drake had his own mage globes in play now. He focused them on Tremayne, ignoring the linked sorcerers fuelling the earl.

It was a moment of utter fairness, but she swiftly realized the futility. Take out Tremayne's sorcerers and he wouldn't have the strength to face Drake.

Bishop would see the sense in that, but then sometimes he swayed too far into the darkness. Drake was his complete opposite.

"Can I get through Drake's wards?" she shouted in Ianthe's ear.

The other woman swayed. Not from fatigue, but from the sheer force of power she was allowing to conduit through her. "Physically, yes! Don't translocate through though. Sorcery can't penetrate them." She blinked over her shoulder, drawing just enough of her attention away from the fight. "What are you going to do?"

"I thought I might distract his little ring of sorcerers."

Ianthe ground her teeth together. "It's a nice idea, but there's a lot of sorcery being flung about. Bishop won't thank me if I hand you back to him in pieces. Drake can handle this."

Then she turned her attention back to the exploding gamut of battle globes.

Something hissed and fizzed at the ground beside Verity. She looked down and saw the edges of Drake's oil-slick ward crackling at the bottom, much the same way Horroway's had when Lady Eberhardt was infiltrating them. What on earth...?

Instinct propelled her to look around. A shadow moved out there in the dark, a person in a black hood waving their hands as they muttered under their breath. She thought she saw someone else out there too, just waiting until the wards lifted.

These were tactics she knew. Send in somebody flamboyant to steal Drake's attention and then attack when his back was turned.

"Ianthe!" She pointed to the wards. They'd lifted almost a foot off the ground by now.

Ianthe's face paled.

"I'll stop it," Verity said, and then ran toward the base of the wards. She slid onto her knees and side, sliding through the snow under the ward. The second she was through, a weave of something dark and deadly flung toward her, but she was ready and vanished.

Verity reappeared behind a tree, and ducked immediately as a battle globe of violent red drove toward her face. It hit the tree, which exploded into flame as she dove away, her skirts tangling in her legs.

More of them. How many...? Verity panted as she punched through time and space, flickering in and out just enough to count. At least a dozen black-robed figures slipped through the woods, waiting for the wards to fail.

There was no time to be nice about this anymore.

Verity snagged a tree root in one of her hops and then reappeared directly behind the sorcerer infiltrating the wards. She slammed the tree root across the back of his head, but it met some sort of resistance and she got the hell out of there the second she realized, just as a net of woven sorcery threads was flung toward her.

Landing in a tree, she peered down, breathing hard. She had no other weapons, and it was clear that they were watching each other's backs, with wards in place, and spells for the unwary.

"Bishop!" She threw the thought out into the world, hoping that he'd pick up on it somehow. She wasn't remotely telepathic but he'd trained himself to be so, and if there was still that link between them.... *"We need you!"*

The ward was halfway up. Sweat darkened Drake's face now, and he cast an uneasy glance at it.

No time to lose.

Well. She had a few tricks up her sleeves.

The black robes started hammering Drake's ward with battle globes, as if they knew they'd been discovered. Lucien turned to face the threat, his own wards expanding out to slip beneath the skin of Drake's. Blood trickled from his nose and he stared blankly, face straining with effort as he tried to hold.

And Verity focused on the nearest black robe, watching as he drew back his hand to throw the red globe forming in his fingertips. Needed to time this exactly right....

She stepped outside of time and reappeared, grabbing his sleeve and dragging him back with her. When they landed, the battle globe flew from his fingertips,

Verity swayed, the weight of taking him with her weighing heavily on her strained resources. Another sorcerer turned to look at her, and drew back his arm....

She punched behind him and reappeared with him directly in front of another of the black robes. They both unleashed dangerous magic, knocking each other off their feet, but she was gone again, collapsing with her back to a distant tree.

"Stop!" one of them screamed, and the barrage on the wards disappeared.

She didn't have it in her to make another leap, but they didn't know that.

A tickling sensation brushed against her mind. This time she recognized it and opened herself up to it the way Bishop had taught her.

"Verity!" Bishop bellowed.

"Right here," she grumbled back, pressing her fingertips to her temples. *"You don't have to yell."*

"What the hell is going on?"

"Ambush." She felt something alien shift through her skin. *"What are you doing?"*

"Looking out through your eyes."

"Oh." She let him.

"Do you trust me?" he asked.

"Of course I do."

A hesitation came. *"I'm going to strengthen the bond between us, so that I can act as a conduit for you. It will give you my strength momentarily, somewhat like an Anchor and Shield bond."*

"A what?"

"No time," he shot back. *"Without runes, it's only temporary but it will help. Can you handle my strength?"*

"I can handle anything *you can give me."*

Another hesitation. *"Was that an innuendo?"*

Verity smiled, and knew he felt it.

"Agatha's a bad influence," he muttered, then pushed something toward her. *"Here. Accept the link."*

Verity clawed after his link, and nearly fell out of the tree as an enormous surge of power shot through her. She felt like she could move mountains. *"Jesus Christ."* He was so strong.

"Watch your back, and remember this is borrowed strength. You'll pay the price for this tomorrow. I'm coming."

Then his connection cut down to a narrow thread. She knew he was still there, a link stretching between them, but they both needed to concentrate right now.

"Right," she muttered, her gaze locking on a black robe. She looked at the fight in the center of the clearing, then the sky above it. Time to get her bearings. Time to pack some punches.

Verity swooped, punching in and taking the black robe with her. It was growing easier the more often she did it. Reappearing above Tremayne, she let the black robe go as gravity sucked at them both, and punched out, landing flat on her back in the snow behind a birch tree.

The black robe screamed and plummeted out of the air, landing where Tremayne had been standing mere seconds ago. Tremayne darted aside, looking around and then up with a curse. Drake smashed at him with another wave of force, and Tremayne staggered back into the arms of a snow-laden birch. A circle of bare earth lit the ground around the ward where magic had melted the snow.

Verity moved. Flickering in and out. Grabbing another black robe and performing the same trick. This time above one of the linked sorcerers.

She hit the ground hard and rolled under a shrub as a black robe appeared out of nowhere and dived for her. Then she was gone again, reappearing behind him as he scrambled under the shrub for her. Verity grabbed his ankles and hauled him flat in the snow.

"Bitch!" the black robe hissed, and turned to shoot a sphere of pale blue light at her.

Verity vanished again.

Bishop's energy wasn't endless. She collapsed into the hollow of a tree, pausing to catch her breath as the fight raged around her. Drake and Ianthe were winning now, with red-robed sorcerers falling faint in a ring around them as they hammered at them with magic. Tremayne screamed in pure rage as he pushed his way out of the birch and took stock of his plot and how it was failing.

"Time to finish this, Drake!" he bellowed, and pulled so much energy into himself that the ground began trembling.

The black robes around her looked down in dismay. One of them screamed and turned to run.

"Get back, you coward!" the main one bellowed again, but the rest of them could see the way the tide was turning. One of them bolted straight past her hollow with her cloak flapping. Verity got a good look at her face.

Violent explosions of light detonated in the clearing. Again. And again. Verity buried her arm in her sleeve as a rush of pure force slammed her back into the hollow, her hair tearing from her chignon and whipping past her.

When it was done, Verity looked up from her arm. Her ears were ringing and white bars flashed across her vision, blinding her partly. She could make out figures standing in the clearing, but she wasn't sure precisely who. The stink of burned flesh made her wince.

Translocating closer, she crept out from behind a bush, relief flooding through her as she saw that her little party was all still alive, though both Ianthe and Drake were flat on their backs, as if knocked there. Lucien lowered a shimmering ward, Eleanor and Cleo clamped tightly to his side. He looked for Ianthe, then hurried to her side, helping her to sit up. Ianthe winced as she saw the burning red robes lying in the snow around them.

Including Tremayne.

Drake pushed to his knees, cursing under his breath. "You bloody fool." He reached forward and vanquished the flames licking greenly at Tremayne's fallen body.

Cleo clapped her hands to her lips as she took a half step toward Tremayne. "Father," she whispered.

Drake cast her a glance. "I'm sorry. The only way to stop him was to ward him in with all that energy."

The young woman nodded, swallowing hard. "I know." She squeezed her eyes tightly closed. "I know."

Verity crept out of the shadows, looking around. She'd seen what Order sorcerers could do when they set their minds to it. But the sheer scale of this astounded her.

Bishop charged out of nowhere. He paused when he saw the circle of fallen sorcerers, his breath coming hard. "Are you all right?" he demanded, striding toward her.

She slid into his arms, thanking every god under the sun that he'd returned to her safe and whole. Bishop looked surprised, but squeezed her gently. The link between them surged at their proximity, and she looked up in surprise.

"I'd like to keep it open for the rest of the night, if it's all right with you?" he asked her. *"This is not over yet."*

Verity nodded, her hand slipping into his, as Cleo knelt by her father's side and reached out to gently close his open eyes.

Drake gently squeezed the young woman's shoulders. Tears wet her pale cheeks. Verity didn't know her well, but it had to hurt to watch her own father die, regardless of his crimes.

"Two down," Bishop murmured, watching the scene with an aloof expression.

He was speaking of Horroway, and now Tremayne.

Sometimes it chilled her to the core how pragmatically he could view this. A bad feeling assailed her. Two to go, if one considered both Morgana and his other brother, Sebastian. As he'd said, this was not over yet.

"Promise me that you won't do anything that will destroy your relationship with Drake," she whispered.

He looked at her. "Ver—"

"Promise me."

Bishop's lips thinned. "He's a threat to all of us. I won't sacrifice you. Nor my father. Nor any of the rest of our little group, out of hope that this brother has one small ounce of humanity left inside him."

"Not everything or everyone in the world has to be a threat," she replied. "All you see are shadows sometimes. What if there's a chance that he could be saved?"

"You don't believe that."

She looked toward Drake, who was pulling the steel masks off the red-robed sorcerers, wincing as he saw faces he obviously recognized. "He does."

That gave Bishop enough doubt to make him scowl a little. "My father sees what he wants to see."

"He thought he was getting through to Sebastian."

"Maybe he was wrong." Bishop shook her off him.

She caught his wrist. "This would destroy your father. You know it." And worse, it would destroy Bishop's relationship *with* his father, which she knew was vitally important to him, even if Bishop didn't speak of it. "Promise me."

He took a long time to answer. "I promise... that I won't act precipitously, Ver. But if push comes to shove, then I won't stand aside and let Sebastian destroy the people I love."

He stalked away, pausing to collect Eleanor and help her steady herself. If not for the rare gentleness he showed, like now, she'd sometimes wonder if he truly had a heart.

But then he had just said *the people I love*, and that included her.

Maybe there was a darkness inside him that would never go away, but maybe there was light there too?

CHAPTER TWENTY-NINE

TORCHES FLICKERED AROUND the grotto, highlighting over two hundred red robed shapes. Drake threw back the hood on his cloak, taking a torch from the wall as he walked to the channel of oil that lined the circular grotto. A shiver ran down Bishop's spine. This was it. He couldn't help feeling like disaster hovered over them.

"And so it is"—Drake lit the oil with his torch and it flared to life—"that my time is done and I pass the flame to another."

Flame ran along the narrow channel, making a hissing noise. The channel formed a circle in the heart of the grotto, with a bridge at either end leading to the stone slate in the center. A collective whisper echoed through the chamber.

Agatha stepped forward, wearing the white robe of one of the Triad Council who ruled beneath Drake. "All those who stand as candidates for the position of Prime, step forward and take a torch."

Three stepped forward: Madrigal Brown and two others that Bishop recognized, but whose names he couldn't quite recall. At his side, Lucien gave his wife a nudge and with a very faint sigh, Ianthe slid her hood back from her raven-dark hair and stepped forward as well.

Madrigal's gaze settled on her like a snake's. She knew who the competition was.

"Madrigal's *Sicarii*," Bishop whispered under his breath, knowing that Ianthe would hear him. "She has the gift of Foresight and has never lost a battle before. She'll see any move you make three seconds before you make it."

Ianthe tilted her head toward him, but gave no other sign that she heard him.

The ceremony drew one of the strange sorcerers into the circle to face Madrigal.

Agatha withdrew a handkerchief from her sleeve and held it aloft. "Yield," she called, her voice ringing through the room. "Or die. If you step outside the circle, then you are effectively yielding. The winner moves through to the next round, where they will face their final opponent." Glancing at Lord Hamersley, another Councilor, she arched a brow. "If you'll do the honors of warding the ring?"

He bowed his head and wove a faintly glimmering ward around the ring that would contain all sorcery within it.

Madrigal and her opponent stepped inside and faced each other, watching the handkerchief in Agatha's hand. Agatha dropped it and instantly the man launched a scathing attack on Madrigal, who merely warded herself and let the sparks shoot off her bubble-like ward.

It ended swiftly, as he'd predicted it would. Madrigal simply countered everything the fellow threw at her, until a well-timed battle globe knocked him off his feet, setting his coat on fire.

"I yield!" he bellowed, crawling back along the slate as Madrigal advanced.

She paused, glancing toward Agatha.

"Madrigal Brown advances as candidate," Agatha called.

Lucien shifted uncomfortably as his wife stepped into the ring to take Madrigal's place, turning to face her opponent, whom Bishop finally recognized as Lord Darville, a pompous popinjay who was nevertheless very dangerous.

"She'll win it," he murmured to his half brother.

"I know," Lucien breathed, never taking his eyes off her. "She's good."

Ianthe was better than good. She countered everything Darville threw at her, though her face was paler than usual. The fight in the forest had taken something out of her, however, and she stumbled briefly as Darville hit her with battle globe after battle globe.

"Come on," Cleo breathed.

"You can do it," Verity said, at his other side, bouncing up and down on her toes.

Bishop watched the interplay. "She's not giving it everything she has," he murmured, watching as Ianthe deflected another battle globe of burning red. He'd seen her fight before. Knew she had more in her. He'd missed most of the earlier battle, but Ianthe should be stronger than this.

Lucien's lips thinned. "She's conserving energy," he murmured. "For Madrigal."

She had to get there first.

But it seemed his doubt was misplaced. Ianthe finally countered the second Darville took a breath, and he realized that this was what she had been waiting for: Darville to overextend himself. Ianthe's fingers wove her sorcery into glimmers of shadows that circled her skirts, and she muttered under her breath, watching Darville the entire time. Her shadows took shape and form: shadow constructs. They stalked toward Darville and he swallowed hard, taking a step back. Flames brushed against his coat, forcing him to look down. One more step and he'd be out of the circle.

"Curse you!" he spat, flinging a red-tinged mage globe that flickered weakly. It went straight through the shadow construct that leapt for him. They dove on him and began pulling at his clothes, dragging him closer to the ring of flames. Nothing he did made any difference. "Yield!" he finally screamed as they threatened to cast him into the flames.

Ianthe flicked her hand, and the shadows melted into the floor. Darville shot her a hate-filled look, but she merely turned and waited for Madrigal to enter the ring again.

Both women faced each other. Madrigal wore her usual white gown, overflowing with lace, and her coiffure remained elegant. Ianthe, on the other hand, looked like she'd been through a storm and back, but there was power in the cool expression on her face, and intent burning in her eyes.

"It's time for a new Order," Madrigal told her, settling into a defensive stance.

Ianthe merely arched her brow. "We shall see."

"Wait."

The lone voice echoed through the grotto and heads turned, here and there, to see who had cried out. Both women stepped apart, turning to face the newcomer.

Snow crunched beneath a man's boots as he made his way through the press of the crowd. Bishop could feel it in his belly; a knot of power, like a vortex hovering just beneath the stillness of the water. It was immense, threatening to crash and burn over the top of them all. The hairs along his arms rose and he saw Lucien look down in shock before their eyes met.

Sebastian, Lucien mouthed.

So this was what it felt like to be in the presence of both of his brothers. He'd been kept out of the action last month, when Lucien and Drake faced Sebastian.

Perhaps his father had feared even then what Bishop might do.

"I claim a chance to contend for the seat of the Prime," Sebastian called, and the last few people stepped out of his path, revealing a tall man with silver-gray eyes, short dark hair, and a sinister smile.

Madrigal's entire face paled. "I yield," she cried out, as if she'd seen something in those moments that terrified her.

Ianthe glanced once at her husband and Bishop saw her swallow. Even at her best she was no match for Sebastian's wild, unpredictable power.

"Don't," Lucien breathed, taking a half step forward. He too had paled.

Ianthe stared at him for another long moment before shaking her head grimly, and turning to face Sebastian.

"Damn you." Lucien moved for the circle, but Bishop grabbed his arm.

"Wait," he growled, under his breath. There was something strange about Sebastian.

"State your name," Agatha called, though she looked a little uneasy.

Sebastian stepped through the ring of red-hooded sorcerers, and leapt up into the slate circle, clearing the flames with inches to spare. He turned, gracing Ianthe with a dangerous smile. "Sebastian Montcalm."

Everyone could see his face now. There was no hiding the fact that he was Drake's son. Every line of his face was a perfect echo of their father's.

"And I am here to become Prime."

He turned to face Ianthe.

It was the longest moment of Bishop's life. He'd promised Verity he wouldn't hurt his half brother, but this... this was disaster. If Sebastian was challenging for the seat of Prime he'd win it, based solely on strength. And if he sat as Prime, then his mother would be pulling his strings.

Verity caught Bishop's arm as if sensing the thoughts racing through his mind. He shook his head at her. He had a duty to protect the Order. "I can't stand aside, Ver."

"Wait," called another voice, clear and ringing.

Heads turned. Cleo stepped forward, her gaze locked on Sebastian, even as her hands curled in her skirts as if she were nervous.

"You have something to say, gel?" Agatha prompted, resting both hands on the heavy staff. Drake stood at Agatha's side, staring at Sebastian as if he represented a puzzle Drake couldn't quite solve.

Something felt wrong. A chill ran down Bishop's spine. Even before Cleo said it, he knew exactly what the problem was.

"That is *not* Sebastian Montcalm," Cleo announced firmly, meeting Sebastian's suddenly glittering eyes. "It's his body, but he's... no longer inside it."

The demon.

Gasps echoed through the room. Bishop was watching his father, and he saw the moment Drake realized what had happened and why he could no longer reach

Sebastian. It shivered across Drake's face like a blow, his mouth parting in shock, in horror. *"No,"* he whispered soundlessly, and Bishop's heart clenched at his father's pain.

The prophecy spoke of sacrifices. Perhaps this was what it had meant? Lucien had been meant to be the demon's vessel, but Ianthe had fought for him a month ago, averting his fate. Maybe it had never been about the three of them dying, but about what they might lose to the demon. Their sanity, their lives, or perhaps even control over their own body?

"You have proof?" Agatha demanded.

Cleo nodded firmly. "I'm Sebastian's wife. And we are bonded by a soul-bond. I cannot sense him... inside." Her voice dropped to a whisper. "Not anymore."

The demon smiled. "I do wish you hadn't done that."

Agatha took a sideways step, eyeing Sebastian uneasily. "You have no right to be here, creature." She suddenly bristled, and Bishop took a step forward. *Shit.* "Begone from this meeting."

The demon laughed, a chilling sound that echoed through the room. Power suddenly began flowing into his appropriated body, immense power. "And just *who* is going to stop me? Morgana, I think it's time for a little get-together."

A woman stepped out of the crowd, sweeping back her red hood and removing the silver mask she wore. All of Drake's anger turned on her—the ex-wife that had poisoned his nephew, stolen his heir, and then lied that she'd aborted the baby. "How dare you come here," Drake spat.

Bishop had never known her, but she'd hurt his father. That was cause enough. He slipped through the crowd toward her, with a murmur for Verity to stay where she was, a knife slipping from his inner sleeve into his palm. There was still an execution warrant with her name on it out there.

"Why hello, Drake," Morgana purred. She had to be in her fifties, but there was a lush sensuality about her despite the streak of silver in her hair. "Looks like you didn't manage to kill me last month, after all."

"Let us remedy that," Drake suggested.

"I don't think so." Morgana snapped her fingers. "I brought friends, just in case the deception was revealed too soon."

A half dozen red cloaks toppled, and out of the chaos of each cloak launched a pair of hell spawn who had obviously stood on each other's shoulders to pass as human. The imps' coppery skin gleamed over lean muscles as they bounded through the crowd, leaping on sorcerers and tearing apart flesh with their gleaming claws.

Jesus.

Chaos erupted. Wards sprang into being with a harsh buzz and mage balls flickered to life. Bishop squeezed the knife in his hand, looking for Morgana, but there were too many fleeing people between them.

And the chaos of the crowd meant that the people on the stage were quite unprotected.

Sebastian faced Drake and Agatha, power brewing until the air felt electric. He lashed out, and Drake drove Agatha to the floor as the entire rock wall behind them exploded with the force of the blow. Bishop launched himself through the circle of flames, landing just behind his half brother, preparing to throw the knife. The demon turned and flung another wave of pure force at him. It swept the knife aside with a clatter.

Bishop snapped his wrists together to form a ward but the force hit him like a giant's fist, sweeping him off his feet and flinging him across the stone circle. Ianthe tumbled with him, landing half beneath him.

Head ringing, vision faltering, Bishop looked up as the room fell still again, surprised to taste blood in his mouth.

Hell. He rolled onto his back, facing the demon who wore his brother's body. Everything that he'd feared had come true. There were no limits to Sebastian's strength, and now the demon owned all of it.

I should have killed him when I had the chance.

Finding his feet, he pushed for Ianthe to run, even as the demon began sweeping immense bouts of power around the room. It wasn't sorcery. There was no control, no spell craft, no ritual to control the power. Simply Expression. Manipulating energy driven by the rage of emotion.

"None of you can stop me," the demon hissed, sending a half dozen sorcerers tumbling like croquet balls. Imps tore into them, but Verity and Lucien were trying to rally some of the sorcerers to their side to fight.

He didn't have time to keep his gaze on her. Verity could handle herself. He had to trust in that.

There was only one person, however, who could take care of Sebastian. *If* he could get close enough.

"That's not entirely true," Drake called, stepping between Bishop and the demon, as if sensing the tide of his thoughts. "I vanquished you once," Drake spat, his coattails flapping in the wind the demon's sorcery had wrought. "Don't doubt that I can do it again."

The demon smiled and held its arms open wide, gesturing to the body it wore. "Last time you cut my body out from under me. Go ahead."

Drake froze.

The demon's arms dropped to its sides. It took a menacing step toward his father. "Oh, I've been waiting all these years for this moment, Drake. You're right. You're the one person who could stop me. So I had to find the right weapon to use against you." It chuckled. "And here it is, one of three people you won't destroy. No matter what."

It lashed a whip of power at Drake and he fell backwards, tripping over Bishop and landing heavily atop him. Bishop knelt at his side, trying to help him sit up, but there was a look on his father's face that he'd never seen before.

Drake never gave up. He didn't know what defeat was. But the demon had found his weakness, and now it would destroy everything and nobody could stop it.

"It's too late," he whispered, holding his father's hand. "He's already gone, damn you. It's too late! We have to kill him!"

Drake's eyes shimmered with unshed tears. "That's the problem with possession." Slowly, he hauled himself upright. "He's still in there. He's just no longer in control."

"No." Bishop shook his head. He glanced at the demon, an etheric blade springing to hand. If Drake couldn't do this, then he would.

Bishop leapt forward, but the demon closed its fist and immense pressure suddenly drove him to his knees, his ribs forced tightly beneath that crushing pressure. He screamed, the blade vanishing into nothing as he clutched at his aching skull.

Someone yelled something and the pressure was gone. Bishop collapsed onto his hands and knees, panting hard. One of his ribs had cracked. He could feel it.

"What did you say?" the demon asked.

"I said, let him go." Drake took another limping step forward.

"And if I do?" This time, the demon's smile held success.

"Drake, no!" Ianthe screamed, fighting her way forward with Lucien at her side. The pair of them fought against the winds. "You can't bargain with it!"

"*Don't,*" Bishop blurted, his lip split and bleeding. No bargain with a demon could ever be a good thing. They only ever paid the price when they had all the cards in their hand.

Drake stood alone before that massive onslaught of pure energy. It whipped around him, tearing slivers of his coat and shirt and raking through his hair. "What do you want?"

The demon laughed. "You know what I want. A vessel strong enough to contain me...."

One brother for another. Ianthe cried out and clasped her husband's hands where the winds were threatening to tear them apart. Drake looked down, his eyes hooded, but Bishop could see his father suddenly still, as if a decision had been made.

"A vessel... strong enough to hold you," Drake murmured, and Bishop's gut dropped.

Drake wouldn't. Bishop surged forward, hand outstretched. He caught his father's sleeve. "No!"

Their eyes met and Drake's resolve firmed. "We cannot fight it, not like this. And I will not sacrifice one son for another."

"Don't do this!" he begged. "Please. I need you." He looked around, desperate for help. "Lucien and Ianthe need you! And the Order."

Drake cupped his palm over Bishop's hand, his voice raw with pain. "Look after Eleanor for me. And if you cannot bring me back, then find the Blade of Altarrh and drive it through my heart. It will kill both of us."

"No! I cannot. You're my father." A flash of his mother's face sprang to mind, pale and listless, etched with pain. *"Please, Adrian. Let me go."* Bishop swallowed. "I cannot do this again."

"You're the only one that I think can." Drake cupped his cheek. "I've made mistakes, Adrian, but you were never one of them. And perhaps because I felt that I had you, I never feared for you as much as I did the other two. I didn't see what was happening to you right beneath my nose until Agatha pointed it out to me. You're strong and you've fought so hard, and I am proud to call myself your father." He pressed their foreheads together. "But you need to stop being afraid of what you are and stop pushing away the one person who could love you. You'll need Verity for what's to come."

"Damn it." There was a lump in his throat. "Damn it, *please*—"

"I walked away from him, Adrian. I walked away last time and left him to die, because there was no other choice. This time I don't have to do that and he needs someone to make that sacrifice for him, to prove that he is worthy of a parent's love. Without it he can never be saved." Drake squeezed his hand hard. "And you are not to kill him. He's your brother. You and Lucien...." Drake looked past Bishop's shoulder. "I need you to put aside your differences with Sebastian. I was wrong to keep you apart. I was afraid that the prophecy would take you both if you came into my life, but I should have known better. One cannot hide from prophecy. Everything I've done, every choice I've made has only served its purpose, to bring the three of you together here, now. This was always the moment it decreed. Well, maybe I can change the prophecy a little? Maybe by taking Sebastian's place, I can alter the course of what is to come? *Trust me.*"

No. Bitterness welled within his chest.

"You cannot stop me, Adrian," Drake told him firmly. "My decision is made. Just... bring me back or kill me, please. I'm sorry."

Before he could refute his father, Drake turned. "You want a vessel? Then I offer you my body and I offer it freely. But you will not take my sons."

The demon's face lit up. "So be it."

"The terms are these," Drake shouted, pausing in the center of the maelstrom. "I grant you my body and my power to use as you desire, but you may not use it to hurt Eleanor, my sons, or their wives and children. You may not use me to cause direct harm to the Order, or harm to any innocents. The second you do, the terms are forfeit and control of my body returns to me."

"Done." The demon's leer spread wider as it stepped forward and clasped Drake's hand.

A scream of pain overtook Drake and he fell to his knees, his body arching backwards and light streaming from his mouth. Runes of darkness crawled over his skin as the demon's magic latched on to him, creeping up Drake's throat and then prying apart his mouth and vanishing inside. Wind lashed Sebastian's hair and then his expression of rapture faded. Became slack and shocked.

"*No!*" Bishop came back to himself, screaming the denial at the edge of the circle. Someone held him back. *Verity?* "No!"

Drake slumped to his hands and knees as Sebastian simply dropped to the slate tiles like a puppet with its strings cut.

His father was gone.

CHAPTER THIRTY

THE FIGHT WAS not over, even if the main player was lost. Bishop crawled after his father as the demon turned and walked away, a tide of imps parting to let him through.

"*No*," he whispered as Drake vanished. Of all the outcomes he'd expected today, his mind had not even come close to the disastrous possibilities of this choice.

Rage fuelled him. He sank onto his haunches, screaming his loss to the ceiling. Power flooded through him. For a second he was no longer in control as his magic lashed out, whip-cracks of lightning detonating around them.

Expression.

Dangerous, whispered the part of him that knew what it felt like to hold a lifeless body in his hands because he'd lost control. But he crushed down the thought as he turned his hooded gaze upon Sebastian.

His brother had collapsed. Bishop didn't care. All he could see was his father screaming as the demon took him over. Lurching to his feet, he staggered closer. All Sebastian had ever been was dangerous. This needed to end now.

Then Verity stepped between them, her skirts shredded and her hair in loose knots that were barely pinned up.

Bishop froze.

"No," she said, tilting her chin up to look him firmly in the eyes. "I won't let you do this."

"Step aside." Chilling, the way his voice came out. He felt like someone else had said the words.

"You made your father a promise," she pointed out, her green eyes flashing fire. "And you will regret this forever if you hurt him."

Bishop stabbed a finger toward Sebastian and screamed, "He cost my father *everything*! Look around you, Verity. All of the blood, all of the bodies here, all of this catastrophe... it's on *him*!"

"I see this quite clearly," she retorted. "A lot of people made choices that brought them here tonight. Your father made a choice. Morgana made a choice. You and Ianthe and Agatha all made choices. Even I made a choice. But you had friends and family around you, whereas he had none from what I can tell." Her expression softened, and she took a half step toward him. "Adrian, I know what it's like to be backed into a corner and to feel like you don't have any more options left. I never wanted to join the Crows, but it was that or starve. Or lift my skirts for coin. I made the best choice I could at the time, and I've spent years stealing and dabbling in cons ever since. I always knew it was wrong. I always felt shame to do so. But I didn't have any other option. Maybe Sebastian didn't either, when the demon made him the offer."

Bishop shook his head. *No.* He couldn't believe that she was daring to defy him. "You know nothing."

"I know you're hurting right now," she shot back, fearless as always. "So I won't take that personally." A tear slid down her cheek. "I want to help you. But I can't let you do this. You said that you loved me."

He flinched. "I do."

"Then trust me now. This is not you. This is the *maladroise* speaking, your emotions, everything.... If you still feel this way in three days' time then I will step aside, but you're not thinking clearly now."

"Don't tell me what I am or aren't thinking," he snarled. "You don't know me. You don't know what I'm capable of." A killer. It burned his soul. That was all he was, all he ever could be. The *maladroise* lurked over his shoulder, haunting him. Horroway's gift or not, he would never escape the sins of his past, and nor would she.

But at least he could finish what he'd started. Stop those who threatened the Order and the people he loved. His gaze locked on Sebastian, but all he saw was his father's face. "Get out of my way."

"Don't do this," she warned, her eyes pleading with him as he took a step forward. "Please don't do this, Adrian. I love you. I want to protect you from the world, from your grief, but protecting you means protecting you from yourself."

Something shifted to his side. Bishop half turned, seeing a man in a cloak lift something toward him.

A pistol.

"Adrian!" Verity screamed.

He tried to form a ward just as the pistol discharged. Too slow. Too damned slow. His life flashed before his eyes in the second it took for the bullet to arrive.

Verity slammed into his arms, translocating out of nowhere, her body jerking and her eyes going wide. "No!" he screamed, wrapping his arms around her.

Not her. Please, not her. Damn the gods, take me instead!

Verity coughed and blood wet her lips, her knees going out from under her as the whisper of death slid through his veins. "Adrian," she whispered, her eyes wide and shocked. He could almost sense that small glimmer of perfect white light lifting from her as her soul began to separate. Catching it desperately in his metaphorical hands, he slammed it back inside her with his magic.

"No!" Bishop lowered them both to the ground. "Verity! Verity! Stay with me!"

There was blood on her dress, and as he pressed his fingertips to the wound, he felt the sucking draw of power as her light slowly began to extinguish.

Agatha's heart had pushed him to the limits of his healing talents, but this.... This exceeded them. Her lungs were punctured on the left, and fluid filled the pericardial sac surrounding her heart, plus the bleeding into her abdomen. An artery ruptured even as he psychically examined the wound. Those leaf-green eyes met his, wide and frightened, and he squeezed her hand.

"You're not going to die," he told her. "I won't let you die."

But where to start? Her lungs? Her heart? He could feel her slipping through his fingers, like sand.

Bishop looked up into a face he didn't know. The pistol was still smoking, the shooter's hand trembling as he lowered it, his mouth dropping open in shock.

"I didn't mean for her...." Osiris's voice, from a face he barely recognized as some other sorcerer in the order.

Bishop saw red. Thrusting out his hand, he curled his fingers and ripped at Osiris's soul with some kind of power he'd never felt before. Osiris's body collapsed as that small soul light streamed toward him. Bishop's hand closed over it, and power roared through his veins.

Death surrounded him. The *maladroise* hovered there, on the edge of his consciousness, but it didn't pull at him as it usually did. "I can't lose you," he whispered, stroking her precious face. "Not you too."

She couldn't speak. There was no breath in her lungs, and only the faintest hint of lucidity glimmered in her green eyes. But she somehow mouthed the words, *Love you.*

Bishop forced all of that power from Osiris's death into her. He healed the artery even as it ruptured again. Forced the liquid in her lungs to reabsorb. Too much. Too much damage. *Please. Please. Please.*

But she was dying, and he knew it.

CHAPTER THIRTY-ONE

VERITY GROANED, TURNING her head into something soft as she slowly woke. The room was dark and warm, but she felt bone-deep exhaustion.

"Easy," Adrian murmured, and then there were gentle hands helping her to slowly sit up and holding a glass of water to her lips.

Oh, goodness. She drank thirstily until someone—Bishop—took the glass away. "Careful," he murmured, "or you'll be ill."

"Well," Lady E muttered. "Didn't you give us half the fright?" Her pale face swam into view, those black eyes meeting Verity's. Lady E looked like she'd aged another decade, but tension dissolved from her shoulders at the sight of Verity, and she gave Verity's hand a squeeze. "Good to have you back in the land of the living."

"What happened?" Verity moaned. She had a vague recollection of the fight in the grotto, of Drake's sacrifice, and then her standoff with Bishop. Not much else. Or too much, perhaps. She kept getting images of carrying a young woman in her arms and shoving her into the carriage. Of blood on her hands. Ianthe taking charge of a bunch of sorcerers Verity didn't know. Of complex weaves and healing and... and looking down on an image of herself lying motionless in the bed.

How strange. She knew she hadn't done any of that.

"Ianthe won the seat of the Prime by default, as Sebastian was technically not human. Drake sacrificed himself to the demon, so that Sebastian could be free. Then someone tried to shoot Bishop," Lady E said. "You took the bullet meant for him." Lady E swallowed, then enveloped Verity in a rough hug that squeezed the breath out of her. "Thank you, my girl. Thank you for saving my boy."

Verity saw it then: the hooded man stepping out of the chaos, as if he'd somehow appeared from nowhere. His gaze had locked on Bishop, and he withdrew the pistol from his sleeve. A strange thing for a sorcerer to use, but with all the magic and wards being flung about, nobody would ever expect a simple bullet.

It had happened so quickly. She didn't think about it. Just slammed into Bishop, a shockingly breathless pain punching through her.

Lady E drew back, patting at her wet cheeks. She cleared her throat. "Now don't *ever* do that again."

Verity paled. She could *feel* how close to death she'd come. "You healed me," she said to Bishop.

"Barely." Lady E snorted, and exchanged a long look with her apprentice. "I daresay you're hungry. Perhaps some of that nice soup you were all foisting on me after my... bout of incapacity."

Without waiting for an answer she bustled toward the door, leaving Verity alone with him.

Nervousness sank through her. She couldn't remember everything, but she very distinctly remembered their fight. "Bout of incapacity?" she asked dryly, using humor to mask her true emotions.

Bishop's hand slid over hers, squeezing. "I'm an idiot," he said hoarsely. "Christ, I nearly lost you, and I said all of those horrible things to you. You have no idea what that felt like. To see you like that."

"What happened to your father?" He shook his head, and she didn't press. "Sebastian?"

His face blanched, and he scrubbed his hand across his forehead and through his hair. Lady E wasn't the only one who looked like they'd aged. Adrian's cheeks were gaunt, his eyes feverishly bright in his hollow face. He'd lost ten pounds, seemingly overnight, and his coat hung off him. "Sebastian's alive. Lucien and Ianthe took him into custody."

"You didn't kill him."

Bishop's gaze lifted. "I was a little distracted." He paused. "And you were right. It's been three days, and... I'm not thinking the way I was then. He's a threat, that's true, but... I have been thinking of other ways to manage the situation. Thank you."

"What happened to you?" she whispered. "Are you unwell? You've lost so much weight."

He breathed out a laugh that was no laugh. "Ver, do you remember what happened?"

"Not really."

Taking her hand, he rested it against his chest, just over his heart. His heartbeat thumped beneath her palm, strangely reassuring.

"What are you doing?" she asked.

He pressed his fingertips between her breasts, the lawn of her nightgown ruffling. Instantly, she realized that her heartbeat kicked along at the same pace as his. A part of her felt that touch in other places too, but she was far too weak to even think of sex.

"Are you ready?" he whispered.

"For?" She could feel something brushing at her mind, as though he was trying to talk to her psychically.

"I've been shielding you from the bond, but I can show you what happened."

Verity opened up to him, and suddenly memories slammed into her, only she was seeing them from *his* eyes.

Blood slid between his fingers as he ground his hands over the wound. "I'm losing her!"

"You can do this!" Lady E snapped. "Concentrate."

"You don't understand." There was a mess of blood, a ruptured artery pumping too fast beneath his/her mental touch. "I'm not a Healer! I'm not! Every time I repair something, the bleeding ruptures it again. I don't have time to work my way through this! Not like when I was healing you."

A sense of loss so profound that Verity had never felt the like washed through her. He/she looked up at Lady E, feeling like a helpless child again. "I don't know what to do!"

"There's one thing you could do," Lady E whispered, sliding a hand over his/hers.

"What?" Desperation choked him/her.

"A soul-bond," Lady E replied, tears wetting her cheeks. "Link her life to yours, and you'll keep her alive long enough to heal her. But if you fail, you'll both go under." Regret warred with responsibility on her expression. "I don't want to lose you too."

"I can't let her go without a fight." Determination filled him/her as he/she began to trace a rune on her forehead in blood. "I love her."

Verity blinked as the memories receded and the room spun back into being. She could sense him now, intertwined psychically with her to the degree that she didn't know where she ended and he began.

There were no walls between them. Not anymore. She could sense his regret at the words he'd said to her, sense the dull grief he'd hastily patched over and pushed aside, and the gut-wrenching loss he was pretending he didn't feel. She also knew that he was terrified she'd reject him.

"I had to do it," he said in a raw voice. "It was the only way to save you. Healing you took too much time and I used up a great deal of energy. That's where all the weight has gone. My body began to consume itself." He paused, then slid onto the bed at her side, clasping her hands in his. "Verity, forcing a soul-bond on you without your consent... I would never have done it if there'd been any other choice. Neither of us can ever break it. But if you were unhappy, or decided you wanted... something else... then I could mute the bond. You'd never hear me, never sense me. You could do whatever you wanted with your life."

But he'd sense *her*. She knew it, just as she realized the thought hadn't been hers.

"Is that what you want?" she asked in a small voice.

"I took your choice away from you." Bishop squeezed her hand. "And I'm shielding you again, but no." Those molten brown eyes met hers, thick with emotion. "I want you to be my wife. I was going to ask you that last night we lay together but I didn't think it was the time, not with Horroway's blood still wet on my hands and so much going on. I wanted.... I wanted to prove I was a better man before I asked. I wanted to be rid of the *maladroise*."

Relief flooded through her. She tugged on his hand. "Lie down with me."

"Is that a yes?" he asked hoarsely, stretching out beside her.

Verity smiled. This man was everything she'd ever wanted in life. "Of course it's a yes. I'm madly in love with you, Adrian. And if I'd even known there was such a thing as a soul-bond, I would never have objected. We've linked before." She stroked the hair from his face as he lay beside her. "And when we're linked," she admitted, her voice dropping, "it's the only time I don't feel so alone anymore."

She'd never have thought he had so much doubt in him, but she saw it when she said she loved him. It wasn't the first time she'd said the words, but she'd not been privy then to his innermost thoughts. And he was letting some of them through.

It hurt to see how poorly he thought of himself. A man with too much blood on his hands and too much death in his future. All he saw when he looked in the mirror was someone whose only gift was killing. And when he looked at her, he hated that that was all he could offer her.

"You fool," she whispered, tears stinging her eyes. "That's not the only thing you can offer me."

And she let her heart swell with everything she thought about him, everything she loved. His gentleness, his chivalry, his determination to help her build a new life without asking for anything in return. The way he kissed her. The way he could build practically anything, and craft amazing spells with his power. His protectiveness, and how he would do anything for those he loved—for Drake, for Eleanor, for Agatha and Marie—even if it meant that he bore the weight of that on his soul, and not them.

"With you by my side," she whispered, cupping his cheek in her hand. "I will never be alone. And neither will you."

Tears wet his eyes at the words and the grief erupted. Verity dragged him into her arms, her heart bleeding for all that he'd lost.

"We'll get him back," she whispered, wishing she could take his grief for him. "Drake's still alive, and that means there's a chance to get him back. Then we can deal with the *maladroise* now that there's a chance to heal you of it, and marriage, and the future. There's always hope, Adrian."

"You are my hope," he rasped, lifting his face and kissing her. "You are my everything. I love you, Verity, and I will spend the rest of my life proving that to you."

She smiled and slid her hand underneath his shirt. "Why don't you prove it to me right now?"

EPILOGUE

Five days later...

THEY'D THROWN HIM in an old potato storage shed, chained to the drainpipe by some sort of manacle that stopped him from touching his power.

Sebastian slumped in the corner, wrapped in the blanket that Lady Rathbourne had given him when she came to deliver his meals. Perhaps they thought this was punishment, but then they knew nothing of what his life had been like. He almost felt like laughing. Three meals a day, a blanket, a lantern, and peace.... God, they knew nothing of torture, these people.

As if to prove him wrong, the lock clanked and the door slowly opened, revealing a tall man clad all in black. Sebastian winced, forcing his eyes to adjust to the sudden change in light. He clambered to his feet, the manacle sliding up the drainpipe as a thrill ran over his skin.

It happened every time he came face-to-face with one of his brothers.

The door shut with a soft click and then Adrian Bishop slowly tugged off his gloves as he looked around.

His breath misted in the air. Bishop surveyed everything else in the room, before slowly, slowly, letting his gaze settle on Sebastian.

Dark hair. Dark eyes. They were nothing alike, except there was a coldness in this man that Sebastian recognized within himself.

His assassin brother. Morgana had shown him the file on Bishop, and Sebastian knew there was only one reason this man could be here, especially alone.

He reached desperately for his power, but it was like trying to bucket water with a sieve. It slipped through his fingers as if he couldn't get a grasp on it. Sebastian took a step back as Bishop stepped forward, and Bishop froze, thoughts racing behind his expressive eyes.

"I'm not here to kill you," he said.

"You tried," Sebastian pointed out, straightening to his full height. He'd caught enough of the conversation between Lady Rathbourne and her husband as they cast him in here to know that. Apparently, he owed Verity Hawkins his life.

Bishop slapped his gloves against his thigh thoughtfully. "You're right. I was considering the idea quite strongly. You're dangerous and out of control—"

"You should know," Sebastian shot back. "You were out of control the other night yourself." He'd seen it all play out through hazy eyes, as if smoke clouded his vision. Being a passenger in his own body reminded him of being blissed out on opium the one time he'd tried it. No longer in control, heavy, forced to ride along as his body reacted and did things he had no say in. He'd thought it wouldn't be so bad, to get revenge on all those he hated, but it had been.

"I was temporarily overwhelmed by grief. You cost me my father."

Something ached inside him. Guilt? "Drake made his choice."

"You're right. He chose your life over his."

The words flayed him where fists would not have touched him. Sebastian tugged at the manacle again. Uselessly. Bishop's silence only aggravated the feeling.

"What do you want? Are you here to gloat? To hit me? What, damn you?"

More silence. When he met his brother's eyes a part of him wanted to run away screaming. For it was not condemnation that he saw, but a sudden sense of compassion.

"Why?" Sebastian whispered. "Why did he do it?"

Dark lashes shuttered those expressive eyes. "Perhaps he saw something in you that others did not."

Sebastian sank to the floor, pressing the heel of his palm into his forehead. He didn't understand any of this, and he'd spent days trying. There was no possible manipulation his father could have found in this. No game to play, no twist, nothing but loss on Drake's behalf.

He had actually sacrificed everything he owned for a chance for Sebastian to be free.

A lump formed in his throat. Nobody had ever given a damn about him, except for Cleo. He had no defense against this. No way to rid himself of the guilt he felt, or the whiplash of emotions that flayed him.

Looking up, he sought answers from the last person he'd ever have expected to get them from. "What do I do now?"

Bishop knelt, resting his wrists on his knees. Reaching inside his pocket, he pulled out a simple brass key and tossed it toward him.

Sebastian caught it reflexively.

"They've been arguing about what to do with you," Bishop told him. "It was decided that I get the final vote."

His hand curled around the key. "You're setting me free?"

"No. I decided to hand you the key for the sheer enjoyment of it."

"You don't know me. The second this is off"— Sebastian wriggled his wrist and the manacle clanked—"I could kill you."

"You might try. But if push comes to shove, I know who walks away from a confrontation between the pair of us. You have strength beyond my comprehension, but strength is not enough when it comes to sorcery. I could tie you in knots and deflect everything you throw at me with ease. You have no training. No control. Just a child lashing out with big fists, destroying the world around him. You're dangerous."

"You didn't tie me in knots the other night."

Bishop's gaze narrowed. "The other night I'd been flinging sorcery around for over an hour. Now I'm rested."

Sebastian jammed the key in the lock on the manacle and twisted. The second it sprang free, he could feel the sweet flush of power rushing through him. He stood, rubbing his wrist, and Bishop mirrored him. There was a moment, just a moment....

"So what now?" he asked. "You just let me walk out of here?"

"I have a proposition for you."

Of course. "Thanks, but I've heard that before."

Bishop's jaw tightened. "Like I said, you have no control. I could tie you in knots right now. But Drake asked me to look after you before he sacrificed himself. That's what I intend to do."

"Do I get to call you big brother?" Sebastian started shaking off the muscle aches of the last few days, eyeing the door.

"You can call me master."

The way he said it beckoned another quip, but Sebastian looked at him thoughtfully. What did that mean?

"Someone reminded me that there is more than one way to deal with a threat. I am offering to teach you to control your sorcery."

"*What?*" Morgana had taunted Sebastian for years over his lack of knowledge. It was the only means she had of keeping him under control, when his power reservoirs overwhelmed hers. This Bishop must be toying with him.

Bishop reached inside his coat pocket and withdrew a flask, tossed it toward him. "You want to learn how to wield your sorcery? Then I will teach you. All I ask in return is that you help me and Lucien free Drake."

Sebastian twisted the cap and sniffed suspiciously. "Water?"

Bishop headed for the door. "You were expecting poison?"

"Who knows?" he muttered, starting after him. None of this made any sense.

Light streamed in through the doorway. Bishop held it open for Sebastian, gesturing him through first. A knot of something—hesitation—speared through him. He didn't understand any of this. People didn't just help you out of the goodness of their own hearts. And Bishop didn't like him, that much was clear.

So what was the catch?

"Seriously, I've seen virgin brides with less reluctance than you," Bishop growled. "Speaking of which, there's someone who wants to see you."

Cleo would be waiting, no doubt.

"No," he said with more force than absolutely necessary.

Bishop quirked a brow, and Sebastian looked away. She'd given up so much already for him. He couldn't... simply couldn't see her again. All he would bring into her life would be destruction. She'd already lost her Sight, her major gifts, because of him. Guilt pounded down again. First Cleo, and now Drake. *You will ruin all of those around you.* His mother whispered poison in his memories. *That's all you are, Sebastian. All you will ever be....*

He ought to get the hell out of there. Leave this entire mess behind him, and get away before he brought Cleo more grief. But Bishop's offer to teach him was far too tempting. Control equaled *freedom.* Nobody would ever enslave him again. It also meant vengeance.

"She's your wife," Bishop said.

"A marriage of convenience to meld the truce between my mother and her father," he replied coldly. Then realized that he lied. She'd become so much more to him in such a short time.

Better off without him. He just had to convince himself of that.

"Perhaps it's for the best," Bishop said slowly. "You need to learn to stop relying on Expression when you wield your power, and she clearly stirs up your emotions."

"Just...." Sebastian hesitated, feeling that ticking link that stretched away into the distance, where Cleo lay. "Just keep her away from me."

Bishop stared at him for a long moment, then nodded. "As you wish. Best come up to the house and get some rest. We start tomorrow. We have a demon to find, and five years' worth of training to push into your head."

COMING 2017...

If you enjoyed *Hexbound*, then get ready for *Soulbound*! Book three in the Dark Arts series; it will deal with Sebastian and Cleo's HEA. It's available in early 2017, so make sure you sign up for my newsletter at www.becmcmaster.com to receive news and excerpts about this release!

Can't wait for more *Dark Arts* action and romance? Then check out my *Burned Lands* series. I recommend starting with *Nobody's Hero*, featuring bad-boy hero Luc Wade, and Riley Kincaid. Kidnapping Riley is the worst mistake Wade makes in his quest for revenge, but she may also be the only thing that can save him from the dark within... Expect lots of intense action, a tortured hero, and a heroine who intends to go down fighting.

Thank you for reading Hexbound. I hope you enjoyed it. Please consider leaving a review online, to help other readers find my books.

Not ready to leave London? Read on for a preview of what's next for Sebastian and Cleo.

SOULBOUND

BOOK THREE: THE DARK ARTS SERIES

A dark force is rising in London...

Sebastian Montcalm knows freedom for the first time in his life, but it has come at a cost. The father he never knew made the ultimate sacrifice: offering his own soul to a demon so that Sebastian could be free. To save his father, Sebastian must learn to control his reckless, uncontrollable powers, but control proves elusive as guilt and numbness flay him. The only thing that stirs him is the innocent touch of the woman he was forced to marry. The one woman he cannot have.

She could be his salvation...

Cleo Sinclair knew her father only ever loved her for the power of her visions, but when he bartered her away in marriage to a man she'd never met or seen, she realized how little value she truly had. Her husband, Sebastian, was nothing more than a dark warmth in her bed, a stranger who refused to touch her. And now he won't even look at her.

...Or he could be her destruction.

When Cleo receives a powerful vision of the demon's plans to tear London apart, they must work together to defeat it. But is Sebastian the one who can end this prophetic doom, or the one bound to begin it? And can Cleo finally reach the tortured soul he hides within?

ABOUT THE AUTHOR

Bec McMaster is the award-winning author of the London Steampunk series. A member of RWA, she writes sexy, dark paranormals, and adventurous steampunk romances, and grew up with her nose in a book. Following a life-long love affair with fantasy, she discovered romance novels as a 16 year-old, and hasn't looked back.

In 2012, Sourcebooks released her debut award-winning novel, *Kiss of Steel*, the first in the London Steampunk series, followed by: *Heart of Iron*, *My Lady Quicksilver*, *Forged By Desire*, and *Of Silk And Steam*. Two novellas—*Tarnished Knight* and *The Curious Case Of The Clockwork Menace*—fleshed out the series. She has been nominated for RT Reviews Best Steampunk Romance for *Heart of Iron (2013)*, won RT Reviews Best Steampunk Romance with *Of Silk And Steam (2015)*, and *Forged By Desire* was nominated for a RITA award in 2015. The series has received starred reviews from Booklist, Publishers Weekly, and Library Journal, with *Heart of Iron* named one of their Best Romances of 2013.

When not poring over travel brochures, playing netball, or cooking things that are very likely bad for her, Bec spends most of her time in front of the computer. In 2016, she debuted the Dark Arts series with *Shadowbound*, the Burned Lands series with *Nobody's Hero*, as well as the second London Steampunk: The Blueblood Conspiracy series, with *Mission: Improper*.

Bec lives in a small country town in Victoria, Australia, with her very own Beta Hero; a Staffordshire terrier named Kobe, who has perfected her own Puss-in-boots sad eyes—especially when bacon is involved; and demanding chickens, Siggy and Lagertha.

Connect with Bec at Facebook and Twitter. For news on new releases, cover reveals, contests, and special promotions, or join her mailing list at becmcmaster.com.

ACKNOWLEDGMENTS

This story has lived in my head for at least ten years, a trilogy about three brothers who needed to save the world–or London, at least. Poor Bishop's HEA was always going to be marred by what happened to Drake at the end, but there is always hope. He has Verity now, and the three brothers are finally together. Let's just say this is the dark moment before the storm erupts.

As for Sebastian–his and Cleo's story is coming. And I promise there is light at the end of the tunnel!

I enjoyed every second of writing this book, but as with every project I take on, I couldn't have done it without a lot of help from these amazing people:

I owe huge thanks to my editor Olivia from Hot Tree Editing for her work in spit-and-polishing this manuscript until it gleamed; my wonderful cover artists from Damonza.com for taking everything I described and giving me the cover of my dreams; and Marisa Shor from Cover Me Darling for the print formatting. To the ELE, and the Central Victorian Writers groups for keeping me sane, and being my support groups! Special thanks go to my beta readers, Kylie Griffin and Jennie Kew–who always find something. And to my family, and my other half–my very own beta hero, Byron–who has always been unabashedly proud of this dream of mine, even when I didn't know if I could do it.

Last, not least, to all of my readers who support me on this journey, and have been crazy vocal about their love for the London Steampunk series, and anything else I write! I hope you enjoy this crazy little detour into a dark, sexy world!

CPSIA information can be obtained
at www.ICGtesting.com
Printed in the USA
LVOW10s1852061217
558857LV00013B/1432/P